DARKER THE NIGHT

A Novel

DARKER THE NIGHT

A Novel

LISA LONDON

Deep River Press
Sanford, North Carolina

Deep River Press, Inc.
918 Twin Oaks Farm Rd
Sanford NC 27330

Cover design by Alan Herberger
Edited by Susan Sipal

Library of Congress Control Number 2015951770
ISBN 978-0-991-16355-7

The following is a work of fiction inspired by the experiences of a remarkable woman, Hilde Sensale. The courageous acts are hers. The others were conceived in my imagination, including relatives, characters, places, and incidents. Any resemblance to actual events, or persons, living or dead, is entirely coincidental.

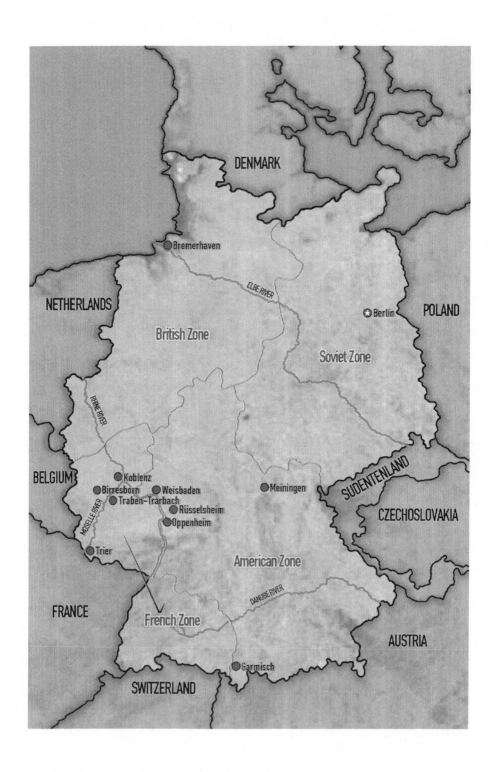

Rüsselsheim

1944

No enemy bomber can reach the Ruhr. If one reaches the Ruhr, my name is not Göring. You may call me Meier.

HERMANN GÖRING— Founder of the Gestapo,
addressing the *Luftwaffe*— September 1939

"Get up, Hedy! It's for real!"

The shrill blast of the air raid siren pierced the air. Hedy opened her eyes, slowly registering the empty beds around the room. Jumping from her tangled covers, she flew from the barracks, only steps behind her friend Ada.

The Allies' planes illuminated the night sky with thousands of green flares parachuting to the ground. The flares sparkled gaily in the air like ornaments, a deceiving contrast to the destruction they foreshadowed.

"The Christmas trees." Ada pointed to the sky as Hedy sprinted across the wide gravel drive to the bomb shelter.

The roar of the bombers grew louder. The repeating shots of the anti-aircraft guns on the roof increased as the teenage girls struggled to open the heavy wooden doors to the shelter below. Debris crashed around them. The smell of smoke combined with the deafening noise rendered Hedy nauseous. She focused her strength on opening the massive doors. As the hinges swung open, the screeching of an approaching shell startled them. Instinctively, she shoved her thin friend into the dark shelter. Vibrations reverberating from the explosion slammed Hedy into the shelter, throwing her down the long, stone stairs.

Her world went dark.

~

The sharp corner of the cold concrete stair cut into Hedy's back. As she pulled herself to a sitting position, pain shot from her head to her tailbone. Blinking, she attempted to orient herself.

The electricity was out, leaving the cellar pitch black. Rubbing the back of her head, Hedy strained to see through the darkness and patted the rough concrete around her. Her hand brushed against a leg to her left, and she jerked back.

"Oh, no. Ada, are you all right?"

The figure moved although Hedy was unable to hear Ada's response, only a thrumming in her ears. Scooting closer to her friend on the floor, she repeatedly hit the side of her head with her palm. Dull ringing replaced the silence. In the dark, she barely perceived Ada's lips moving and lowered her head nearer.

Ada groaned, "Did you really have to push me that hard?"

In spite of herself, Hedy smiled.

Birresborn

1937

Melanie would not win. Her reign was finished.

Tossing back her thick brown ponytail, Hedy Weiß positioned
her right foot at the edge of the start line. Her sleeveless, white shirt
was already damp with sweat. She glanced over at the long-legged
blonde next to her, who sneered confidently back. Hedy's eye's
narrowed. This would be her day; she was sure.

The bang from the starter's pistol jolted her attention forward.
Hedy pushed her legs into action. Her arms pumped. She flew down
the field, focused only on the finish line. Two more strides and Hedy
would be the champion.

Without warning, a blond blur passed her, claiming the gold.
Hedy's knees went weak. Not again. Did Melanie have to win every
event?

Gerda Schmidt, breathless from her extra plumpness, slapped
her on the back. "*Gratulation.* You won second place."

Hedy glared at her best friend. "I didn't beat Melanie."

Shrugging her off, Gerda pointed towards the champion. "No
one does. Her legs must be two-meters long."

"*Achtung.*" Ahead, Frau Bertha's deep voice demanded both girls' attention. The group leader clapped her sturdy hands and rested the intertwined fingers on top of her generous girth until all eyes were focused on her. "Once again our Melanie has brought great pride to our group." She pulled a medal on a ribbon out of her pocket and placed it over the winner's head. "The Führer himself would be pleased with such accomplishments."

The dozens of girls in matching dark skirts, white blouses, and black neckerchiefs who had watched the competition applauded. Hedy wiped her sweaty palms on her dark shorts before she put her hands together without enthusiasm alongside the other competitors.

Frau Bertha laid her arm around Melanie's shoulder. "Your achievement in honor of the Third Reich has earned you a position in the Youth Gathering in Cologne this summer."

Hedy's eyes grew wide, mirroring Melanie's.

"But I'm not in the League of German Girls," said Melanie as she fingered the medal around her neck. "I'm not fourteen yet."

"An exception has been granted for first and second place winners this year." Frau Bertha searched the crowd until her eyes settled on Hedy. "Hedy, you will be joining them."

Gerda seized Hedy's arm to save her from falling.

"It is a very special honor this year as Herr Hitler will be in attendance." An indulgent smile cracked her thin lips as Frau Bertha allowed the girls a few moments of excited commotion before regaining control. "You are dismissed. Melanie, Hedy, tell your parents I will be contacting them shortly."

Hedy could barely walk straight. Words poured out of her mouth. "I've never been to Cologne. There will be thousands of people there. I may get to meet the Führer."

Gerda steered Hedy toward home, letting the excitement bubble out of her friend. As they turned the corner, Hedy bumped into a tall, young man with broad shoulders and a cleft chin wearing the black uniform of the SS.

"Whoa." Jaeger Wolf grasped her shoulders and peered at her through narrowed eyes, studying her features. "Is this beautiful young lady the postmaster's daughter?" He swatted her ponytail. "The same one who used to follow me around my father's grocery store?"

Hedy's mouth went dry. Amazed such an important and handsome man would remember her, she inhaled deeply and stepped back to gaze at him. "*Guten Tag*, Jaeger." Staring at his uniform, she sputtered. "I can't believe you are in the SS."

Jaeger laughed. "Neither can my father. Come on." He placed his arm around her shoulder. "I'll walk you home, and you can ask me a thousand questions like you used to."

Saying goodbye to Gerda, Hedy stood taller and picked up her stride. Daring a quick glance over her shoulder, she noted the daggers shooting from Melanie's eyes. She may not have won the race, but Hedy was being escorted by the most attractive fellow in town.

Turning her attention to Jaeger, she shared her exciting news about attending the gathering.

"I will be there," he informed her. "It is my duty to protect the Führer."

Hedy's hand covered her heart as her lips parted. "What is he like in person?"

They stopped in front of the steps of a two-story brick building. "I believe this is your house." Glancing at his watch, Jaeger added, "I've got to go. I'll tell you all about him next time I am in town." He gently yanked a section of her hair as he sauntered off. "Say hello to your parents for me, pest."

Waving goodbye, she raced up the steps by twos. Hedy burst through the front door and jerked to a stop. Her father sat in his overstuffed chair, reading a paper. From the other side of the room, music from the piano stopped as her mother, Marlene Weiß, glanced up and narrowed her eyes at the sight of her daughter's sweaty shirt. "Hedy, what have you been doing?"

"The *Jungmädel* group races were today." She bounced on the balls of her feet.

Her mother rolled her eyes. "Oh, yes, the Hitler Youth meeting." She resumed her playing.

Her *Vater*, Fritz, motioned her to the table. "Who did I hear you talking to outside?"

She ran to her father's side. "Jaeger Wolf, the grocer's son. He protects Herr Hitler." Hedy paused for a breath. "And he was nice enough to walk me home. He is so sweet."

Muttering under her breath, Mama flipped a page of music. "That will change."

"What do you mean, Mama?" Hedy tilted her head towards her mother.

Mama started to speak, but Vater flashed her a warning look. Her eyes focused back on the music. "He has an extremely serious job. I am sure he will become very serious too."

Vater stood and laid his arm across Hedy's shoulder. "So how did you do today?"

"I almost forgot." Hedy's voice rose and the words poured out. "I get to go to the Youth Gathering in Cologne this summer with the League of German Girls."

A discordant key was struck, and her mother's fingers froze above the piano. She turned on the bench to confront Hedy. "But you are only eleven. Why would you go with the older girls?"

Hedy dashed to the piano. "I won second place in the race." She threw her chest out. "Melanie isn't the only one to go."

Mama and Vater grew silent and avoided Hedy's eyes. Pushing herself away from the keyboard and heading to the kitchen, Mama waved away the idea. "I am afraid you won't be able to make it. Your cousins will be upset if you don't spend the summer with them on the farm."

Hedy followed her mother with outstretched arms. "But Mama, I go to the farm every summer. The trip is paid for." She stomped a foot. "Besides I have earned the honor."

Turning, Mama attempted to moderate her voice. "Your cousins are expecting you. You love spending summers on the farm."

"I'll go after I get back from Cologne."

"You are not going and that is final."

The sternness in her mother's speech surprised Hedy. She focused on her father. "Vater, please. The Führer will be there. I have to go."

Vater sunk into the chair. "You are spending the summer on the farm."

She dropped to her knees beside him. "But, Vater, why?"

With sad eyes, he shook his head. "There are things going on you can't possibly understand. The farm will be a far better place for you this summer."

Hedy stood and stormed towards her bedroom. She stopped to get in a last word, but remained silent as Mama stepped towards Vater, eyes blazing. "You said it would be safe to let her join that ridiculous group. The brainwashing is unreal. Why would they send such a young girl?"

Vater pushed himself out of his chair and lowered his voice. "We had to let her. Besides, Birresborn is too Catholic of an area to let the fanatics take over. Frau Bertha from church promised us she would stop the group from becoming anything more than a fun time."

Mama held onto Vater. "I hope you are right. But I don't have to like it."

Frowning, Hedy snuck into her room. She wondered why her parents were always talking in whispers. They obviously didn't want her to know something. But she wanted to go to Cologne.

The Farm

1937

The light wind at her back on the late spring day gave Hedy wings under her feet. She loved the two-hour walk to the family farm. Although it was difficult to be upset on such a stunning day, her thoughts kept drifting to Cologne. Melanie might have been meeting the Führer right that minute.

Hedy drew a breath and focused on the well-worn path. Trees, standing tall and proud, dotted the rolling hills and magnificent mountains of western Germany. The lilacs were in bloom; their fragrance filling the air. Lush green grass on either side of the path tempted Hedy to take off her shoes and run barefoot. Her mother's stern expression kept her shoes on her feet. Mama preferred tea in the café with her friends over running among the mountain fields.

"Slow down, Hedy, and wait for us. You are eleven now. I trust you will behave like a proper young lady this summer."

Her father snickered and coughed. "Be helpful. Besides, I'm sure your cousins Konrad and Anton will enjoy bossing you around."

Hedy teased her father back. "If we had taken our bicycles, we would already be there."

"*Süße*, your mother doesn't ride a bicycle. Don't worry. We'll ride together when you get back at the end of the summer."

"I will miss our Saturday rides, Vater." She hiked on, watching the goats, sheep, and cattle grazing the mountain fields.

"Tag, Hedy. You're it." Her father chuckled as he touched her shoulder and sprinted up the next hill. Hedy followed as fast as her thin legs would let her. Once close enough, she dove to tag her father before he twisted out of her reach.

"Hedy Weiß, get out of the dirt." Mama crossed her arms. "And Fritz, what are you thinking? We are almost there. Can't you help keep her clean for a few more minutes?"

Her father offered Hedy a conspiratorial wink. "Yes, dear."

As the trio crested the final hill, the geometric patterns on the walls of the half-timber and stone farmhouses in the valley came into view. The stone barns with red-tiled roofs filled Hedy with joy. The barns held such delightful memories. What trouble she and her cousins had gotten into with the neighboring farm children. The combination of the grunts, moos, and bleating sounded like a symphony as she gazed at the pig, cattle, sheep, and oxen in the corrals of rough-hewn timbers.

Two boys raced up the ancient stone path from the closest farm to greet them. "Tante Marlene, Onkel Fritz, we are glad to see you," the youngest shouted, brushing his uncombed hair out of his eyes.

"Only because it got you out of splitting wood this afternoon, Aldrich." The teenager punched his brother on the arm.

"Konrad, stop tormenting your little brother," called the stout woman stepping out of the farmhouse below. "Let our guests get into the house."

Tante Claudia ushered the travelers into the dark kitchen with its exposed beams. Hedy paused to inhale the smell of fresh baked cookies and drying herbs. She rushed to hug her grandfather. "Opa, I have missed you," she said as she reached behind him to sneak a piece of gingerbread.

~

As soon as Hedy had waved goodbye to her parents, a mischievous expression crossed Konrad's face. "Hedy, I have a special job for you this summer. You have earned the right to harness the ox."

Aldrich pulled on his brother's shirt and shook the hair from his face. "The harness weighs more than her."

Ignoring the warning in her gut, Hedy shoved Aldrich aside and ran to Konrad. "Ok. What do I do?"

"I still don't think it is a good idea." Aldrich crossed his arms and frowned.

Konrad sauntered to the corral, with Hedy hurrying to match his stride. He easily picked up the weathered, solid oak harness and positioned it in Hedy's outstretched arms. Her knees sank from the weight, and she swayed left and right as she tried to keep it off the ground.

"You will need to carry it to the old ox and put it over his head." Striding to the corral gate, he swung it open.

Aldrich attempted to stop her. "Hedy, you don't have to do this alone. I'll help you."

"Don't you dare, Aldrich. I can handle it." Hedy slowly and cautiously took a step toward the ox. The harness lurched to the left, causing Hedy to spread her legs farther apart to maintain her balance. The harness tilted to the right, and Hedy's slow, cautious walk became an elaborate, though not graceful, dance through the corral.

The ox watched Hedy and the swaying harness, flicking his tail. Konrad's taunting laughter provided her with the determination she needed to continue. As Hedy approached the ox, it dawned on her she would have to lift the heavy harness above the ox's head. Was she strong enough to do it?

Watching the realization cross her face, her cousin mocked her. "Too bad you are only a girl or you would be able to lift it."

Glaring at Konrad, Hedy straightened and mustered all of her strength.

Aldrich whispered in her ear, surprising her. "I'm right behind you. Take a deep breath and lift up and away as far as you can. The ox knows what to do. You can show Konrad."

With that Hedy closed her eyes, inhaled, and practically threw the harness onto the ox at the moment her grandfather stepped out of the house. "Hedy! What do you think you are doing?"

Startled, Hedy stumbled and fell on her backside. Konrad whooped in disbelief, "You actually did it."

Hedy struggled to stand and looked around. The ox had moved just enough for the harness to land exactly where it belonged. When she realized the harness was in place, she strode towards the house, but not before she flashed Konrad a satisfied smile.

~

For the rest of the summer, Hedy woke up early to milk the cows and assist her aunt with breakfast. During the day, whatever the boys were doing, she insisted on helping. Evenings were spent with her aunt and uncle on the porch, listening to her grandfather and cousins playing music or telling stories.

"Opa, tell us what you did in the Great War," Hedy begged.

"Surely you would rather hear something more cheerful than that." Opa leaned back in his chair and motioned toward his grandson. "Konrad, why don't you play something on your violin?"

Hedy watched as her cousin positioned his chin on the violin. She scarcely believed her obnoxious cousin could stroke such pleasing sounds out of those strings. With his music, she wanted to laugh one moment and to cry the next.

The summer flew by and soon it was time to go back to Birresborn. Konrad punched Hedy on the shoulder as she headed back with her parents.

"I might even miss you," he teased. "I guess Aldrich will have to do my chores now."

Hedy grinned at him and turned to Aldrich. "Ignore him. He's all bark."

Aldrich's sad expression took her back. She gave him a long hug before heading home with her parents.

The Caves

1938

"Hey, Hedy. Look over here," Günter Werner shouted as the skinny thirteen-year-old boy scurried above the pile of boulders.

"Wait up, I want to see." She scampered up the rocks behind him, trailed by Gerda, whose flushed face emphasized the small beauty mark on her lower left cheek.

Various spiky plants made it difficult to reach Günter. By the time Hedy and Gerda caught up with him, their arms and legs were scratched and Hedy's dress was stained. Günter pulled a small lantern from his backpack and waved it along the entrance of a cave. The mouth was mostly hidden behind a jagged boulder and measured about a meter and a half high.

Raising her eyebrows, Hedy peered into the darkness. "Have you ever been in there before?"

"No, I don't think any human has."

She stepped back. "Are there are animals living in it?"

"Let's find out."

Gerda stopped them. "That is a horrible plan. Who knows what might be in there?"

Günter glared at Gerda, "Oh come on, don't be a *Weichling*."

"I am not a softie." Gerda crossed her arms and rolled her eyes. "I'm smart enough not to go where I might get hurt."

Whirling towards Hedy, Günter offered his hand. "I'll protect you."

Hedy stepped in front of him and announced, "I don't want your protection. I am going in first."

"I'm staying out here." Gerda plopped on the ground and wiped the perspiration dripping from her forehead. "Someone will need to run for help when you two get attacked by some bear or crazed lunatic hiding in there."

Hedy elbowed Günter as he rolled his eyes at Gerda and inched toward the opening of the cave. Leaning with her hand behind her right ear, she listened. Her foot nudged a small rock, polished smooth by time. Picking it up, she tossed it into the darkness as far as she could.

"You throw like a girl," Günter teased.

"Quiet." Hedy jumped back. A whirlwind of bats flew out, filing the air with high-pitched screeches. She and Günter plunged to the ground and crossed their arms over their heads.

"I told you it wasn't safe." Gerda stayed away from the action.

Once the bats flew off, Hedy stood and stretched her neck into the opening. "It's too dark to see anything. Günter, hand me your lantern."

Not believing Hedy was actually going into the cave first, he started to hand her the lantern, but pulled back. She scowled at him. Günter shrugged and relinquished it. Side by side, they crept cautiously into the darkness. The cavernous opening gradually narrowed and snaked considerably further back than anticipated.

The light from the lantern barely penetrated the darkness. A musty smell permeated the entire cave. The two explorers continued their journey in silence as if afraid to awaken what might sleep within. With each step, their feet crunched unknown objects on the cave's floor, sending shivers up Hedy's spine.

When she reached the end of the cave, Hedy tentatively stroked the wall. Her fingers grazed the rough markings etched into the stone. Trembling, she shone the light on the rough artwork. The figures resembled humans and animals. "I don't think we are the first people here."

"This is one of the caves the Neanderthals lived in. Remember Herr Huber telling us about them in class last week?" Günter rubbed his hand along the etchings. "I wonder what they mean."

"Who knows? Maybe we can get a field trip out here and have him explain them to us. Herr Huber is always going on about Germany's glorious past."

"No," Günter cried, searching the dark recesses of the cave's interior. "Let's keep this our secret. We can come back and try to decipher it ourselves. I'll bring some of Mama's canned fruit and beans, and we will have our secret hideout forever."

"But what about Gerda?"

"Who care—" Günter stopped himself. "She is too afraid to come in. It might make her feel bad if we tell her about it. Especially when she can't experience it for herself."

Moving her left hand up and down her right arm, Hedy hesitated. "I don't like keeping secrets from her."

"You don't want to make her feel bad, do you?"

She pondered for a moment. "I guess you're right. We better go back before she gets worried."

With that, he smirked, confusing Hedy. They headed out of the cave, still cautious, but moving more quickly.

Once she was able to see the sun hanging low in the sky, Hedy inhaled the fresh air. "I never realized how good the spring air smells."

Gerda sighed with relief. "I was afraid I'd have to come in after you. Discover anything interesting?"

Günter rattled his head back and forth. Hedy frowned and hesitated. "Not especially, but I wish you had come with us."

"No thanks." Gerda motioned towards the sun, just touching the tops of the steeples in the town below. "We'd better get back, or we'll be in trouble."

Once again, they climbed amongst the spiky plants and found slight footholds to crawl over the boulders. Hedy's hand slipped as she struggled to climb up.

"Here, Hedy. Let me give you a hand." Günter pushed Gerda out of the way.

Gerda scowled, "Watch it, or you'll have to carry us both back."

At the top of the boulder, Hedy held tightly to Günter's shoulder. "Are you sure you don't want to share our discovery with anyone?"

"No way." He deliberated for a moment. "Maybe someday. We'll bring our child here so he can realize how adventurous his parents were."

"What child?" Hedy snickered as she headed down the path toward town. "I'm not marrying you, silly."

Moving to Trier

1938

The German people in Austria, Prussia, Bavaria, in all the German Gaue, are free because of Adolf Hitler.

Weekly poster issued by the *Gaupropagandaleitungen*—April 10, 1938

"Why is Onkel Fritz making you move to Trier?" Aldrich snaked his way down the steep hill between Hedy and Gerda. The girls were walking her cousins partway back to the farm after their visit to say goodbye.

Hedy let Konrad and Gerda pass her on the narrow trail. She stopped and lifted her cheeks to catch the waning rays of the afternoon sun. "Vater wants me to go to the best school possible."

Aldrich frowned. "It is bad enough that Konrad has to go into the army, but now you are moving too."

Hedy smiled at Aldrich as Konrad punched her lightly on the arm. "I'll try to stop by Trier if I get a furlough."

She punched him back. "I hope the army teaches you not to punch." Her voice softened. "Please be safe."

"Hedy, you don't have to worry about a thing. Herr Hitler has made Germany so strong, we won't need to fight." He puffed out his chest and threw his elbows back. "Look at the *Anschluss*. The Austrians want to be a part of Germany."

Grimacing, she shook her head. "I don't think it will be that easy. Besides I don't want you in any danger."

"Can we change the subject?" Aldrich shifted from one foot to the other as he avoided looking at his older brother. "Gerda, surely you can give me some good stories about my cousin?"

Gerda eyes twinkled mischievously, and she waved her hand towards Hedy. "Not good, but you might ask about her sweetie."

Konrad chimed in, "Sweetie? Indeed, Hedy?"

"I don't have a sweetie." Hedy sat on the ground. "I have no idea what Gerda is talking about."

Gerda's eyes rolled to the top of her head as she sat beside her friend. "Fine, Hedy." Spinning back to the boys, she said, "What do you call it when Günter is always passing notes, taking Hedy for picnics near the boulders, and generally showing off every time he is around her?"

Aldrich knelt in front of Hedy. "Sounds like a sweetie to me. Who is this Günter?"

Blood rushed to her face. "Günter Werner, but he isn't a sweetie; just a friend I have known for years."

"Why is he telling everyone he is going to marry you?" Gerda was obviously enjoying Hedy's displeasure.

"Because he can be a bit obnoxious." She glared at Gerda as she rose.

Creases appeared in Konrad's forehead. "Wait. Scrawny, arrogant guy? Quite irritating?"

"That's him." Gerda replied with a smile, struggling to stand. Aldrich straightened and offered Gerda a hand.

"Oh, knock it off, you two," Hedy insisted as she started back down the hill. "He does like to brag a bit, but he is kind, sensitive, and goes out of his way to be polite and helpful."

"To *you*." Gerda called after her.

Spinning around, Hedy batted her eyes innocently. "My, how late it has gotten. I think Gerda and I need to head back home."

Konrad punched her again as he ran down the hill past her. At the bottom, he twisted around and called to her. "Hedy, I'll be in uniform next time you see me." Sadness in his eyes betrayed him as he attempted a joke. "You'll have to salute me."

Blinking back the tears, Hedy vowed she would. "Remember, you promised to stay safe."

He bowed before addressing his brother with an exaggerated salute. "You are officially in charge of keeping Hedy in line. It is a big responsibility, but I'm certain you are up to it."

Aldrich returned the salute. "I'll do my best, *Sir*."

~

The raised voices of her parents arguing greeted Hedy when she returned home.

"Marlene, I had to join to get the transfer to Trier."

"But, Fritz, you've seen how crazy some of them get. Ever since our neighbor Sigmund got his brown shirt, you would think he was a prison warden. 'Keep your curtains closed. Follow the rules for *Eintopfgericht* tonight–donate what you saved by eating stew instead of dinner to the Nazi Party. Do what I tell you.' He has become quite the ass."

"Marlene, I'm shocked to hear you talk like that. I like it even less than you. How else are we going to get Hedy into the schools in Trier?" Her father stood and drew Mama into his arms. "I would not have gotten the transfer if I hadn't joined the Party." He grimaced. "As long as I pay my dues, at least I don't have to attend the meetings."

"But, Fritz—" Mama stopped when she noticed Hedy standing in the doorway.

"Vater, you said you wanted to move to Trier." Hedy's eyes narrowed as she searched his face for understanding.

Her father released her mother and slowly came over to Hedy. He tilted his head towards the ceiling. "I do, dear." Patting her on the shoulder, he added, "Don't worry about a thing."

Scratching her head, she glanced from her father to her mother, wondering what she was missing. They seemed to be speaking over her head again, as was happening a lot lately. But exciting visions of big-city life in Trier soon wiped those worries from Hedy's mind.

Kristallnacht–Night of Shattering Glass

1938

H edy loved the abundance of activities in the city. What impressed her most was Trier's Roman history. Grand arches topped with rows of smaller arches created the *Porta Nigra*, the massive ancient sandstone gates. Thick ancient walls circled the city and reeked of security as if nothing could touch them.

Walking from school with her new friends, Kiki and Inge, Hedy inquired about an ancient ruin they passed, a sign marking it a prison called *Sieh um Dich*. Kiki, basking in her role as a descendant of German aristocracy, stood on her tiptoes to look toward the old prison. "If a prisoner escaped 'Look Behind You'." She snickered at the name. "And reached the *Hohe Domkirche St. Peter*, there," she pointed to towering spires of the oldest cathedral in the country a block or so away, "he was allowed a trial under the jurisdiction of the Church."

"I guess he would have a better shot at a fair trial than one by the Romans," Inge added, pushing her brunette hair from her long, narrow face.

Kiki giggled. "Maybe if he had some of the lingerie from your aunt's shop, he could disguise himself long enough to sneak away."

"But what would the priest say when he got to the church?" Hedy chuckled.

The blaring of the public announcement speakers interrupted their conversation. The dozens of people on the street stopped and stared at the siren.

Fellow Germans

The great power of Germany has been shown again without a single shot fired. The Sudetenland is now back under German rule. War has been averted by your Führer.

Immediately after the announcement, the national anthem played. Hedy, Inge, and Kiki saluted the Führer and sang along. At the song's conclusion, the entire street buzzed. "Can you believe that?"

"First Austria, now the Sudetenland. Herr Hitler is amazing."

"All German people will be reunited once again."

Hedy clapped her hands. "That means my cousin Konrad is safe."

"My cousins, too." Hugging her goodbye, Kiki headed home, taking Inge with her.

Turning onto the street for her home, Hedy passed the local synagogue. A dark-haired girl stepped from a side door. Rachel Rosen waved, motioning Hedy to wait for her. "Did you finish your French assignment?"

Hedy stopped to let her friend catch up. "Almost. How about you?"

"I don't know when I am going to get it done. I need to help my father in the jewelry store this afternoon."

Pointing to the loudspeakers, Hedy said, "Did you hear? Our Führer got the Sudetenland back without a fight."

Rachel's eyes narrowed. "Which country will he want next?"

Tilting her head to the side, Hedy squinted. "What do you mean?"

"Never mind." Rachel searched the street around them before waving goodbye. "I'll see you soon. I have to drop these books off before I go."

"Call me if you want help." Hedy waved goodbye.

Raised voices from the kitchen reached her as she opened the door to her home. Her father sat at the table with his brother, her Onkel Georg. Hedy did not see the family resemblance to her father she had always noticed before. Instead her uncle's red face was almost the color of the armband around his brown shirt.

Rising from the table, he pressed his palms against the table. "My daughter is getting married under the large oak tree. We don't need the church. The Führer himself said religions are all alike no matter what they call themselves. They have no future—certainly none for Germans."

Her father's nose flared as he glared in disbelief at his brother. "Georg, you were an altar boy with me. What has happened to you?"

Onkel Georg stormed out, almost hitting Hedy with the door. "If you don't want to come to the wedding, then don't come."

Vater held his head in his hands. Hedy walked over and put her hand on his shoulder. "What happened, Vater?"

Her mother strode into the room. "Since Georg got his brown shirt, he has become insufferable."

"Onkel Georg is taking his new job too seriously." Her father let out a slow sigh. "He came to invite us to the wedding."

Searching her father's face for some sort of understanding, Hedy asked, "So are we going?"

Mama walked to the stove, staying silent. Her father lowered his eyes. "I am afraid we are no longer welcome."

Biting her lip, Hedy placed her hand on her father's back. "I'm sorry, Vater."

~

On Sunday, Hedy strolled to the ancient cathedral for mass with her parents. Dragging her hand along the walls to the church, she felt the inspiring presence of the early Christians. As the ancient Latin service flowed over her, she traced the lines of the soaring arches to the ceiling and to the elaborate altar. The spicy, smoky aroma of incense and candles swirled around her.

"What good is it, my brothers, if someone says he has faith but does not have works?" The *Pfarrer* had started his sermon.

Hedy sat up straighter and tilted her head toward Pfarrer Weber.

"Can that faith save him? If a brother or sister is poorly clothed and lacking in daily food, and one of you says to them, 'Go in peace, be warmed and filled,' without giving them the things needed for the body, what good is that? So also faith by itself, if it does not have deeds, is dead."

Hedy's brow creased as her mind focused, drowning out the remainder of the sermon. What did she need to do to help others? Beside her, Mama gasped, jerking Hedy from her thoughts. "What is wrong, Mama?"

Putting her finger to her lips, her mother gave her a slight shake of the head. After mass, Pfarrer Weber received the parishioners with a gracious smile and kind eyes as they left the church. Vater grasped the priest's hand and whispered into his ear. "You should be more careful. Men have been sent away for lesser comments."

Pfarrer Weber pulled back. "No, Fritz. Think of Deuteronomy 31:6. 'Be strong and courageous. Do not fear or be in dread of them, for it is the Lord your God who goes with you. He will not leave you or forsake you'."

Mama clutched her bag tightly. "But we need you here. It is not necessary for you to put a target on your back."

"Thank you for your concern, Frau Weiß. I will be fine." He excused himself to greet others leaving the church.

Hedy pulled on her father's arm. "What did he say?"

Her father scanned the faces of those around them before answering her. "He is upset with the Führer for sending individuals who don't agree with him to *Konzentrationslager*."

"What is a concentration camp?"

"It is a prison with strict security for political prisoners."

Hedy bit her lip. "They wouldn't take Pfarrer Weber there, would they?"

After a reassuring embrace, Vater grasped her hand and started down the street. "I certainly hope not."

~

The fall weather became colder. Bundled in her winter woolens, Hedy greeted her father at the base of the stairs coming home from school. They climbed the stairs together, to be met by a Strauss waltz on the radio.

Opening the door, Vater escorted Hedy in. "Shall we dance?"

Giggling, she dropped her books by the door and assumed her place at his arm. Mama tapped her foot in rhythm as she stirred the soup on the stove. They danced until the music abruptly stopped. Through the static on the radio, a voice stated:

We interrupt the program for an important announcement from our Minister of Enlightenment, Joseph Goebbels.

Joseph Goebbels's deep cadence boomed across the room.

The Führer has decided that demonstrations should not be prepared or organized by the party, but insofar as they erupt spontaneously, they are not to be hampered.

"Oh, dear." Her mother laid down the wooden spoon with a shaky hand and rubbed the back of her neck.

"What does he mean, Mama?"

Vater sat Hedy down at the table. "A Jew killed Earnest von Rath, who was a diplomat at the Embassy in Paris. People like your Onkel Georg are extremely upset. Your mother and I are afraid there are radicals who will do bad things to the Jews as revenge."

"What kind of bad things?" Hedy bit her lip. A picture of her friend leaving the synagogue flashed in her head. "Will Rachel be all right?"

Mama stepped to her daughter's side. "Don't worry, dear. I am certain everything will be fine. Come help me finish getting dinner ready."

There was little conversation at dinner. Any attempt to ask more questions was stifled. The food lost its flavor. Throughout the entire meal, Vater and Mama gave each other worried glances, even when the conversation was mundane.

Concerned, Hedy went to bed early, but she found it difficult to sleep. Why would a murder in Paris cause problems in Trier? There weren't any bad people here. What were Mama and Vater not telling her?

Hedy fell asleep only to be awoken by yells from the street and the crashing of windows breaking. She fled from her room.

Across the parlor, her mother strained to peer out the window. "Mama, what's happening?" Hedy clutched her arms to her chest.

"I don't know, Hedy. We are safe here." She raised her eyes and made the sign of the cross. "Go back to bed and try not to worry."

Hedy's hands became clammy. "Where is Vater?"

Mama averted her eyes from her daughter. "He left to see what is going on."

Hedy's throat clogged with fear. She flew back to her room and threw on clothes. Grabbing her coat, she ran towards the door. Mama leapt up to stop her as her disheveled father entered the room.

"Where are you going, Hedy?" The severity of his voice stopped her.

"I was going to look for you." She stared at him defiantly.

Taking off his coat and locking the front door, her father shuddered. "No one is going back out tonight. It isn't safe." He wiped the ash and dirt from his hands onto his pants.

Mama rushed to his side. "What is happening?"

He sank into the overstuffed chair, rested his elbows on his legs, and held his head in his hands. "It is terrible. The synagogue is burning. I was able to help the rabbi get some of the books out while others attempted to put out the fire. The brown-shirt mob came over and stole the hoses." His voice faltered as tears streaked down his soot-covered face.

Hedy had never seen her father cry before. Her entire body tensed. She knelt beside him and positioned her arms around his legs. Mama sunk onto the couch. "Oh, Fritz. What is next?"

The family sat in silence. Shouting and echoes of rocks being thrown continued throughout the night. No one slept.

~

The next morning, Hedy and her parents ventured out to the market streets. The overcast sky added to the feeling of gloom filling the area. Glass was strewn everywhere. Graffiti stating awful things about the Jews cluttered the walls. Numerous shops had been looted. Noticing the blood stains on several of the doorways and sidewalks, Hedy shivered. The lingering smell of hatred permeated the air.

How could such a thing happen in her town?

Not a word was spoken. As the Weiß family wandered in silence, Hedy clutched her father's hand and squeezed tightly. She stopped in front of a lingerie shop. "Look. Inge's store wasn't damaged."

"They aren't Jew–" Vater began, but Mama stopped him. She pulled Hedy a bit closer to her, and they continued their slow walk amongst the destruction.

Treading further up the street, Hedy dragged her father back to a storefront with the windows shattered and hateful sayings painted on the walls. "The jewelry shop. That is Rachel's father's."

"Shush, Hedy." Vater scrutinized the street, before lowering his head. "I know."

Alarm rising in her chest, she yanked on her father's arm repeatedly. "Are Rachel and her family all right?"

"They have plenty of money," Vater answered without conviction. "They can move."

"But, Vater, why should they have to leave their home and friends? We were going to study together today."

Vater stopped and knelt in front of Hedy. "It's not fair, *Süße*. For their sake, I pray they do."

Mama linked her arm within Hedy's and hurried her away.

By My Own Efforts

1939

By the new year, the market street had been cleaned up and the Jewish-owned businesses closed. The synagogue was habitable and services held, however few congregants attended. Coming home from school one day, Hedy saw a familiar figure hunched over in a coat.

"Rachel, wait up." Hedy increased her pace to walk with her friend. "I haven't seen you at school lately. Where have you been?"

With glaring eyes, Rachel stopped. "Don't you realize I am a Jew? I am not good enough to go to school with you."

Involuntarily stepping back, Hedy raised both her hands. "I don't care if you are a Jew."

Rachel's tone softened. "It isn't your fault. I would love to be back in school with you." Eyes darting, she scanned the street. "You had better go. I don't want to get you in trouble."

Lowering her head, Rachel left. Hedy stared after her, the creases in her forehead deepening.

~

Walking with the throng of parishioners on the Feast of Corpus Christi, Hedy followed the holy parade. Clouds covered the early June sun as the robed members of the procession led the way for Pfarrer Weber holding the monstrance with the Blessed Sacrament aloft. The congregants paraded down the streets in their neighborhood before returning to the church. As they mounted the steps to enter the sanctuary for the benediction, they were interrupted by the pounding of drums from a marching band. Everyone stopped and stared down the street.

Rows and rows of uniformed Nazis came around the corner, each with one arm raised high. Singing loudly, they marched straight through the middle of the religious procession. At the end of a row trooped Onkel George, glaring at Hedy and her parents as he rallied by. In all of her thirteen years, she had never seen anything so rude.

Vater let out a heavy sigh and rested his hand on Hedy's shoulder. The priest, holding the monstrance high, began singing, "*O thou who at thy Eucharist didst pray.*" One by one the parishioners joined in as loudly as possible while entering the church.

After the service, Hedy leaned towards her father. "Vater, why did the Nazis parade on Corpus Christi? The church always has a festival today."

He patted her knee. "There are those who don't want us to go to church. They schedule demonstrations during the services to force the party members to choose which to attend."

"But Onkel Georg marched with them."

Dropping his head and closing his eyes, he answered, "Please pray for him."

"Oh, Vater." She rubbed his shoulder lightly. "I will."

~

With fall approaching, Hedy walked home from school early one afternoon with Kiki. The two girls passed the almost deserted synagogue. "I haven't seen Rachel in a while." Kiki's body shivered.

"Me neither. Vater heard from someone in the synagogue they moved to another country to allow her father to start his jewelry store again."

"I hope she is all right." Kiki lowered her voice as Hedy strained to hear her. "My aunt said a few of her Jewish friends have been taken away."

Hedy gave her friend an incredulous stare. "Where to? Why would anyone do that?"

Kiki shrugged. "I don't know. She tells me people are disappearing."

They arrived at the Weiß's apartment building. Hedy waved goodbye and headed up the steps to join her parents for the main meal of the day. The smell of sausages and sauerkraut for their *Mittagessen* welcomed her.

"Mama, it smells delicious."

Mama embraced her and continued to set the square wooden table. The radio played the usual patriotic music over the local station. Waving Hedy over, her father inquired about her day. But before she could answer, the Führer's voice broke in amid the static on the radio.

The wave of appalling terrorism against the inhabitants of Poland, and the atrocities that have been taking place in that country are terrible for the victims, but intolerable for a Great Power which has been expected to remain a passive onlooker. ... I see no way by which I can induce the government of Poland to adopt a peaceful solution. But I should despair of any honorable future for my own people if we are not, in one way or another, to solve this question.

Vater pushed his food around on his plate and rose from the table to switch off the radio.

"What is wrong, Vater?"

Turning slowly, unwillingly, towards Hedy, he sighed. "I am afraid we are headed to war."

"But the Führer has to protect the Germans in Poland, doesn't he?"

Mama gripped her daughter's hand as Vater headed back to work without answering.

𝔏ife in the 𝔉atherland

1940

One late spring day, Hedy accompanied her mother to the *Marketplatz* to shop for groceries. Mama pointed to the bakery and said, "You get the bread. I'll run to the butcher."

Before Hedy could answer, the public service speakers screeched. Everyone on the street stopped.

We have marched into France and conquered.

The cheers were deafening. Shoppers set down their packages and congratulated one another. Hedy hugged her mother. "If we've taken France, the war should be ending soon."

Mama clasped her hands together in prayer. "I hope you are right."

The national anthem blared from the speakers. Hedy saluted and sang *Deutschland, Deutschland über alles* with the others.

After the song concluded, Mama grinned at Hedy. "With the announcements of all the victories the Führer has had, I can barely get my shopping done."

Hedy giggled, before becoming serious. "Mama, my teacher says since I am fourteen, I ought to be helping the war effort. What can I do?"

A large group of young men in uniforms were walking toward the railyard. Mama motioned towards them. "The hospital can always use help rolling bandages or reading to the soldiers."

Hedy followed her mother's movements; her eyes lighting on the soldiers' faces. She recognized one as a friend's older brother. A shiver ran through her body as she contemplated her mother's suggestion.

Hedy pointed at the soldiers. "You don't think they'll be hurt, do you? We are winning all of the battles."

"It is a war, dear. Even if we are winning, people are getting hurt."

Hedy glanced from the young men to the public address speakers and closed her eyes.

~

The brick building loomed in front of Hedy. What had previously been a busy local hospital was now a military medical and surgical facility. Nurses in their large white aprons and scarves hurried into the building. Men in uniforms wheeled patients through the doors. Beside her, Kiki hesitated. Hedy nudged her friend sharply, practically pushing her into the main hall.

A catchy military march played on the radio. Patients sitting up in their beds waved to the girls. A nurse assistant in a loose-fitting grey and white striped dress and white rounded collars straightened her apron before approaching them. "Can I help you with something?"

"We would like to help." Hedy looked around the room. "Is there anything we can do?"

"I'll take you to the *Oberschwester*." The assistant escorted them to the head nurse.

The tall woman in a full nursing uniform introduced herself. "I am Schwester Kristine. We can use your help in a number of areas." She pointed to other volunteers sitting in the corner rolling bandages. "We have girls your age serving meals, pushing wheelchairs, running errands, rolling bandages, writing letters for the disabled, and reading to patients."

They followed the nurse to a supply room where she provided

them with lengthy white aprons complete with thick straps and two oversized pockets. "You will wear these while you are here working, however you must leave them each evening. After you are dressed, join the volunteers rolling bandages across the hall."

Hedy attempted to position the straps over her shoulders and across her back. After several frustrating tries, she flung her hands up. "Kiki, how am I supposed to get these wrapped around my waist?"

Giggling, Kiki straightened the straps, wrapped them around Hedy's waist and tied a large bow in the back. "There. Now you have to do mine."

Repaying the favor, Hedy tied Kiki's apron. "How will I get dressed if you aren't here?"

"We'll learn. Surely it will get easier." Kiki twirled, making her apron spin. "We look like real nurses."

Hedy caught her arm to stop the spinning, and, arm in arm, they strolled towards the other volunteers. A patient with his arm wrapped in bandages called to them as they walked by. "*Schwester,* could you bring me water?"

Hedy looked around to see to whom he was talking, before realizing he thought she was a nurse. "Of course, *mein Herr.* Please give me a moment. I am new here."

Dashing off to the kitchen, Hedy smiled. This was exactly what she should be doing.

The Duchess

1941

Never did the German people harbor hostile feeling against the peoples of Russia. However, for over ten years, Jewish Bolshevist rulers had been endeavoring from Moscow to set not only Germany, but all of Europe aflame.

ADOLF HITLER—Declaration of War on the Soviet Union —June 22, 1941

"You must come with me to the family estate for the summer," Kiki said as she and Hedy headed to their English class.

"You mean to stay in a castle with your aunt, the Duchess of Saxe-Meiningen?" Hedy gasped.

"We will be staying in the hunting fortress, actually. *Veste Heldburg.* Nobody lives in the castle anymore."

Nothing could dampen Hedy's enthusiasm as she twirled around, picturing herself as a real princess. "I'll be staying in a fortress."

~

The summer break could not come quickly enough for Hedy. When the day of her trip arrived, she was packed and ready to go.

"I'm worried about two young girls on a train by themselves." Mama fiddled with the collar on Hedy's dress as they headed to the station. "You have never been that far east before. It is almost to Slovakia."

Hedy huffed. "Mama, I am fifteen. I'm not that young."

Vater patted Mama's back gently. "Don't worry, dear. She can take care of herself."

The public speakers blared, and the family stopped to listen.

Wir haben die Briten auf die Knien gebracht.

"What does it mean to have the British on their knees?" The playing of the national anthem interrupted Hedy's question. The trio stopped and sang before continuing.

Vater patted her shoulder. "It means the war is going well."

"I assumed it would be over by now."

Her father shrugged. "We all did."

Mama held her hand as they arrived at the train station. "Act like a proper young lady for the Duchess. Remember, you are not on the farm with your cousins."

Hiding the eyeball roll from her mother, Hedy hugged her parents and dashed toward Kiki, who stood nearby. Hand in hand, they skipped onto the train. The girls froze as they entered the compartment. Passengers filled every seat and bags were stuffed everywhere.

"I think we get to sit on the floor." Hedy pushed her way in, with Kiki right behind. On their way to the back of the car, they passed a tired mother with a child on her hip, an older, overweight man who reeked of cheap cigars, and three handsome soldiers in their pressed uniforms.

Using her jacket to brush the dirt on the floor aside, Kiki laid it out. "The floor appears reasonably clean."

Hedy did the same, squirming around before finding a somewhat comfortable position. As the train lurched forward, Hedy elbowed Kiki and pointed to the handsome soldiers.

One of the men saw the girls gawking and waved. Hedy jolted her head in the other direction, staring up at the ceiling. Try as hard as she might, she was unable to suppress her giggling.

"Hedy, you need to be more subtle," Kiki chided.

Placing her hand under her chin and batting her eyes, Hedy retorted, "Oh, look at me, soldier boy. I'm Kiki."

The girls burst out into laughter, causing the other riders to stare. The three soldiers gave them knowing glances as if they were humoring their younger sisters.

The train ride to Meiningen went quickly. Arriving at the station, Hedy tapped her foot as the passengers in front of her dawdled. Grabbing her bag, she stepped out to the small station.

"Let's walk to the front. My aunt said she would send a ride." Kiki pulled her friend towards the door.

In front of the station waited two matching horses hitched to an elaborate coach. The coachman bowed to the girls.

Hedy clutched Kiki's arm. "I am truly in a fairy tale."

"No, you silly goose. My aunt uses the coach because petrol is so difficult to get."

Hedy didn't care why. She loved having the two splendid horses pull the elegant coach up the hill to the palace. She gasped as they approached the massive brown circular tower with its red roof. Semicircular buildings formed a high wall around it. Heavy wooden gates secured the entrance. On each of the gates hung the family crests with its four parts. A black rooster with a red crown sat in the left corner. The upper right side displayed a standing lion with a gold crown on its head. Below these stood a flag of red and white alternating squares and a green crown.

"I cannot believe your family lives here." Hedy barely remained seated.

Kiki explained that within the walls lived her aunt and her cousin Regina, the coachman, who doubled as the groundskeeper, and his family, and a private teacher who tutored Regina. "My father is studying in China for two years, so I am staying here when I'm not at school."

Once the horses brought the coach to the front door, a dignified woman with grey streaked hair and dark circles under her eyes greeted them. "Kiki. You are home safely." The Duchess embraced her niece, before addressing Hedy. "And you must be the lovely Hedy my niece speaks so highly of."

The girls were ushered to their rooms. After putting away their clothes, Kiki invited Hedy to explore the property. Enormous trees surrounded the castle, but when Hedy climbed to the top of the tower, she felt she could see all of Germany.

The ceilings of the palace were so tall, the wood paneling only went up three quarters of the way. Hedy's favorite room was the library, a two-story tall room with an enormous fireplace. The family crest hung over the fireplace, and every available bit of wall space was covered in bookshelves. The balcony to reach the second story of books was accessed by rolling ladders throughout the room. The books ranged from simple children's readers to first editions of famous stories.

The Duchess invited the girls to join her in the rather substantial garden. With a high chin and broad arm movements, she motioned towards the rows of vegetables. "Girls, we need to all help in the war effort, even if Hitler is a fool."

Hedy's eyes bulged. She had never heard anyone say anything so blatant against the Führer.

The Duchess continued. "I'm proud the estate is self-sufficient. Between this garden and the cattle, chickens and pigs, we produce most everything we need. With my husband and sons gone to war, I need your help with planting, weeding, and harvesting while you are here."

Hedy and Kiki readily agreed to help. Once the Duchess stepped out of hearing range, Hedy confronted Kiki. "I can't believe she insulted the Führer."

Kiki stepped closer to the fence. "My uncle, the Duke, was a supporter when the Nazis came into power. He and my aunt believed Herr Hitler would do a lot for the country."

She stopped and glanced over her shoulder. "And he did. The unemployment lines are gone and everyone has food. Germany has become respected again." Kiki picked up a flower petal that had fallen and studied it before continuing. "But then people began to disappear. Some of our Jewish friends were chased out of the country. When the Führer decided to invade Russia this year, the Duke attempted to talk him out of it. Instead of listening, Hitler sent him to the Eastern Front." She tossed the petal onto the grass. "My aunt is furious."

Biting her lower lip, Hedy felt helpless. "But it isn't our fault we are at war. The Führer said he didn't want a war. The Allies insisted."

Kiki shrugged. "I don't know. It doesn't help that my cousin was shot down over France a few months ago. The Duchess has been trying to get his body back for burial since then."

"Oh, Kiki." Hedy rubbed her friends arm gently. "I am so sorry. I didn't know."

Hedy pictured Konrad, worry filling her heart. There hadn't been any letters lately. Had he been shot and killed? What if he was buried in a foreign land and Tante Claudia never knew. Closing her mind to the fear, Hedy struggled to focus on the beauty of the estate.

~

When she wasn't needed in the garden, Hedy joined Kiki and Regina exploring the hills nearby or dressing up in antique dresses from the attic. The Duchess loved the theatre and encouraged the girls to act out plays in the evening. Hedy could not ask for a more pleasant summer.

One misty day, as everyone sat for the *Mittagessen*, two German officers with grim expressions arrived. The Duchess left the room to speak to them.

"That cannot be good," Regina spoke with dread.

The ominous murmur of voices from the next room was followed by the front door opening and shutting. The Baroness stepped back in the room, her eyes lifeless, and her movements slow and deliberate. Everyone sitting around the table waited for her to speak.

"My son Friedrich will be escorting the remains of his brother Anton home next week. Now, if you will excuse me." Her sentence trailed off as she left the room.

~

For the next week, the household became a flurry of activity, preparing the tower for the burial and planning the funeral. Working with Kiki, Hedy aired out the rooms for Friedrich and his friends and made the beds. The Duchess remained stoic, but frequently requested to be left alone.

Before Friedrich arrived, the Duchess received more heartbreaking news. The Duke was missing from the Eastern front and assumed dead. Grief hung in the air. How could one woman handle so much at once?

"What can I do to help?" Hedy bit the inside of her cheek.

Kiki blinked back her tears. "I don't know, Hedy. I don't know," she answered before running into her room.

~

Friedrich arrived with his brother's casket and several military friends. His starched uniform matched his solemn countenance. The next day, a simple ceremony was held at the chapel. The mourners trailed the casket to the circular tower for the burial.

The priest raised his arms and began with a profound, reassuring voice. "Because God has chosen to call our brother Anton from this life to himself, we commit his body to the earth, for we are dust and unto dust we shall return."

Turning away as the casket descended, tears splashed down Kiki's face. Hedy reached for her hand. Kiki squeezed, leaving nail marks in her palm. Watching her friend suffer, Hedy felt so useless and in the way.

She considered returning to Trier after the funeral service to let the family grieve alone. Friedrich's friends, however, rendered this unnecessary. Following the service, they joined efforts to bring their friend out of his sorrow.

"Come on, Friedrich."

"We all miss Anton, but we only have a few days of military leave."

"It's our responsibility to cheer you up."

Laughter helped lift the mood of the castle. Friedrich's friends flirted with the three teenage girls, and they played games in the parlor each evening. Hedy especially liked her time with the strong jawed Friedrich. She stared at his short blond hair as he directed her to numerous books in the family library, recommending to her stories she had no idea existed. Endeavoring to sit next to him whenever possible, she questioned him about the world outside of Germany.

A few days later as Friedrich prepared to depart, Hedy stood next to him with her chin near her chest and gazed up at him. "Will you write me after the war?"

"I can't," he responded. Friedrich bent down to whisper in her ear. "Once the war is over, I plan to enter the monastery."

Hedy blurted, "But you are the only male heir left." Her two hands flew to her mouth.

Friedrich watched as the shock washed over her. "My mother isn't too happy either." He grimaced and mimicked his mother's voice. "'You need to carry on the family name'. But this is my calling, and if I make it through this war alive, I'll be at the monastery."

~

A week after Friedrich and his friends left, the Duchess stepped out into the garden with Kiki and Hedy. She invited them to sit with her on a bench. "Kiki, after you take Hedy back to Trier, I would like you and your mother to move to the hunting lodge in Austria with me."

"But why, Tante? You like to hunt buck, but I can't shoot."

The Duchess patted Kiki's knee. "It isn't the hunting. I don't like the news I'm hearing from the Eastern Front. Stalin is burning Russian farms to stop us from advancing. He is terrorizing his own country. Imagine what he would do if he marched into Germany. Our home is too close to the border."

Hedy was flabbergasted. "But the Führer will not allow the Russians into Germany."

"Hopefully not, Hedy. Nonetheless, we must be prepared."

Biting her lip, she bowed to the Duchess and left the two alone.

~

Back in Trier with the start of school, Hedy resumed her volunteer work at the hospital. Though she enjoyed her work assisting the patients, it had gotten considerably busier by December. Wounded soldiers arrived daily and she missed Kiki. One afternoon, as she leaned against the counter, waiting for the cook to hand her food for the injured, Hedy rapped her fingers to the music on the radio.

Picking up the full plates, she hummed. Static overtook the music. The Führer's speech filled the room. She sat the plates down and listened.

...Although Germany on her part has strictly adhered to the rules of international law in her relations with the United States of America during every period of the present war, the government of the United States of America from initial violations of neutrality has finally proceeded to open

acts of war against Germany. It has thereby virtually created a state of war.

The government of the Reich consequently breaks off diplomatic relations with the United States of America and declares that under these circumstances brought about by President Roosevelt, Germany too, as from today, considers herself as being in a state of war with the United States of America.

Hedy's stomach clenched as she stared at the cook. "We are at war with America?"

"I am afraid so."

Groaning, she picked up the plates. "This war will never end."

The Hospital in Trier

1942

They see in the dangers and burdens a chance to prove their mettle, which they know they must do if they are not to be weighed in the balance of fate and found wanting.

JOSEPH GOEBBELS—Radio address *Our Hitler*—April 28, 1942

H edy rolled bandages with the other volunteers and listened to a patriotic march as a new group of injured soldiers arrived. The flurry of activity always amazed her. How did the nurses know exactly where to place everyone? How did the medics remain so calm? Who should be helped first?

The girl next to her tapped her shoulder. "Hedy, pay attention. Schwester Kristine is calling you."

Hedy reported to the nurse. An unconscious patient needed to be lifted onto a bed. "Hedy, take the corner of the sheet near his left foot. On the count of three."

Holding her hands up, Hedy whispered, "But I have never done this before."

The nurse rolled her eyes. "Simply lift and follow my lead."

Hedy and a medic moved into position. The nurse barked, "*Eins, zwei, drei.*" They lifted the patient in unison and slid him over to the bed. The patient groaned, opened his eyes, and began to scream.

Her first response was to run away. She stood frozen in place as the soldier became more agitated and flailed. Shoving Hedy out of the way, the nurse laid across the soldier's chest and arms to keep him stable. His legs remained motionless.

The medic reached over and injected him with a sedative. After the patient calmed down, Hedy asked the medic, "Why did he do that?"

The medic checked the patient's pulse. "He was scared. He has been hurt, he can't move his legs, and he feels out of control."

The rest of the day, Hedy watched the patient and the others struggle with the impact of their injuries. The fear on their faces eventually drained, only to be replaced by grief. It required all of her inner strength not to run out of the hospital and hide.

A medic rolled a patient in a wheelchair near her and left. Lethargy overwhelmed the injured soldier; depression showed on his entire body. Hedy set down the bandages and went to him. "*Mein Herr*, is there anything I can get for you?"

"You can make me walk again."

Inhaling sharply, Hedy searched for help. "I, I don't know..."

A voice behind startled her. "She can't, but I can."

Hedy whirled around to see Schwester Clotilda, a stout woman dressed in a full Red Cross uniform with strong arms and intelligent eyes.

"I doubt it," the man grumbled.

"There is a new field of study called *Heilgymnastik*. It is physical therapy for limb injuries. From what I have studied, you may be able to walk again with the right exercises."

"You cannot be serious." The patient focused his full attention on Schwester Clotilda.

So did Hedy. She supposed the same thing.

"I cannot promise you anything. Your spinal cord does not appear to have been permanently damaged, so with serious work on your part, you ought to be able to walk again." The nurse addressed Hedy. "You will help, won't you?"

"I'd love to, but I've never heard of physical therapy."

"It's an innovative concept. There are only a couple of universities which train students in the procedures."

"Can you actually make his legs work again?" She leaned closer, wanting to point, but dared not.

The therapist glanced at the patient. "With his injuries, I should be able to." Patting his shoulder, she added, "It takes a lot of work on your side, though."

A slim, young man in a hospital gown inched across the room using two canes. The physical therapist motioned towards him with a satisfied air. "Here comes one of my success stories, Herr Kurt."

Kurt leaned on his cane and offered his hand to Hedy. "I'll be ready to take you dancing any day, Fräulein."

Lightly taking his hand, Hedy curtsied. "I would be pleased to go, Herr Kurt."

The three laughed. She spent the rest of the afternoon helping the therapist, quizzing her the whole time.

~

Hedy burst into her parent's apartment. "Mama, Vater, I know what I want to do with my life." Without stopping to catch her breath, she continued. "Remember how Pfarrer Weber said those who are strong should help the weak? There are so many people being injured in the war; I can help them."

Mama rotated on the bench of the black upright piano to face her. "Slow down, Hedy. What are you talking about?"

Her parents were unfamiliar with *Heilgymnastik,* but with Hedy's excited explanation, they understood its importance. "Why don't you research which universities offers such a program?" her father suggested. "We can see if it makes sense to send you there."

Hedy's pulse raced as she explained she had already explored the options. "The therapist I worked with at the hospital said the Institute in Berlin is the best."

Her mother stood, fingering the gold cross at her neck. "But Berlin is a ten-hour train ride away. Isn't there anything closer?"

"No, Mama." Hedy's head shook defiantly. "It is the premier place to study physical therapy."

"You are too young to go so far."

In a gentle tone, Hedy reminded her mother, "I am sixteen years old. I only have one more year of high school, Mama. I will be moving away somewhere."

"There are countless opportunities in Trier. You don't need to go to Berlin." Mama paced the floor. "You can get an office job. Once the war is over, there will be plenty of opportunities for intelligent women right here."

Hedy clenched her fists. "What if Konrad was hurt? Wouldn't you want me to be able to help?" She paused, her eyes daring her mother to argue. "I am going to Berlin."

"Fritz, talk to her." Mama's eyes pleaded with her husband.

Vater patted her on the arm. "Marlene, if Hedy thinks this is her calling, we need to investigate it. She has another year of school before she has to decide."

Mama refused to acknowledge either of them and strode off towards the kitchen.

"Oh, Vater. Thank you. And Mama." Hedy followed her mother and kissed her on the cheek. "Everything will be perfect."

Future Plans

1942

"Mama. Vater. I've been accepted. I'm going to Berlin this fall." Hedy waved the acceptance letter in the air as she danced around the room.

"That's wonderful, dear," her mother said quietly as she focused back on her piano.

"I know you are happy, Hedy," her father replied while moving to his wife's side. "We need to work out the logistics, though."

Hedy cringed. The retaliation of the Allies for all the bombing in Britain was intense. The *Tommies* were bombing the rail lines going to Berlin on a regular basis.

"I will find a way."

~

As the weeks turned into months, Hedy tuned into the radio every night, listening for news of Berlin. The bombings continued.

She paid attention to the chatter at the hospital from soldiers who had come from the east. Her heart sank into her stomach. Over and over the only response was, "Unless you are in a tank, you aren't going to Berlin."

Finally acknowledging her dream of studying in Berlin was not in the cards, she informed her parents of her decision.

Mama crossed herself and rushed to Hedy, smothering her. Vater held Hedy's hand. "I know you are disappointed, *Süße*."

"I'm not giving up. I will become a physical therapist."

He squeezed her hand. "You will. The war can't go on forever."

Hedy went to work, researching other options for studying physical therapy. She discovered the University of Strasbourg in the east of France offered a program and applied. The acceptance letter from Strasbourg arrived, surprising Mama and Vater. "But we didn't realize you had applied."

"I didn't want you to spend any more time worrying than you already are, Mama."

Her mother paced the floor. "The war is still going on. It isn't safe to leave the country."

"France is under German control, so I will be safe." Hedy attempted to reassure her. "I can perfect my French and save our soldiers."

Arbeitsdienst

1943

Since we do not want to be a dying people, our goal is to increase our birth rate. But for a growing population we need space if we do not again want to see large amounts of German blood emigrating to other nations, as was the case before the World War.

"People without Space" —Geography Textbook—1943

Hedy dashed through the pouring rain into the house, smiling. "Good news, Vater." She shook her coat and hung it to dry. "The Red Cross nurses think I will complete my nurse training this summer before I head to France."

Handing her a letter, Vater regarded her with sad eyes. "You need to open this."

Hedy accepted it with trembling hands. The seal of the *Arbeitsdienst* Board glared at her. Slowly opening the envelope, she slid the letter out of the envelope, scanning the contents.

> *You have the honor of being selected to serve the fatherland at Weiblicher Arbeitsdienst of Gonsenheim. Report to Gonsenheim on May 1st for your six-month duty.*
>
> *No changes of clothing or extra shoes are needed. All clothing will be assigned. Small personal items such as combs, hand mirrors, and writing paper are allowed.*

"No." Hedy crumpled the paper in her hand. "I am going to be a physical therapist."

"Remember, *Süße*. The darker the night."

"The brighter the stars." The scorn in her voice bled through as she finished the saying. Waves of emotions flowed through her. She was seventeen and she knew what she wanted to do with her life. Hedy was going to make it happen. "I am going to the *Arbeitsdienst* Board. They must understand how important it is for me to become a therapist."

~

Smoothing her skirt, Hedy glanced up the towering flight of steps toward the massive stone building. The office of the *Arbeitsdienst* Board was on the second floor. She carried the crumpled letter in her left hand and information from the therapist at the hospital in the other.

She merely needed to explain how her plans for becoming a therapist were better for the country. She managed the first step. What was she thinking? Hedy stopped and gawked at the edifice in front of her. Throwing her shoulders back, she bounded up the remaining stairs to the front door.

"*Guten Tag, Fräulein*," the guard greeted her.

"*Guten Tag*." She gathered her courage. "I am here to speak to someone from the *Arbeitsdienst* Board."

"Ask for Herr Zimmerman. He'll assist you."

Thanking him, she climbed the stairs and stood outside the door of the office. Should she knock? Or just walk in? She hesitated a moment, almost leaving. Instead she grasped the knob and swung the door open.

A secretary squinted at her. "May I help you, Fräulein?"

"I... I would like to speak to Herr Zimmerman."

"Have a seat. He will be with you shortly." She walked down a hallway behind her desk.

Hedy hovered on the edge of her chair, trying to smooth out the wrinkles of the letter in her hand. A short, stout man with a pointed chin and dark eyes called her back. She stepped into the dark paneled office with an oversized desk. "How may I help you?" he asked.

Her well-practiced speech flew out of her head. Her tongue stumbled as she struggled to explain.

Herr Zimmerman stopped her. "Sit down." He pointed to a solid chair in front of his desk. "Take a moment to compose yourself and explain why you are here."

Steadying herself, she stared him straight in the eye. "It is my lifelong desire to assist the fatherland by helping our soldiers recover from their injuries. I have been accepted to the University of Strasbourg to study physical therapy and am scheduled to begin in two months." She paused to see if her words had an effect. "Here is a letter from a therapist explaining the importance of the program."

Hedy pushed it towards the officer, who waved it away.

"I believe this is more valuable than going to Gonsenheim, therefore, I respectfully request a waiver." She exhaled deeply.

The *Arbeitsdienst* officer appeared unmoved. "As admirable as your goals are, there is a more immediate need to harvest the food from the fields. Our men are fighting for our country." An intense expression overtook his face. "It is your duty to put your personal desires behind those of the Reich."

Hedy opened her mouth, but the officer silenced her with a wave of his hand. "You can go to school after your six-month assignment has been completed. You are dismissed."

Her throat tightened. With sagging shoulders, she rose and left without another word.

~

Obeying orders, Hedy headed to Gonsenheim with rather ambivalent feelings. On one hand, her carefully planned future had been abruptly altered. On the other, she was helping her country. Besides, she was a bit curious about life in a semi-military camp. As an only child, Hedy had never lived with a group of girls and imagined what fun it would be to share a room.

She stepped off the train onto the busy platform. The smell of smoke combined with the mass of bodies and sounds of countless people talking at once caused her heart to palpitate. Jostling her petite travel bag among the crowd, she noticed seven other girls all carrying similar bags. She tilted her head knowingly in their direction, afraid to speak, as she glanced around.

Across the street stood a huge compound enclosed by an extremely high fence with a locked gate. The gate cast a shadow over the young women. A sign read *"Weiblicher Arbeitsdienst of Gonsenheim,"* or as Hedy interpreted it, "home for the next six months."

A knot formed in her stomach as she stared at the giant fence. Was it to prevent unauthorized persons from coming in? Hedy shivered. Or her from leaving?

The gate swung open for the young women. A short, chubby woman, around thirty and dressed in the official uniform of brown skirt, white blouse, and matching brown jacket, waved the girls over and received them. At her side was an immense, white Siberian wolf hound. The sight of the matron stroking the beautiful dog and smiling nearly relieved Hedy's anxiety. After welcoming them, Frau May handed the group off to her assistant, Fräulein Hannah, a younger woman with large-rimmed glasses and a tour guide patter.

The tall, gangly girl with mousy brown hair next to Hedy smiled. "I am so nervous. I don't know anything about farming."

"Farming doesn't scare me, though I've never been to a military camp before." Hedy bit her lower lip.

"I keep telling myself if my brother is brave enough to be on the Eastern Front, I should be able to handle farm work. Besides, I'd like to believe some of the food will go to him directly."

The sweet concept brought a grin to Hedy's face. Encouraged, the girl continued. "I'm Frieda." She rambled on without stopping. "Papa was happy when I got my letter."

Hedy stared at her. "Seriously?"

"He thinks I eat too much and with rations getting harder to find, he assumes I will be fed better here." Frieda snorted. "Then he might get a full meal."

Fräulein Hannah led the group to a wooden shed behind the food pantry. She issued the new recruits the standard *Arbeitsdienst* wardrobe, consisting of:

- black gym shorts and a tee shirt
- sweatpants and a top
- a modest blue work dress
- a cloth shoulder bag

- a thick grey apron
- a heavy work shirt
- a head scarf
- a rain jacket
- two pair of wool socks
- and the heaviest work boots Hedy had ever seen.

"Change into the blue work dress and give me your traveling clothes. Frau May will store them in the main building until your service is completed."

The girls groaned. "I'll never be pretty again," whined Frieda.

"You are responsible for maintaining your clothes during your stay," Fräulein Hannah explained. "Including yourselves, there are forty-eight girls here. Besides your work outside the camp, you will take turns helping in the compound. Over the next six months, you will be rotating in weeklong work details within the camp."

The girls followed Fräulein Hannah's arm motioning toward the sterile compound.

First she pointed to the main building, a two story house with dozens of windows. "Four girls will clean the big house from top to bottom. When you are on this assignment, you will also be responsible for cleaning the toilets in your barracks."

"Yuck," exclaimed a voice from the crowd as others groaned.

Lowering her head and glimpsing over her glasses, Fräulein Hanna elaborated. "Your mothers are not here to wait on you. You are adults and will be responsible."

She strode toward the kitchen. "Four will work in the kitchen assisting Fräulein Bucker. In the process, Fräulein Bucker will train you how to cook for fifty people."

Hedy strained her neck, wondering what a room that could cook for fifty was like, but the crowd pushed her on as the assistant continued.

"Four will work in the gardens with Frau Berger. She will have you weed, plant, and harvest as well as maintain the plantings around the compound." Her hand pointed to several large plots with rows and rows of small green plants. They were meticulously labeled and without a single weed. "If you pay attention, you will be able to grow your personal garden when you return home."

The assembly moved on to a cement building, and the Fräulein continued. "Two will be in charge of the laundry and will keep the shower room cleaned and maintained. All of you who are not on these duties will be going out to help on the local farms."

Finishing the tour, Fräulein Hannah lined the young women up in a vast clearing with a flagpole and saluted Frau May.

Frau May slowly scanned the women before speaking in a booming voice. "Your country and our brave soldiers appreciate your willingness to assist in the war effort. It will take a strong effort on everyone's part to defend our fatherland and bring our soldiers home victorious."

She let her statement sink in before continuing. "We run a regimented schedule from which there will be no deviations. You will rise at 5:30 for a morning run and exercises. At 6:00, you will change into your work dresses and properly make your bed before given breakfast. At 6:30, you will attend the raising of the flag and the singing of our national anthem."

Inspecting the women's faces to assure she had their attention, she continued, "You will get on the 7:00 a.m. train and continue for three stops. At the third stop, there will be farmers in wagons to take you to their farms. If the farmer is satisfied with your work, you will continue to go to his farm as long as he needs you."

Pausing, she added in a more serious tone. "I sincerely hope I do not receive reports a farmer is dissatisfied with your effort."

By the expressions around her, Hedy knew all the girls hoped so as well.

Frau May continued, "At 3:45 the farmers will bring you back to the station to return to our camp. That is your schedule from Monday through Saturday. Sunday afternoons you will have two hours of liberty. If you have visitors at this time, you will entertain them in the assembly room."

The girls' eyes tracked Frau May's arm as she motioned to the buildings on the left. "Now you will be accompanied to your barracks to stow your items and make your beds."

The group marched by the dining hall with its lengthy tables, the spacious assembly room, and the damp communal showers. Eyes darting, Hedy was especially anxious to see the sleeping quarters, having no hint what to expect. Fräulein Hannah stopped the group in front of three identical, elongated wooden buildings used as barracks.

Hedy stepped into the barrack; she blinked and shook her head. This room was nothing like neither her home nor anything she had imagined. The four double wooden bunk beds on either side of the room had a narrow makeshift closet between each bunk. A bulky, black, potbellied stove in the middle of the room supplied the only source of heat.

The narrow front and back walls held the only windows. The rear faced a forest, shading the natural light from the back. From three ceiling fixtures hung small light bulbs.

The dark, cramped space stole Hedy's breath. As she stepped to a bunk, she gasped. Instead of a mattress, a tattered sack cloth scarcely filled with straw and wrapped in a thin sheet covered the wooden slats. A second sheet and a thick wool army blanket lay folded at the foot of the bunk.

Hedy had never slept on anything but a feather bed before. Tentatively, she touched the pillow, expecting the rough straw to poke her hand. To her surprise, feathers brushed her fingers. Exhausted from the extensive trip and all of the surprises, she put away her newly issued wardrobe. Searching through her stack, Hedy noticed there were no pajamas.

"Excuse me, Fräulein. What are we supposed to wear to sleep?"

"Look under your pillows. Your sleep shirts are there."

As each of the girls moved the pillows, there were exclamations and laughter.

"Did the delivery truck made a mistake?"

"These are Grandpa's nightshirts."

Hedy held up the one-size-fits-all men's night shirt. The oversized shirt had a single pocket at the chest and a slit cut part-way up each side for ease of movement. She slipped on her new gown and modeled it for Frieda. The girls snickered together.

Frieda snagged the lower bunk first. Ready to hit the hay, Hedy chuckled at her own joke as she attempted to discover the best way up without stepping on Frieda.

"Hedy, watch it. That is my knee."

The bunks had no ladder. Putting one foot on the rail of the bottom bunk and a hand on the next bunk over, Hedy was able pull herself onto the bed.

"Lights out, Fräuleins. Morning will come early." Fräulein Hannah flipped the light switch off and left the building.

Exhausted as Hedy was, sleep escaped her. The straw had been used for several months, making the mattresses as flat as pancakes. Her spine scraped the wooden slats of the bed frame through the straw. She tossed and turned, moaned and groaned, and eventually, slept as best she could.

~

As she climbed down the next morning, Hedy's oversized nightshirt caught on a ragged edge of the bunk. Hearing the rip of the fabric caused her to cringe. "Please don't let this be an indication of my day." She changed into her gym shorts and joined the others for the morning run.

The smell of fresh straw reached the young women as they jogged around the camp in the early morning light. She elbowed Frieda. "That better be for our beds. I would like to sleep tonight."

Frieda yawned in agreement as she stopped jogging and laid her hands on her knees.

The group changed into their work dresses and ate breakfast before gathering at the flag for the singing of the anthem.

With her Siberian at her side, Frau May stepped in front of the assembly and issued instructions. "Take your mattress out of the barracks and dump the old straw into the field to the north. Refill it and return it to your barracks and make the bed. You have one hour, after which you will receive your work assignments."

The girls ran back to the barracks to grab their mattresses. Dragging her sack mattress out of the barracks, Hedy dumped it out and carried it to the fresh straw. Using both arms, she dug into the pile with a vengeance. "I am *not* going to sleep on a thin mattress again."

"Good idea, Hedy." The other girls copied her lead. After packing the mattresses tight, the women struggled to drag the unwieldy, overstuffed bags back into the barracks. With considerably maneuvering, and more than a few obscenities, they hoisted the mattresses onto the bunks. Hedy fell to the floor, exhausted. Several of the other girls followed suit as Frau May entered the room.

Frau May dispensed strict instructions on how the beds were to be made. "You will make your beds properly each morning before breakfast. If it is not completed to my standards, you will start over and redo it until it is."

Perhaps Frau May's previously welcoming appearance was not indicative of her natural demeanor. Hedy attempted to tuck the corners of the sheet under the mattress as directed, however the mound of straw made it difficult. She was the last one to receive the matron's approval.

~

With the beds made, the young ladies reconvened under the flagpole and whispered amongst themselves.

"I don't want to go to a farm with animals."

"How can I cook for 50 people?"

"With my luck, I'll be stuck cleaning toilets for six months."

"*Achtung.*" Frau May read down the list of names, assigning jobs to each of the girls. Hedy shifted her weight from one foot to the other and tried not to bite her lower lip. Finally, Frau May reached the end of the alphabet. "Hedy Weiß, you will be working on Herr Meyer's farm."

Exhaling strongly, Hedy nodded. "I enjoy working on a farm. Konrad and Aldrich made certain of that."

~

The rest of the day was filled with learning procedures and meeting everyone. The sun hung low in the sky as they headed back to the barracks after dinner. "I don't think I can keep my eyes open for another moment." Frieda yawned.

"At least we will sleep better with our thick mattresses." Hedy covered her open mouth with her hand.

She attempted not to step on Frieda as she climbed up to her bunk. She snagged her night shirt again and growled. "I'm going to spend the next six months repairing this shirt."

Instead of sinking into the soft bed Hedy had imagined, the overstuffed bag was as rigid as the boulders outside of Birresborn. She tried to snuggle into the bed, but lost her balance and rolled off the mattress. Catching herself by grabbing onto the next bunk, she managed not to hit the floor. The *rip* of her nightshirt catching on the nail was the icing on the cake.

After climbing back up, she attempted to perch on the stiff mound. This time, she fell to the floor.

"Ouch." Frieda hit the floor beside her. "I can't stay on my bed."

"*Oomph*. Watch out." Karla in the next bed over grabbed the side of the bunk as she rolled off.

One by one, the girls plopped to the floor. Some rubbed their backsides as others fought to climb up again.

"Hedy, this is the last time we are listening to you." A pillow hit her on the head.

"Worst slumber party ever." Another pillow flew at her, followed by a giggle from Frieda.

Grinning, Hedy picked it up and swung back. Frieda seized a pillow and returned fire. Soon all of the girls were throwing pillows and shrieking. Laughter, squeals, and feathers filled the room as they fell on top of one another.

The door of the barracks flew open. "What is going on?" Fräulein Hannah stopped in disbelief and surveyed the pile of giggling girls.

The girls struggled to stand up and all began speaking at once. Fräulein Hannah waved her hands to stop the chatter. With her body shaking and the corners of her mouth rising, she could not manage to appear dismayed. "You had better find a way to remain in your bunks before you wake Frau May."

Hedy climbed back up to her bunk and punched the straw down enough to stay atop the mound. With any luck, it would work its way down. She settled into another fitful night's sleep.

~

The 5:30 wake-up call sounded exceedingly early. After the morning run in the dawning light, Hedy came back to the barracks to change into her blue work dress and make her bed. She was ready for breakfast and the singing of the national anthem with three minutes to spare.

At exactly 7:00 am, she joined the other young women assigned to work on the farms and boarded the train. At the third stop. Herr Meyer, a thin man with calloused hands, picked her up at the station and drove her to the farm in a beat-up panel wagon drawn by two old mares.

"If you need help with the animals, let me know." Hedy volunteered. "I have spent my summers on my cousins' farm."

Herr Meyer did a double take. "We usually get city girls who are afraid to get their hands dirty. By the time we train them to be useful, it's time for them to go somewhere else."

Hedy beamed with pride. When they arrived at the farm, she was introduced to his wife and two boys, seven and fifteen. Herr Meyer guided her to the field, where two day workers were already planting.

She worked hard all day in the field. The sun felt warm on her shoulders, and she whistled softly as she worked. Tired, but pleased with her day, Hedy climbed into the wagon to return to the train station. Frau Meyer stopped her and said, "You are a good worker, Hedy. Thank you," as she slipped extra sweets into Hedy's canvas shoulder bag.

On the train ride back, Hedy discovered most of the other girls did not find the farm work as pleasant. Griping filled the car.

"The cow charged me."

"I'm not strong enough to lift all those bags."

"Sunday's liberty can't come quickly enough for me."

Hedy merely shrugged. It wasn't bad at all.

Even with dozens of girls sitting around the extended dinner tables, the meal was quiet. Hedy barely held her head up. By the time she arrived back to the barracks, she doubted she had enough energy to climb to her bunk. "I won't move once I'm up there. At least, I shouldn't fall out tonight."

Frieda groaned. "I may be asleep before I close my eyes."

~

On Sunday, the girls woke up giddy. Shouts of "No farm work today" echoed around the room. Camp chores were assigned and completed before the young women were issued their liberty clothes— brown skirts and jackets with white blouses and a simple hat. The girls chattered amongst themselves.

"I am ready for a ball."

"At least it isn't those horrible work dresses."

"These shoes are ugly but they aren't work boots."

Hedy agreed. "My work boots are two sizes too small. My feet will never be the same."

At two o'clock, the substantial iron gates to the compound opened. Giggling ensued as the group of girls headed into the small town. Once they arrived, Hedy found the lone café to have ice cream and cake, but with no empty seats.

"I guess we'll take a tour of the city until a table comes free." Hedy elbowed Frieda.

"We aren't at camp." Frieda laced her arm in Hedy's.

"Or working. It's a perfect day."

Liberty

1943

The routine of the camp continued. After a couple of weeks, Hedy missed going to church. With a slight tremor to her voice, she addressed the matron. "May Frieda and I take our liberty on Sunday morning instead of the afternoon? We haven't been to mass since we arrived and would like to go."

Frau May narrowed her eyes. "Liberty is for two hours in the afternoon."

"But Frau May, we want to go to church."

"No exceptions." Frau May marched away.

Hedy stared after her, confused.

~

The next morning, the matron strode into the barracks for inspections. She paced between the beds. The young women stood at attention, not daring to move.

"Hedy Weiß, your bed is not made properly." Frau May tore the sheets and blankets off of her bunk.

Grabbing the sheets from the floor, Hedy immediately remade the bed. She took extra care to make the corners as tight as possible. As she was smoothing out the last wrinkles, she sensed the matron's hot breath on her neck.

"Can you not learn, Fräulein?" Frau May pitched the bedding to the floor and walked on.

After two more tries, the matron finally allowed her to go to breakfast. Hedy sat at the table and began eating when Frieda came over and tugged on her sleeve. "Hurry up, Hedy. We have to be at the flag raising or we'll be punished."

Hedy stuffed a whole sausage in her mouth as she hurried to catch up with Frieda. Swallowing, she complained. "I can't believe she made me remake the bed four times."

"I had to redo mine twice."

Hedy snatched Frieda's arm. "She doesn't do that to the other girls. Why is she picking on us?"

Frieda trembled. "I don't know. The ones who have stayed at camp to clean tell me she is a bear to deal with. But if we don't get to the flag raising, it will only get worse."

Releasing Frieda's arm, Hedy sprinted ahead of her.

~

A few weeks later, Hedy approached Frau May once more about attending mass. The response was the same.

"She makes me so mad," Frieda pouted. "It's not like we are causing trouble. We only want to go to church."

The next morning, Hedy made an extra special effort to have her bed perfect.

Frau May came to her bunk and examined it. "Fräulein Hedy, are you intentionally this incompetent?"

The matron pitched the sheets and blankets onto the floor and strode away. Hedy scowled at her, daring not to say a word. She remade the bed and rushed to breakfast.

"Hedy, you've got to get to breakfast earlier. You are going to be late—" Her well-meaning friend shrank under Hedy's glare.

The rest of the week followed the same pattern. Frieda and Hedy were held back to remake their beds every day.

"Why us?" Frieda whined. "We fix the beds as well as the other girls."

Hedy reflected for a minute. "I finally figured it out. She is punishing us for wanting to go to church."

"Surely not," Frieda responded. "Why would she do that?"

Fuming, Hedy dropped her voice. "Because she is a brown-shirt. In Trier, they would schedule parades during mass times purely to interrupt the service."

Frieda shuddered. "You might be right. We are the only ones who have asked to go to church."

"Someday, I'm going to get even with Frau May."

Clearing her breakfast plate, Frieda's gaze moved towards the door. "Shush. Don't think that way. You'll only invite more trouble."

~

At least on the farm, Hedy didn't have to worry about the matron. The sun warmed her back as she cut stalks of corn and propped them against each other to dry. She stepped back to admire the structure, accidentally hitting the stalks from the previous day. Startled mice scurried away. A devious notion formed in her head.

On the train ride the next morning, several of the girls complained they were being mistreated by Frau May. Hedy leaned forward and listened for a while, before asking, "Would you like to get back at her?"

The other girls gawked at Hedy. "What can we do?"

She motioned for them to come closer. "Look in the middle of the stalks. There are always mice. Tie one up in your scarf and bring it back in your bag."

"*Eww.*" The girls grimaced. "Why?"

"Trust me. It will be fun." Hedy rubbed her hands together.

~

That evening, the young women gathered at the flagpole in rows for the evening ceremony. Frau May stood in front of them calling for order. Hedy maneuvered herself near the middle of the group.

She scanned the area, her shoulder bag wiggling. The girls from her train glanced away. The public loudspeakers played *Deutschland, Deutschland über alles*. Right arms were raised and Frau May's song rang above the rest.

A dozen mice ran out from the rows of girls towards the matron. Frau May screamed hysterically and ran to the big house. After a moment of shock, the girls jumped and squealed. The entire group screamed as they ran to their barracks. Hedy did her best to feign terror as she stifled a laugh.

Frieda saddled up beside her. "That was beautiful. You are a genius."

Hedy picked up her pace. "I don't have any idea what you are talking about."

"Nor do I," Frieda answered. "Nor do I."

~

Everyone in the camp tiptoed around Frau May for the next several days. The employees talked about the mice infestation as if there was a camp-wide problem. Eventually it wasn't mentioned again.

Hedy crossed her arms. "I'm going to ask about attending mass this weekend."

"You already know what the answer will be." Frieda was not optimistic.

"It will be no if I don't ask. What do I have to lose?"

Frieda stared at her. "We'll have to miss breakfast because we are remaking our beds a thousand more times."

Frau May strolled by with her Siberian wolf hound. Summoning up all of her courage, Hedy approached her. "Frieda and I would like to take our liberty tomorrow morning instead of the afternoon."

The matron presented her with a withering stare. "Fräulein, I have already explained there are no exceptions. If you and your friend are not busy enough," she stopped and petted her dog, "you can clean out the dog pen and bathe Siegfried tomorrow. Good day."

Walking back to Frieda, Hedy slapped her palm to her forehead. "I am so sorry. We have to clean out the dog pen in the morning."

Frieda groaned. "Yuck. The dog pen is the messiest work of all."

A mischievous grin crossed Hedy's face. "Wait, we may enjoy tomorrow after all."

Wrinkling her nose, Frieda was worried. "What are you thinking?"

"Trust me." Hedy's eyes twinkled.

~

The next morning, Frau May provided instructions on cleaning the cage and retired to her office. Hedy began to shovel out the cage while Frieda played ball with Siegfried to occupy him. Edging closer and closer to the gate, Frieda "accidentally" unfastened the gate. She screamed for effect as the hound, smelling freedom, raced down the road in a flash. The two girls chased the dog as he headed to town.

"Siegfried has his ID on his collar, so he will be returned home." Hedy slowed down her gait once they were out of sight of the camp.

Together, Hedy and Frieda headed into town and attended mass. After church, they sauntered back to camp. Greeting them near the bushes at the front gate was the missing hound, who managed to find his way home alone. Frieda slipped the leash over his head. Stifling their grins, the young women mussed themselves up a bit and entered the gates triumphantly.

Frau May saw the girls and rushed out to meet them. "Thank you for searching for my dear dog." She clasped each of their hands. "For your dedication, you are excused from any assignments for the rest of the day."

Careful not to glance toward Frieda, Hedy attempted to suppress her smile, but she vowed to say an extra Hail Mary tonight in penance for her deception.

~

The weeks dragged on. Homesickness permeated the camp. Reports from the front no longer carried glorious news.

"I am almost afraid to open letters from home," one girl lamented.

Frieda held a letter, her eyes glistening. "My cousin lost a leg on the Eastern Front."

Hedy's hand trembled as she tore her letter open. She exhaled slowly with relief as she read her mother's accounts of the daily life in Trier.

Morale became so low, Frau May gathered the girls together. "We have informed your families that they may visit next Sunday. You will get the entire day off rather than the two hours of liberty."

The cheers were deafening. The mood of the camp lifted instantaneously. Hedy counted the days until her parents arrived.

~

On Sunday, Hedy rose early, and put on her dress uniform. The main gate swung open and the parents filed in. Hedy searched the crowd. Her mother's slim build and thick dark hair came into view.

Hedy rushed into her arms. "Mama, I've missed you so."

Eyes filled with tears, Mama stroked her daughter's hair. Hedy lightly pushed back from her mother. "You are going to get my jacket wet if you keep that up." She looked around and observed her father break away from the crowd.

Letting go of her mother, Hedy lurched toward him and held tight. She inhaled his aroma as he engulfed her. "Careful, Vater, you'll make me cry like Mama."

She showed them around the camp, introducing them to her friends as they went. When Hedy finished the tour, they sat on a bench, and her parents caught her up with the news back home.

"The Nazis arrested Pfarrer Weber." Her father's shoulders sagged.

"No, Vater. Why?"

"The baker's daughter was engaged to a boy. He became a brown shirt and didn't want to get married in the church. The priest advised her she should not marry a man who did not share her values."

Hedy gasped as her father continued. "The boy notified his superiors, and they arrested Pfarrer Weber."

"Will he be all right?"

"We must have faith. From what we understand, he was taken to Dachau." Vater shook his head. "There are other priests there."

Mama made the sign of the cross. Taking Hedy's hand, she said. "Your cousin Konrad is in Italy and doing well. His parents received a letter last week."

Hedy squeezed her mother's hand. "Wonderful. I have been worried about him. How is Aldrich doing?"

"Aldrich is helping on the farm, but—" her voice faltered.

"What is it, Mama?"

Papa placed his arm around his wife. "The Nazis have required Aldrich's *Hitlerjugend* group to train with guns."

"They can't send him to war. He isn't even sixteen yet."

Patting Hedy's shoulder, her father attempted to alleviate her fears. "They aren't sending him to war. They are simply training him."

A cloud covered the sun. She shivered and bit her lower lip. "Is the war going that badly?"

Mama picked up a small rock from the ground. Vater's eyes dodged hers. "It isn't going as well as the Führer would like."

Clearing her throat, Mama changed the subject. "I would love to meet the family you have been working with. If we spend the night, may we ride on the train with you in the morning?"

"Of course. You will love them. They have two boys and let me help with the animals. Frau Meyer sneaks extra treats in my bag. They are very good to me."

~

Monday, Hedy stepped outside the gate in her in heavy boots and the work dress. Mama, in her perfectly pressed dress and hat, gasped, "What ever happened to my little girl?"

Her father laughed. "Maybe if we had dressed her like that growing up, you wouldn't have fussed at her for messing up her clothes so much."

Hedy grinned back at her father. "I just wish the boots were my size. My feet are killing me."

Mama instantly straightened and headed to the gate. "We need to get that fixed."

Waving her hands in front of her, Hedy stopped her mother from heading straight to Frau May. "It's fine, Mama. The other girls and I can trade around."

"Hedy can take care of herself, Marlene." Vater put his hand on his wife's arm and glanced back at his daughter.

~

At the train station, Hedy introduced Herr Meyer to her parents. He complimented their daughter as he drove them to the farm. "I could not ask for better help. Hedy is a hard worker."

Her father agreed. Hedy stood a bit taller.

"In fact, if my son was older, I would want him to marry her."

Hedy's face caught fire. Herr Meyer chuckled. "I didn't mean to embarrass you. Your service will be up soon. Would you like to stay longer to help past the fall harvest?"

Hedy's heart raced. Surely he wouldn't ask Frau May to make

her stay? She collected herself. "I am sorry, Herr Meyer. I have enjoyed working with you and your family, but my studies in physical therapy will be starting shortly."

Herr Meyer sighed. "I understand. If you change your mind, let me know." After a tour of the farm, he addressed her parents. "I'll take you back to the station to catch the next train."

~

The next weekend, the girls finished lunch and were waiting for their two-hour liberty to start, when squeals sounded at the camp entrance. "Oh my. There must be a hundred young men."

The ladies sprinted to the front gates. A complete company of *Arbeitsdienst* men in full uniform marched into camp. Frau May's eyes moved from the giggling girls to the rows of men. She threw up her hands and announced, "Liberty time for all for the next three hours. Be back to camp by 4:30 for coffee and cake on the lawn."

Hedy peeked over at Frieda, sheepishly. "When she does something this nice, I feel guilty about deceiving her."

Frieda snickered. "Don't. The dog appreciated it. Besides, remember all the beds you had to remake and all those missed breakfasts."

In less than ten minutes, all forty-eight girls had changed into their official Sunday outfits and chattered amongst themselves.

"It is like they brought in dates for our day off."

"He is so handsome."

"Which one?"

"All of them."

The sunny day was the perfect setting for an outing. The men appeared to be as pleased to discover so many young women as Hedy was to see so many young men.

Frieda tilted her head towards two men walking towards them. "The blond on the left seems interesting."

Elbowing her friend, Hedy agreed. "His friend is awfully cute too." She strived to compose herself as they drew closer.

"*Hallo*, I am Johan," the young man Hedy had noticed said. "And this is my friend, Ernst."

Hedy returned the greeting, noting his steel blue eyes.

Ernst, who couldn't keep his eyes off of Frieda, said, "We are being sent to a camp a few miles from here."

Focusing her attention on Johan, Hedy explained, "We are almost to the end of our duty, but we haven't heard much news. What is going on in the world?"

Johan let out a low sigh before answering. "The Allies have bombed Rome. The Führer is sending troops to Italy to help."

Her eyes widened. "He doesn't think the Italians can hold them back?"

Wringing his hands, he leaned closer to Hedy. "I understand the Allies have Sicily already." Standing upright, he changed the subject. "Enough about the war. Let's go explore the town." He offered his arm.

Hedy shrugged off thoughts of the war and accepted his arm. They strolled off to town.

~

As the final weeks dragged on, the carefree moments became fewer and further between. The later crops were now ready for harvest, and the farmers needed more help.

With her sternest expression, Frau May gathered the young women together for an announcement after dinner. "The Führer needs all Germans to work harder for the war effort. Starting tomorrow, we will have buses brought to the camps to allow you to arrive at the fields earlier and work until dusk. It is our duty to get the harvest to our fighting men."

Stifling her groan, Hedy headed to the barracks. "Well, Frieda, we better sleep well tonight, because it sounds like we will be working hard tomorrow."

"We are already working hard." She held up her hands. "These callouses will never go away."

~

The shrill sound of the air raid siren jolted Hedy awake. Fräulein Hanna rushed into the room and barked commands. "Fräuleins, change into your sweat pants as quickly as possible. Grab your uniforms and bring them to the cellar, *now*."

The girls fell out of bed and scrambled, pulling on their clothes and shoes. Hedy's nightshirt caught on a loose nail and ripped once more. She leapt to the floor and threw on her clothes. While trying to pull on the too-small boots in her hurried state, she fell to the side, knocking Frieda down.

Shoving her back, Frieda fussed. "Watch it. We have to get out of here."

With her feet shoved halfway into her boots, Hedy snatched her uniform and hat. She was the only person left in the room. Fräulein Hanna stood in the doorway, waving for her to hurry. "Hedy, get to the shelter immediately."

Bombers roared overhead. Hedy dashed to the shelter, if she could call it that. The room was simply a cellar, not a true bomb shelter, and barely fit all of the girls.

"Is this what sausage feels like when it is stuffed in the casing?" Frieda moaned.

At the door, Fräulein Hanna spoke to Frau May, waving her hand and pointing to Hedy. Frau May stared at Hedy and curled her lip.

A tingling sensation rose up Hedy's spine. She elbowed Frieda and struggled to focus on something else. "Have you ever been in a bomb shelter before?"

"No. I didn't think the *Luftwaffe* would let them come this close." Frieda's voice faltered.

Hedy scanned the scared faces around her. The fear in the room was palpable. *Please God, let it be over soon.*

Finally, the all clear signal sounded followed by huge sighs of relief. Frau May opened the door and allowed them to return to their barracks. As Hedy squeezed by, the matron gripped her shoulder. "You might have been hurt. Prepare yourself better for the future."

Staring at her feet, Hedy slinked back to the barracks.

~

The sun rose, filtering into the barracks. "Why should we have to get up early after spending last night in the shelter?" Frieda moaned.

Hedy was too worn-out to answer. Dragging her feet after breakfast and the flag raising, she loaded onto the bus and headed to the farm. At least the matron had cut out the morning run in order to spend more time in the fields. The day was long and filled with back-breaking work. Back at camp, she fell exhausted in her bed and was sound asleep in minutes.

Within a few hours, the sirens blared, shocking her awake. "Again?" Hedy groaned as she hopped off the bunk, trying not to catch her nightshirt on the nail. "We will never get a good nights' sleep."

After pulling on her sweat pants and grabbing her boots and uniform, she arrived at the shelter before most of the others. Frau May nodded, approvingly.

~

The nightly raids continued. Anger and frustration replaced the fear from the first night.

Frieda growled. "Why must we go to the shelter? The bombers don't care about us. They are on their way to Mainz and Frankfurt. I want to stay in bed and sleep."

Sniping and growling supplanted the cheerful comradery as the sleep deprivation worsened. The next weeks were grueling.

Crawling up into her bunk, Hedy complained to Frieda. "I can barely move after slaving on the farm, and the siren wakes us every night. We only have a little time left, but I don't think I can stand it."

Frieda's gentle snores responded. Lying there alone in the dark, homesick and tired, a tear escaped Hedy's tightly closed lids. Picturing her mother's smiling face and her father's warm hug, she prayed, *I want to go home.*

~

Several days later, Hedy waited in front of the big house for mail, standing in line with Frieda. "Only one more week. I'm thrilled to be going home, but I'm afraid I'll never see you again."

"How will I be able to sleep without you stepping on me?" Smiling, Frieda passed a letter to Hedy.

Hedy ripped into her letter with a grin and read it. Dropping the letter, she cried. "No. It isn't fair."

Everyone gaped at her as she sank to the ground.

"What is wrong, Hedy?" Frieda rushed to her side.

"Vater's letter. I have been drafted to work in a factory for my *Kriegsdienst.*" Hedy stamped her foot. "I need to go to France to become a physical therapist. I've already done my work service." Her voice cracked. "Why should I have to do war service too?"

Frieda lowered her head, eyes darting back and forth. "Mama tells me all Germans are expected to be working harder for the war effort."

"The Führer said Germany was stronger than all the other countries. Why haven't we won yet?"

Shaking her head and lowering her voice, Frieda responded, "My brother says it's terribly bad on the Eastern Front. They are freezing and don't have enough food."

With a pinched mouth, Hedy punched the ground beside her. "It was insane for Hitler to invade Russia."

Horrified, Frieda stopped her. "You cannot talk about the Führer like that."

Hedy scowled. She got up and began to walk away. Stopping she wrapped her arms around Frieda. "I guess I'm off to Rüsselsheim. I'll miss you."

"At least we learned we can handle anything life throws at us." Frieda pointed at Frau May's dog in the pen. "Even if it takes a slight deception."

Kriegsdienst

1943

The longer the war lasts, the more this idea will unite this Volk, give it faith, and increase its achievements...It will destroy whoever attempts to shirk his duties. It will wage this fight until a clear result is obtained, a new January 30, namely, the unambiguous victory.

ADOLPH HITLER—10th anniversary of the Nazi regime —January 30, 1943

"Again?" Hedy slammed her small bag down on the train floor with the announcement of another delay.

What should have been a simple three-hour train trip home was fraught with delays and detours. With the tracks on the direct route bombed, she was forced to take four different trains. Moving from one train to another, her chest tightened. How had the *Alliierten* been able to get by the *Luftwaffe*? Germany's air force was supposed to be the strongest.

The delays robbed her of one of her three precious days off. Finally, Hedy arrived in Trier. Exhausted and ravenous, she sat at the table. Her mother placed a bowl of watery soup in front of her.

"Everything is being shipped to the fronts. We must make do with what little is left." Her mother's eyes displayed her sadness as Hedy bit into the small boiled potato.

"I didn't realize. No wonder they wanted me to work such long hours during the harvest." She drained the bowl.

Her father laid his hand on her shoulder. "*Süße*, your cousin Konrad has been captured by the *Alliierten*."

"No." Hedy's head jerked up.

"Don't worry. He is uninjured. There are rumors the POWs are being shipped to the US because the Allies can't handle all of them. The Red Cross will let his parents know for sure."

Mama made the sign of the cross. "Thank God he wasn't on the Eastern Front."

"I haven't gotten any real news in a long time. What is happening?"

Mama stopped the discussion. "You are only home for another day. We are not going to spend it discussing this horrible war." She encouraged Hedy to share stories from the camp and filled her in on her friends around Trier.

~

After tear-filled goodbyes, Hedy boarded the train to Rüsselsheim. Her jaw clenched as she tried to tamp down her frustration over the loss of her schooling for the second time. *Only six more months,* she repeated over and over to herself. *Only six more months.*

The train pulled into the station. Hedy was stoic. She would make the best of this situation. Stepping onto the platform, she met up with the other twenty-three women who had been drafted.

Letta, a tall, strawberry blonde, introduced herself to Hedy and compared notes. "You had to deal with Frau May? Poor thing. My sister did her *Arbeitsdienst* there and shared the worst stories about her."

"We came to an understanding," Hedy explained as they walked into the compound.

The facilities impressed her. Compared to the *Arbeitsdienst* camp, these furnishings were luxurious. In place of barracks, the sleeping quarters were in a building laid out like a house with a comfortable dining room and a spacious living room. The walls were painted a light color and had several substantial windows to let in the natural light.

Hedy stepped into the sleeping room and sniffed the air. No straw. Wonderful. Instead, soft bedding and blankets graced the beds.

"I miss my old-fashioned nightshirt." She grinned as she viewed the bunk bed. Dashing to the side of the bed, she clapped. "Oh, a real closet."

The woman next to her chuckled. "Quite a surprise." She offered her hand to Hedy. "I'm Ada."

"Looks like we are bunk mates." Hedy gestured towards the beds.

Letta walked in and tossed her bag next bunk over. "I'll be next to you, Hedy. You'd better not snore."

"I'll do my best." The women laughed and stowed their clothing.

~

Though the surroundings were more pleasant than the farm camp, life was still strict and structured. Frau Horn, the *Kriegsdienst* matron, maintained a tight operation and expected the women to follow the rules exactly. "You will work Monday through Saturday in the factory. Breakfast will be served here, with your *Mittagessen* in the factory. Sundays are your free day. There will be food in the kitchen, but you are expected to cook for yourself and clean up afterwards."

Hedy motioned to catch her attention. "Is there a church in town?"

Frau Horn frowned. "There is, but I should think you would not find it necessary."

Not again. Hedy shook her head and walked away.

~

The next morning, Hedy reported to the Opel factory with the other girls. Rather than cars on the assembly line, there were dozens of cockpit shells of single engine planes dangling from an oversized conveyor belt. The importance of this factory was obvious.

The conveyor moved across the air, transporting the shells from stations on the first floor slowly to the second floor. From floor to ceiling stood metal scaffolding. Following the movement of the cockpits with her eyes, Hedy felt as if she'd been shrunk and placed inside her cousin's Erector set.

The supervisor directed Ada and Letta to another supervisor and ushered Hedy to the second level. "Once transported to the second level, the cockpit walls will be filled with bundles of multicolored wires. It is your responsibility to place each wire into its proper slot."

Hedy stepped back, brows drawing together. "I'm not familiar with electronics or airplanes."

"I don't expect you to be." He showed her an extensive blueprint with instructions. "These are the work drawings. You will follow the steps exactly."

Tension shot throughout Hedy's shoulders. "What if I wire one incorrectly?"

The supervisor spoke in a quiet voice. "I will be checking all of your work. Sit here." He pulled a chair on wheels over to Hedy.

"I have to move while I'm wiring?" She grew pale.

"The conveyor moves exceedingly slow. You will inch alongside it and connect the wires. When you reach the end, you will roll your chair back and start on the next one."

Waving her hands in front of her chest, Hedy stepped back and shook her head. "I can't. How could I live with myself if one of our brave pilots crashed because of me?"

The supervisor peered above his glasses, unsympathetically. "Then don't mess up."

~

As the months passed on, Monday through Saturday had the same routine: wakeup call at 6:30, breakfast at 7:00, and to the factory by 8:00. Hedy's work attire consisted of plain beige coveralls and sturdy work boots. Life was regulated, but the food was adequate.

News of the war rarely came through. Censors marked up letters from friends and relatives at the front lines. As a result, they were barely readable. What was the government hiding?

One evening, Hedy was alone in the living room. She ignored the bright orange tag attached to the radio dial warning civilians against listening to the wrong stations and twisted the knob until English words streamed forth. Her brow creased. The English-speaking voices spoke of Italy declaring war on Germany.

It wasn't possible. The Italians were on their side. She leaned in closer, twisting the dial to clear the static. A muscled woman's hand seized the knob and switched off the radio. "Those are stations you should not listen to."

Startled, Hedy realized Frau Horn was frowning at her. She stuttered. Frau Horn waved her away. "I am certain there are more constructive uses of your time."

Hedy hurried to her bunk and flung herself down. Staring at the ceiling, thoughts raced round her head. What did Frau Horn not want her to know? It was evident the war was coming to the fatherland. Shouldn't she be prepared with all of the information available? With these disturbing notions, Hedy fell into a fitful asleep.

~

"I have a surprise," Letta whispered to Ada and Hedy the next evening as she passed them in the community room. She was carrying a small bag and motioned them to step outside. They trailed behind her. Hedy grinned as Ada raised an eyebrow.

Letta pulled a bottle of wine and tiny tasting glasses from her bag as Hedy and Ada sat on a bench. "Care to join me? We deserve a treat once in a while."

They each raised a glass as Letta poured the red nectar from the bottle. "*Prost.*" The friends toasted one another. Pulling up a wooden stump, Letta sat in front of them. Several toasts were offered. They laughed and told silly jokes.

"I don't think we are holding our wine well." Ada snickered.

"They should serve it with dinner, to better prepare us," Letta recommended.

Hedy offered the last of the bottle to her hostess.

"Wait, wait. I heard a great joke." Letta gulped the wine straight from the bottle and giggled loudly. "Hitler and Göring were standing on the roof of a tall building overlooking Berlin."

Ada stood, finger to her mouth. "Shush, Letta, someone may hear you." She hauled Letta off the stump. "Besides, it is almost lights out."

"No, let me finish." Letta waved her arms in front of her. "It is hilarious. Hitler turns to Göring and says—"

Hedy grabbed Letta's hand and pulled her towards the barracks. "Ada's right. We should stop telling jokes and go to bed."

Leaning on Hedy, Letta let out an exaggerated sigh as she staggered. "Fine. But you are missing out. It really is funny."

~

The next evening, Ada chewed on her fingernail at the dinner table. "Letta was pulled from the line this afternoon."

Hedy dropped her fork. "What are you talking about? Where did she go?"

"I don't know. She didn't come back to the factory, and she's not here for dinner."

Searching the room, Hedy whispered to Ada. "You don't think someone overheard her last night, do you?"

"*Ja*, Fräulein. Someone heard her."

Hedy jumped, almost knocking over her water glass. Frau Horn was breathing down her back. "You and Fräulein Ada will follow me."

Hedy dared not glance at Ada. Her entire body trembled as she ran to keep pace with Frau Horn. They sat in two stiff chairs in front of the matron's desk. Frau Horn stared in silence. After what seemed an eternity, she spoke. "It is against the law to speak ill of or make jokes about the Führer." Her glare caused Hedy to sink lower in the chair. "It is also the law you must report persons doing so."

Biting her lower lip, Hedy focused at the floor under her feet.

Frau Horn waited, glaring at one girl and then the other. "Have you anything to say?"

"Letta was, I mean we all were drinking, Frau Horn." Sweat beaded on Hedy's forehead. "She didn't realize what she was saying. And she didn't tell the joke. She stopped."

"I know." Her penetrating eyes stayed on Hedy. "That is why you and Ada will not be punished. Though you did not report her as required, it is my understanding you stopped her from continuing her rant."

Ada exhaled loudly. Hedy glanced in her direction.

"I recommend you be careful of the company you keep." Frau Horn stood and motioned towards the door. "I also recommend staying away from wine. It obviously dulls your senses. You are dismissed."

Trembling, Hedy rose to leave, with Ada beside her. When she reached the door, she faced the matron. "What will happen to Letta? She was drunk and didn't mean anything."

Frau Horn pointed to the door. "It appears she had too much time on her hands. She will be taken to a more appropriate camp."

Hanging her head, Hedy left the building. Once outside, she shook Ada's shoulders. "They are taking her to a camp for political prisoners. For a stupid joke."

"Shush, Hedy. Thank God she didn't finish the joke; it might have been worse."

"How can it be worse? We don't know what they are going to do to her." Hedy chocked back her tears.

Ada dropped her voice. "Hedy, we can't talk about this. We don't know who reported her or who may be listening."

The two friends observed the women who were strolling around the compound, talking. Which of them had turned Letta in? Hedy's shoulders sagged as she headed to bed.

~

The earsplitting buzz of the air raid siren jolted her awake. Hedy glanced back and forth across the room as she laid in bed watching everyone jump from their bunks. Her brain finally registered she needed to get to safety.

Frau Horn pointed at her and yelled. Hedy leapt out of bed, seized her coat and shoes, and rushed outside. Sprinting alongside the other women, leaving footprints in a light dusting of snow, Hedy rushed into the thick shelter and squeezed between the other girls along the wall.

Several lights glowed in the cavernous room. The lights flickered but remained on. The roar of aircraft grew louder. Anti-aircraft guns fired. Hedy cowered as the noise of the bombers came closer. The sturdy walls reassured her. This was a true bomb shelter, not the makeshift cellar from the previous camp.

Tension crawled through Hedy's body. She had been to the shelters at the work camp more times than she cared to remember. Here she worked at an airplane factory. Previously the Allies had no reason to bomb her. Now they did.

She leaned her head against the wall and prayed.

Eventually, the all clear sounded. Everyone stood, stretched, and quietly shuffled back to their beds. Exhausted, Hedy fell asleep almost immediately.

~

As the morning light worked its way up the window, Frau Horn barged into the room. "Many of you were slow last night."

She glared at Hedy as the women in the room hopped out of bed and stood at attention. "It is imperative you collect your clothing and proceed to the bomb shelter the moment the signal sounds. Besides your personal safety, it is crucial to the war effort that you fulfill your duties."

Frau Horn strode out of the room. Ada rubbed absently at her arms. "It's a good thing we are needed for the war effort, or we might as well be killed."

Hedy cringed and sunk her head in her shaking hands.

~

Chilly but sunny, Sunday finally arrived. Hedy craved time outside. The grating creak of the gates to the compound caused her to spin around. Two dozen soldiers marched in, smiling at the women as they entered. Their commanding officer stopped them and sent for Frau Horn.

The officer allowed the soldiers to relax while he met with the matron. "These men are assigned to man the anti-aircraft guns on top of the buildings. Can you make arrangements for their quarters?"

"Certainly." Frau Horn led him to her office to finalize the arrangements. News of men on the premises circulated around the camp. The women rushed to the entrance, slowing their gait as they grew closer.

One of the soldiers moved towards the women and asked, "Anyone from Cologne? I'd like to hear news from home."

A frail girl with a small turned-up nose approached him. "I am from Cologne."

Town names were bandied around as the men and women introduced themselves. One particular soldier, with broad shoulders and amusing eyes, gazed at Hedy. She glanced at him from under lowered lashes, and he came to her side. "My name is Richart. This is my first month of *Kriegsdienst*."

"I'm Hedy. You are brave to work the anti-aircraft guns."

Puffing his chest ever so slightly, Richart nodded. "It is serious work, but—" he stopped to smile, "—at least I have the afternoons off."

The two chatted about their assignments. Richart pointed out a couple of his friends in the unit. They came over to meet Hedy. Ada joined the group and whispered in Hedy's ear, "It isn't nice to take so many for yourself."

Her jaw dropped, recovering when Ada winked. Hedy quickly introduced her to the men and waved a few of the other girls over. The young people all talked and laughed until the soldiers were required to return to work.

Richart touched Hedy's elbow and drew her attention from the group. "Will you go into town with me next Sunday for cake?"

"I would be delighted." Her heartbeat raced.

That evening, the women tittered with delight as they headed to the dining hall, comparing notes on all the men.

"I want to stand next to you next time men come through, Hedy. You seem to attract them like honey."

Another added, "Seriously, Hedy? Hogging four of them?"

Though the girls acted as if they were saying these things in jest, Hedy sensed a different undercurrent. She pulled Ada aside. "Did I do something wrong?"

Ada rolled her eyes. "No, Hedy. They are jealous the boys noticed you instead of them."

~

The gentlemen were a distraction from the mundane work and sleepless nights. For the next several days, the nights were all the same. The sirens sounded, the women rushed to the shelter, but nothing else happened.

"I am exhausted." Hedy climbed into bed before leaning down to talk to Ada. "I believe we could set our clocks by the bombers. Shouldn't they have run out of bombs by now?"

Ada tossed her lengthy blond hair out of the way as she fluffed her pillow. "I would surely like one full night of sleep. I can't believe we still have to go to the factory after being kept up all night."

"The *Yanks* won't even let me dream about Richart and my's first date." Hedy pulled her blanket over her head and fell into a deep slumber.

The Bomb Shelter

1944

The end of this war will bring with it either the end of European history and any historical meaning from our point of view or our victory will give our continent a chance for a new beginning.

JOSEPH GOEBBELS—*Our Hitler*—April 20, 1944

"Get up, Hedy! It's for real!"

The shrill blast of the air raid siren pierced the air. Hedy opened her eyes, slowly registering the empty beds around the room. Jumping from her tangled covers, she flew from the barracks, only steps behind her friend Ada.

The Allies' planes illuminated the night sky with thousands of green flares parachuting to the ground. The flares sparkled gaily in the air like ornaments, a deceiving contrast to the destruction they foreshadowed.

"The Christmas trees." Ada pointed to the sky as Hedy sprinted across the wide gravel drive to the bomb shelter.

The roar of the bombers grew louder. The repeating shots of the anti-aircraft guns on the roof increased as the teenage girls struggled to open the heavy wooden doors to the shelter below. Debris crashed around them. The smell of smoke combined with the deafening noise rendered Hedy nauseous. She focused her strength on opening the massive doors. As the hinges swung open, the screeching of an approaching shell startled them. Instinctively, she shoved her thin friend into the dark shelter. Vibrations reverberating from the explosion slammed Hedy into the shelter, throwing her down the long, stone stairs.

Her world went dark.

~

The sharp corner of the cold concrete stair cut into Hedy's back. As she pulled herself to a sitting position, pain shot from her head to her tailbone. Blinking, she attempted to orient herself.

The electricity was out, leaving the cellar pitch black. Rubbing the back of her head, Hedy strained to see through the darkness and patted the rough concrete around her. Her hand brushed against a leg to her left, and she jerked back.

"Oh, no. Ada, are you all right?"

The figure moved although Hedy was unable to hear Ada's response, only a thrumming in her ears. Scooting closer to her friend on the floor, she repeatedly hit the side of her head with her palm. Dull ringing replaced the silence. In the dark, she barely perceived Ada's lips moving and lowered her head nearer.

Ada groaned, "Did you really have to push me that hard?"

In spite of herself, Hedy smiled.

~

"I'm so sorry." Hedy's stomach tightened as she attempted to assist Ada. "I might have gotten you killed."

"It's not your fault. I supposed it would be like all the other nights, too." Cautiously, Ada worked herself up to a sitting position. "How close was that bomb?"

"Too close." Hedy leaned against the wall and slowly pulled herself into a standing position. "Can you stand?"

She positioned her hand under Ada's shoulder and helped her up.

"I don't think anything is broken," Ada murmured, "but Frau Horn is going to have a fit we got here so late."

"We'd better find the other girls before she finds out." Hedy's hands quivered. "I can't believe we are more afraid of her than the bombers."

With the ringing in her ear subsiding and her eyes becoming

accustomed to the dark, Hedy managed to lead the way down the long stone hallway to the room with the others.

Finding a minor bit of unoccupied wall space near the doorway, Hedy scooted against it and gently leaned her bruised back against the cold stone. She lifted her thick hair and folded it behind her head to act as a cushion.

Pulling a rosary out of the small pocket on her nightshirt, Hedy's fingers tightened around a tiny white bead. "Hail Mary, full of grace. The Lord is with you. Blessed art thou—" She became distracted by the next wave of approaching airplanes. "Blessed art thou among women and blessed is the fruit of thy womb Jesus. Holy Mary, Mother of God..."

Another explosion hit the ground. The masonry showered miniscule particles of dust onto the young women. Hedy prayed faster. "Pray for us sinners now and at the hour of our death."

Though she had known the prayer her entire life, it was difficult to hold the words straight in her head. The roar of the airplanes, the tat-tat-tat of the anti-aircraft fire, and the vibrations of the shells hitting the ground brought frightening visions to her head. Unconsciously fingering the rosary, bead by bead, she scanned the thick walls of the shelter. They continued to rain dust, but seemed to be holding. The expressions of the women next to her mirrored her particular terror and concern.

Hedy kept the rosary low in her lap, away from Frau Horn's prying eyes. She didn't really worry about being reprimanded for praying. Frau Horn was probably saying a few prayers herself.

Her fingers grasped a bead. "Hail Mary, full of grace. The Lord is with you," she began again. The bombing continued. The darkness became more ominous with each explosion. Beside her, Ada's petite body trembled as her friend attempted to hold in the sobs.

"Come on. We should be getting used to this." Hedy tried to hold back her anxiety while comforting Ada. "We've been in this cellar every single night this week. I'm thinking about asking if we can decorate it or maybe move our bunks down here."

Ada shuddered. "The lack of sleep makes it scarier. I'm exhausted, sore, and scared. We can't tell anyone about our close call or we'll get punished for not having come down sooner." Wiping her tears, Ada fidgeted as she attempted to settle into a more comfortable position. "Besides, the bombers haven't been anywhere near this close before."

Silently, Hedy agreed. The preceding explosion sounded as if it might have hit the factory. The airplanes were the reason the Allies was bombing them. *Oh Gott.* She needed to concentrate on anything else.

Another bomb exploded, further away. Her hand loosened the grip on the rosary slightly. Though the overall nervousness in the cramped shelter seemed to abate, Hedy wanted to crawl out of her skin. The feeling of anxiousness overwhelmed her. She would go insane if she didn't get out of the cellar.

Hedy allowed her head to rest against the damp, uncomfortable stone wall. She made do as best she could. Attempting to distract herself, she imagined her next date on Sunday. Sunday was only two days away, and she drifted into a fitful dream about the most handsome soldier at camp.

A shrill piercing cut through the air, rattling her from her trance. The ground shook as cement dust and plaster rained around them.

Stillness settled in the basement. Collectively, the group held their breath, waiting to see if the building would fall on them. After what seemed like an eternity, the all clear signal wailed in the distance. A cheer went up as the girls scrambled towards the door, pushing each other in the crowded cellar. Claustrophobia overtook Hedy as the bodies propelled her into the hallway.

Frau Horn stopped the shoving by raising her hand and clearing her throat. "We are not aware of the damage, stay back while I open the door. We will leave slowly in a single file line and wait outside the building."

The matron cautiously pulled at the door, but it would not budge. Two of the girls started to cry. Frau Horn glared in their direction, stopping them. "We can't go out this way," she stated matter-of-factly.

The girls searched the basement for an alternate exit. The only other option involved a small window adjoining the ceiling.

"I need a volunteer to crawl out this window and find out why the door will not open." The matron surveyed the room.

Immediately Hedy volunteered, her face flushed and her breathing shallow.

Ada yanked her back. "What are you thinking? You don't know what is out there."

"I can't remain in here any longer." Hedy trembled, knocked Ada's hand off of her arm, and maneuvered her way to the window.

Frau Horn positioned a chair under the window and steadied Hedy as she climbed to the glass. After a firm push, the window opened. The dark night did not allow her to distinguish anything outside. She pulled herself up to the window, maneuvered her legs out one by one, and, shoving herself off the sill, slid down with a scream.

Stunned from the drop, Hedy rubbed her head and struggled to focus. She steadied herself in the bottom of a sizable crater, smoke billowing from pieces of debris around her. The stench of the smoking debris along with the realization of how close the bomb had hit caused a wave of nausea to overtake her.

"Hedy. Hedy. Are you ok? Where are you?" The girls in the cellar yelled out the opening.

"Quiet. How are we to hear her, if you are all yelling?" demanded Frau Berger. "Hedy, can you answer?"

Struggling to hold back the nausea, Hedy explained the situation to those stuck inside. "There is a deep crater right below the window. Give me a moment to figure out how to climb out, and I'll try to open the door."

Climbing out of the crater, her bruised body aching, she tiptoed around the rubble to the other side of the building. The blast which had thrown her into the shelter earlier caused the walls to shift and the doors to jam.

Looking around for help, Hedy realized the supply warehouse next to the airplane factory had been hit with an incendiary bomb and was ablaze. She returned to the crater and called to Frau Horn.

"Are there any men available to help?" Frau Horn wondered.

"Everyone is running around trying to put out fires. The warehouse has been hit."

"What will happen if we exit through the window?"

"Everyone will need to go feet first and be ready to slide down. I'll go back down and clear any shrapnel in the way." Grimacing, Hedy inched her way back down the crater. Using her boots, she kicked away the smoking debris. Frau Horn barked orders above her. Involuntarily, she grinned at the matron's extreme efficiency in organizing the escape.

"Ooohhh." The first girl pushed herself out of the window, hit the side of the crater, and slid down to the bottom as if on a bumpy playground toy.

Ada appeared in the window as Hedy helped the first girl out of the crater. Landing with a thud at the bottom, Ada rubbed her bottom. "For the second time tonight, gravity has not been my friend."

Hedy hustled Ada out of the way for the others. The flurry of activity in and around the crater amplified. Ada and the other girl climbed to the rim to offer a hand to those climbing out.

Ada called down to Hedy. "We are a bunch of moles."

From below, gentle pushes were given to help the momentum of those climbing. The choreography of those escaping the building and those assisting reminded Hedy of an elaborate dance.

"We may need to get lard to smear on the edges of the window to squeeze her through," snickered Ada, as Frau Horn managed to wiggle herself out the small window.

"You are going to get us in trouble yet, Ada." Hedy cringed in pain with each snort.

~

Once out of the crater, the young women comprehended exactly how close the bomb had come to hitting them. Hedy watched the realization cross their faces. A few more feet and they would not have gotten out alive.

Sobs began. Frau Horn cleared her throat before addressing the frightened young women. "Focus on the future, Fräuleins, not what could have happened. Let this firm your resolve to do your best work to help fight the enemy. Go get some sleep. You've earned it."

The group, dazed, shuffled to their sleeping quarters. Within minutes, the girls were in their beds. Though thoroughly exhausted, the near-death experience kept Hedy's mind racing, making sleep impossible. She was being bombed at an airplane factory instead of studying at the Institute of Strasburg. Her stomach cramped as she tossed and turned in her bunk before finally falling asleep.

~

The morning light showed the destruction from the previous night. While the men hauled away the considerable debris, Hedy penned a letter to her parents sharing the events of previous night, assuring them she was okay. She intentionally omitted the part about her almost not making it to the shelter, not to worry them. She also wrote Konrad, hoping he would receive it wherever he was.

After posting the letters, Hedy treaded across the compound looking for Richart. She knew his position involved the top of one of the larger buildings, but she wasn't sure which one. Working her way around the wreckage, she recognized four of his friends.

Rushing over to them, Hedy hugged each one. "I am glad you are safe. Where is Richart? I want to tell him how much I'm looking forward to this Sunday."

The men's expressions went blank. None would look Hedy in the eye.

Feeling the blood rush from her face, she stumbled back, her hand flying to her mouth. "No!"

Richart would not ever be joining her again. Tears pooled in her eyes, and she hurried back to her room.

Lying in her bed, a sharp pain pierced her abdomen. The pangs of agony amplified until they became so severe, she dragged herself to the sickbay. The doctor on staff blamed it on stress and female irregularity, and ordered warm compresses. Between the painful abdominal attacks, an idea formed in the back of Hedy's mind.

~

Days later, Frau Horn assembled all of the draftees together. "I have magnificent news for you. Your work has been noticed by the officials in Berlin. They are tremendously pleased with your progress."

Her announcement was met with a splattering of applause. Ada's eyes narrowed as Frau Horn continued. "You only have one month left in your service. Due to your exemplary work, you have been chosen to remain here at the factory for an extra six months serving your country."

Groans filled the air. Frau Horn's features hardened. "Remember, girls, we are at war. We must achieve what we can to win for our fatherland. Do not underestimate how well you are treated here. You are fed and kept safe. It is not as easy in other places."

The crowd grew silent. She dismissed the assembly to go back to work.

"I refuse to stay another six months." Hedy stomped her foot, almost stepping on Ada's. "My coursework starts in Strasbourg, and I *will* be there."

Sadness covered Ada's face. "I don't believe you get a choice, Hedy."

With clenched hands, Hedy glared back at her. "Maybe I do."

~

Ada rushed in to the infirmary, startling Hedy, who gazed at her friend and moaned. "My lower back is killing me."

Worry showed in Ada's eyes as she squeezed Hedy's hand. "I came as soon as my shift ended. Are you all right? This is the third time this week you've been in the hospital."

Eyeing the door to assure no one could hear, Hedy explained. "I told you I would not be staying for another six months. If I am going to die for my country, I want to be helping soldiers in a hospital, not sitting in a factory."

Gasping, Ada's eyes grew wide. "Do you realize the trouble you will be in if you are caught? Think of Letta. If she was sent away for a mere joke..."

A flit of doubt crossed Hedy's mind, but she shrugged it off. "I am complaining of women's problems. The male doctors haven't a clue how to deal with them. I asked my parents for my family doctor to request my discharge."

"But then I'm stuck here without you." Ada shivered at the idea.

"Wait a few weeks after I'm gone, and you can try it too." Hedy elbowed her friend, and the two snickered, carefully keeping quiet.

Evacuating Trier

1944

Adolph Hitler declared war on the United States 11 December 1941. The American bombers give their answer: ATTACK. ...This leaflet was dropped by an American bomber.

American propaganda leaflets dropped in Germany—1943-44

Stepping off the train, Hedy spotted her mother and father's gaunt faces. She clasped her travel bag and pushed her way beyond the crowd to greet them.

"Whoa, *Süße*, you'll knock us over," her father teased as she threw herself against them in a giant embrace. He picked up her bag while her mother linked their arms together for the walk home.

The main streets of Trier were deserted. The cafes were practically empty. The tourists who had always filled the ancient city in March were nowhere to be found. The whole town appeared to be in mourning.

"Mama, Vater, where is everyone?"

Her father's mouth formed a grim line. "Last week, the town's administrators announced women and children must report to the railway station the next morning. When the families arrived at the station, officials shipped them east to host families in the center of Germany."

Her mother interrupted her voice cracking. "The host families have not volunteered their extra rooms; instead they are required to take the refugees."

"I can't imagine that is a good situation." Hedy pointed at the empty tables in the cafes. "But why the evacuation?"

"Our extensive railroad yard system. It is simply a matter of time before we are bombed. The *Alliierten* are pushing eastward. Rumors of an invasion are rampant." Vater shook his head. Focusing his attention on Hedy, he explained. "The postal administration office is moving to Koblenz next week. I've made arrangements for the two of you to stay with my sister Gisela in Noviand where you should be safe."

Hedy mulled over his statement. "Vater, isn't Noviand as close to the fighting as Trier?"

"It is, but it is a farming community. There is no reason for the *Alliierten* to bomb it."

Hedy knew Noviand well as she and her father had spent countless weekends cycling across the countryside to visit his sister. As nice as it would be to visit her cousin Rosemary, she hated to be separated from her father once again. This was one more thing beyond her control.

A selfish notion crossed her mind. "I assume this means my schooling in Strasburg is on hold again." Hedy's whole body sagged.

"I'm afraid that is the least of our worries, *Süße*. I'm not sure how much longer we will hold Strasburg."

She gasped. "You can't be serious. We are losing France?"

His eyes grew dark as he nodded and clasped her elbow. "Let's get packed."

"Now?" She jerked back.

"You are the only reason your mother was allowed to stay. I convinced the mayor she needed to wait and bring you with her."

"But I need to get a ration card."

Her mother reached for Hedy's hand. "There isn't time. We have to leave today."

~

Nothing would ever be the same. Hedy stood in her bedroom, staring. Resigning herself to the reality her home could be bombed, she packed the scarce number of clothes she could still wear and her hope chest. Carefully she wrapped each piece of china and crystal in the linens she had collected to take to her own house someday. Closing the lid, she patted it gently and sighed.

Vater loaded the chest into the bed of a borrowed pickup. Squeezing herself between the kitchen stove, mattresses, the bicycle, and bedding, Hedy bit her lip and buckled down for the bumpy ride. Trier faded into the distance.

~

"Rosemary. It is wonderful to see you." Hedy stumbled towards her thin cousin, trying to unkink her legs from the truck ride. "I am sorry we have to intrude on you and your parents."

"Oh, Hedy." Her cousin hugged her tightly almost knocking off her thick glasses. "We want you here. We have been so worried. The radio says we shouldn't be, but there have been terrible reports and rumors about bombings all over Germany."

"Marlene, Hedy, come into the house and get settled." Tante Gisela turned towards the large three-story brick structure which served as both their home and the local schoolhouse. "Marcel and Fritz can take the big things." Climbing the steps, she explained, "Your Onkel Marcel is now the senior teacher in town. We are up to thirty-five students with all the evacuees from the cities. The classroom takes up most of the second floor.

On the window sill at the second story landing stood a large statue of Christ. Hedy crossed herself and silently asked him to watch over her family.

"Your rooms will be on the third floor," Tante Gisela continued. "Hopefully the children's noise won't bother you."

Rosemary chimed in from behind them. "Papa asked me to help as his assistant. If we get too loud, let me know, and I'll take them to the courtyard. It doubles as our playground."

Reaching the third floor, Tante Gisela pointed to a room at the right. "Hedy, you will stay with Rosemary." Motioning to the left, she added, "Marlene, there is a room for you." Her voice weakened. "I am sorry it is so small."

Mama opened the door. Sunshine from the lone window shone on the worn pastel quilt covering the small bed which filled most of the room. "Gisela, it is perfect. Thank you."

~

Once the women were unpacked and the Weiß's belongings stowed in various corners of the house, Vater headed back to Trier to begin his move to Koblenz.

Hedy searched for her uncle. "Onkel Marcel, I don't have a ration card. I don't want to use up your food."

Her uncle shook his head and crooked his index finger at her. They strolled into the dark-paneled dining room. "Behind those panels is our dry storage. We have flour, sugar, and rice. We have to be frugal," he lowered his voice, "but if the war doesn't continue more than another year, we should survive."

"I am glad you have it, but," Hedy hesitated, "isn't it against the law to hoard food?"

He rose and headed to the kitchen. "It's called planning, not hoarding. However, I would appreciate you not mentioning it to anyone outside the family."

Hedy drew in her breath, following him. "Of course not." She reflected for a moment. "I don't want to be an inconvenience to you or to run down your supply. With my *Arbeitsdienst* experience, I should be able to earn my keep, if you would introduce me to the local farmers."

Onkel Marcel pulled out a bottle of wine and poured a glass. He pushed his thin spectacles up his long sharp nose. "Very admirable of you, Hedy. The hills around Noviand have communal grapevines. You can start there to meet the various families." He sipped the wine. "I should warn you, though. The hills are very steep. It is difficult work."

"I don't mind the hard work now that I don't have to deal with camp matrons." Hedy shivered at the memory. "If the grapes are for the whole community, where are they stored?"

The impish expression which crossed Onkel Marcel's face startled her. He pointed to his courtyard. "Our home is not only the schoolhouse. The wine is stored and aged in giant casks in the cellar. Besides grapes, the local apples are also processed and aged here."

"The *Viez*." Hedy wrapped her arms around her shoulders. "I love apple wine warmed on a cold night. It has precisely the right amount of kick."

~

For the next two months, Hedy worked six days a week in the vineyards or fields for whichever farmer needed help. Payment consisted of extra food, which she brought back for Tante Gisela's kitchen.

One day in early June, she dragged her drained body back home, too exhausted to notice the rumbling in her belly. Her feet ached from the too-small shoes, but there were no shoes available to buy. All she wanted to do now was to sit, but the entire town was congregating on the main street near the schoolhouse. Excitement and uncertainty filled the air as everyone spoke over each other.

One man stepped backwards, bumping into Hedy. "What happened?" she asked.

"The Yanks have invaded France. The *Invasionsarmee* is headed to the fatherland."

The woman to her right clutched her arm. "Millions have come from the sea."

"They will be here in Germany soon," another shouted.

A flush of adrenaline swept through Hedy. The long-expected Allied invasion had finally occurred. Recalling the ease the bombers had displayed flying over the airplane factory, Hedy recognized it wouldn't be long before Allied tanks arrived in Germany.

"Maybe then this stupid war will be over." Clasping her hand to her mouth, she prayed she hadn't spoken out loud.

The Field Hospital

1944

I believe that our Leader should expect his people to be as firm and resilient as they have shown themselves to be, and I believe that these virtues should be prized because these are the virtues which will win us the war.

JOSEPH GOEBBELS —Speech to Berliners—July 8, 1944

H edy walked to the kitchen sink and scrubbed the remnants of the vineyards from under her nails. "Mama, these grape stains will never come out."

Mama put away the plate she was drying and picked up another, her dress hanging loosely. "Purple is a beautiful color on you."

"I hope it complements the callouses I've acquired since coming to Noviand two months ago." Leaning over to kiss her mother on her bony cheek, Hedy was careful not to drip water on her. "Mama, I am going to volunteer at the field hospital."

The dish in her mother's hand fell onto the counter with a clatter. "What are you talking about? What field hospital?"

Hedy picked up the plate and set in on the shelf. "The priest told me the resort hotels in Traben-Trarbach have been converted into army field hospitals. The number of injured is increasing, and they desperately need help."

"It is 100 kilometers between here and there." Clutching her daughter's arm, Mama continued, "There is a war on. The enemy is on its way. You can't simply head into it."

"The enemy isn't in Germany yet. The summer weather has been wonderful for travel. I will be fine." Hedy dried her hands and tried to peel her mother's fingers from her body. "Besides I'll be more helpful taking care of our soldiers than picking grapes."

Mama seized her daughter's shoulders to confront her directly. "Hedy, no. You aren't a nurse. You didn't finish your training."

Shrugging her off, Hedy planted her feet. "Mama, I can still help." Her stomach gurgled loudly. "Besides, they will feed me. I won't have to use everyone else's rations."

"You bring home more than your share from the farms. Besides, we are doing fine with the food. I don't eat much."

Hedy placed her hand on her mother's back and stroked her spine. "I can feel every bone. You must eat more."

Shaking off her daughter's touch, Mama's eyes narrowed. "A young girl cannot go traipsing around the countryside in a war."

Tante Gisela and Rosemary stood in the doorway, not wanting to interrupt. Hedy marched to her aunt and dragged her into the kitchen. "Tante Gisela, please explain to Mama. I'm eighteen and an adult. Our country needs me."

Gisela glanced from Hedy to Mama and lowered her eyes. "I don't know what to tell you."

Pushing the dark rim of her eyeglasses back onto her nose, Rosemary chimed in. "You should go, Hedy. The hospitals need the help. I would hate to think of Willis hurt and the hospitals not having enough nurses." She looked around the room. "I'd like to join you, but Papa needs help with the school."

Mama straightened and, refusing to acknowledge Hedy or Rosemary, marched out of the room.

Gisela watched her sister-in-law leave and patted her niece's hand. "Hedy, you aren't a burden on us. I wish you would change your mind. Your mother will be worried sick, and she isn't as strong as you."

Hedy's chest expanded with gratitude towards her aunt. "I can only go because she will be in your capable hands."

Tante Gisela stepped outside, leaving the cousins alone. Hedy sat next to Rosemary. "Have you received word from Willis lately?"

Rosemary beamed. "He's hoping to get a week furlough next month." She scooted a little closer to Hedy.

"He is a dear. How long have you been seeing each other?"

"Almost a year." Rosemary appeared ready to explode. "In his last letter, he said he has something important to ask me on his next leave."

Laughing together, Hedy twirled her cousin around the room.

~

Dressed in a worn blue dress and equipped with a small backpack, Hedy offered her mother a hug goodbye.

Her sobbing mother stopped her. "I'd like to give you something before you go."

Mama unclasped the chain from around her neck and held up the simple gold cross for Hedy to see. "My mother gave this to me when I was eighteen. I would like you to have it." She hesitated, giving her cracking voice a moment to recover. "May it protect you on your journey."

Hedy embraced her mother while she attached it around her neck. "Thank you, Mama. I promise everything will be fine." She patted the cross reassuringly and mounted her bicycle.

"Hedy, please be careful." Her mother wiped her eyes with the back of her hand. "The enemy may be anywhere along the road or who knows where else."

After assuring her mother she would, Hedy pedaled off. The beautiful spring day cleared her mind, and she closed her eyes to breathe in the smell of honeysuckles. A pothole jarred them back open and she struggled to maintain control of the bicycle.

The road had not been maintained for years. As she pedaled further down the road, detours became a frequent occurrence. After an hour, there was still no one else on the road. "I guess I should not expect many travelers. Who can get petrol?" Her eyes searched the woods ahead for activity.

The whine of an engine behind her caused her to jump. Her bike wobbled as she dashed to a clump of trees. Hopping off, she hid. A flatbed truck filled with crates of produce driven by a farmer with a worn face drove by.

Shaking her head, Hedy chastised herself. Mama's excessive

worrying had made her jumpy. Riding on, she pushed up the mountain range. After hours of biking and with aching legs, she crested the final hill.

Her heart raced as the black slate roof with miniature spires of the resorts first came into view. She rode closer, noticing how the red painted half-timbers contrasted beautifully with the whitewashed walls to form triangles and rectangles across the elongated building. The impeccable landscaping and one long side of the building reflected in the crystal clear river.

Stopping to catch her breath, Hedy surveyed the valley and absorbed this picturesque view. This was the right decision. Filled with a second wind, she coasted down the hill to the front entrance.

~

The serene atmosphere of the resort was swept away as she pedaled closer. Ambulances lined up outside the door, with medics pulling patients on gurneys out. The ornate front doors of the resort were propped open to display the frantic activity inside. The smell of antiseptics and lingering death combined, knocking Hedy back. One section of the resort had been set aside for surgery. Along all of the other walls, cots stood almost on top of each another. Worse still, patients filled every one. None of her previous volunteer experiences prepared her for this.

Hedy stood at the door unable to move. An orderly bumped into her as he wheeled a patient around her. "Fräulein, can I help you with something?"

Finding her voice, she answered, "I would like to volunteer to help, if you need it."

"Do we?" The medic waved to a haggard nurse. "Schwester Marga, help is here."

A middle-aged nurse with a few strands of hairs peeking from her cap strode over. Hedy introduced herself.

"Your help would be greatly appreciated." Schwester Marga called a doctor over. "Which official classification do we assign to her?"

"I don't know," the distracted doctor said. "Is there money to hire her?"

Hedy waved her hands to get their attention. "I am here strictly as a volunteer. You don't need to pay me. If you give me a place to sleep and meals, I will help as much as I can."

"Can't argue with that." The doctor handed her to the nurse. "Schwester Marga will get you set up and trained. She is the best around." He took off towards the surgery.

Schwester Marga provided her with a quick tour of the hospital. Walking briskly, she introduced Hedy to the skeleton staff working in the makeshift facility: the surgeon, another doctor, and a number of medical orderlies. Three of the local civilian women worked as cleaning ladies.

Two hours later, Hedy was fed and sent to a volunteer's house across the street. She climbed the stairs to the small attic. It had no heat and only a tiny window. At least a comfortable bed awaited her. Exhausted, she fell fast asleep.

~

"*Guten Morgen*, Hedy." Schwester Marga handed her the standard shapeless grey and white striped dress topped by a thin collar to be worn as part of the nursing uniform. From a shelf in the supply closet, she pulled out a white apron with outsized front pockets and a white scarf. "You are not trained as a nurse, correct?"

Hedy accepted the uniform and responded with a shake of her head. Schwester Marga continued, "Then you don't need the Red Cross pin for your neck." She pointed to a room down the hall. "Change and I will show you what needs to be done."

Changing, Hedy carefully wrapped the wide apron straps across her back and tied them in the front. Smiling, she recalled how long ago she had to rely on Kiki to tie her apron. She stepped back into the hallway and searched for the nurse.

"Your hair is to be kept tucked under the scarf at all times. Keep yourself as clean as possible." Schwester Marga ticked off instructions as Hedy accompanied her on the rounds. "Take a second uniform when you leave tonight, so you always have a fresh one. They are yours to keep."

Unable to take her eyes from the nurse, Hedy thanked her.

"A typical day, if we were to ever have one," the nurse began, "starts with rounds at 7:00. We serve breakfast, asking the ambulatory patients to help. Next, bandages are changed, temperatures taken and recorded. *Never* forget to record the temperatures—it is important we track how the patients are doing over time. Beds need to be made or straightened, and medications must be distributed."

Hedy repeated the instructions in her head and nodded. "I received plenty of experience making beds during my *Arbeitsdienst*."

"Good." The nurse strode down the hall. "We are a field hospital. We stabilize the soldiers before they are transferred to the larger hospitals in the center of the country. There are the better facilities and many more doctors."

She paused for a breath. "Mid-morning, the doctors will make their rounds and we will record their orders on charts. For the patients well enough to be transferred, you will assist them in preparations for the trip." With a long slow sigh, she added, "Unfortunately, as soon as one bed empties, more injured arrive."

Schwester Marga stopped at the foot of a soldier's cot. "Geoff, you are looking considerably better today. How are you feeling?"

Geoff smiled weakly at her and shrugged. "Better, Schwester."

She patted his foot before continuing her instructions to Hedy. "After checking in the new arrivals, you will assist in getting everyone their *Mittagessen*. Usually we can stop for a quick bite ourselves, but be prepared to work during the meal when necessary. The rest of the afternoon will be spent checking on the patients, reading to them, or assisting with their correspondence."

For the first time, the nurse stopped and faced Hedy directly. She lowered her voice. "Try to call them by name if possible. Most are young boys, hurt and away from home, and need to feel like someone cares. Some do not think they will make it home. The best medicine may be the knowledge they still matter."

Hedy's hand flew to her mouth. She crossed herself before finishing the tour.

~

The difficult days drained Hedy. Her shift finished at 6:30 each evening. A sandwich in the hospital kitchen barely provided her energy to cross the street and climb up the stairs to her attic room. Closing her scratchy eyes, sleep came straightaway, as did the alarm at 6:30 the next morning.

After several days of training, Schwester Marga pulled her aside.

"I have been impressed with your work, Hedy. Rather than waiting for direction from me, I would like you to be responsible for the less seriously wounded."

Hedy stood taller and pulled her shoulders back, feeling like a peacock.

"Schwester Hedy," a patient called to her.

She raised her chin and strode over to him. His face and the complete right side of his body were burnt. Her pride dissipated when she realized the pain he would have to live with.

He refused to speak of his experiences on the front line. The horrors were etched deeply into his face. In the Trier hospital, there had been a strong sense of pride in the war by soldiers and the staff. Here that pride was nonexistent.

~

Changing the bandages on a new arrival a few days later, Hedy noticed the clenched jaw beneath his day-old rubble. She stopped immediately. "*Mein Herr*, am I hurting you?"

"No, Schwester." He sighed. "This war is hurting me."

She patted his hand. "Come now. You shouldn't think that way."

The patient responded with a bitter sneer. "We are losing this damn war. Countless lives have been wasted." His chin trembled. "It has all been in vain."

Hedy steeled herself. She would not let the anger and tears show. "Don't focus on the war. Let's focus on getting you better." Finishing dressing the wound, she rubbed his shoulders, but could not look him in the eyes.

~

Other days were easier. The men searched for distractions to release their frustration. Hedy was a favorite topic of conversation.

"Schwester Hedy, where are you from?"

"How is your family?"

"Did you receive those full lips and great smile from your mother?"

"What are you going to do after the war?"

And the most popular question, "Do you have a boyfriend?"

Loving the attention, she gently flirted back. An expert at throwing the questions back at the patients, she encouraged them to open up about their lives. Often, the soldiers would start to reminisce about more pleasant days and, Hedy hoped, to forget about the pain for a little while.

The local Great War veterans were also a blessing, as a living reminder to the soldiers' that life would go on once the war concluded. They brought books, magazines, playing cards, and their wives' home-made cookies. Their advanced age, however, did not stop them from flirting with Hedy. "These boys are too young for you. Women like mature men," one 70-year-old teased.

Hedy tilted her head demurely. "You are so right. When do you think I will find a mature man?"

He slapped his knee. "Don't mess with Schwester Hedy."

~

Her responsibilities grew each day as the number of injured increased. One day, the doctor asked her to join him in the surgery room. "I am performing an extremely complicated procedure and need you to hold a book with the diagram steady, so I can reference it."

Her chest tightened. She began inhaling rapidly. She had never seen an actual surgery, let alone assisted. What if she got sick? Or dropped the book?

Schwester Marga read her mind. "You will do fine. You have seen worse on the hospital floor and handled it. Stop worrying and go help the doctor."

Trembling, Hedy scrubbed and entered the surgery. The doctor handed her an oversized book opened to an illustration of the internal anatomy of a human body. Positioning her by the operating table, he barked instructions. "Right there. Try not to jerk or move your hands. I need to see where to cut."

Steeling her arms, Hedy did her best to center her attention on the book and not stare at the opened body next to her. Her eyes darted away. The doctor pushed a pile of man's entrails to the side. Trying to control her quivering hands, she swallowed and prayed the surgery would be finished soon.

Schwester Marga grasped her elbow. This offered Hedy enough time to compose herself and train her eyes on the opposite wall.

Finally, the surgery was complete. The doctor washed up and thanked Hedy for her help. "Are you ready to head to medical school now?"

Vigorously she shook her head. "*Doktor*, I like physical therapy better. Less blood."

~

On her rounds, Hedy stopped at a bed with a sleeping child in it. Frowning she searched for the head nurse. "Schwester Marga, are we taking the local children?" She pointed to the child's bed.

The nurse's voice became flat, almost monotone. "I am afraid he is a solider."

"He can't be fourteen years old." Hedy widened her eyes.

Bitterness replaced the flatness. "They claim he is sixteen. The government is making sixteen year-olds serve."

Heat rose throughout Hedy's body. She struggled to modulate her voice. "If we have to send children to war, we have already lost."

Schwester Marga gently placed her hand on Hedy's back. "Try not to let it get to you." She regarded the hospital floor, covered with cots. "And don't let the injured see your reaction. They have enough to deal with."

Hedy resumed her work, trying to regulate her rage. She pictured her cousin Aldrich playing on the farm. Was he sixteen yet or still fifteen? A commotion near the entrance interrupted her thoughts. The doctor, the nurse, and two medics were frantically trying to save a patient.

"This man needs a transfusion immediately or he will bleed to death. Is there anyone who hasn't given lately?" The doctor's gaze searched down the hall until it lit on Hedy. "What is your blood type?"

She stood frozen. Finally, she stuttered, "I-I don't know."

He waved his hand to rush her down the hall. "Will you donate blood if you qualify?"

"Y-yes." What had she agreed to?

One of the medics poked her arm with a needle and ran to the lab. "Ouch." Hedy rubbed the spot. Time stopped, and the hall grew completely silent, until the medic barked, "It's a match."

The room became a beehive with all the activity fixated on Hedy. Her scalp tingled and her heart raced as a medic laid her on a wheeled stretcher and rolled it next to the patient's bed. An IV was inserted in her arm causing her entire body to tighten. A clamp opened, and bright red blood flowed into a cup.

In the cup was her blood. The room spun. Once the cup filled to the half-way mark, the medic closed the clamp and poured the cup of blood into a contraption attached to the patient. The room appeared cloudy, but Hedy managed to relax.

Just as the fainting feeling subsided, the medic rushed back to her and opened up the clamp again. "Wait," she cried as he extracted another half cup of blood. Would she have any left? The room blurred. Hedy drifted into a fog.

The doctor cheered, *"Wir haben's geschafft.* We did it. He is coming around."

Applause filled the hallway as the doctor kissed Hedy on the forehead. Her body floated with the movement of the stretcher. The medic murmured in her ear, "It was a direct transfusion of blood. The patient is going to live."

Eyes fluttering, Hedy's head slumped to one side. Maybe she would understand better in the future. For now, she only wanted to sleep.

~

Hedy slept on the stretcher for the night. The doctor donated his office to her, and the kitchen staff prepared special muffins. After breakfast, the doctor checked in on her. "There is someone who would like to speak to you."

He assisted her to the bedside of the patient with her blood in his veins, and left to finish his rounds. With great effort, the patient sat up and gently hugged her. Tears flowed from his bloodshot eyes. "Because of you, I will hold my wife and children again."

She gingerly sat on the edge of his bed, trying to blink back the tears. "Tell me about them."

After sharing stories of the friends and family back home, Hedy rubbed his hand. "What happens to you now?"

"I'm being transferred tomorrow to a hospital closer to home." His trembling voice revealed his excitement. "They have promised me a discharge." He squeezed her hand.

Talk of going home affected Hedy more than she realized. Her stomach clenched as the homesickness overtook her. Wiping the moisture from her eyes, she waved goodbye and searched out Schwester Marga. "May I take a few days off to check on my family?"

The nurse embraced her warmly. "Only if you promise to come back. You have been a blessing."

Günter

1944

The German Volk survived the Romans; it survived the invasions by the Huns, countless wars, the Thirty Years' War, the Seven Years' War, the War of the Spanish Succession, the World War. It will survive this, too.

ADOLF HITLER—Speech at the *Platterhof*—July 4, 1944

Hedy wanted to ask for a full week off, but the number of wounded increased daily. Rumors abounded about how close the American tanks were to the German border. Though a volunteer and not required to stay, she couldn't in good consciousness be away from the hospital for that long. There were so many in need. Instead she requested a two-day leave.

"How will you get home?" Schwester Marga fretted. She dropped the skimpy tuna sandwich from her hand onto the plate. "It is October and there is already snow in the mountains. I don't want you bicycling over the range again."

Holding up her hand until she swallowed the tuna in her mouth, Hedy dismissed the nurse's concern. "Onkel Randolph lives in Bernkastel. I will take the train, and he can take me to Noviand. I'm sure he won't mind visiting his sister for a day or two."

~

The trip went as planned. When Hedy hopped out of her uncle's pickup and into the schoolhouse, she was taken aback by her mother's shallow appearance. Her dress hung on bare bones. "Mama, are you well? Are you getting enough to eat?"

"I am fine, dear, now you are here. I have been so worried about you." Hedy's mother doted on her. "Thank goodness the enemy isn't bombing hospitals. Come into the living room and sit down. I'll bring tea."

While her mother fixed the tea, Hedy quizzed Tante Gisela. "Why does Mama look so weak?"

Diverting her eyes, Tante Gisela wrung her hands. "She worries too much. I can't get her to eat more. Besides her concern for you and your father, she is afraid we will run out of food before the war is over."

Taking her aunt's hands, Hedy leaned over to her. "What can I do?"

Mama interrupted them, carrying in two cups of tea. She set them in front Hedy and Gisela. Gisela stood. "You sit and talk to Hedy. I want to visit with my brother." She left the two alone.

"Has Vater been able to visit?"

Mama's smile answered her question. "Though, he was not pleased to find you gone. He is going to try to visit you in Traben-Trarbach."

"That would be wonderful. I miss him so."

Pulling a letter out of a basket at her side, her mother beamed. "Good news. We finally received a letter from Konrad. The Americans have taken him to the US, even so he is in fine spirits. You will love his letter."

Hedy snatched it from her mother's hand.

> *Dear Onkel Fritz and Tante Marlene,*
>
> *I hope you and Hedy are doing well and staying safely away from the fighting. I am, even if I'm not supposed to be. The Allies captured my unit in Italy. There were so many of us, they decided to ship us to the US. The POW camp is somewhere in a place called Texas. It is unbelievably hot and humid this summer, but the winter should be great.*
>
> *The food is abundant and they treat us well. We can walk around camp; it is barely guarded. I guess they assume we wouldn't know where to go if we left.*

Something about swamps in one direction and rattlesnakes in the other.

Tell Hedy the practicing I did on my violin for her entertainment all those summers has paid off. One day I overheard an American playing a violin rather poorly. I asked if I could give it a go, and he handed it to me.

While I played, a couple of officers ran out of the officers' club. "Would you be willing to play in the band at our club?" they asked.

I could hardly believe it. I'm a German and a POW and they want me to play in a band at the officers' club. Of course I agreed. I get to sleep in (because I work into the wee hours of the morning), play music instead of duties, and, even get a drink or two pushed in my direction.

It's almost a pity the war will be ending.

I miss you all.

Love,

Konrad

Hedy fought back tears of happiness. All those months of worrying about him and he was playing in a band without a care in the world. She laughed aloud. "What about Aldrich, Mama?"

Mama crossed herself and lifted her gaze to the ceiling. "Drafted. Into a tank unit. Tante Claudia thinks he may be close by. She gets some letters from him, but they are few and far between."

"But he isn't old enough." Hedy's lip quivered.

Bitterness filled her mother's reply. "Herr Hitler is making boys as young as sixteen go to war. They don't have guns for them." She took a deep breath and exhaled slowly. "They are sent to the front line and ordered to pick up a dead soldier's gun as soon as one is available."

Hedy's whole body shook. She flung her arms around her mother and held tight. Neither said a word.

~

The hours flew by. Too soon, it was time for Hedy to return. After extracting a promise from her mother to take better care of herself, she rode back to Bernkastel with her uncle. He left her at the train station with plenty of time to spare. She sat on a bench and began reading.

"Hedy? Hedy Weiß?"

A well-built young man with broad shoulders, a strong jaw, and thick blond hair waved to her. Though dressed in a regular army uniform, there was nothing regular about him. She returned his greeting, although she was clueless who this Greek god might be.

"It's Günter Werner—from Birresborn. We used to explore the caves together."

"The scrawny boy from school?" Hedy cringed as the words left her mouth.

Günter chuckled as he straightened his generous chest. "Not so scrawny anymore."

"No, you look great." She held her book up to hide the fire burning in her checks. "It has been more than five years. How did you ever recognize me?"

He stepped towards her. "Your thick black hair and perfect lips."

Hedy almost dropped her book as she turned her head. After checking with the stationmaster, Günter discovered the train would not be coming for another two hours. "There is a cozy little *Weinstube* close to the station. Come have a drink with me before you go."

Opening the heavy wooden door of the wine tavern, they stepped into the dark room lit by candles on each table and warmed by a generous fireplace. The smell of wine and cigarette smoke permeated the room. Günter motioned Hedy to the corner table where she slid into the booth. He squeezed in next to her.

Bottles of wine laid on top of one another in diamond shaped boxes filled the wall behind the bar. Coats of arms of German nobility lined the other walls. Hedy pointed to the wine. "I wonder which of these bottles I helped harvest."

Günter ordered two glasses of the best *Moselwein* Hedy had ever tasted. "This must have been one of them." His glass clinked against hers. "It tastes ideal."

They reminisced about their Birresborn days. "Do you think those preserved fruits are still there?" Hedy chuckled.

"We'll have to go investigate. They have probably fermented. In which case we could sell them to this tavern." Günter's gaze never left her face.

"Do you think Gerda ever found out about the cave drawings?" Her fingers traced the rim of her glass. "I can't believe you wouldn't let me tell her about them."

"Come on, Hedy. You loved having a secret as much as I did."

The waiter brought more wine as they caught up on the past five years, skirting over anything related to the war as best they could. Günter brushed his hand against Hedy's as he raised his glass for a toast.

She felt her heart race. From such a light touch? Surely the wine was going to my head. Hedy offered the next toast. His leg touched hers. She licked her lips and swallowed. They enjoyed another glass.

"I need to get back to the station." She rose to discover her legs were unsteady. Holding her elbow, Günter escorted her through the cobblestone streets.

Once they arrived, he held both her hands in his. "When the war is over, I'll find you."

She drew back. "Of course you will," she teased. Tossing her hair back, she offered an exaggerated pout. "After you fling off all the beautiful girls who will be crawling all over you."

He gazed deeply into her eyes. "I'm serious, Hedy."

The train pulled into the station, allowing Hedy a chance to change the subject. After giving him a quick hug, she boarded the train without glimpsing back.

The evening train contained few passengers. An elderly man with a cane sat near the door. Two rows behind him sat a woman with a half-empty shopping bag. A couple of soldiers with their arms and legs in bandages stared straight ahead on the other side. Hedy weaved her way past the other passengers and claimed an empty seat. Blackout curtains covered the windows. She only needed to go three stops to be back in Traben-Trarbach.

The train started its journey. The car swayed gently back and forth. The other passengers stayed silent. She settled comfortably into her seat, relaxed from the several glasses of wine, and reflected on her evening with Günter. A wide smile crossed her face as she drifted off to sleep.

Jolted from a lovely dream by the train conductor's call of "*Endhaltestelle*, last stop," Hedy slapped her forehead. She had missed her stop.

"Excuse me. When is the next train?"

The conductor glanced at her over the top rim of his glasses. "Fräulein, this is the final train of the night."

"Oh, dear. How far back is Traben-Trarbach?" Her eyes darted around the emptying train.

"About five kilometers."

Hedy groaned. She stepped out of the train onto the platform. The clouds parted, allowing the moon to shine on the road, showing her only path back. No cars appeared. She shouldered her small backpack and began the trek to the hospital.

Each step required such effort. How could she have been so stupid? Why did she drink too much wine?

Arriving at her room near midnight, Hedy fell into bed fully clothed and overslept the next morning. Once at the hospital, she confessed to her previous evening's adventure, expecting a reprimand. Instead, she received the staff's laughter and more teasing than she would have preferred.

~

The wounded continued to flood the hospital. Food supplies dwindled. The nonstop work drained Hedy of the energy to make it up the stairs to her attic room at night. The weather grew colder, but huddled under a thick, old quilt, she barely noticed the lack of heat in the room.

After a month without a break, a summons into the administration office surprised Hedy. A phone call waited for her. "Hedy? It's Günter. I have a week's leave and will be visiting my parents in Braubach. Can you join me for a few days?"

Some vacation time with the handsome young man was extraordinarily appealing. Hedy agreed.

"Is this the fellow who caused you to miss your stop?" the doctor teased. "You might want to refuse any wine he offers."

~

Hedy packed the sandwich from the hospital kitchen into her bag alongside her faded blue dress and stockings. Wearing a pair of light brown slacks, topped with her favorite wool jacket, she actually felt pretty. The black double-breasted jacket was sprinkled with white specks resembling tiny snowflakes. Freedom from her nursing uniform for a couple of days brightened her spirits even more.

The trip required a change of train in Koblenz. Once there she realized the train to Braubach wasn't scheduled to depart for two hours. She wished she had thought to tell her father she was coming through. Oh, well. The rather sparse station offered a solid slab for a bench and she settled in to read. She fidgeted, trying to find a comfortable position.

"Excuse me, Fräulein." A burly soldier dressed in a brown shirt with a swastika wrapped around his arm interrupted her. "If you are waiting, we have more comfortable chairs in the shelter below the station."

"That would be lovely." Hedy followed him around the station and down several steps. She stopped halfway down as the shelter came into view. Couches and overstuffed chairs filled half the room. The other half of the room encompassed tables laden with food and wine.

"Are you hungry?" He politely pointed towards the wall. Bread, meat, pastries, and fruit filled several tables. It was more food than Hedy had seen in months.

She held her growling stomach. "Isn't everyone?"

"Not us." He snickered and brought her a thick roast beef sandwich with brown mustard dripping off the side. "There are benefits to belonging to the Party."

"Hear, hear." Another Nazi lifted an expensive bottle of wine.

She bit into the sandwich and closed her eyes. The flavors woke her taste buds. Inhaling deeply, she savored the treat while listening to the chatter of the Party members around her. The brown shirts were comparing their latest feasts and sagas of their so-called bravery. The more she heard, the less appealing the sandwich became.

A quarter of the sandwich was still in her hand. She motioned towards the tables. "How can you have such an abundance of food? I work at the hospital, and we can barely get enough to supply the injured soldiers."

One man jerked his head toward the food table. "You have to know where to look."

"If you are tired, there are beds in the next room," another offered with a wink.

She swallowed the bile rising in her throat. *I have got to get out of here.* Mustering all of the calm she could, she excused herself. "The air is affecting me. I'll go for a walk before my train arrives."

Once outside, she tossed the remainder of her sandwich to a mangy dog and hurried to the station. Luckily, no one approached her again until the train pulled in. She sighed with relief as she entered the car.

~

"Sorry, Fräulein," said the station master at the last station. "We don't have petrol to run the buses anymore. You'll have to walk to Braubach. It is a pretty decent road, and you can probably catch a ride."

"Another ten kilometers." Hedy headed up the road. "At least I'm used to walking." Several kilometers later, not a single car had passed her.

Did no one use this road? Trekking on, Hedy stumbled on a pile of rags. The rags moved, making her jump.

Under the rags laid a scruffy man, barely more than a skeleton. He growled. "Watch it." Eyeing her bag, he demanded, "Do you have food?"

Backing up, Hedy was dumbstruck. Her hand touched the small gold cross on her neck. The man sat up; a crazed look covered his face. "I need food. What is in your bag?"

She started to run, but his bony hand seized her leg. "I don't want to hurt you. I haven't eaten in days."

The pain in his request stopped Hedy from struggling. She dug in her bag. "Where are you from?"

"Poland. They dragged me here to farm. The fighting came and everyone left." He stared at her. "What am I supposed to do now?" The desperation in his voice was tangible.

"Oh." She handed him the thin sandwich from her bag. "You are a displaced person."

The man snatched it from her and devoured it, all the while glaring at her. "You mean slave of you Germans."

Terrified, Hedy ran. Scraping of metal against metal sounded behind her. She slowed enough to look behind her. The displaced person was fleeing into the woods. The noise grew louder. Overwhelming smells of oil, petrol, and smoke surrounded her. A Panzer tank with three passengers dressed in street clothes perched on top appeared. She stared in bewilderment.

A head poked through the cupola. "Need a ride, Fräulein?"

Hedy blinked. The tread circled two metal wheels almost as high as her head with eight smaller wheels in between. Dwarfed by its size, she glanced down at her traveling clothes. From atop the tank, a young woman around her age called out, "Come on. It's slow, but fun. Far better than walking."

"I'm glad I wore slacks today." She cautiously attempted to climb aboard.

"I need to punch your ticket," teased the soldier as he hopped out of the center console. He guided her to an open space to the left of the gun barrel, where she sat clearly in his view.

"I'm afraid I must have left it in my other coat." Grinning, she searched for something to hold to as the forty-three tons of steel lurched forward.

The other passengers welcomed her. Herr Muller, a paunchy middle-aged man, decided to educate her about her ride. "This is a Panzer IV. The word panzer comes from the Latin work *pantex* which means belly. The Old French referred to a coat of mail as *panciere*, literally, armor for the belly."

The tank lurched as it powered through a sizable pothole. Everyone held on as Herr Mueller continued. "But we don't care what the French did. In Middle High German, *panzier* simply means armor. It seems only fitting armor with five men in its belly should be called a Panzer."

Hedy started to ask a question but was stopped by the lanky civilian on the other side of the garret. "If you humor him, he'll talk your ear off. I'd rather hear from the young ladies on our coach."

"Me, too," shouted the soldier above Hedy.

"And I." Another soldier's upper body sprung out a window on the side of the center column, startling her.

Cruising at only twenty kilometers an hour, the soldiers had plenty of time to question and flirt with the ladies. Sooner than she realized, they entered the town. All of the soldiers in the tank hopped down and wanted to assist her. She thanked each of them with a quick hug and continued down the street to Günter's house.

A modest dwelling with two bedrooms, Günter's home was built on the side of a hill. While waiting for Günter to return, his parents offered her tea in the spacious kitchen next to a generous family room. They remembered her from Birresborn and asked for news of her family.

Günter and his fifteen-year-old brother Ralph burst into the house. "Hedy. You made it." Günter grabbed her around the waist and spun her around.

"Hey, my turn," Ralph interrupted.

"Wait a minute," Hedy cried. "You don't want to spin me after tea."

Laughing, the three of them sat and chatted. "Let's go for a walk before it gets dark." Günter stood, offering his hand to Hedy. Ralph leapt up to join them. Günter stopped him. "I think Papa needs you to help him."

Once outside, Hedy scolded him. "Poor Ralph. You should have let him join us."

Günter shrugged and guided her into the woods. "Let him find his own girl." He motioned to a downed log overlooking a clearing. The sun dipped into the horizon, displaying a glorious array of red and orange light. Günter reached over to hold Hedy's hand. "It was wonderful to stumble onto you in the train station."

She stared into his steely blue eyes, her mouth dry. "I'm glad you did. It's delightful seeing you again."

Günter leaned towards her, gently touching her lips with his. Surprised, Hedy hesitated, closed her eyes and replied in kind. His hand circled around her waist, and he pulled her closer to him.

"Mama said to call you for dinner," Ralph shouted from the edge of the woods. Günter and Hedy leapt apart. "What is taking you two so long?"

Thankful for the evening shadows, Hedy hid her blushing face as she straightened herself.

That night, the brothers offered their bedroom to Hedy, and they retired to the living room. Stripping down to only her undergarments, Hedy crawled under the thick handmade quilts with a smile and sleep engulfed her.

~

"Come on, sleepy head. It's time to explore the world," shouted Ralph as he barged into her room the next morning.

Horrified, Hedy pulled the covers up as far as possible. "Please let me sleep a bit more," she begged, realizing she had no robe and dared not move any more than necessary.

Ralph would not allow it. "We have so much to do today. I'm not going to let Günter hog all your time again."

She finally convinced him to leave and got dressed. Ralph definitely had a crush on her.

The brothers escorted her around town, showing her the sites. They stopped for tea and cake at the local café, where a group of the Nazis were making a racket. Günter noticed her staring. "Is there something wrong?"

"I hope they aren't the same ones I met in the train station." She failed to hide her disgust.

Concern showed on Günter's face. "Did they bother you?"

"No, they were quite friendly and offered me food and drink."

He frowned. "Why are you upset?"

Her heart raced as her voice rose. "You would not believe their luxurious surroundings at the train station. There was enough food to feed an entire division. Hidden solely for them."

"Quiet, Hedy." Günter patted her hand. "They had food and were nice enough to offer it to you. I don't understand why there was a problem."

Dropping her fork to the table, she glared at him. "Do you realize how little food we have to offer the wounded at the hospital? I needed to work in the fields near Noviand because I didn't have a ration card. If I had gotten one, it wouldn't have mattered. There is hardly any food in the stores. The brown shirts steal from our soldiers and families, and you expect me not to be upset?"

Shaking his head, he attempted to pacify her. "They have permission from the Party for the things they do. It may not seem fair; nonetheless, it will work out."

"I can't believe you are standing up for them." She attempted to pull her hand away. "They should be run out of the country when we lose this war."

Günter's hand tightened around hers. "We are *not* going to lose, Hedy."

She yanked her arm back. "If you believe that, you are delusional. You would not believe what I am seeing in the field hospital. The radio reports are worse."

"What radio reports?"

"The ones in English and French. We listen to them at the hospital. They give us a better indication of the number of wounded to expect than the allowed stations do."

He set his jaw. "They are Allied propaganda. The Führer has plans." His fist clenched. "We will win the war."

"You are a fool if you actually believe that."

The anger in his eyes caused Hedy to shiver. She twisted in her seat to turn her attention on Günter's brother, who sat staring wide-eyed at the two of them. "So what did you have planned next, Ralph?"

The trio wandered around the town. Ralph regaled them with silly stories. Hedy kept the conversation light, but the twinkle in Günter's eyes had been replaced by dark glances. The afternoon, though pleasant, had lost the intimate feeling of the previous night. Günter's mood lightened eventually, which relieved Hedy tremendously. But, for her, the spark was gone.

~

Finally, the time came for Hedy to catch her train back to the hospital. Günter's strong hands grasped her waist and easily lifted her onto the back of a flatbed trailer. "Sorry I couldn't commandeer a tank for you."

They laughed, and, determined to leave on a positive note, Hedy reminisced once more about the caves of Birresborn on the way to the train station. Standing in the station as the train pulled in, Günter grasped her hand and spun her close to him. "You will wait for me after the war."

"Silly." Hedy grinned as she twirled back out from his arms. "You are a dear friend, but I told you when we were twelve, I wouldn't marry you." With that she boarded to the train and turned back to wave.

Günter stood, silently staring, his gaze intense. She dropped her hand, and her throat thickened.

Evacuation of the Hospital

1945

Therefore, I expect every German to do his duty to the last and that he be willing to take upon himself every sacrifice he will be asked to make; ... I expect city dwellers to forge the weapons for this struggle, and I expect the farmer to supply the bread for the soldiers ... I expect all women and girls to continue supporting this struggle with utmost fanaticism.

ADOLPH HITLER—Radio address—January 30, 1945

C hristmas came devoid of the holiday spirit. More wounded arrived, overwhelming the cots available. The townspeople helped as much as possible, giving up a share of their personal rationed food to prepare Christmas goodies for the wounded. The local bakers worked overtime to supply the Christmas *Stollen*—thick, sweet bread with dried fruits and powdered sugar.

"Any room for this?" Several of the older men of the town carried in a tree they had chopped down for the occasion. Their wives followed with tinsel and ornaments from their attics.

Schwester Marga clapped her hands. "We will make room."

The local church offered a service at the hospital Christmas morning. Even the most adamant Party members did not argue. The priest, wearing a long white robe and a gloomy countenance, was accompanied by two altar boys, scarcely ten years old. He preached a quick mass, praying for the wounded and offering solace to those away from their families.

Hedy clutched her rosary. She knew the unspoken prayer on everyone's lips— *'Let this war finally be over.'*

The partial choir, who barely fit into the room, sang *"Stille Nacht"* without musical accompaniment. Tears welled up in the patients' eyes as they heard *"All is calm; all is bright."* Sobbing overtook most of the staff. By the end of the first verse, even the choir could scarcely sing. Hedy dug into her giant apron pockets for her handkerchief.

~

New Year's Eve brought morale to an all-time low. The enemy had reached Germany. Sub-zero weather and profound snow slowed the Allies' advances. Proclamations on the radio bragged about the German army's ability to use the bad weather to stage serious attacks on the Allies. The great German army had managed to break through the Allied forces near Ardennes and was threatening the Allies' ammunition and fuel dumps.

"We won't hold them back long." A medic bringing the wounded from the front line whispered. "The *Alliierten* are regrouping, and we have nothing left to stop them with. They will be here soon. Expect a lot more casualties."

Hedy gasped. All around her, the incredulous staff murmured amongst themselves. "How many more can there be?"

"Do we have any men left?"

"This stupid war is lost anyway."

The invasion of the fatherland had begun. Evacuation orders to move the hospital inland would arrive shortly. Preparations and planning started. Sleep was a novelty with the staff barely getting six hours off at a time. Hedy found herself having to double check every task. She was too drained to think about the anything but the task at hand.

~

"Alles Gute zum Geburtstag. Happy birthday, Hedy." In spite of the load, the staff wanted to celebrate Hedy's nineteenth birthday, which fell on the feast day of St. Valentine. One of the doctors managed to find, or perhaps was willing to share, a bottle of a fine *Moselwein.* Her new friends, now like family, offered toast after toast

to Hedy, to St. Valentine, and to a smooth evacuation, even after the wine disappeared.

The next morning, the evacuation orders arrived. No one had a moment to sit. Medical equipment was loaded into trucks, supplies were boxed, and patients were made ready. The intense atmosphere made Hedy restless and trembling.

Frantically tying a sixteen-year-old soldier to his bed for transport, Hedy motioned to the head nurse. "How much time is left?" The boy's eyes grew wide, although he didn't say a word.

"Everyone must be out tonight. The *Invasionsarmee* is close, and the ambulances will be traveling in the dark." Schwester Marga paused briefly at Hedy's side. "Which vehicle are you assigned to?"

She shook her head furiously. "I am not going with you. I must get back to my mother in Noviand."

A medic walking by overhead her. "Why would you do that? The enemy tanks are headed that direction. They will be in Noviand in a few days."

"Which is why I must go." She pulled the strap tighter on her patient.

Schwester Marga tapped her foot. "It isn't safe. You need to come with us."

Standing, Hedy planted her feet in front of the head nurse. "My mother needs me. I am going."

"How will you get there?" The medic opened his palms. "You can't go on the main road. There are enemy scouts, or worse, our own retreating soldiers may shoot without knowing who you are."

After pointing her thumb over her shoulder, Hedy crossed her arms over her chest. "I'll go over the mountain."

"At night? In February?" The medic ran his fingers through his hair.

"Don't be ridiculous," Schwester Marga fussed. "You can't think straight after working so many hours without sleep. You are going with us."

Hedy inhaled deeply. Her lips flattened into a straight line. "I am familiar with the vineyards. I used to work in them. They are planted in straight rows on both sides of the mountain." She paused a moment, working out the plan as she spoke. Her expression softened.

"Think of it like a hidden road to Bernkastel. There I can stay with my Onkel Randolph, before heading on to Noviand."

"It is still a bad idea. I want to talk you out of it." The nurse attempted a smile. "But having worked with you this long, I realize you are going to go anyway."

Hedy embraced her. "Don't worry about me. Take care of them." She patted her patient gently on the arm.

The ambulances and trucks were loaded with no time for heartfelt goodbyes. Hedy's heart ached. She was losing a part of her family. For almost a year, they were her teachers, companions, and friends. The final vehicle pulled out. She was totally alone. Reaching for her bag, she trooped over to her bicycle. Now she needed to make her way home.

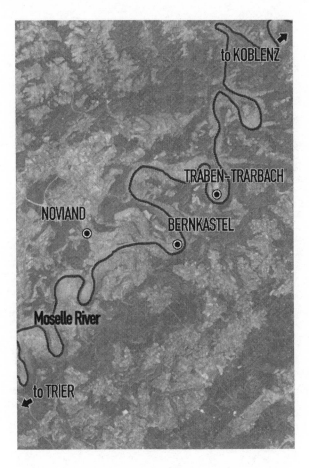

The American Tanks

1945

Throwing her wool coat on top of her Red Cross uniform, Hedy had no time to reflect. She must find a way home. The time for planning had vanished. With only a bicycle, a small backpack, and worn shoes, she must journey over a mountain in February, without being spotted by the enemy. *What could she possibly be thinking?*

Negative thoughts were not going to carry her to her mother. Closing her eyes, she pictured the terrain between Traben-Trarbach and Bernkastel. It was a steep climb up the mountain from the river where she stood, but the slope was planted in vineyards. Vines staked in perfectly straight rows would serve as her trails. With the frozen ground under her feet and the clear evening sky above her, she would not get lost if she stayed within the vines. Even without their leaves, the woody stalks could serve as cover if Allied troops were in the area.

The night sky sparkled with thousands of stars, lighting her way. She visualized her father counseling her. Surely he'd been preparing her for this moment all along; the darker the night, the brighter the stars.

At least there was no snow to trudge through. She mounted her bicycle, but pedaling across the frozen ground was problematic. She would have to push it up the mountain. Her tattered shoes allowed each rock to dig into her weary feet. Blisters arose and would have been painful, except the cold numbed her senses. Her backpack, filled with her second uniform and the few changes of clothes that she could still wear, had seemed light on her trip to Traben-Trarbach so many months ago. Now it weighed against her as if filled with stones.

The medic's warning about the Allies reconnaissance teams and retreating German troops heightened Hedy's concern. Her nerves were on edge. Every noise was a threat. Her eyes constantly scanned the area in front of her. Wind hissing through the plants caused her to drop to the ground.

Cursing under her breath, she reprimanded herself. Hearing ghosts behind every leaf was not going to get her home. Rising, Hedy pushed on. An owl hooted behind her, scaring her enough to drop her bike. Shivering, she continued her trek, trying to disregard the rustling noises.

Around midnight, she left the vineyard rows and cautiously crested the top of the mountain. The walking was less cumbersome, but she was visible if the enemy was near. Stopping to rest, she perched on her bicycle so as not to sit on the frozen ground and scanned the valley below. Where was Bernkastel?

No light from the town could be seen. Doubt entered her mind. Had she walked too far along the ridge? Was she mistaken about the location of the vineyards? Hedy could hear her mother fussing at her for being impulsive. Fighting back the tears, she tried to work out where she was.

It finally dawned on her exhausted mind that the town had blackout curtains. Of course, there wouldn't be any light. Exhausted, she didn't want to move, but it was far too dangerous to sit on top of a mountain in February, exposed to the elements and enemy forces.

Mustering up the few reserves she had left, Hedy lifted the bike. A few steps further allowed her to make out the staked grapevines on the Bernkastel side of the mountain. Now she had the trail she needed. Hedy carefully wheeled her bike down the mountain towards the vines. Her sense of security returned as she walked between the stalks once more.

The steep decline gave her more grief. The bicycle wanted to roll ahead of her, making her arm muscles spasm from trying to keep it close. Creeping between the rows to stay under the branches caused her knees to ache with each step. She walked like the arthritic old men from town. She had no water and no way of telling how much further she needed to go. Silently, Hedy repeated the Hail Mary. When she chanted the line, *pray for us sinners now and at the hour of our death*, she wondered if this may not be the hour.

A small animal scurried across her foot. Hedy screamed, and the bicycle plunged to the ground. Squatting to hide between the bare vines, she slapped her palm to her forehead. If any enemy scouts were around, they knew where she was now.

She stayed hidden until she couldn't stand the cold ground any longer. Holding herself back from the overwhelming desire to race down the mountain, Hedy slinked between the rows, staying alert to all the nocturnal dins.

Finally, she reached the base of the mountain. Stepping out from the vineyard, she oriented herself. With a last search of the stars, and a thank you to Our Blessed Mother, Hedy stumbled the remaining few blocks towards her Onkel Randolph's house. Thank goodness her father had so many brothers. After propping her bicycle against the half-timbers, she banged on the door.

After what seemed an eternity, Onkel Randolph peeked out the side window. His expression almost made her chuckle. He had seen a ghost. Opening the door, he stammered, "What are you doing here?"

Prying her way in, she responded, "Wouldn't you like to invite me in to get warm first?"

He fixed her a warm cup of tea and listened to her story. With a shaking voice, he said, "I can't believe you crossed the mountain in the dark, you fool."

But in the end, he agreed staying off the main road was necessary. Hedy begged to go to sleep and fell fully clothed into bed.

~

Morning arrived almost instantaneously. Hedy crawled out of bed, afraid to put weight on her legs. After a moment or two of groans and stretches, she was able to join her aunt and uncle for breakfast. They begged her to stay another day and rest, but her gut told her Mama needed her.

"Let me find some petrol, and I'll drive you there," Onkel Randolph offered.

Knowing the preciousness of gas, Hedy declined. "This leg of the trip will be considerably easier."

She climbed onto the bike and waved goodbye. Her aunt made the sign of the cross and blew a kiss. Her uncle just shook his head.

~

The clear road allowed her to ride the bike rather than pushing it. The sunshine and her desire to be with her family filled her with the strength she required. As Hedy neared Noviand, heavy guns rumbled in the distance. She shuddered. It wouldn't be long.

As she pedaled finally into town and used the last of her strength racing to the schoolhouse, she saw her cousin out hanging laundry. Sighting her, Rosemary dropped the clothes basket she was carrying. "Hedy? Is that really you?"

Inside the house, someone squealed. *"Gott sei Dank. Gott sei Dank."* Her mother dashed out of the house and squeezed her before Hedy dismounted. "Thank God you are safe. Where did you come from?" She showered Hedy with kisses. "Are you all right?"

Burying her face in her mother's bony shoulder, Hedy didn't say a word. After breathing in the familiar lavender soap, she held her mother tighter. She felt so fragile, Hedy loosened her grip, but refused to let her go. Her eyes reddened.

For the next several hours, Hedy regaled her family with the story of her nocturnal journey over the mountains.

"Unbelievable."

"What were you thinking? It was too dangerous."

"Are you insane?"

She simply smiled. "I knew I needed to be with all of you."

Throughout the day, the rumblings of large guns grew louder, signaling the advance of the invading forces. "They will be here soon. Should we hide in the hills?" Rosemary paced the floor.

"The fighting is all outside of town. They have no reason to bother our village." Tante Gisela reassured her, but mouthed a silent prayer.

Near the end of the day, four German soldiers without weapons stopped by. Their uniforms hung loosely on their emaciated frames. The dark circles beneath their deep-set eyes were the only color left in their faces. Tante Gisela invited them to stay for a meal.

While they ate, the soldiers reported being under heavy shelling from the advancing Allied forces. As the only remaining soldiers of their company, they had loaded their wounded into the final vehicle and sent them to locate a field hospital as far from the front lines as possible.

Emotionless, the senior member explained their final task. "We remained behind to carry each of our dead *Kameraden* to the church yard. The Red Cross transport will be here shortly to pick up, identify, and bury them."

It was difficult to face the soldiers. The horrors they'd faced were beyond Hedy's comprehension. As she shook the vision out of her head, someone tapped her arm. "I noticed your uniform. May I ask a favor?"

"Please do."

"A young boy and his mother were injured by shrapnel during the fighting outside of town. Are you familiar with Frau Berg?"

"Yes." Hedy's forehead wrinkled. "Are she and Walter badly hurt?"

He heaved a sigh. "We treated the wounds as best we could. The mother won't be able to clean and re-bandage the wounds by herself. If you can help, they should be able to recover."

"Of course. I'll do whatever I can. We don't have any medical supplies. Do you have any left?"

The soldier frowned. "We used the last of them earlier today."

Tante Gisela lowered her head. "*Meine Aplogies*, but where do you go now?"

The senior officer patted her arm. "We are going to surrender to the Americans. Pray for good weather. The POW camps don't have enough shelter. We understand they were unprepared because there are so many of us." He sighed. "Hopefully, they'll have food."

Seeing the horror on the women's faces, he reassured them. "We are used to it. We haven't had decent shelter or food for a while. The good news is we won't be fighting." He stood and motioned for his men to join him. Their chairs scraped the floor as they rose wearily.

One of the soldiers said, "Thank you for the meal. It was greatly appreciated."

They stepped outside, and the officer paused. "The Americans will be here tomorrow. You have nothing to fear from them. They have been treating the German civilians well." He trudged up the road alongside his men.

Mama watched them walk away. "The poor souls. They have no spirit left. I can't imagine what life will be like for them as POWs."

Sadness engulfed Hedy as she waved goodbye to the men. She crossed herself and said a quick prayer for their brave soldiers.

~

The next morning, the household awoke to the bark of gunfire and the thunder from the tanks immediately outside the village. Everyone ran outside, congregating near the town fountain, not knowing what to expect, and worrying as to what to do.

"Grab a bed sheet and tie it to a beanpole. We want the enemy to recognize us as civilians and not soldiers," instructed an aged Great War veteran. "Do not hide in the houses. We are Germans. We will meet the enemy head on."

"We are lucky it is the Americans coming. The stories about the Russians are terrifying," stated another.

"Better than the French." An old woman nudged her companion. "Remember them after the Great War, Evert?"

"Don't remind me." Evert grunted.

As mothers clutched their children tight and grandfathers scanned the far-off plumes of smoke with eyes that held the ghosts of past horrors, Tante Gisela shared what the retreating soldiers had conveyed. Silence engulfed the group. Everyone stood and stared from one to other; fear and worry filled the air.

Onkel Marcel's schoolhouse was, by far, the largest house in town. By the time the shooting stopped, someone had mounted a bed sheet on top the tallest wall in his courtyard. Hedy changed into her Red Cross uniform to await the enemy's arrival, hoping the universal symbol of neutrality and aid would keep her and her family safe.

The scraping of metal and the racket of heavy equipment

entered the town first. The rumbling of engines was periodically punctuated by high pitch squeals. Hedy's entire body stiffened at the sound. Two tanks entered the lower village. Uniformed soldiers sprouted out of the tops of the tanks pointing their rifles in every direction, reminding Hedy of a vase of daffodils. She shook her head at the strangeness of that thought.

The smell of gunfire, smoke, and oil filled the air. Hedy wanted to run away; however, fear and the spectacle unfolding in front of her kept her glued in place.

Leading the tanks on foot was an officer. The tall man reeked of importance, not at all diminished by the size of the tank behind him. Wearing riding boots and a helmet, he carried two pistols by his side, one in each hand. His dark sunglasses masked his eyes; she couldn't tell where he was looking.

Signaling the tanks to stop, his resonant voice called out in English, "Any German soldiers in the village?"

From the top of the first tank someone shouted in broken German, *"Wo sind die Deutschen Soldaten?"*

"You speak English," Onkel Marcel whispered. "You are in uniform. Go talk to them." He shoved Hedy towards the enemy.

Stumbling in front of the intimidating figure in sunglasses, her voice disappeared as she struggled to recall her high school English. The pistols and several rifles pointed directly at her did not help.

"No, no German soldiers in village," finally squeaked past her constricted throat as she waved her arms back and forth.

The answer seemed satisfactory. The pistol-toting officer barked instructions and pointed to Onkel Marcel's house. The riflemen hurdled down from the tanks. Her knees trembling, Hedy rushed back to her family.

She translated the Americans' exchanges as best she could. "The commander is ordering some of the men to search the houses for soldiers. The others are to come up to our courtyard and move into the schoolhouse."

The courtyard became a flurry of activity. An ambulance pulled up as did a few jeeps. The soldiers unloaded supplies of all kinds and carried them into the house. The commander chose the smaller house next door for himself and his officers, making it the command center.

"What do we do?" Tante Gisela's eyes were wide and her hands covered her cheeks at the sight of Americans running in and out of their home. Mama stood, trembling. Onkel Marcel was frozen in place.

Hedy's cousin Rosemary headed towards the house. Not knowing what she intended to do, Hedy sprinted to catch up with her. When Rosemary reached the house, a soldier shouted, "Out, Out."

Rosemary's hands flew in the air and she yelled, "No."

"Out. Out." Using his gun, the solder pointed to the door.

After numerous repetitions, Hedy interrupted, using the English she remembered. "We live here. Where are we supposed to stay?"

The soldier motioned to the cellar in the back yard. The girls shook their heads. Seeing he was about to lose his patience, Hedy motioned him to watch as Rosemary opened the cellar door. The tiny dank space had a dirt floor and was used for coal and wood storage. Finally understanding, the soldier suggested the girls find another house to live in. "Just go."

Hedy elbowed Rosemary and pulled her back to the street with their family. The two rejoined their mothers. Rosemary mentioned the parish house with its two extra rooms.

"Good idea, Rosemary. While I go talk to the pastor, why don't you and Hedy go get clothing and bedding from our house?" Onkel Marcel headed to the rectory.

"With all the soldiers in it?" Hedy stared at her uncle in disbelief.

"I am certain they won't bother two pretty girls like you."

Her face blanched. Was he actually that much of a coward? Hedy bit her tongue.

The girls entered the house, and motioned to the soldiers they wanted to gather their belongings. As they started up the stairs, a soldier holding his rifle and helmet dashed passed them, seemingly to check the second story. He almost reached the landing when he stopped and gaped at the large statue of Christ standing alone on the window sill. Slowly, reverently, he crossed himself and backed down the stairs.

Hedy wondered what had crossed his mind. They continued up the stairs and opened the door to Rosemary's bedroom. The room was already claimed. Strong odors arose from the boots by the door.

Equipment and dirty clothes decorated the furniture and bedspread. A violin case caught her eye, making her think of Konrad. She didn't see any men, but yanked Rosemary out of the room anyway.

"But I need to get my things." Rosemary pulled away from her grasp.

"Do you want the soldiers to think we are waiting in the bedroom for them? We need to get out of here immediately."

They hurried down the stairs and gathered bedding from a storage closet. As they were leaving, the girls were startled by boisterous cheering and laughter emerging from the kitchen. Hedy's curiosity got the best of her and snuck over to the door.

"You said we should leave." Rosemary poked her arm.

"Shush. Look." Peeking around the corner, Hedy pointed to her aunt's normally pristine countertops. Tante Gisela's fruit preserves spilled across the counters and tables. Covered with apple, pear, peach, mirabellen, blueberry, and cherry jams, the group of soldiers had hit a jackpot.

Rosemary gasped. The soldiers jerked toward the door, hands reaching for their rifles. Embarrassed, they did not say a word.

Realizing this was probably the first treat the soldiers had encountered in a while, Hedy cried, *"Guten Appetite."* Giving the thumbs up gesture, the soldiers relaxed, returned the smiles, and continued their feast.

Cheers rose from the courtyard as the young women headed out of the house, arms filled with bedding. Hedy set down the bulky blankets and walked to the rear of the house. She cracked open the back door enough for Rosemary and her to see. The Americans had discovered the community wine cellar and were making the most of it. Some were stripped down to their tee shirts, pants, and helmets; others wore complete uniforms and rifles. Each held a small tasting glass from the cellar in his hand.

One soldier yelled, "I just heard. We're gonna get Combat Infantry Badge."

"Does that mean extra pay?"

"Hell, yeah. I think we've earned it, don't you?" The men all cheered and gulped down another swig.

Most were not terribly steady on their feet, and a few were

alternating gulps of wine with target practice. Unfortunately, the targets were Tante Gisela's chickens.

"This is a good time to get out of here," Rosemary whispered to Hedy.

"I agree." Hedy moved from the door. "I shouldn't laugh, but it is a sight."

Rosemary cringed. "Let's not mention this to my mother. I don't think she needs to know what is happening to her chickens."

They quietly shut the back door and hurried back to the pastor's house, balancing the unwieldy bedding as best they could.

"It may be terrible," Hedy glanced sideways at her cousin, "but watching drunk Americans try to shoot chickens was the funniest thing I have seen in a long time."

~

Mama and Hedy woke up squeezed together on a spare bed in the rectory. When Mama tried to get out of bed the next morning, she fainted.

"Rosemary, come help me," Hedy cried as she struggled to get her mother off the floor. Using the techniques she had learned at the hospital, she struggled to resuscitate her mother, without success. She threw a coat over her nightshirt and raced to the house where she had seen a Red Cross truck.

"*Doktor, Doktor.*" Hedy stormed into the soldiers' quarters. Twenty rifles were simultaneously trained on her by men in undershirts. She froze in place, but concern for her mother overwhelmed the fear.

"At ease." One of the Americans stood and motioned to the others to lower their guns. "What is the problem, Miss?"

"*Meine Mutter ist krank.*" In the excitement, Hedy's English escaped her. The man continued to question her. She could only respond with "my mother is sick" in German. With her hand to her forehead, she dramatized a faint. "*Kein Arzt in der Stadt.* There is no doctor in town."

Finally understanding, he dressed, seized his medical bag, and motioned Hedy to show him the way. Within minutes, they arrived at her mother's bedside. Hedy stood to the side to let the doctor kneel next to her mother. After a quick exam, he shot an injection into her arm and massaged it.

Mama's eyes fluttered open and became wide. "Who is touching me?"

The American explained to her mother that he was a doctor there to help her. Hedy appreciated his reassuring voice. Though he spoke in English, which her mother did not understand, his friendly tone calmed Mama. The doctor left medicine and vitamin tablets, before promising to come back the next day.

Grateful, Hedy accompanied him to the door and worked up the nerve to give him a big hug. Surprise registered on the doctor's face, replaced by a blush. "Your mother needs more nutrients to restore her strength. I'll send food over this afternoon."

~

With her mother stable, Hedy remembered the family the German soldiers told her about. "I need to go check on them."

"You can't go there," Rosemary reminded her. "It is too far. You won't be back by the curfew the Americans set. Besides, you don't have any clean bandages or supplies."

"The Americans do. I've barged in on them once already; I might as well try again."

Rosemary stared at her cousin as if she were insane. "You do recall they are the enemy. The invaders, right?"

"Yes, but they have the supplies."

Hedy changed into her Red Cross uniform. Back to the schoolhouse she walked slowly, silently practicing what she wanted to say in English. When the door opened, she asked to speak to an officer. She prayed it wouldn't be the pistol toting one.

Her prayer was not answered.

"What can I help you with, Miss?" The intimidating officer came up behind her from the smaller house, startling her.

Shrinking back, Hedy resisted the urge to stare at the pistols on his hip. He lifted his sunglasses to study her and revealed an extraordinarily handsome face. Focus. She needed to focus. "A-a young boy and his mother outside town were injured by shrapnel. I would like to help but will need to be out past curfew."

He replaced his sunglasses and nodded. "That should not be a problem. You have my permission to be outside after curfew as needed." He began to walk away.

Hedy channeled her courage. "Um, I also need medical supplies. There are none left."

Without a word to Hedy, the officer stopped and motioned to a red-haired soldier. He spoke briskly. The soldier dashed off and came back with a hefty bag of medical supplies, which he passed to her.

The supplies would last for weeks. Their generosity overwhelmed Hedy. Her well-practiced thank-you speech became a jumble of German and English words. Impulsively, she threw her arms around the officer and hugged him. Horrified by her action, she stepped back. A warm smile etched its way across his stern face. He told her to wait a moment and stepped out of the room.

Reappearing moments later with two chocolate bars, he handed them to her. "For the boy."

She left quickly, afraid she would burst into tears. She never expected such kindness.

~

The boy and his mother lived a mile or so outside of the village. As Hedy walked closer to their house, she shivered. The countryside was pitted with artillery holes. Pieces of shrapnel protruded from their front yard. When Hedy knocked on the door, Frau Berg ushered her in, wanting to hear everything that was happening in town. Hedy filled her in as she changed the dressings on their wounds.

"The medics did a very good job on your arm, Frau Berg. I am certain you will heal nicely. I'll be back to change the bandages again in a few days." Handing the chocolate to Walter, Hedy explained it was a gift from the American commander. After spending a few hours helping do the chores Frau Berg could not do, she headed back to the parish house.

She passed her uncle's house on the way. The sun shone on the soldiers outside, some washing their laundry in the public fountain and cleaning their equipment. Others played a type of ball game. Many of the soldiers stopped what they were doing as she walked by. Uneasy from the whistles and comments, she kept her eyes forward and picked up her pace.

~

That night, as promised, the doctor sent dinner to Mama, with enough extra to share with the rest of the family.

"This is more food than we have seen in weeks." Tante Gisela clapped her hands together.

For the next several days, the doctor stopped by with medicine early in the day and sent dinner at night. One morning he did not come, but in his place sent a medic. After giving Mama her medicine, the medic handed Hedy a box filled with cigarettes, crackers, canned meat, chocolate, candies, dextrose tablets, and chewing gum. Hedy clutched her cousin's arm. "Rosemary, we can use the cigarettes to barter for more food."

~

News traveled through town that Hedy had medical supplies and skills. She spent her days traveling around the town and neighboring farms to help anyone who needed it. Besides the curfew, the occupying troops put few requirements on the townspeople. Her mother continued to improve, thanks to the medicine and the additional food.

Walking in front of the soldier's quarters was less intimidating. They continued to whistle and greet her when she walked by. Now she responded with a friendly wave, safely on the other side of the street.

~

After five days of occupation, activity around the school house increased.

"What is happening?" The townspeople gathered as the soldiers packed up their belongings.

The commanding officer stepped out and addressed the crowd. "We have been ordered to move on. Thank you for your assistance this week."

Hedy translated. Within an hour, the soldiers loaded all of the jeeps. The townspeople waved good-bye to the troops and wished them good health.

"I guess if we had to get invaded, we couldn't have asked for a nicer group," an older lady noted.

"It is difficult to believe those polite young men are the terrible enemy we have been warned about for all these years," Tante Gisela observed.

Hedy followed her aunt and her cousin into the schoolhouse. All pleasant thoughts of the Americans dissipated immediately. Boots, clothes, and blankets filled every corner. The smell of body odor permeated the furniture and the curtains. All the pots, pans, and dishes had been used. Not a single one had been washed. Food and wine stained the walls and counters in every room. Cigarette burns marred the chairs and couch. And the two bathrooms. Hedy had never seen anything so disgusting.

Tante Gisela cringed at the sight. Working together, they piled the clothing and army supplies near the front door. A neighbor stopped by with an armload of clothes, wondering what she should do with them. Tante Gisela pointed to the pile and invited her to add to it. Several other villagers did the same.

Rosemary headed upstairs. Within moments, a scream pierced the air. Hedy and Onkel Marcel raced up the stairs as her cousin rushed out of the bedroom and slammed the door shut.

"What's wrong?" Marcel stopped and slowly began backing down the stairs.

"There are strange metal boxes with wires under the bed," Rosemary wailed. "They wouldn't leave a bomb here, would they?"

Marcel stopped, deliberated for a moment, and strode upstairs to lock the door to the room. "Girls, I am sure it is not a bomb. Let's go downstairs and relax for a bit." He ducked down to the cellar and brought up a bottle of wine. Pouring it into a glass, he said, "*Lass doch*. Leave it. We will worry about it later."

As if on cue, a knock sounded on the door, and an American stuck his head into the house. "We understand someone who speaks English lives here." He and another solder explained in broken German with a spattering of English that they were the clean-up crew for anything left behind.

Rosemary and Hedy began chuckling. The men stared at the giggling young women. When they were shown the ever-growing pile, they understood the response. "We will need to come back tomorrow with a larger truck," the first soldier said, grinning back at the girls.

"Share a glass of wine with me before you go." Onkel Marcel poured two more glasses. When they finished, the Americans rose.

Hedy stopped them, "Would you examine some strange boxes left under the bed?"

The soldiers followed her upstairs. She stayed safely outside the room. Pulling the first box out, the American stated, "This is odd. These are radio transmitters. They aren't dangerous, but they shouldn't have been left."

He carried them downstairs and threw them on the pile to be picked up the next day. "Obviously, the clean-up crew isn't terribly worried about them." Hedy shrugged.

"It seems awfully wasteful." A faraway look crossed Rosemary's face. "Willis is out there with barely enough clothes to keep him warm." She hesitated, staring at the mound of American clothing. "And they just leave it behind."

~

True to the soldiers' word, they picked up the total pile the next morning. Then the real cleaning began. A rather particular person, Tante Gisela proceeded in an efficient manner to assign duties and gave everyone a role in restoring the house.

"Rosemary, do you think there is any food left? Those soldiers ate through the preserves like candy," Hedy fretted.

"Most of the canned food is hidden in the formal dining room, Hedy. Maybe they didn't notice it."

Tante Gisela inventoried her dwindling stock of food. The cold, dark room must not have appeared inviting to the soldiers as the cupboards remained untouched. "There isn't much here, but that isn't the soldiers' fault. Thank God the war is finally over. Now maybe we will be able to buy food."

Hedy held her arms over her gurgling stomach as she agreed.

Heading to Trier

1945

Once more the armies of the enemy powers storm against our defensive fronts. Behind them is the slavering force of International Jewry that wants no peace until it has reached its satanic goal of world destruction. But its hopes are in vain.

JOSEPH GOEBBELS—His last *Our Hitler*—April 20, 1945

O ver the next month, very little news trickled in. Radio batteries had long since died, and the availability of electricity was sporadic. Worse, there was no word from Vater since the Americans had left. No one knew if the Allied troops had captured Koblenz yet. "Remember what Vater said, 'No news is good news'," Hedy attempted to reassure her mother.

The weeks wore on. Hedy became anxious, not knowing if they had a home left to go to or how her friends had fared. Finally, she could stand it no longer. "I am going to Trier tomorrow."

Her mother gasped. "Hedy, the *Alliierten* bombed the city back in December. Our house was most likely destroyed."

Hedy paced the floor. "But I need to see for myself what we have left. We can't help anyone sitting around here."

Once again her mother attempted to talk her out of a journey. "Don't be ridiculous. The war isn't over. Everything is so unsettled."

"If I hear shelling, I'll come back, Mama."

Her mother's voice rose. "We don't know where the *Invasionsarmee* is."

"It has been two months since the Americans came through. Surely they have crossed the Rhine by now. The waiting is driving me insane." Hedy stopped and held her mother. "I will be fine. I'll be in my uniform. Remember how nice the Americans were? They supplied you with food and medicine." She allowed her mother a moment to let it sink in. "Trier has been captured. There won't be any more fighting."

Mama sat and rapped her fingers on the table. "How will you get there? There are no buses, trains, or petrol."

"I'll take my bicycle. It has taken me further than that." Hedy slid onto the bench opposite her.

"By yourself? That is far too dangerous." The tapping sped up. She called Onkel Marcel into the kitchen.

Her uncle sided with Mama. "It is foolhardy for a young woman to travel by herself."

"I will find a way," Hedy responded stubbornly.

Tante Gisela walked in and hung her jacket on a peg by the door. "Find a way to do what, Hedy?"

"I would like to get to Trier."

"So would Herr Kessler and Herr Schellenberg. They own music stores there and are wondering if anything is left. Poor souls have been stuck at the guest house in town for months."

An idea raced through Hedy's head. "I'll be back in a bit." She dashed out of the house. Tracking down the stranded men at the guest house, Hedy introduced herself and explained her plan. "I am familiar with the roads and shortcuts from here to Trier. My father and I used to bike them frequently. If you are interested, I can lead you there by foot."

The men were surprised. "Isn't it over forty kilometers?" asked Herr Kessler, a slim man of medium height and white hair.

"And mountainous?" chimed Herr Schellenberg, a shorter man whose build gave the appearance of having been much heavier earlier in the war. "We aren't spring chickens."

"It is quite a way, but as there is no petrol or trains, I'm not aware of any other way for you to get there. We can leave early, pack light, and drink water from the public fountains along the way. We ought to be able to make the trip in one day."

After mulling it over, they agreed to meet at 6:00 am in two days. Happily, Hedy sprinted back to the house to get things ready.

"Hedy, you will put me in an early grave." Her mother refused to face her. "If you must go, look for your father's friend, Moritz Haas. He is back in Trier. You can stay with his family."

~

The beautiful April morning sun peeked above the horizon when Hedy left the schoolhouse, leaving her tearful mother behind. When she entered the town square in her Red Cross uniform, Herr Kessler gulped. "Are you traveling as our nurse or our guide?"

She chuckled. "I certainly hope you won't need a nurse."

The travelers headed towards Klaussen. Hedy explained to her companions the town had a church with a public fountain and would be a good rest stop. From there, they would follow the main highway to Trier. To avoid an extended walk through town, Hedy lead the men down a shortcut to an old path.

"There is a wide gully, but it has a footbridge which puts us near the church and the fountain." She pointed to the path ahead of them. "This will save us several kilometers of walking."

When they arrived at the gully, Hedy's hand flew to her mouth. To her dismay, only remnants of the bridge remained.

"Do you think the Yanks did it?" Herr Kessler said.

"Who knows?" Herr Schellenberg stared at what was left of the bridge. "Our troops might have taken it down while retreating. We only know it isn't here anymore." Examining the crossing, he pointed to the long ropes stretched across the gully. They had a series of knotted lines tying them together in an elongated V shape. "Looks like the locals fashioned a rope bridge. You won't get me on that thing."

Herr Kessler pointed at the knotted cords and at Hedy. "Are we supposed to cross that?"

Sheepishly, Hedy nodded, "That or walk the long way around."

The three gawked at the ropes, the gulley and the path, contemplating the options. The church bells rang, excusing attendees from the morning mass. A middle-aged man strolled towards them. With a friendly *guten Morgen*, he hopped onto the rope bridge and easily crossed to their side.

Seeing their astonished expressions, he offered, "Would you like assistance?"

Hedy nodded. He held onto her arms and inched her across. Scarcely daring to glance down, she focused her attention on following the stranger's movements. Her heart pounded as her foot slipped, but the stranger's strong grasp shoved her onto the bank on the other side.

"Thank you, *mein Herr*." She called back to her traveling companions. "It really isn't that bad."

The man hopped back across and, with a bit more hesitation, Herr Kessler and Herr Schellenberg accepted his help. Once the three had crossed the bridge, the helpful man waved goodbye, whistling as he sauntered on his way.

~

By ten o'clock, Hedy spotted an isolated farmhouse ahead and suggested they stop for a drink. The farmer offered apples for the road, which were gratefully accepted.

After another hour, they finally reached the main road. Hedy had hoped to hitch a ride, but the highway was deserted. A few hours later, a farmer driving a small tractor with an empty trailer stopped. Gratefully, Hedy and the men hopped onto the bed of the trailer. For the next half hour, they covered their ears from the roaring din of the engine and breathed through handkerchiefs to protect themselves from the black exhaust fumes. When the farmer stopped to turn off the highway, none of them complained about walking.

Ready to stop for their midday meal, they stumbled upon another farm and requested water. The family was finishing their *Mittagessen* and invited Hedy and her companions to join them. Even after explaining they had their own food, the family insisted they sit for dessert.

Hedy's eyes widened at the site of the delicious pudding and cupcakes. "These are delicious. I haven't seen cupcakes in years," Hedy thanked the farm wife.

The leathery-skinned woman beamed. "I am glad you enjoyed them. I am getting a lot of experience baking with honey and what we can grow on the farm."

Back on the highway, the travelers walked until a flatbed delivery truck picked them up. Hedy practically jumped with delight. "What luck. We should be in Trier well before dark."

"Good." Herr Kessler pulled the shoe off his right foot and

rubbed it. "I can't believe I let you talk me into this."

"Don't worry," Hedy responded with a twinkle in her eye. "Remember, you brought your private nurse."

The truck driver delivered the travelers to the military checkpoint outside of town. Nervously, Hedy and the gentlemen offered their identification. American soldiers welcomed them with a friendly hello and inquired about their journey, setting them at ease.

One soldier questioned them. "Since the bombings last December, there are few habitable spaces in town. If you do not have a place to stay, we can't allow you to enter."

Each showed proof of residency and provided the addresses.

"Are you working in a hospital?" The soldier pointed at Hedy's uniform.

"I am applying to work at the *Bruderkrankenhaus*."

"Good idea." He grinned. "It is now our military hospital, and we can use you."

This information startled her, even though she shouldn't have been surprised. Hedy couldn't help but marvel at what it would be like to work in an American hospital.

With passes in hand, Hedy and her travelling companions headed into the town, passing an American behind the wheel of a jeep, who was watching them intently. The helmeted soldier wore an officer's uniform with a pistol in a bulky holster strapped across his chest. Hedy shivered at the sight.

Passing by what was left of the Roman gates, she blinked, not believing the scene in front of her. The bustling tourist town with its ancient walls stood in ruins. Empty facades stood as ghosts of what had once been modern, beautiful, active buildings. The ancient Romans walls, which once gave Hedy such a feeling of security, had sections of barely more than rubble. Buildings which seemed untouched at first glance revealed entire sections missing. Rubble littered the streets, broken glass everywhere. It was difficult to reconcile this scene with her memory of one year ago.

She glanced at the men. They were dumbstruck. Wandering in a daze, they gaped at the destruction. They continued past the ancient Roman baths and the high rise concrete bunker.

"The *Hochbunker* survived the bombings." Herr Kessler pointed at the towering bunker.

"I should think so." Herr Schellenberg growled. "That is why they built it."

Hedy shut her eyes. "I hope it saved some lives."

Herr Kessler patted her on the shoulder. "It did. Besides, most everyone had already evacuated."

Shaking her head, Hedy disagreed. "I heard over 400 souls perished in December alone."

The three continued walking without another word. At the next intersection, Herr Kessler broke the silence. "My place is this direction. Thank you, Hedy, for helping me."

Herr Schellenberg took his leave. "Do your friends live close by, Hedy?"

"Don't worry about me. Herr Haas lives around the corner from here."

When she arrived at Herr Haas' home, he greeted her with a strong handshake. His wife, Barbel, their son, Egon, and daughter, Mechthild, all offered Hedy big hugs. Five other travelers had also camped there and more were expected. The three story house resembled a dormitory with mattresses thrown everywhere. Though everyone was pleasant, Hedy wanted to be alone.

"I'll be back before curfew," she told her hosts. "I'd like to see what is left of our house."

The pity in Frau Haas' eyes was almost more than Hedy could bear. She left with more despair than hope.

~

Hedy knew she was on the right street, however nothing jogged her memory. She took a few more steps and searched the area. Wait. That building was familiar. She looked again and walked back a half block. Realizing her location, Hedy stared in awe at the scene in front of her.

The Weiß's house was part of four attached multi-story structures. A shell had come in at such an angle that the first building had only the roof taken off, the second lost the top floor, and the Weiß's building lost the top two floors. The fourth building was completely destroyed. In spite of a strong urge to flee, she inched her way closer.

It wasn't possible. There on the open second floor stood her mother's piano, seemingly untouched. It balanced on a support beam, while everything around it was shattered. She rubbed her arms up and down, trying to suppress the chill racing through her body. It simply was not possible. Their home destroyed, but the piano survived.

Repressing the urge to vomit, Hedy bolted from the area. She slowed when reaching the market area and fought back the tears pooling in her eyes. Instead of crowds of shoppers and loud speakers blaring the news, there was only a stray dog and silence. Wandering among the empty streets, she lost herself in her thoughts and reminisced about the shop owners and the goods that had been sold there.

The corner of a leaflet stuck out from the rubble. Moving the debris, Hedy picked up the torn paper.

Once again, there are two possibilities:

Either one slaves away for foreigners until the end of his life without ever seeing his homeland and his family again, or one gets a shot in the back of the neck a little earlier.

Since both of these last possibilities end in death, there are no further possibilities.

Therefore:

There are not two possibilities.

There is only one.

We must win the war, and we can win it. Each man and each woman, the entire German people, must call forth their utmost in work, courage, and discipline.

Shivering, she hurled it to the ground and wiped her hand on her apron. The war was lost, but the damn Nazis still wanted her countrymen to die. She spat on the paper and headed the other direction.

Turning onto *Nagelstrasse*, she recalled the specialty shops she used to visit. Inge's family's lingerie store had been on this street. She wondered if it survived. A few steps later, she found it. The front of the building appeared almost untouched. Her smile vanished as she stepped closer and realized one of the walls was substantially missing and the back of the building gone.

Hedy stopped and made the sign of the cross, praying for Inge's safety. Voices drifted down from near the top of the building. Was she hearing ghosts? There was no way a human lived in such destruction. But the voices continued. Cupping her hands to her mouth, she shouted. "Inge, are you up there? It's Hedy Weiß."

Footsteps. The sound of buckets pushed across the floor. Now she was sure she was hearing things. Spooked, Hedy stepped back as a dark-haired woman popped her head out from a bombed-out window above. "Hedy? Is it actually you? Wait a minute. We're coming down."

Inge worked her way down the steps tailed by a short blonde, both dressed in Red Cross uniforms. Hugging her tightly, Inge started asking questions, one right after another. "What are you doing here? Is your family safe? Where have you been staying?"

Raising her hands, Hedy stopped her. "Hold on. I just got to town from Noviand. By the way," she glanced at the blond woman, "I'm Hedy."

"Hedy, it's Gerda. We attended school in Birresborn together." She pointed to the beauty mark on her left cheek.

"Gerda?" Hedy did a double take at her previously chubby classmate. "Is it really you?" She hugged her old friend. "What are you doing in Trier?"

"I met Inge in medical school. The bombing has gotten so ridiculous in Berlin; we decided to check on her family's shop."

Inge gestured towards what was left of the second story. "Would you like to come into our castle? The maid couldn't make it today, but the fresh air is plentiful."

Hedy worked her way up the rickety stairs as they explained their system of intruder alarms using buckets of debris and a seeming maze. The slanted living room floor had buckled, and broken glass was swept to the side.

The two intact walls and two partial walls somewhat enclosed the space. Hedy waved her arm around the room in disbelief. "You can't possibly stay here."

Snickering, the two women responded, "Yes we can."

"It is quite cozy." Gerda slowly motioned around the room. "We don't have to worry about anyone bothering us. No one believes it is livable."

Hedy raised her eyebrows. "I'll grant you that."

Gerda proudly showed her their sleeping arrangement of blankets and lingerie from the shop piled on the floor. "Most luxurious beds in town. Spun from genuine silk."

"Feel free to go shopping, if you need lingerie." Inge pointed to the various pieces of clothes around the room. "We have all sizes."

Laughing out loud, Hedy picked up a camisole. "I could use clothes. Besides this uniform, I haven't had anything new in four years." Slowly spinning in place, she added, "And my figure has changed a bit."

Gerda stuck out her generous chest. "Not as much as mine."

Hedy carefully folded the camisole. "But I wouldn't think of robbing you of your bedding."

Inge invited Hedy to spend the night.

"I have a place to stay." After a moment, she added, "With walls."

For the next hour or so, Inge and Gerda regaled Hedy with stories of surviving in Berlin and the devastation taking place.

Shuddering, Hedy exhaled deeply. "I had planned on going to Berlin to school. I guess it is a good thing I didn't."

"Climbing over boulders with you growing up was good training for living in wartime Berlin." Gerda attempted to lighten the mood.

"I understand needing to get away from Berlin. How are you surviving here in Trier?"

Inge explained. "We volunteer as nurse assistants at the hospital. As long as we work, they give us at least one meal a day." The co-conspirators glanced at each other. "The hospital staff assumes we are staying in the less-bombed area of town."

Hedy pointed toward Gerda. "I can't believe the same girl who wouldn't go in a cave with me in Birresborn is living with a rubble alarm."

"Obviously you were a bad influence. What have you been doing?"

When Gerda realized Hedy had been at the field hospital in Traben-Trarbach, she became excited. "My mother lives there. I'm going next week to live with her and work in the hospital."

Hedy clapped her hands. "I'll come visit you once you get settled." She noticed the sun hanging low in the sky outside the bombed out wall. "Oh, dear. I've got to get back to the Haas' before curfew."

"You'd better." Inge grimaced. "If the Americans catch you, you'll have to work in their military kitchen for three days,"

Gerda held her growling stomach. "They'd feed you, though."

Hedy swallowed. "As good as that sounds, I promised Mama I'd get right back to Noviand." She sighed. "I'd better not get caught."

Elbowing Inge, Gerda suggested, "Maybe we should go hang out after curfew, Inge. I'm hungry."

"With our luck, the soldiers would have us picking up rubble," Inge growled back.

The women guided Hedy back around the maze to the street. "I'll be back tomorrow. We have plenty of catching up to do." Hedy waved and then hurried down the street.

The Soldier in the Jeep

1945

The lack of lights in the city allowed the first stars of the evening sky to shine through. The evening offered plenty of light for Hedy to make her way back to Herr Haas' home. Heading towards the 2000-year-old town gate, she reached *Simeonstrasse*. When she first moved to Trier, she remembered worrying about how long it took to cross this street. It was the widest in town, with dozens of shops and hordes of shoppers scurrying about. Now it was empty. Almost.

Engrossed in memories, she barely noticed the military jeep that slowly passed her. It stopped, allowing Hedy to make out the young helmeted driver as she walked by. A pistol was strapped to the center of his chest like the soldier she had seen earlier in the day, and his jeep had a tall rod extending straight up from the center of the front bumper. The fading evening light added to the eeriness of the sight.

Hedy picked up her pace. The vehicle kept pace with her. The driver pulled up next to her, almost on the sidewalk. She shortened her stride, hoping he'd pass. He addressed her with a friendly smile and, surprisingly, near-perfect German. "Excuse me, Fräulein."

What did he want from her? She pivoted away from him and kept walking. Perspiration beaded on her forehead.

"May I offer you a ride?"

Hedy stared straight ahead and continued her walk. "No, thank you, sir. I'm not far from home." Two MPs turned onto the street several blocks ahead of her. If she wasn't already nervous enough, she now had to worry about getting back before curfew.

Behind her, the jeep crept along, keeping pace with her. He didn't leave. After she had stepped a bit further, the soldier tried again. "Could I ask for your assistance with an address?" He pulled a piece of paper from his pocket. "How do I get to the *Moselufer*?" he said with a gentle voice.

Hedy stopped and accepted the paper without looking at him. She recognized the address instantly. Though close by, the street was outside the bombed center of town. Herr Haas had told her the lovely homes there had been left untouched.

"It is not far and easy to find." Pointing down the street, Hedy explained which roads to take and expected him to drive away. She handed back the paper.

He flashed a generous smile. "I mean no harm and it is close to curfew. Are you sure you wouldn't like a ride?"

"No, no thank you, sir. I am fine." Hedy spun away from him and hurried down the street.

He pulled up next to her. "Are you sure?" He pointed to his watch and to the two MPs ahead of them.

Kitchen duty in the barracks or a quick ride with a polite stranger? Either way, she was trusting her fate to foreign soldiers. Hedy impulsively climbed into the jeep as the MPs drove by. They offered the jeep driver an exaggerated salute. "I hope this wasn't a mistake," she said out loud.

The driver waved away her anxiety. "Don't worry." He drove slowly, asking for directions. When he approached within a block of the house, he stopped the jeep and turned toward her.

"This is not the right street." Alarmed, Hedy swung her leg out the side of the jeep.

He gently touched her arm. "Please don't go. I'm not going to hurt you. I simply want to talk. I saw you earlier today near the checkpoint with two older men and was happy to catch sight of you again."

Hedy relaxed slightly. "I must be getting back to Herr Haas's home. I am required to return before curfew, and I don't want to worry them."

"I'll get you back for curfew. I'm Johnny Merenda." He showed her his Counter Intelligence Corps ID, rank, and orders stationing him in Trier.

Hedy pulled out her pass, but Johnny waved it off. "No need. Please, tell me your name."

Shifting in her seat, she murmured. "Hedy Weiß."

"Hedy. A lovely name." His eyes never left her. "Was one of the gentlemen with you at the checkpoint your father?"

She tried not to stare at the gun strapped across his chest. "No. They were two businessmen who needed help finding the way from Noviand."

"Wait." Johnny's eyes grew wide and his brows rose. "You walked all the way from Noviand today?"

A grin surfaced. "You sound like my mother. How else was I supposed to check on our home?"

"Your mother is a wise woman. Tell me, is yours a large family?"

Clasping her hands in her lap, she replied, "It is only my parents and me."

A thoughtful expression crossed his face. "I always wondered what it would be like to be an only child. I'm from New York, and my parents are from Italy. With all my brothers and sisters," he gestured, "it gets rather loud."

"Sounds like fun." In spite of herself, Hedy relaxed. "I'm only in Trier a couple of days. I want to check on our home and inquire about a job at the hospital. Then I'm going back to Noviand and my mother." She stopped, realizing the time. "But I must get back before my host is worried."

Johnny's next question surprised Hedy. "May I see you again? I'd like to invite you to dinner."

Hedy laughed incredulously. "We have such a huge choice of restaurants available in the city. Where would we go?"

"No restaurant. Come over to my villa and have dinner with my partner Fred and me."

She simply stared at him. He could not possibly be serious.

Watching her, he added, "If you are uncomfortable coming by yourself, please bring along friends."

Finding the conversation ridiculous, Hedy answered flippantly, "Certainly. How many can I bring?" Surely that would bring the conversation to a halt.

"How many would you like? If you will give me their addresses, Fred and I will pick them up."

It dawned on her he was actually serious. "I don't know."

"Please?" Puppy dog eyes stared at her.

"I suppose you and Fred will do the cooking?"

He frowned. "No, we have a cook."

The young man and his offer tempted her. "I'll think about it. Let me check with my friends and let you know." She pointed to his watch. "But it is after 9:00, and I don't want to worry Herr Haas."

Johnny drove her to the house. "I will stop by in the morning to confirm our dinner date and to introduce you to my partner Fred. It has been a pleasure to speak with you."

Hedy hurried into the house, amazed at his considerate manner. She was met by a hoard of people all throwing questions at her. The entire household must have been watching out the window when the mysterious soldier in the jeep brought her home.

"Who was that?"

"Are you okay?"

"Were you arrested?"

She answered their questions and told them about her evening, trying to downplay how much she had enjoyed it.

~

After an hour, Herr Haas' son Egon sprang into the living room shouting, "A jeep is in the street outside."

Everyone in the room stared at Hedy.

"Don't look at me. How would I know what's going on?"

A solid bang sounded on the porch. Being in a war zone, everyone jumped. Hedy stole to the window and pulled back the curtain. "I can't see anything. Egon, go find out what it is."

Egon clutched Hedy's hand and dragged her with him to the front entrance. He slowly opened the wooden door, glanced around, and quickly shut it. "It is a box." He poked a finger at her chest. "Go get it."

"Why didn't you bring it in?"

"What if it's a bomb?"

"I rather doubt that." She opened the door and pulled the cardboard box inside. Bringing it into the kitchen, she pried open the top flaps as everyone in the house crowded around her.

"Someone raided the American's supply room."

"Fresh fruit. It isn't possible."

But it was. Filled with candy and chocolate, cookies and crackers, apples and oranges, coffee, tuna fish, packs of cigarettes and gum, and more, the gift surprised everyone.

"Why did you get this?" Herr Haas studied her suspiciously.

She felt her face flaming. "Why are you assuming it is for me?"

"No one else has been escorted home by an American."

"In that case, help yourselves." Hedy motioned toward the box and, grabbing an apple, skipped up the stairs to her designated mattress on the floor.

~

Sunshine streamed through the window, waking Hedy. She wondered how much of yesterday had actually occurred and how much had been a dream. At 8:00 am, her questions were answered.

True to his word, the mysterious soldier arrived. Herr and Frau Haas escorted Hedy outside to greet him. Standing several inches taller than her with dark, wavy hair, Johnny's Italian heritage showed. His strong jawline offset his gentle eyes. He carried himself with such ease, confidence, and perfect politeness, Hedy couldn't imagine anyone having a negative thought about him.

"*Guten Morgen*, Fräulein Weiß." Johnny offered his hand.

Lowering her head, she accepted it. The warmth of his large hand enveloped her smaller one. "*Guten Morgen.*" Pointing to her hosts, she added, "This is Herr Haas and his wife."

He tipped his hat. "Herr Haas, Frau Haas. Please understand my intentions are honorable, and Hedy and her friends will be safe with us. This is my partner, Fred Smith."

"Morning, sir, ma'am. It is a pleasure to meet all of you." Fred faced Hedy. "I am glad you and your friends are joining us for dinner."

The Haases looked at each other and nodded. Fred continued, "If you give me your friends' addresses, I will pick them up while Johnny comes to get you."

Concern crossed her face. "I haven't had time to ask them if they can attend."

Johnny interrupted, "May we assume they will agree? If so, we'll be back at 5:00 to pick you up."

Hedy agreed and waved goodbye as they left.

"He seems like a nice young man," Herr Haas noted.

"He does," Frau Haas noted. "But, regardless, I am glad you are taking friends with you to dinner tonight."

Inhaling deeply, Hedy was pleased they approved. Within the hour, she braved the rickety stairs and makeshift rubble alarms to visit Inge and Gerda.

"Hedy? What are you doing here so early?" Inge dropped the lingerie she was organizing.

Stopping to catch her breath, she exclaimed, "I need chaperones for dinner with an American."

Inge glanced from Hedy to Gerda. Gerda glanced at Inge and they broke out laughing. "We aren't agreeing to anything until we get the full story."

Once Hedy detailed the events from the previous evening, her friends agreed to join her.

"I wouldn't miss it for the world," Inge stated.

"*Ooh, la, la,*" teased Gerda. "I want to see what this mysterious officer looks like."

"Well, be ready by 5:00." Hedy waved goodbye. She hurried to the hospital to inquire about a position.

The hospital administrator explained that as greatly as they needed help, he couldn't give her a definite answer. The Americans would be moving out, and a new unit would be taking over. "I expect it to be the French army," he said. "Each of the Allied countries will be handling different areas of Germany."

Hedy hid her dismay at this prospect. The old veterans had spoken of the condescending attitude of the French after the Great

War. Besides, she could not imagine the French would be nicer this time after being occupied for all these years. In contrast, the Americans had been courteous and helpful.

Back at the house, she spoke with Frau Haas. "Why did I agree to this?" Hedy paced the floor.

"You will have a lovely time." The middle-aged woman ran her fingers through her thinning hair. "He impressed me by stopping by to introduce himself and his partner. Besides he agreed to let you have two chaperones."

"Actually, I said I was bringing friends, not how many. He might think it is four or five. I assumed he was joking." She twisted a lock of hair around her finger as she rambled.

"Calm down, Hedy. Even if you don't enjoy his company, you and your friends will get a real meal."

"It seems wrong to have dinner with a man who stalked me in a jeep."

"You obviously have quite an effect on men, dear. Have some fun." Frau Haas pretended to dance, causing Hedy to chuckle.

~

Johnny and Fred arrived at exactly 5:00 pm. While helping Hedy into the jeep, Johnny suggested she give Fred the address to fetch her friends while they waited at the house with Jo, the cook.

"If I gave you the address, you would not be able to find them."

"You don't seem to give me any credit." Fred put on a fake pout as he stepped into the jeep. "That's okay. Tell me where to go.

Arriving at the lingerie shop's street, the two Americans gawked at the debris. "Hedy," said Johnny. "You must be mistaken. There is no way anyone is living on this block. There is nothing left."

She stifled a smirk. "You'll see. Pull up to the next building."

Fred stopped in front of Inge's half-destroyed home, and Hedy hopped out and called up to her friends. "Inge, Gerda, your ride is here."

The officer's expressions as two women stepped out from the debris were priceless. "I wish I held a camera to take a picture of your faces." Hedy chuckled.

Fred regained his speech first. "How do you live up there?"

The women grinned as they crowded into the back of the jeep.

Gerda responded in broken English. "Very carefully."

Laughing, Fred waited for Johnny to climb in the jeep and the group headed to dinner. Both Inge and Gerda fidgeted next to Hedy. "Sit still or you are going to fall out of this thing," Hedy whispered.

Inge hissed back. "Sorry, but I am a bit nervous. Where are we going? What are we supposed to talk about?"

The jeep slowed. Approaching the row of homes requisitioned by the Americans, Hedy recalled where she had seen this address recently. She tapped Johnny on the shoulder. "I thought you needed directions to this house."

Turning his head back toward her, he shrugged. "You wouldn't talk to me any other way. Can you blame me?"

Though he faced the road, Hedy could feel the smile on his face.

The Italian cook, Jo, greeted them at the door and ushered them into the dining room. Communicating became comical as Inge and Gerda only spoke rudimentary English, Jo spoke Italian and French and a touch of German, Fred spoke only basic German besides his English, and, though Hedy could handle French fairly well, her English limited her. Johnny was the only one who understood each of the languages.

"You ladies cannot possibly live in that building. There are no walls." Fred threw up his hands.

Running her hand through her hair, Inge responded hesitantly. "We like to think that with proper accessories, we can live like princesses in our open air castle."

"You sound like my sisters." Johnny gestured as he spoke. "They are always talking about accessories." He looked at Fred and pretended to be confused. "Do you have any notion of what that is about?"

The women laughed. Hedy listened, impressed with Johnny's ability to put everyone at ease. In spite of the language difficulties, it did not take long for the stories to begin in earnest.

Inge spoke to Fred, "My English is limited, but I know what intelligence means. What does counter-intelligence mean?"

"Counter usually means against, which would make us against intelligence, wouldn't it?" Fred chuckled. "Johnny and I are responsible for using intelligence to track down war criminals and trouble makers."

Feigning a scared expression, Gerda asked, "That wouldn't include girls living in lingerie shops would it?"

"Only if they had walls."

Hedy elbowed Gerda. "I guess you are safe."

Jo exited back to the kitchen to prepare the plates, while Fred shared humorous stories of meeting his wife and of his three-year-old son's antics. Obviously anxious for the war to be over, he talked of going home to wrestle with his young heir. Gerda explained the mechanics of rubble burglar alarms, and the hysterics continued.

With the rest of the crowd caught up in the storytelling, Hedy used the opportunity to observe the young American officer sitting opposite her. His wavy dark hair and dark brown eyes contrasted with the light olive complexion of his skin. The curve of his cheeks drew her gaze to his perfectly straight teeth. Johnny glanced over and noticed Hedy watching him. His disarming smile flashed at her, highlighting his spirited eyes.

With a playful wink, he said, "Are you ready for a spectacular meal by our private chef, Jo?"

The ladies applauded and Jo entered with trays of food. Ham with pineapple slices, sweet potato puree, cranberry sauce, and dinner rolls filled the table. The aroma of such a freshly prepared feast caused Hedy to sigh. Fred poured glasses of *Moselwein,* and everyone toasted each other's health.

The conversation came to a halt as the girls wolfed down serving after serving. Jo stopped in, observed the women's healthy appetites, and said something in Italian to Johnny. Johnny hushed him but seemed to agree. Certain her eating habits was the topic, the heat rose in Hedy's face, but she didn't care. The meal was heavenly.

When Jo came around with yet another platter of food, Hedy decided she should have better manners and stopped eating to speak to him. "You obviously aren't an American. How did you end up with these two?"

Jo's charming smile vanished. "Johnny saved my life. I was captured by the Germans and forced to work on a farm. When the Americans grew close, the Germans beat—."

Putting his hand on Jo's shoulder, Johnny interrupted. "You always exaggerate my role. He said he was from Italy and could cook. I jumped at the chance for food like my mother made. You ought to taste Fred's cooking sometime. It is hardly edible."

Jo gazed up at Johnny, his eyes glowing, and cleared the plates. As he came near Hedy's seat, he whispered, "Johnny is a very good man." He pointed at the gold cross on her necklace. "Catholic, too."

Once again, Hedy felt the blush rising in her cheeks.

After dinner, the cookies and chocolates were barely touched as Hedy and her friends had already eaten so much. Inge pointed to the clock on the wall. "It is close to 8:00 and we have to get up to our quarters while it is still light. Our intruder alarm system takes a bit of time to set up."

Fred offered to drive them home, leaving Hedy and Johnny. Inge and Gerda glanced knowingly in Hedy's direction. She nodded and they left with Fred.

"Let me help with the dishes." Hedy stood.

"No, you are my guest. Please come join me." Johnny motioned toward the couch.

Hedy sat, and Johnny followed, a respectable distance apart. "I am a bit confused. Are you Italian or American?" she asked.

Johnny grinned. "Born in the US, although Mama and Papa are both Italian. Papa plays bassoon for an American philharmonic orchestra, but Mama preferred living in Italy, so I have bounced between the two countries. How about you?"

"I have always lived in Germany. I wanted to study physical therapy in France, but the war got in the way."

Johnny nodded knowingly and scooted closer to her. "I understand. I found out my mother died in Italy after I landed on the beaches with the invasion."

Hedy detected the pain in his eyes, moved closer, and laid her hand on his. "How sad. You didn't get to go to her funeral."

"I did visit her grave."

"How?" Hedy tipped her head and stared at him.

"Let's merely say I convinced my CO I knew my way around Italy well enough to get there and back."

Hedy eyes grew wide. What an unusual man. As they talked,

sharing memories of childhood and the war, Hedy noticed the space between them on the couch had disappeared.

Johnny nestled his arm around her shoulder. She snuggled into his chest and let out a satisfied sigh.

"Is everything all right?" he asked gazing down.

"Perfect. Thank you." She fixated on the slight dimple on his left cheek.

Their lips met. Softly, slowly at first and then more passionately. Johnny pulled slowly away. "I need to take you home now, or I may never let you go."

Hedy stood. "Herr Haas has given me his key, but I don't want to worry him. Besides, I have to get up early. I'm walking back to Noviand tomorrow."

Standing next to her, he shook his head. "No you aren't."

"Excuse me?" She stepped back.

Johnny held her right hand. "I will pick you up at eight tomorrow morning and drive you there."

"You don't need to do that. I realize you are busy."

Placing her hand on his arm, he escorted her to the door. "I am driving you." He leaned over and gazed into her eyes. "I also want to promise you no matter where they assign me, I will find a way to get in touch with you."

Hedy was speechless. She lost herself in his soft brown eyes, knowing, though they had just met, he meant it. Overwhelmed with emotion, she blinked back the tears and hugged him.

Johnny took her hand. "Let's get you back to your lodgings on time, and I'll see you in the morning."

~

When he arrived with his jeep the next day, Hedy was standing at the door in her uniform. A young soldier sat in the rear seat. Johnny threw her pack in the back with the soldier. "You need to sit in the front, and if anyone asks, I will tell them you are being taken in for questioning."

She tilted her head and raised one eyebrow. "So, I am technically a prisoner of the US Army?"

The soldier in the back stifled a snicker. Hedy enjoyed the ride and used the opportunity to ask about the pistol strapped across Johnny's chest.

"I spend most of my time traveling in the jeep. It was difficult to reach my pistol quickly while sitting behind the wheel, so I designed this harness to hold my gun at my chest where I can access it as needed."

"Well, I'll confess, when I first saw you with that contraption I was scared."

"Good." He turned to grin at her. "I'd like to scare any bad people I might come across."

"What is that thing?" Hedy pointed to the iron pole welded on the center of front bumper. It rose straight up about four feet in the air.

"The retreating forces will sometimes string wire across the road at neck height." Johnny scrutinized Hedy's face with concern before continuing. "The iron rod catches it before the wire catches us."

Involuntarily Hedy moved her hand to her neck. With the fun the previous night, she had almost forgotten a war still waged.

Johnny asked her about Noviand. Though not impressed with Onkel Marcel when he heard about the tanks entering the village, he chuckled about the soldiers taking over her uncle's house. "I apologize for my Army brethren's slovenliness," he graciously offered with a smile.

They arrived in Klausen and stopped near the church. "Let me out here. It is a short walk to Noviand." Hedy pointed across the gulley.

Johnny shook his head. "I'll drive you the rest of the way."

"You may notice the bridge is out." She waved toward the rope structure she had crossed on her way to Trier. "It will take you too far out of your territory to drive me all the way."

Hedy collected her backpack, thanked the soldier in the back, and swung across the rope bridge. Turning to wave good-bye, she chuckled.

Johnny shook his head and blew her a kiss. She spun back and strolled towards Noviand.

Gerda

1945

Thunderbirds who last week still wondered why we fought the Germans and their beliefs got their answer at the Dachau prison camp where death claimed victims by the carload and murder was a wholesale sadistic business.

45th Division News—May 13, 1945

The walk allowed Hedy time to focus on the events of the past forty-eight hours. The preceding two days were part nightmare, part dream. The war continued, her family's home was in ruin, and her future was uncertain. Yet, from an enemy soldier, she experienced kindness, consideration, and generosity in ways she had never dreamed possible. It was too overwhelming for her to absorb.

"Hedy. I can't believe you are back already." The thin figure of her mother running towards her pulled Hedy back to the present. Her aunt trailed right behind.

"Let me take your bag for you." Tante Gisela looped it off of Hedy's shoulder. "It weighs a ton. What did you bring back?"

Hedy had not noticed. Following the women into the kitchen, she gaped when apples, oranges, and chocolates spilled out of the bag.

Her mother's eyes darted between the contents of the bag and Hedy. "How in the world did you get these?"

Hedy beamed. Johnny had snuck them in. She did her best to explain the events of the previous few days.

"You accepted a ride from an enemy soldier and had dinner with him?" Disbelief covered her aunt's face as she watched her niece.

Mama didn't say a word.

"He was a perfect gentleman. Herr Haas approved." Her lips parted slightly. "Did you hear from Vater while I was gone?"

Her mother's drawn eyes answered her before the words came out. "Since the invasion, the mail and trains have not been running. I'm certain he will return any day. We need to stay in Noviand until he does."

"Has Koblanz been taken yet?" Hedy wondered.

Shrugging, her mother struggled to answer. "We don't think so. No one knows for sure."

"This damn war is lost. Why can't it be over?" Hedy sank onto the hard bench and bit her lip.

~

Over the next week or two, Hedy continued to check on Frau Berg and her son and assisted other villagers with minor medical needs. It was a distraction from the constant waiting.

Coming into the kitchen wearing her uniform, she plopped her empty bag on the table. "I have run out of bandages from the Americans. I hope everyone who needed them has been taken care of."

"You have been such a blessing, dear." Tante Gisela positioned a bowl of watery soup in front of her.

"There isn't much more I can take care of here. I think I will visit Gerda. She should be in Traben-Trarbach by now."

Her mother stood and leaned on the table. "Hedy, the war is still going on. You must stop wandering around the countryside. It isn't safe."

"It is our country, Mama. We should be able to go as we need." She stared defiantly back, ready to argue more.

Mama stormed out of the room, fuming.

"I'd recommend you take your bicycle by way of the road instead of the vineyard route," Rosemary teased her, trying to lighten the mood.

Her mother came back, calmer. "If you must go, would you mind stopping by to check on the Begons on your way home? They are in Ürzig, and I'd like to find out if they are all safe."

Hedy kissed her mother on the cheek. "They live above the post office, right?"

~

The ride went quickly. Hedy stopped at the resort to check if Gerda was working. Though still being used as a field hospital, the resort at Traben-Trarbach was now run by the Allies. The environment was not nearly as frantic as it was before. The cleaning ladies were the only ones Hedy knew as the rest of the German staff left when she had.

Leaving the hospital, she cycled past the middle of town, near the marketplace. All around were civilians with armloads of linens and household items. As Hedy came closer, she noticed an American soldier backing away from a rather insistent German woman.

"I don't know what you want." The soldier shook his head and held his hands in front of him as the woman pushed a blue and white linen at him and spoke rapidly in German.

Hedy swung off her bike and approached them. In English, she addressed the soldier. "Can I help you with something?"

"Thank God, you speak English." The soldier tipped his hat to her. "I'm Bud Smith, from Kansas. This woman keeps handing me her tablecloth. I don't understand."

"She would like to sell it to you or trade it for food."

"I don't need a tablecloth. Can I give her cash?"

Hedy stopped him. "We might have lost the war, but we remain proud people. She isn't asking for charity. She wants to trade."

Bud understood. "My sister Lorene is on a farm with her three boys. She would love a pretty tablecloth like that. Would you assist me?"

Hedy spoke to the woman. Negotiations complete, the GI tipped his hat again. She saluted with a grin, and headed toward Gerda's home.

~

Gerda welcomed her with a huge hug and introduced Hedy to her mother. "Mama, this is the girl who got us a feast in Trier."

After catching up on the news, Hedy dragged her friend out of the house to walk along the river.

"Do you ever run into anyone else from school?" Gerda kicked a stick from the no longer maintained path.

"I'm not sure I'd recognize any of them." Hedy thought for a moment. "Oh that is not quite true. Remember Günter Werner?"

"Sure, the scrawny kid who told everyone he was going to marry you?"

Hedy raised a brow. "He's not so scrawny anymore. Actually, he is quite handsome. I bumped into him last year at the train station."

"*Ohh la.* Does he still want to marry you?"

She gave Gerda a gentle pinch. "Cut it out. We had a lovely visit which made me miss my stop and caused me to walk back several kilometers."

"So you've dated." Gerda's eyes narrowed as her voice became more serious. "Is he as obnoxious as before?"

"Gerda, we haven't dated." She bit her lip before she continued. "I did visit his family, but we got into an uncomfortable discussion about the Nazis' excesses. I haven't heard from him since. Nor do I care to."

Their discussion progressed to the status of the war. Gerda became intense. "I simply refuse to believe the things the Allies are saying about the concentration camps. No one could be so evil. Certainly not our own people."

Hedy stopped and stared absently across the river. "I don't want to believe it either; however, I am afraid it may be true."

"You believe our countrymen—our soldiers, the boys we attended school with—could possible annihilate countless innocents for no reason?" Gerda's pitch rose.

"I don't believe most of our soldiers would do such things." Hedy hesitated. "The reports are rather detailed and convincing."

"Propaganda. It has to be." Gerda moved to block Hedy's line of sight. "The Allies know they have won and want to humiliate us more. Once the war is over, I am going to the camps to view them myself."

"I lived in Trier, down the street from the synagogue when they destroyed all the Jewish businesses. I had never seen such hatred in my life." Hedy walked past her friend, dodging the low hanging branches muddling the previously landscaped path.

Gerda reached for her arm. "There is a big difference between breaking windows and killing thousands of people."

"My friend Rachel Rosen had to leave." Hedy shuddered. "Or was taken. The Nazis imprisoned our priest from Trier."

"I don't believe it." Gerda grew louder. "There is no possible way our country did such horrific things."

Sweat appeared on Gerda's forehead. Hedy decided she needed to change the subject. "See that house there?"

As the women headed back to Gerda's house, Hedy regaled her friend with stories of her time at the field hospital. After dinner with Gerda's mother, they called it a night. The next morning with promises to visit each other, Hedy started back to Trier via Ürzig.

~

Hedy easily located the post office and met the Begons in the apartment above. As they caught up on the events of the past year, a honking vehicle and men shouting outside interrupted them.

Herr Begon leaned out the window and, after a few moments, addressed Hedy. "Are you in some kind of trouble? There are two American soldiers looking for you."

Hedy jerked straight up. Sticking her head out the window, she cried, "I'll be right down."

Quickly, Hedy explained why American soldiers sought her and hugged the Begons goodbye. Rushing down the stairs, she flew outside and landed in Johnny's arms.

"Wow. Quite the welcoming embrace." Johnny's dimple deepened.

Embarrassed, Hedy stepped back and offered Fred a quick hug. Spinning back to Johnny, she said, "What are you doing here? How did you find me?"

"I had the day off and drove to your uncle's in Noviand."

"But you didn't have his address." Hedy narrowed her eyes.

"I'm Counter Intelligence—remember? We can track anyone." Johnny grinned as he continued. "Besides you told me he lived in the schoolhouse. It wasn't hard to find."

"I have obviously been talking too much." She crossed her arms.

"You must have said something good about me. Your mother advised me where to find you."

Hedy caught her breath. "Mama did?" Smiling, she recovered. "Of course I said nice things about you. I didn't want her to worry about my having dinner with an American."

He led her to the jeep and tossed her bag in the back. "Let me drive you back to Noviand. I have something I need to tell you."

With that, Fred strapped Hedy's bike to the jeep. The three hopped in, with Fred in the back and Hedy next to Johnny in the front.

"Am I a prisoner of the CIC again?"

Putting on an exaggerated somber expression, Johnny answered, "General Eisenhower has a strict non-fraternization policy, so yes."

Hedy became serious. "I don't want you to get in trouble because of me."

Johnny patted her hand. Jolts of electrical current shot up Hedy's arm. "Don't worry about me, Hedy. Is there anything you need? Anything I can do for you or your family?"

Hedy simply shook her head. "What was so important you needed to track me down?"

"I have received orders to move to the CIC office in Oppenheim. It is quite an honor," Johnny hesitated, "but unfortunately, I'm not sure when I'll be able to see you again."

Hedy couldn't respond. A bolt of electricity floored her. As odd as it seemed for this almost stranger to search her out, the realization it would be a long time before she saw him again left her speechless. They weren't supposed to talk to each other, but she was thrilled when he made such an effort to track her down.

How could she be so attracted to an enemy soldier? She was incapable of reconciling the feelings of her heart with those of her head.

~

It was late afternoon when they arrived in Noviand. Hedy formally introduced Johnny to her mother. "John, thank you for escorting Hedy home. She worries me so, running around the countryside with all the unrest out there."

"It is my pleasure, Frau Weiß." He tilted his head toward Hedy. "I wish she would stay in Noviand, too. It would be much easier to find her that way."

Mama invited the men into the kitchen for a cup of tea made

from local herbs. They sat at the large roughhewn table. Fred and Johnny regaled Hedy and her family with humorous stories from America.

When it was time to leave, Johnny asked for a moment with Hedy outside. He withdrew a camera from the jeep and asked if he could take her picture. In spite of the fire in her cheeks, she agreed and smiled for him.

The repetitive clicks of the camera were so numerous, she stopped him. "Don't waste so much film on me."

Stowing the camera, Johnny placed a small picture of himself in her palm. "That would never be a waste." His voice softened. "Please don't forget me. I will find you again soon."

Addressing her mother, he added. "I will see you again. Please believe that."

And with that, he drove away. Flipping the picture over, Hedy read, *Affectionately yours, Johnny Merenda.* She held it to her heart and stared down the road after him.

War is Over

1945

GERMAN MEN AND WOMEN: When I addressed the German nation on May 1 telling it that the Führer had appointed me his successor, I said that my foremost task was to save the lives of the German people. ... I ordered the German High Command during the night of May 6-7 to sign the unconditional surrender for all fronts.

ADMIRAL KONRAD DONITZ—Radio announcement—May 6, 1945

Sitting at the kitchen table, Hedy, Mama, Tante Gisela, and Rosemary stared at the radio. Mama crossed herself.

Hedy leapt up. "Thank God it has ended."

Rosemary leapt up, tears streaming down her face. "Finally. Please God, let Willis can come home quickly."

~

Over the next several months, the lucky men returned from the fronts, many physically injured and most scarred emotionally. The mood of the town vacillated from happiness the protracted war was finally over, to grief for their deceased family members, to despair over the lack of food and housing.

"We are fortunate to have not been bombed and to be near farms for food. The poor city dwellers are having a far more difficult time." Tante Gisela waved a letter in the air. "My friend in Cologne tells me very little housing is available. With ration cards no longer usable, they can't get food. The *Invasionsarmee* hasn't let the authorities establish new rations yet."

~

After working a long day with a local farmer on the harvest, Hedy stepped into the kitchen and plopped down on the bench next to her uncle. Pouring a glass of wine, Onkel Marcel asked about her day.

A jeep pulled up outside. Marcel leapt to his feet, stared out the window, and headed to the cellar, taking his wine glass. She hurried to the window. The sight of Johnny in his jeep had her pulse racing. She glanced towards the cellar as Onkel Marcel shut the door. Coward.

Hedy pulled open the door as Johnny and another soldier appeared. Trying to refrain from flinging herself at him this time, she teased. "American soldiers aren't supposed to be fraternizing with the enemy."

Johnny grinned and stepped back with a bow. "I see no enemies."

Her heartbeat quickened as she ushered them in. How could this soldier from the invading army make her feel so good? "What are you doing in Noviand?"

"Steve and I are headed back to Trier and wanted to bother my favorite German. Steve, this is Hedy."

Steve tipped his hat. "Pleasure, Ma'am. Johnny was not exaggerating about you."

Hedy cleared her throat. Her cousin approached them carrying a basket of tomatoes. "Johnny, this is my cousin Rosemary. Rosemary, this is the soldier I told you about."

He shook her hand solidly. "I am proud to meet you, Rosemary. Hedy told me about your bravery when the tanks came through." He hesitated. "I am sorry my brethren chased you out of your home."

Blushing from head to toe, Rosemary simply nodded. Hedy invited them in to sit at the table for a glass of *viez*. As the group sipped the apple wine, the conversation ranged from Steve explaining the CIC agents were drawing straws to pick who would accompany Johnny on his "finding Hedy" visits to Rosemary detailing the unfortunate episode of using chickens for target shooting. The men buried their heads in their hands. Hedy wasn't sure if they were embarrassed or trying not to laugh out loud.

When it was time for them to leave, Johnny asked Hedy, "I want to know if you need anything. What can I bring your family next time I come?"

She waved him off. "Nothing, Johnny. We are fine."

Rosemary knocked her glass over, dowsing Hedy. As she dried herself off, Johnny stood. "I am sorry I can't give you any warning when I am coming. I will try to stop by as often as I can." After a warm embrace, he and Steve left.

Her cousin grasped Hedy's arm. "Why didn't you ask him for meat? Or bread? The Americans have everything."

Hedy glared at her cousin. "I won't take advantage of his kindness."

"You are a fool."

~

News and bits of mail trickled into town. No one understood what losing the war actually meant. Those with batteries for their radios shared any information they could.

A few weeks later, Onkel Marcel offered Hedy a tattered envelope. Her heart leapt when she recognized Aldrich's writing. With trembling hands, she opened it.

> *Dearest Hedy,*
>
> *I pray my favorite cousin is staying safe. Mother tells me Trier has been bombed, and she wishes you and your parents would come out to the farm and stay with her. Knowing you, however, you are probably organizing the townspeople in cleaning up the mess.*
>
> *I enjoyed your earlier letter, though I am certain it is old news by now. I can't believe you ran into Günter Werner. He always had quite an infatuation with you, but he can be something else. I guess I shouldn't have written that, as you might be dating him. I'm sure you have to beat the suitors off with a stick. Luckily the war seems to be winding down, and I can come home and wield the stick for you.*
>
> *Seriously, though, remember that war changes men. In fairness, I guess it has changed all of us. From your letters*

and Mother's, it sounds as if it has given you direction and strength. For me, the changes are far more negative. I've been asked to do things I hadn't dreamt would be requested of another human being. Now I just pray it ends soon and I can wrestle with my demons on my own time.

I'm in big trouble with my commanding officer. We were in battle and captured dozens of American soldiers. The officer wanted us to shoot the captured men in cold blood. As I stared down my rifle site, all I envisioned was Konrad's face. My vision blurred as I imagined the American's hearing of this and taking revenge on my brother. I would rather die myself than cause any danger to him.

Needless to say, I couldn't pull the trigger. The officer was furious. I believed he was going to shoot me. At the last second, he composed himself. I still feel him giving me the evil eye, however we are so cold and busy, who has time to worry about it?

Hedy shuttered, remembering the torn leaflet she had seen in Trier with the threats alluded to for those not fulfilling their duties. Shaking off the thought, she focused back on the letter.

As terrible as it is to realize we have lost the war, I am happy to think I should be home soon. There are rumors a peace treaty is being negotiated. I can't wait to return to the farm and have you milk the cows and take care of my chores for me.

Give your family my love, and I send you my deepest regards,

Aldrich

She stumbled back into a chair and stroked the cross at her neck. "Thank God, he's safe."

~

A week later, Hedy stood in a long line outside the butcher shop, stomach growling, chatting with a neighbor. "I doubt there will be meat left when it is my turn."

Behind her an American jeep pulled up. A familiar voice called out. "Fräulein, would you come with us?"

Hedy lowered her head to hide her expression while crawling into the jeep. Once out of sight of the line, she hit Johnny playfully on the arm. "I can already hear the rumors. I will be a war criminal by evening."

"I don't care. I wanted to see you, if only for a short time." Johnny stopped the jeep and embraced her. She didn't want him to ever let go.

Fred cleared his throat. Hedy jumped away from Johnny and held her hand up to cover her flushing face.

"You should hear the grief the agents give him. 'You are driving four hours round trip to spend a half hour with a girl?'" Fred said. "I informed them I would do the same thing if I was Johnny. Now they all want to ride along and meet you."

"Ignore him." Johnny held her hand and focused on her. "I checked on your father. He is safe in Koblenz and will be home before long."

Her hands flew to her mouth, the sides of her index fingers pressed against her lips in prayer. He continued before she could speak.

"Your cousin Konrad is safe in a POW camp in the States. I was unable to find any record of Aldrich. I am sorry."

"That is okay. I just received a letter from him, so I know he is safe." She embraced him. "Thank you so much, Johnny."

"What do you need? Do you have enough food?"

Unconsciously holding her empty stomach, Hedy shook her head. "You've already done enough."

~

Cheered by the news her father was alive, Hedy bounded with energy. A few days later, as she hung the clothes out to dry, she stopped. A familiar figure trudged up the road. Dropping her work, she sprinted down the road to greet him. "Vater. You are home."

The two embraced. Her father squeezed her tight, tears dripping onto her shoulder. When he finally released her, Hedy wrapped her arm around his waist. Her questions poured out. "Why has it taken you so long to come back? Were you hurt?"

"Whoa, *Süße*. No, I wasn't hurt. Let's find Mama and let me rest for a moment."

Mama had heard Hedy's squeals and was running towards them. Her parents embraced. Hedy turned to give them a bit of privacy. Together they walked to the house.

In the kitchen, Mama motioned for him to sit down. "We have been so worried. What happened?"

Vater inhaled deeply and let out a long breath. "The Allies bombed the city. It was truly awful. We hid in the cellar of the post office and opened packages looking for food. Then in early March, the American tanks came through. There was some fighting, but to tell you the truth, most of our soldiers were glad to see them. We all wanted the war to be over."

Hedy and her mother shared an understanding glance, waiting for him to continue.

"Skirmishes popped up in the streets for a while, before things calmed down. The building I was in was searched, and I was interrogated for a while. Luckily, they realized I wasn't anyone important and released me."

"Not important to them, but very important to us," Mama corrected him.

Papa squeezed her hand and stared into her eyes for a moment. "I was stuck. There was no way to send word to you I was alive. We knew the tanks had gone through Noviand. I prayed every day you two were safe."

Stopping, he pulled both of the women to him. "The Americans in Koblenz were generally polite and well behaved, however we heard stories—."

Hedy snuggled into her father's chest. "They were good to us here in Noviand, too."

Exhaling, he pulled her tighter. "I am happy to hear that."

Mama stood. "You must be starved after your walk. Let me get you something to eat."

Helping her mother, Hedy brought her father food. The women shared many of their stories. Not wanting to worry Vater, Hedy held back the more stressful ones. While he ate, she dashed to her room and retrieved Aldrich's letter. "Look, Papa. Aldrich is well and should be back anytime."

Vater's face darkened. "I'm sorry to tell you, Hedy. Aldrich died in the final days of the fighting. The whole platoon knew the war was lost and headed home. Their commander ordered them to come back and fight. A member of his unit told his mother Aldrich refused, and the officer shot him."

Mama gasped, hands flying to her mouth. The letter fell from Hedy's hand. Warm, salty tears streamed down her face as the realization hit her. Visions of the wounded boys back in the field hospital overwhelmed her, and she crumbled to the floor.

Graben+Trarbach

1945

(ii) To convince the German people that they have suffered a total military defeat and that they cannot escape responsibility for what they have brought upon themselves, since their own ruthless warfare and the fanatical Nazi resistance have destroyed German economy and made chaos and suffering inevitable.

Conclusions of the Potsdam Conference— August 2, 1945

The leaves on the trees fell. Hedy returned to the school house one day to recognize a familiar figure sitting with her mother and Rosemary at the kitchen table.

"Konrad." Hedy rushed and grabbed him from behind, not giving him a chance to stand.

He pried her arms from around him and pushed back the bench. Hopping up, he gave her a proper hug, before gently pressing on her shoulders to see her face. "Can this beautiful woman truly be the irritating little cousin I used to know?"

She beamed. "What about you? Look how tan you are." She squeezed him again and let out a long sigh. He stroked her hair and squeezed a bit harder. "A grown man and a musician."

Laughing, Konrad stated, "Yeah being a prisoner of war was hard work. It could have been a lot worse."

The room grew silent. Thoughts of Aldrich flooded Hedy's memories, and she wiped away the tear developing in her eye.

"Sorry." Konrad's eyes grew red as he drew his arms close to his body. "I always imagined Aldrich and I would raise our families next to each other on the farm. Like so many of our plans, that won't happen."

"I'm glad we have you back." Hedy hugged her cousin again.

He sat back down and motioned for her to sit across the table. "So, Hedy, what is happening here?"

Hedy slid on the bench next to Rosemary. "Vater is trying to get us back to Trier. They have a job for him at the post office. In the meantime, I am helping where I can."

He turned to Rosemary and flashed his boyish grin. "We are both Hedy's cousins, but not related. Is there a name for that?"

Rosemary laughed. "I don't think so, but you are welcome here anytime."

"Thanks, Rosemary. Hedy wrote me that you are engaged. How is Willis?"

Her face fell. "I wish I knew. I haven't heard from him in months. I am worried."

Hedy patted her back lightly. "He'll be home any day, Rosemary."

Rosemary brightened. "I hope so." She challenged Konrad. "Ask her why a certain enemy soldier keeps showing up in town."

Frowning, Konrad stared at Hedy. "Really? What is going on?"

"Nothing. There is a nice American named Johnny whom I had dinner with."

Konrad smirked. "That is why Tante Marlene has been asking me about America. How serious is this?"

"How serious can it be? He shows up for an hour here and there." She brushed away the question. "I want to know everything that happened to you. Tell me all about your travels."

"I was one of the lucky ones. The Allies busted through our lines so fast, they didn't know what to do with us. Next thing I know, I am in a place called Texas."

"You said they treated you well. Is it true?"

"Oh yes. I actually contemplated asking to stay." He pantomimed playing a violin. "I could be a musician there. But—"

Concern filled Hedy. "What's wrong?"

His demeanor turned serious. "I needed to come back. Our

Germany will never be the same."

Rosemary agreed. "What can we do?"

"Come on. Where's your German spirit? We will rebuild and come back stronger." Hedy rallied her cousins.

Konrad shook his head. "That is exactly what the rest of the world is afraid of. This occupation is not going to be easy."

"Well, we will help where we can. When the schools open up again, I'll become a physical therapist and help the wounded."

"Willis and I will move to the city to see what needs to be done there." Rosemary stated, her face warming with a smile.

Hedy rose. "It is a beautiful day. Let's go for a walk."

The three cousins strolled out amongst the trees, catching up. A half hour later, Hedy's father crept toward them, his feet barely moving. She waved, and he joined the group. "What is wrong, Vater?"

Vater's eyes passed Hedy and settled on Rosemary. He placed his arm around her, and they stepped away from the others. "Oh, Rosemary, I am so sorry."

Her eyes grew wide. "Why? What has happened?"

"I spoke to Willis's father." Vater gulped. "Willis was shot during the last days of the war. He died trying to save one of his friends."

"No. It can't be." Rosemary fell into Vater's arms, sobbing uncontrollably.

Hedy's hand flew to her mouth. She rushed to support Rosemary's sagging body. Konrad's face went blank. They helped her back to the house where Tante Gisela ushered her grieving daughter upstairs, leaving Hedy with her father and Konrad.

"It isn't possible. I assumed the bad news would end with the war." Hedy sunk onto the couch, wiping her eyes.

Konrad held her hand while her father sat beside her and patted her knee. "It will be a long time before everything is straightened out." Vater placed his palm under her lowered chin and raised it. "The darker the night."

"I am not seeing brighter stars, Vater."

~

The year progressed on. The Japanese surrendered, finishing the War in the Pacific. The Allies divided Germany, and, as expected, Noviand and Trier landed in the French sector. Food rationing coupons returned, however food rations remained small, less than 1200 calories a day. Worse, even with their ration coupons, there was scarcely any food available to buy.

Supplemental food became harder for Hedy to earn due to meager harvests in the area. In an effort to control the black market, the Allies made it illegal for Germans to trade for food and had banned international food relief packages to German civilians as punishment for the war. The farmers attempted to grow enough crops for the population, but the fertilizer had been used for bombs. Germany was starving.

Coming home one afternoon with only a few potatoes to show for her hard day's work, Hedy plopped onto the kitchen bench and peeled off her too-small shoes.

"Ouch. It is supposed to snow tomorrow, so at least I'll get to rest my feet." Hedy sighed. She glanced at her cousin who was wearing the closest thing to a smile Hedy had seen in months. "Okay, Rosemary, what is going on?"

"A woman from the Red Cross stopped by today looking for you." Rosemary inhaled, allowing for a generous pause. "A young man is looking for you. She wants you to go to the station to give your approval to let them tell him where you are."

Hedy thought for a moment. "That must be Günter."

"Who is Günter?" Mama balanced the canned goods in her hand as she stepped around Hedy to place them on the counter.

"Günter Werner, from Birresborn. I saw him a few times while I was working at the field hospital."

"Oh, I remember his family. Good people."

"And German," Rosemary piped in. "I'll go down to the Red Cross with you tomorrow, if you'd like."

Hedy waved away their comments. "I am not interested in Günter. I see no reason to waste their time or mine."

"Waiting for your American?" Rosemary's voice dripped with condescension. "We haven't seen him in a long time. What makes you think he'll come back?"

Hedy bristled. "He is busy. He will visit as soon as he is able."

"Of course he's busy. He is tracking down all those evil SS members. We've all heard the reports of the concentration camps.

After what he has seen, why would he want to have anything to do with a German?" Rosemary stormed out of the room.

Mama stepped behind Hedy and gently rubbed her back without saying a word. Doubt flooded her thoughts. Surely Johnny wouldn't hold it against her for being German. Her whole body shook as she buried her head in her hands.

~

When the snows cleared, Inge and Gerda sent word for Hedy to come to Traben-Trarbach for a mini reunion. Understandably hesitant, her mother attempted to dissuade her. "I realize the war is finally over. Everything is in such disarray. There are displaced persons everywhere, trying to find their way back to their own countries. You don't know what is out there."

"Mama, I survived the trip from Traben-Trarbach over the mountains at night with a war going on. Going back via the main road on a beautiful day will be a piece of cake. Besides I had no problems last time I went."

"*You did what?*" her father interrupted, face growing red.

Hedy and her mother grinned at each other. "I guess we haven't shared everything, dear." Mama patted her on the arm. "All right, wear your uniform and don't stay long. Herr Haas has found rooms near a grocery store in Trier for us to move into. I am certain your Tante Gisela will be thrilled to get us out of her hair."

Eager to visit her friends again, Hedy headed back over the mountains to Traben-Trarbach. The perfect weather allowed for a pleasant ride until she reached a damaged portion of the main road. A detour onto a smaller, heavily shaded country path was required. The sunshine eked its way amidst the leaves.

Hedy shivered as she rode. Something moved ahead, by the side of the road. Slowing her bike, she reached inside the substantial pocket on her uniform. As she closed in, a scrawny man in torn clothes came into view. He yelled for her to stop. This time she was prepared. She pulled an apple out of the pocket and tossed it to him as she sped by.

"*Danke. Gott beschütze dich,*" he shouted.

"God bless you, too," she called back, waving.

~

"You made it," squealed Inge as Hedy leaned her bicycle against the fence.

"Can you believe the war is finally over?" Gerda linked arms with her friends and walked to the river to catch up.

"So, hanging out with the enemy anymore?" Inge teased. "I haven't had a dinner like that since."

Looking away, Hedy hid her flushing face.

"You have. Hedy, what is going on?"

"He may have tracked me to Ürzig after I left you, Gerda."

"Wow. How did he do that?" Gerda's eyes grew wide as she raised her hand to her mouth.

"Mama told him where I was going."

Inge jerked to a stop. "How did he find your mother?"

"He is very attentive." Hedy raised her face to the sky to avoid eye contact. "He has stopped by once or twice."

"*Oooh*. How interesting." Gerda slapped Hedy lightly on the shoulder.

Hedy could not stop smiling anytime she pictured Johnny. She attempted to change the subject. "Any news when the medical school will open again?"

"You are changing the subject," Inge called her out before shaking her head. "Berlin is in ruins, and the Russians are arguing with the Allies about who controls the area. We probably will never get to finish." Inge's disappointment was palatable. "How about you? Can you go to the school in France? Or will the French let any of us in?"

"I have no idea," Hedy answered. "Vater finally came home and we are trying to figure out how to move back to Trier." She sighed. "It will be a while before I can think about school again."

"I know of a lovely loft above a lingerie store in Trier with an expansive view," Inge offered.

Hedy laughed. "I can imagine my extremely proper mother setting up the rubble alarm every night. Thanks. We have rooms away from the central part of town which weren't bombed. Vater is trying to figure out how to get our stuff from Noviand back to Trier. He can borrow a truck, but there isn't any petrol to be found. I can't carry our stove on my bicycle."

"There is always your handsome soldier," Gerda suggested. She elbowed Inge and pointed at Hedy. "There's the smile and the bright red cheeks again."

"Yes," says Inge. "I recall you two getting rather cozy at dinner. It appeared he'd be willing to do anything for you."

Putting her hands on her hips, Hedy tried, unsuccessfully, to suppress her feelings. "It's starting to rain and will be dark soon. Shouldn't we head inside instead of interrogating me?"

The girls hustled back to Gerda's house and settled down to a light dinner. After clearing the table, they retired to the living room to chat with Gerda's mother. The gentle rain from the afternoon turned into a late thunderstorm. Periodically, the room lit up with a lighting show and vibrated with the responding thunderhead.

Around 10:00 that evening, the living room lit up, although the flash did not go away. In place of thunder, the women heard voices. As they strained their ears and searched out the window, two booming voices called, "Gerda, Inge, Hedy."

"Is that who I think it is?" Inge snatched Hedy's sleeve.

Gerda's mother placed her hands on her hips. "Who is there and why are they standing in the rain calling you girls?"

Hedy started for the door, as Gerda and Inge struggled to explain, talking over one another.

"Stop." Gerda's mother threw up her hands. "Bring them inside, get some robes and bedding, and light a fire in the fireplace."

Hedy stepped out the door and ushered them in. "Johnny, come in before you catch your death of cold. Steve, you too."

"I didn't think we would ever find you." Johnny gratefully accepted the towels and handed one to Steve. "We had the evening off and thought we'd say hello."

Steve chimed in. "Just didn't realize how far we had to go to track you down."

After a quick introduction, Gerda's mother issued orders to Johnny and Steve. "Get out of those wet clothes and hang them up to dry. I will get you a brandy and then go to sleep. We will see you at breakfast." She added sternly, "Girls, good night. I believe you were heading to bed."

Chastised, the young women said good night to the soldiers. Johnny managed to give Hedy a quick hug. "I'll be having sweet dreams, knowing I'll see you in the morning," he whispered.

I won't be able to sleep at all. She kept that notion to herself as her whole body tingled.

It might as well have been an elementary school slumber party. Gerda and Inge quizzed and teased Hedy, wanting her to share all the details of her dates with the handsome officer.

"He keeps showing up when I least expect him. We've barely had a minute alone, but when we are together, it's like we've known each other our entire lives. I can't explain it." Hedy paused, stood tall, and regarded her friends sternly. "And I don't have to."

Gerda nudged Inge. "We need to let Hedy get her beauty sleep for her date in the morning."

Grateful, Hedy laid down. Closing her eyes as tight as she could, she fought to block out the thoughts of Johnny downstairs in order to sleep.

The next morning could not come quickly enough. Gerda's mother fixed a lovely breakfast, and the men shared their story of getting to Traben-Trarbach.

"As usual, when I arrived in Noviand, Hedy was gallivanting around the countryside," Johnny began with a stern countenance. "Steve and I knocked on the schoolhouse door. I'm expecting to greet your mother again, Hedy. Instead, a frowning man asks me why I want to find his daughter."

Hedy gasped. She had mentioned an American soldier to her father, but had downplayed her feelings.

Johnny continued as he glanced sideways at her. "I had assumed Hedy had been singing my praises and her father would want to meet me, however it appears I needed to count on her mother for that."

"Mama?" Hedy gripped Gerda's arm.

"Yes, Hedy. It seems she has mentioned my visits to your father and was happy to tell me once again where you ran off to. A problem arose, however, when neither Steve nor I possessed the foggiest notion of how to get here. Your father rode along to show us how to get around all the detours to the main road, then he needed a ride back."

Looking thoughtful, Johnny added, "We need him at our office. I have never been interrogated so thoroughly before."

Steve chimed in. "For a moment, I thought Johnny was going to have to give him the dates of his baptism and confirmation." Laughing, he picked up where Johnny left off. "By the time we survived the questions, returned Mr. Weiß, and got here, it was late and raining. Your folks didn't know Gerda's address; hence we knocked on doors and asked."

Grinning, Hedy imagined the neighbors' expressions when two American soldiers knocked on the door asking for Gerda's address.

"I'm afraid we'll be hearing stories about Gerda being taken to an American prison," Inge said between giggles.

"I'm more afraid to find out what my father asked," Hedy murmured.

Steve continued, "When we finally got your address, it seemed awfully late to ring the doorbell. We decided to get your attention by calling to you, instead."

"Well, Inge and Hedy," Gerda reminded them, "your names were also being called. I guess we are all going to prison together."

The group spent the rest of the morning chatting until the men announced they had to drive back to Oppenheim. Johnny wanted to take Hedy to Noviand. She reminded him he needed to go the opposite direction, and, with all the detours, he would be late getting back to his post.

As they prepared to leave, Johnny pulled Hedy aside. "I promised you I would keep in touch as best I can. I don't know when I'll see you again, but remember I will."

Hedy's eyes met his. She didn't need to say a word. Detoured roads would not come between them.

"Before I go, is there anything you or your family need? Food, clothing, anything I can do?"

Hedy hesitated. She knew the family desperately needed petrol if they were to move back to Trier, but she didn't want to ask. Johnny noticed the hesitation. "There is something. What do you need, Hedy?"

"We have a place in Trier we can move into and a truck we can borrow, however there is no petrol."

"Say no more, *mia amore*, I shall get you gas. When do you need it?"

"There is a problem. Vater isn't sure when the truck will be available. The driver offered us a week's notice." She bit her lip.

"I'll be on call for you. I can get you gas when you have a date."

When the men drove off, Inge stared at Hedy, hands on her hips. "Just how serious are you two? What haven't you been telling us?"

"What are you talking about?" She batted her eyes. "I haven't seen him many more times than the two of you."

"But he doesn't gaze at us that way," Gerda continued to torment Hedy.

"Since you two can't behave yourselves, I'll head back to Noviand. Besides I don't want to hang around to hear all the rumors about American soldiers performing a house-to-house search for Gerda." Hedy hopped on her bicycle and chuckled.

"I'll tell them the soldiers had the name wrong." Gerda gave the bike a push. "Be safe, Hedy. Don't forget I'll be in Noviand in a week or so."

Pleasant thoughts filled Hedy's ride home. Once again, Johnny surprised her. What trouble he endured to see her.

~

Upon Hedy's return, her father quizzed her as a father should. "Who is this man and why is he stalking you?"

"He is not stalking me, Vater. He has been particularly kind and helpful. In fact, he is going to get petrol for us to move to Trier."

Vater's serious stance lightened. He admitted Johnny seemed to be a fine, upstanding young man, even if he was an American soldier.

"He is, Vater. He is." Her hands flew to her mouth, and she stepped away beaming.

Oppenheim

1946

Keep faith with the American soldiers who have died to eliminate the German war makers.

DO NOT FRATERNIZE

Label on a *Pocket Guide to Germany* published by the US Government for occupation forces.

Back at her uncle's, Hedy was anxious to move to Trier. Though gracious, Tante Gisela obviously would like to have her home back. Onkel Marcel appeared more interested in the wine cellar than the family, and Rosemary's depression since the news of her fiancé's death increased dramatically.

Hedy's relationship with Rosemary became more strained by the day. "I wish I had news about the school in Berlin." Hedy pinned the corner of a tablecloth to the clothesline. "Rosemary, can you get that corner?"

Her cousin did as requested. "Why bother? So you can go help the enemy?"

Hedy picked up a wet towel. "What are you talking about?"

"You go on and on about becoming a physical therapist to help your countryman, then you flirt with an enemy soldier."

"But Rosemary, you met him. He is a good man." She wrung the water from the towel.

Keeping her back to Hedy, her cousin spat. "He is an American.

They can't be trusted. Haven't you heard the stories of *frau bait*? The *Yanks* laugh they can get girls by offering them food."

Hedy's hands clenched the cloth in her hand tighter. She twisted it until her wrists hurt. "How can you say that? The Americans saved Mama's life. Don't you recall how generous they were with the food and medicine? They didn't ask for anything in return."

"We are starving while they eat like kings."

"I realize food is hard to come by, but that isn't the Americans' fault."

Rosemary spun around and exploded. "They killed my Willis." She flung down her laundry basket and pointed her forefinger at Hedy's chest. "You are a traitor." She stormed off.

Shaken, Hedy dropped the towel to the ground. She was not a traitor. Johnny was a good man. It was not his fault he was an American.

~

Making good on her promise, Gerda came to Noviand for a visit. She and Hedy were helping the other women in the garden when Vater returned with good news. "The truck will be available in eight days. Hedy, can your young man get us the petrol by then?"

Rosemary glared, condescension dripping from her voice. "Surely her soldier can do that for her. Those Americans *never* expect anything in return."

Hedy chose to ignore her and responded to her father. "I am sure he can if I could reach him."

"He shows up whenever he pleases." Rosemary picked up her basket and skulked off.

Gerda stared after her before making a suggestion. "Let's ride over to Oppenheim. The weather is good and it isn't far. Surely we can find a hostel for the night."

The wrinkled brow on Vater's face displayed his anxiety. "Oppenheim is more than 130 kilometers."

Hedy allayed his fears. "Vater, we will wear our Red Cross uniforms. They have kept us out of trouble"— she stopped to glimpse sideways at Gerda — "more times over the last few years than you will ever know."

Gerda stifled a giggle. Hedy's mother suppressed a smile.

After more protests, Vater finally consented. "I don't like it, but I guess it is the only option."

"Let's start right away." Hedy headed to the house. "We should get halfway there before dark."

~

After changing into their trusty Red Cross uniforms, the two women mounted their bicycles. With the lovely weather, they made good time to the town of Simmern, about a third of the way to Oppenheim.

"Oh, dear." Gerda's bike wobbled as the chain slipped off the gear. She stopped and reset it. Minutes later, it slipped again. After several attempts to fix it, the women decided it would be better to walk the bike into town and find a repair shop.

The repair shop owner wiped his hands on a towel hung from his belt. "I am closing up. I'll fix it in the morning."

"Is there somewhere for us to spend the night close by?" Hedy inquired.

"Sure." He pointed up the street. "The Langes have a room to rent and are only about six blocks north of here."

After thanking the man, Hedy and Gerda headed towards the Langes. They had not gone far when the military police stopped them.

"Your travel permits and reason for travel, please." The MP wasted no time.

They had no permit. Without a permit, Hedy realized they were in trouble. "Sir," she responded in her basic English. "I have a sister with two children who were evacuated to Oppenheim and need help to return to Trier. I haven't seen my sister or nephews for a year."

He didn't budge. "You are required to have a permit."

Hedy began to argue, but Gerda stepped in front of her. "We would like to speak to Steve Homer in the CIC office, please."

The MP regarded her suspiciously, then at Hedy. "Follow me."

Hedy and Gerda followed him into the center of town. "I hope he is taking us to the CIC office and not to jail." Hedy bit her lower lip. "How did you think of asking for Steve?"

"I remembered Steve saying he was being assigned to Simmern." She rolled her eyes. "If you ever paid attention to anyone but Johnny, you would have known that too."

The MP guided the women to the government building that acted as the CIC headquarters. They waited in a comfortable room as the MP called the commander over and pointed to the women. The two held a low discussion. The MP left to go back on his rounds, and the commander disappeared into his office.

"What now?" Hedy fidgeted.

Gerda shrugged her shoulders and chewed on a fingernail. A Polish woman about Hedy's age quietly entered the room and motioned for them to follow her to a house across the street. In her limited German, the Polish woman explained the commander controlled the house and rented the rooms for travelers needing a place to stay.

At the top of a flight of stairs, the woman opened the door to a small attic room with two beds and a bath. After leaving them to get settled, she came back with a plate of sandwiches and cookies. "Compliments of the commander," she said before wishing them goodnight.

"I supposed we would be in jail tonight," Gerda whispered as they settled into bed.

"It has to be our nursing uniforms. I don't think the MP believed the story about my sister at all."

"Do you think Steve knows we are here?"

"If so, he's probably wondering what kind of crazy girls Johnny introduced him to." Hedy grinned at the thought.

Gerda turned out the light. "Well, if Johnny can track you all over the countryside, it only seems fair we return the favor."

~

The rays of morning light landed on the young women's faces, waking them. After taking a moment to realize where she was, Hedy dressed and walked downstairs with Gerda to thank the family for their hospitality. The Polish woman handed them a package of sandwiches for the trip. "With the commander's compliments. He recommends you go to his office for travel permits."

Once again amazed by the Americans' generosity, Hedy accepted the sandwiches and promised to pay a visit to the commander after they picked up Gerda's bicycle.

"It seems every time we think we are going to get arrested, we get fed." Gerda snickered. "I may have to explore a life of crime."

"It shouldn't be a crime to wander around our own country." Hedy shot back. "Just don't get any other ideas."

After collecting Gerda's bike, they headed back to the CIC office. The guard at the door stopped them. More relaxed this time, Hedy stated, "We are here to meet the commander regarding travel permits."

He called into the building, and a tall, thin officer with shocking red hair came over. "The commander is busy. He asked I get the information from you to issue your permits."

After getting their names and travel plans, he ushered them inside and stepped back into his office. While waiting for him to return, a low voice startled them. "There is a CIC agent driving around in a jeep asking if we've seen two nurses. Would that be you young ladies?"

They spun around. An MP pointed out the window. Hedy started toward the door as the red-haired officer returned to give them the permits. After thanking him for his help, she grasped Gerda's hand and pulled her outside. Searching up and down the street, she couldn't find the jeep.

Gerda mounted her bike. "We must have just missed Steve."

They rode down the street. A vehicle behind them honked. Hedy moved to the side of the road as Steve pulled up next to them. "Hedy, Gerda. I didn't think I would ever find you two. Do you realize how many nurses are in this town?" He bounded out of the jeep. "You can't leave until you have lunch with me."

Gerda thanked him as he loaded their bikes into his jeep and drove them to the CIC house. The seven officers sitting down to their meal greeted Steve, who motioned to the women. "Meet Hedy and Gerda from Noviand."

The agents stood and made room for the ladies. Out of courtesy to the women, they switched to speaking in German. Steve regaled the table with a tale of being called into the commander's office last night. "So I am resting after a hard day at work..." Snickering was heard down the table. "...when I am ordered to report immediately to the commander's office. I start racking my brain; what have I done this time?"

"This time?" Gerda raised her eyebrows. The agents chuckled.

"So sheepishly, I slink into his office trying to figure out what he might have been told, so I don't confess to the wrong thing. The commander stood up from his desk, told me to sit down and said, 'Why are there two German nurses asking for you?'"

With an exaggerated motion, Steve sat up tall to continue his story. "'Two nurses, sir?' I ask him. That was definitely not one of the things I expected to be accused of. The commander explained two attractive"—the Americans around the table all nod in agreement—"nurses were about to be arrested for traveling without a permit when they asked for me."

A thoughtful expression crossed his face as he rubbed his chin. "Well, the most attractive girls I have seen recently were with Johnny over in Noviand. I put two and two together. By the way, I had to vouch for your characters, ladies." He wagged his finger in their direction. "So please behave while you are traveling."

Gerda batted her eyes. "We always behave."

"So, that explains you driving all over town this morning scaring all the nurses on their way to work," shouted an officer.

"I'd have spent all morning tracking you ladies down too," another chimed in.

Hedy and Gerda laughed with the men as they ate their lunch, before realizing how late it had gotten. Hedy stood. "As greatly as we are enjoying your company, we need to get to Oppenheim before dark."

"At least let me drive you after I spent all morning searching for you," Steve offered. "I can't take you all the way, however I'll take you as far as I can."

Hedy gratefully accepted for the two of them.

With the bikes in the back of the Jeep, Steve drove them the next forty kilometers. "It is probably another fifty kilometers to Oppenheim. I have to go back, but I'll try to get a message to Johnny that you are on your way."

~

Back on the road, Hedy and Gerda rode on. After a while, two American soldiers with rifles stopped them.

"What now?" Gerda glanced at Hedy.

One of the soldiers handed a gunny sack with something in it to Gerda. "Rabbit. Umm, *hase*. Food."

Gerda handed it back. "*Nein Danke.*"

Pushing the bag back at Gerda, the soldier tried again. "For you. Rabbit."

Finally, Hedy whispered to her, "Take it or we will never get on our way."

Reluctantly, Gerda accepted the gift. "*Danke.*"

The soldiers smiled and waved as Gerda tied it to her bicycle. "Now, Hedy, what am I supposed to do with a dead rabbit for the rest of the trip?" Gerda groaned.

"We'll give it to someone else down the road. Let's get going. It's getting late."

~

An hour later, a vehicle drove up behind them. They pulled over to let it pass. An American ambulance stopped. "Which hospital are you going to?" The driver called out the window. "Do you need a ride?"

"We're headed to Oppenheim."

"It is out of my territory, although I can carry you part of the way."

Hedy and Gerda stowed their bikes in the back of the ambulance and sat behind the driver and his only other passenger, a soldier who didn't look as if he was old enough to be in the war. Neither the driver nor the soldier spoke German, nevertheless the women managed with their limited English.

Once on their way, the young soldier twisted in his seat to face the girls. He grew pale and seized his rifle. "You have a gun?" he stammered as he stared behind them.

Hedy and Gerda drew back. Raising their hands, they glanced behind them and comprehended his concern. Blood dripped onto the floor of the ambulance. The bag tied to Gerda's bike was stained red. "No, no. No gun." they answered in unison.

Waving her hands in front of her, Hedy explained. "It is a rabbit. Soldiers handed it to us right before you came by. Please, you can have it. We don't want it."

The driver stopped the ambulance, and the soldier tossed the sack with the bloody rabbit into the woods. After giving the soldier grief for his reaction to a dead rabbit, the driver twisted and looked back at them, "I'm ahead of schedule. I can't enter the town, so I'll drop you off at the entrance."

At the edge of Oppenheim, the driver pointed out the sign for the CIC office and provided them directions. They unloaded their bikes and did their best to mop up the blood with a wad of bandages. After apologizing for the mess the dead rabbit had left, Hedy and Gerda thanked the men and rode into town.

~

Arriving at a beautiful two story house with an undersized sign notating the CIC office, Hedy noticed the lack of cars in the drive. She turned to Gerda and shrugged as she rang the bell.

A young woman in a serving uniform composed of a modest-length black dress with a white apron opened the door. Slowly she scanned the two women. "Nobody home." She shut the door in their faces.

"That was rude." Gerda rang the doorbell again.

Cracking open the door, the woman spat at them. "I told you, nobody home."

Hedy knocked incessantly. After several minutes, the door opened again, this time by a familiar young man. "*Signorina* Hedy." He kissed the air near her right cheek and her left, before greeting Gerda the same way. "*Signorina* Gerda. What are you doing here?"

"Jo, I am so pleased to see you. We are looking for Johnny." Hedy hugged the short Italian cook.

"Come in, *amici*, come in. Come, sit on the sofa. I'll put away your things..." he led them to a generous sitting room with a number of overstuffed divans, "...and fix you something to eat."

After putting away the bikes, Jo reprimanded the serving woman. "These are special friends of Agent Johnny. Make sure they have anything they want." He placed a platter of bread and cold cuts and opened a bottle of wine on the end table. "Johnny's room is here in the main house. I'm not sure when he and Fred will be back. Please be comfortable. I'll alert you when he arrives."

She thanked him. After partaking of the cold cuts and a glass of wine or two, Hedy and Gerda fell asleep in the sitting room on the large, comfortable divans.

A few hours later, Jo quietly woke the girls. "Agent Johnny is home." He switched off the lights to the room as he left.

"Why did he do that?" Gerda whispered.

Within moments, the lights glared. The surprised expressions on Johnny and Fred made the harrowing trip worthwhile. They stood speechless and simply stared at the two girls.

Gerda and Hedy grinned. "Don't we at least get a hello after traveling all this way?" Gerda teased.

Johnny rushed to Hedy and squeezed. "I can't believe you are here."

Hedy and Gerda shared their adventures with the men. Fred stared at Johnny and scratched his jaw.

"Is there nothing you two won't do?" Fred wondered. He referred to his watch. "It is late and you can't sleep here. There is a small apartment in a house down the block we rent for visiting officers."

"And crazy girls," Johnny added.

He escorted them to the house. After introducing the girls to the owner, he asked if he might stay for a short while.

"If you won't find me rude, Johnny, I'll go on up to bed," Gerda subtly excused herself.

Finally alone, Johnny stared into Hedy's eyes. "Why on earth did you come all this way?"

"How else could I contact you?" Her voice quickened. "Vater has scheduled the truck to move us back to Trier, but if we can't get the petrol, we lose the use of the truck. It is a terrible bother for you, I know. I didn't see any other option."

He patted her knee. "You are never a bother, Hedy. In the morning, I'll get the gas situation worked out." He pulled his chair closer to hers, until she absorbed his warmth all along her side. "I can't believe you put yourself in such danger."

"I am fine, Johnny. Tell me what has been going on. Has Oppenheim been a good move?"

"It has." His eyes lit up. "I have great news. I received word yesterday I will be transferred to the larger CIC office in Wiesbaden. Not only is it closer to Trier, the main roads are considerably better."

Hedy listened intently as Johnny explained how his fluency in German and Italian were needed and his transfer orders would be arriving. His arms flying, he described the town, the bigger office, and the better quarters. He went on and on.

Hedy sensed his excitement changing into nervousness. "Johnny, there is something else. What is it?"

He inhaled deeply, moved his chair in order to face her, and lifted her hands, rubbing the back of them with his thumbs. A shiver sailed up her spine.

"I have found the love of my life, and I never want to lose you. Will you marry me?"

The room spun, making Hedy thankful she was seated. Stunned with emotion, her thoughts overwhelmed her. Yes, she loved him, but this wasn't a normal courtship. They had not gone on dates. His visits had been more like lightning bolts, filled with electricity and gone in a flash.

"Hedy?" Johnny stared, his brow furrowed.

"Yes," she exclaimed, embracing him tightly. The extended kiss which followed filled her with a warmth like she had never experienced before.

Eventually he pulled away from her. There was no time to make future plans. "I'll get the gasoline and clearance to take you back to Noviand." He hurried out the door, before pausing to look back. "I love you very much."

Hedy stood there, in a daze. Engaged. She wanted to shout it from the rooftop. Climbing up the stairs to the room she and Gerda shared, Hedy sang, "*Ich bin verlobt*, I am engaged," over and over.

Yanking Gerda's blankets off her, Hedy shouted, "Wake up, Gerda. *Ich bin verlobt*."

Gerda rolled over and mumbled, "That's nice. Go to bed and tell me in the morning."

Frustrated, Hedy laid in bed trying to sleep. She replayed every moment of the evening, heat radiating from her chest. Finally, her body forced her mind to go to sleep.

Once the sun rose, Hedy leapt out of bed and shook Gerda

awake. "I'm in love with a beautiful man, and he's in love with me. Unbelievable."

Gerda obviously had not listened to anything from the night before. "It seems pretty obvious to everyone else he's in love with you. Are you finally figuring this out?"

"*Ich bin verlobt.* I'm engaged. Did you not listen to me last night?"

"Are you serious?" Gerda wrapped her arms around her friend. "That is magnificent. Why didn't you wake me?"

With that, Hedy pushed her back on the bed and threw a pillow at her. Laughing, they dressed and strode downstairs, arm in arm.

Hedy was not the only one eager to share the news. When she and Gerda stepped outside, Johnny stood waiting next to his jeep. Across the bottom of the windshield, block letters spelled out HEDY.

Johnny's shoulders rose. "Do you like it?"

"It is perfect." Hedy clapped her hands in delight.

A tall, serious man with numerous patches on his uniform strode up to the jeep. Johnny jumped to attention. The officer stared at the letters on the windshield and at Hedy.

Addressing Johnny, he barked. "Is this woman German?"

Johnny answered, "Yes, sir."

"Are you not aware of the regulations regarding fraternizing with the locals?"

"Yes, sir, but..."

Shaking, Hedy strode over to the officer and interrupted in the best English she could muster. "Sir, I am Hedy Weiß from Trier. Johnny was not aware I was coming and should not be held responsible for my behavior."

Raising his eyebrows, the officer stared at her and at the letters on the jeep. "Hedy, hmmm." He spun back to Johnny. "Is this the same Hedy the agents said crossed the mountain near Traben-Trarbach at night as our tanks were entering Germany?"

An expression of surprise crossed his face. "Yes, sir. It is."

The officer's expression softened. "Agent, perhaps you should bring her to my quarters, and we will discuss this over breakfast."

He left. Hedy's mouth opened.

"Hedy, that was my commanding officer."

"It seems my reputation precedes me. How had he heard about my trip to Noviand?"

Johnny looked sheepish. "Fred and I may have shared some stories with the men." He snatched her hand. "Come on, we have been invited to breakfast. Fred, would you take care of Gerda?"

During breakfast, the officer quizzed Hedy about her experiences during the war. "I have a daughter about your age. I cannot imagine her traipsing across the countryside during a war."

"Your wife probably doesn't have as many grey hairs as I have given my mother." Hedy laughed, before adding, "I only did what I needed to."

As Johnny and Hedy left the table, the officer pulled Johnny aside. After a few moments, they stepped back to Hedy.

"It has been a pleasure, Hedy. Johnny informs me he wishes to marry you."

"He does, sir. And I would like that too."

"Are you aware the army forbids marriage to German civilians?"

"Yes, sir. I am praying it will change soon."

He responded with a large smile. "So am I. Johnny, take this woman home. And, Hedy," he patted her shoulder kindly, "try to be more cautious."

Smiling, she embraced the officer and kissed him lightly on the cheek. Johnny touched her elbow and escorted her out. Fred had finished securing the girls' bicycles onto the jeep with the gasoline. He stared at the couple with a question in his eye.

Johnny grinned back. "She charmed him almost as much as she charms me." He gently helped Hedy into the back seat and settled in next to her.

"I'm not surprised." Helping Gerda into the front, Fred said, "I don't mind driving, but behave back there."

He chauffeured the newly engaged couple to Noviand. Gerda and Fred quickly gave up trying to engage them in conversation. Hedy and Johnny were alone in their world.

~

Once in Noviand, there was no time to visit. The men unloaded the girls, the gas, and the bicycles. Johnny explained to Hedy's parents that he would return in three days and would like to speak with them.

After giving Hedy a quick hug, he headed back to Oppenheim.

Rosemary stood in the window, refusing to come outside. Hedy's smile melted under her glare until her father's voice caught her attention

"Why is Johnny coming back to speak to us, Hedy?"

The sternness of her father's expression surprised her. "He wants to marry me, Vater."

Watching the emotions wash across her father's face caused Hedy pause. Was it fear, concern, or something else? "Don't you approve?"

Blinking his eyes, Vater responded, "He is a good man, Hedy—" Her father hesitated, clearing his throat before continuing. "But you will always be my little girl."

"Vater." Hedy fell into his arms, crying.

Back to Trier

1946

Germany needs all the food she can produce. Before the war she could not produce enough food for her population. The area of Germany has been reduced.

J.F. BYRNES, US Secretary of State—*Restatement of Policy on Germany*—September 6, 1946

As promised, Johnny arrived early the next Saturday morning accompanied by Fred. Vater and Mama invited them to sit at the table. Twisting the edge of his cap, he hesitated before pulling out a chair and sitting down. Fred stood by the door with his head down. "I'll take a short walk around the neighborhood."

As Fred shut the door, Hedy heard a muted chuckle. She shook her head slightly before clutching Johnny's left arm. His right hand trembled when he covered hers. Clearing his throat, he announced in a strong, determined voice, "I would like to marry your daughter when the law allows." Exhaling slowly, he scanned her parents' faces.

Beaming, Mama rose from her chair and stood behind Hedy and Johnny. She squeezed their shoulders in an expansive hug and excused herself as tears began to flow.

Motioning towards Mama's back, Vater stared towards Hedy. "It appears your mother is in favor of the marriage." His gaze shifted to Johnny. "I am glad we had time to talk when you were looking for Hedy earlier, but I would like to have a word with you alone."

Hedy watched Johnny. He smiled and nodded at her. Patting his arm, she stood. "I'll check on Fred."

As she headed out the door, she heard Johnny state to her father, "The army has begun allowing soldiers to marry Austrian women. I believe the ban will be lifted for the German population soon."

Stepping outside, she noticed Fred smoking a cigarette near the jeep. "Everything okay?" he asked.

A tiny stone rested on the sidewalk at her feet. She bent and picked it up. It rolled between her fingers easily. Tossing the stone in her hand, she answered. "Mama is fine." She bit her lower lip. "Vater wanted to talk to him alone."

He tossed his cigarette butt to the ground and stepped on it. "He should. Johnny wants to take away his daughter."

Her eyes grew wide, causing Fred to chuckle. "Your dad only wants to make sure he is strong enough to take good care of you." Scratching his chin, he considered Hedy. "From what I've seen of you, your father knows it is going to take an extremely strong man."

"Fred." Hedy lightly punched his arm. "Stop teasing. You remind me of my cousin, Konrad."

After what seemed like an eternity, Vater appeared at the doorway and called Fred and Hedy in for a toast.

"See," Fred whispered. "I told you it would be fine."

After the toasting was complete, Johnny addressed her parents. "I need to take care of something important." He ushered Hedy to the door. "We will be back before dinner."

"Where are we going, Johnny?" Hedy climbed into the back of the jeep.

Climbing in beside her, he shrugged. "You have to wait and see."

Fred drove through the countryside, taking several detoured roads. After about an hour, he stopped the jeep at a small shop in a rural town. The weathered sign said *Juwelier*.

"A jewelry store?" Hedy said as Johnny led her in. The lively Italian owner received them warmly.

"*Ciao*, Johnny. Is this your lovely bride-to-be? She is even more beautiful than you led me to believe, if such a thing was possible." He waved his arms broadly. "Come to the counter, *Signorina* Hedy. There's something you need to see."

With that, he set two square boxes on the counter. Hedy's eyes widened as Johnny opened the first one with a stunning amethyst ring. The second box opened to reveal two gold wedding bands.

Tears filled Hedy's eyes when Johnny threaded the amethyst ring onto her finger. "I hope you like it. They all need to be sized. I will pick them up next time I come visit you."

Without a word, Hedy threw her arms around Johnny and held tight. She wanted this moment to continue forever. Finally, Johnny pushed her back just enough to stare into her eyes. "We are going to be remarkably happy."

"I know." Hedy barely spoke above a whisper. She leaned back toward him, and their lips brushed against one another. Slowly, gently, their kisses became lengthier and lengthier.

"Umm," Fred coughed at the door. "I hate to break up the party, but we need to be heading back. I'll be in the jeep."

Hedy stepped back, feeling a rosy glow working its way up her face. Johnny glanced at her and laughed lovingly. "It's okay. We'll have permission to do this soon."

Cuddling in the back of the jeep with her fiancé, Hedy exhaled deeply. She had a fiancé. It was official. The adoring look in Johnny's eyes made her snuggle closer.

"I guess if I want any conversation, I am going to have to talk to myself," Fred complained.

~

With the gasoline in hand, Vater arranged for the family to move back to Trier. Hedy, her mother, and her aunt packed up their belongings. Rosemary made no effort to help, or to speak to Hedy. Finally, Hedy couldn't stand it. She marched outside to confront her cousin.

"Rosemary, talk to me."

No response.

"I realize you are grieving, but it is not John's fault. I would like you to give him a chance."

Her cousin scowled. "Don't you dare judge me." Rosemary wagged her finger in Hedy's face. "You who always talked about helping others are reprimanding me? Here comes your ticket out of Germany and this mess, and you are the first one to head for the boat." She stopped to breathe. "Did all of our losses mean nothing to you? Go. Go to America. I never want to speak to you again."

Rosemary ran into the woods behind the house, leaving Hedy speechless.

~

Monday morning, the truck arrived at the school house, ready to be packed.

"I want to be ready first thing tomorrow," Vater instructed. "Let's get everything loaded today."

With the sun shining overhead, Vater and the driver loaded the huge cook stove into the truck first. Onkel Mathias stood by and offered advice. The furniture was next followed by the larger items. Mama and Hedy packed up the final boxes and secured all the breakables.

"Is the tea service in your hope chest cushioned enough, Hedy?" Mama wrapped clothes and towels around the glassware as she eyed Hedy handling the porcelain.

"Mama, everything in here is so tight, nothing can move."

"Good. Here is the last of the breakables. Let's get your father and uncle to load it on the truck."

When Hedy stepped outside, she stopped and stared. The sheer volume of things and the unorthodox method of cramming them into the bed of the truck amazed her. Her father maneuvered boxes in between furniture in ways she never believed possible. Vater tied the heavy chest on the smooth top of the cook stove. Thick ropes crisscrossed over and around the furniture and boxes, tying down anything that was movable. It was like no moving job Hedy had ever seen before.

"Vater, I see a problem."

"What is the matter, Hedy?"

"I assume Mama will ride with the driver up front. How will you and I get to Trier?"

"Isn't it obvious? We will sit on the furniture." Her father grinned. "Be sure to hold on tight."

Hedy slept on the floor that night, having packed all their furniture in the truck. It was not comfortable and she woke up irritable.

~

While Vater reviewed the last minute instructions, Rosemary

stood under a tree in the distance. Hedy approached her, cautiously. "Rosemary, we have been the best of friends all of our lives. I can't bear the idea of leaving like this."

Rosemary turned her back. Hedy laid her hand on her cousin's shoulder and spun her around. "Talk to me."

The anger in Rosemary's eyes caused her to take a step back. "I can't believe you are marrying that man," her cousin spat.

"Rosemary, I love him."

"But he is an American."

Hedy attempted a joke. "Mostly Italian, actually. He spent most of his childhood in Europe."

Rosemary did not appreciate the humor. "He killed my Willis."

"No *he* didn't." Seeing her cousin so miserable shook Hedy. With watery eyes, she whispered. "I can't bring Willis back."

"I realize that." Her cousin sank to the stiff ground and sobbed. "But do you have to marry one of them?"

Kneeling beside her, Hedy encircled Rosemary with her arms. "Johnny isn't one of them. He is Johnny Merenda, my fiancé."

Rosemary buried her face into Hedy's shoulder. Her cousin's warm tears trickled down Hedy's chest. Her chest rose and fell in time with Rosemary's labored breathing. Hedy stroked her hair and said nothing more.

~

The truck driver yelled for everyone to load up. Mama sat in the cab. Vater lifted Hedy up, and she squeezed herself between two boxes. "If this isn't a smooth ride, I am going to get squished."

The truck began its slow journey to Trier. The roads had not been maintained throughout the war, leaving an endless barrage of bumps and potholes.

"Ouch."

"What is wrong, Hedy?" her father called to her.

"Just when I find a comfortable position, the driver swerves to miss a hole in the road and knocks me around. How many holes can one road have?"

Dodging a large rut in the road, the driver cranked the wheel sharply. The thick rope holding Hedy's hope chest broke, and it slid off the cook stove. Hedy watched in horror as the chest burst open, with crystal and porcelain flying.

"Stop. Stop. Stop." Hedy frantically knocked on the back window with one hand and held her father's shirt with the other to keep him from jumping off the truck.

Hearing the commotion, Mama alerted the driver. Opening the door, she saw the cracked lid on the splintered chest with thousands of shards of glass and porcelain and wailed. "We kept your trousseau safe throughout the war and the bombings only to be ruined in a country ditch?"

Seeing her mother in such distress worried Hedy. "Mama, it is ok. We will save what isn't broken."

Vater suggested a glass and porcelain funeral. Even Mama chuckled at his suggestion. Hedy brought out a blanket and wrapped up the limited number of unscathed pieces. "Does this mean all hope is lost?" she wondered, only half joking.

Her father lifted an unbroken piece of stemware. "Hope is never lost."

She climbed back into the pickup. Her father handed her the makeshift bag with the remaining pieces. As the truck drove off, Hedy studied the bag. "No, hope is never lost."

~

As they entered Trier, there were French soldiers at the checkpoint. They checked their paperwork efficiently, but with none of the pleasantness she had experienced from the Americans on her previous visit.

Her father was silent as they drove around the remains of their town. Hedy reached across the piles of furniture to touch his hand. Her heart ached for him as she recalled the horrors she felt on her visit so many months ago.

The truck entered Trier West, an area outside of the bombed center of town. The driver parked the vehicle behind the building that was about to become their home. After a quick lunch of sandwiches, compliments of Tante Gisela, the work began. Two of Vater's coworkers from the post office came to help. Mama stationed herself upstairs in the rooms to oversee the proper placement of furniture, while everyone else made multiple trips up the two flights of stairs.

A large building had been converted into numerous apartments. Her family's living space consisted of five rooms above a grocery store: three small bedrooms, one larger bedroom, and a bathroom. Though small, the rooms encompassed adequate windows and a pleasant feel. The biggest bedroom was transformed into their kitchen. Mama and Vater used the next room for sleeping. Hedy stepped in the smallest room and noticed an angled ceiling. Ducking her head, she assumed this would be her room.

She stepped into the hall and peeked in the bathroom. "Vater, where is the tub?"

"Stolen. Like most everything in town," Vater explained. "I brought up that bulky sink for water and to wash." He paused, frowning. "There is a good-sized washroom for laundry in the cellar with the wood and coal."

"It is fine, Vater. I am thrilled we finally have a home of our own—with or without a bathtub."

Once all the furniture was unloaded, Mama went to work. Her attention to detail shone. The kitchen's large double window's expansive view of the river allowed plenty of light to fill the room. The stove, two cabinets, and the table were positioned with room left for an undersized sofa.

"Perfect for your father to take a quick nap before heading back to the office," Mama moved to the room Hedy would be using. "Let's put your mattress there under the eaves to give you room to move around."

Seeing the limited clearance for her head, Hedy chuckled. "I have a feeling I will learn the hard way to slide out of bed."

The sitting room also had low eaves, so Mama pushed a desk under them. The heirloom grandfather clock stood against another wall, but the room was missing the needed furniture to truly be a sitting room.

"I'm afraid our sitting room furniture didn't survive the bombing." Mama closed her eyes.

Hedy wrapped her arm around her mother's shoulder. "This is perfect. You've done a wonderful job with what you had to work with, Mama."

~

Over the next two months, Hedy and her family settled into life back in Trier. Ration coupons had been issued, and her father's job in the post office paid him in occupation currency, but there was little food available for purchase.

"I wish the farms weren't over the mountain," Hedy groused. "Then I could at least bring food home from work."

"We've survived this long." Mama's stomach growled contradicting her soothing voice. "At least we live over the grocery. We know when food is there."

Johnny's workload steadily increased. He visited whenever possible, but usually could only stay a few minutes before running off again.

"Are you and your family managing all right? Do you need anything?" was his constant refrain.

In spite of the constant gnawing in her belly, Hedy always insisted everything was fine. She refused to take advantage of his kindness.

~

"Umm," Johnny cleared his throat. He only had fifteen minutes to spare, but he'd come to ask Hedy's parents' permission to spend the weekend with him in Wiesbaden. "I have arranged for her to stay with a pastor's widow down the street from my quarters. I give you my word, she will be adequately chaperoned."

Hesitation was clear in Mama's voice. "I am not comfortable with you taking her for a weekend."

Vater held Mama's hand and squeezed. "The situation is not ideal, but Hedy wants to marry him. She needs time to spend with him before taking that step." He let go of her mother and put his hand on his daughter's shoulder. "We can't deny she has proven capable of taking care of herself over the past few years."

Beaming, Hedy hugged her father. "Oh, Vater."

Fred coughed and looked at his watch. Johnny took the hint and climbed into the jeep. Vater held his daughter's hand as she waved goodbye to her fiancé with the other. "What is it, Vater?"

Pulling her close to him, Vater said nothing.

"It will be fine, Vater." She embraced him tighter. "It will be perfect."

~

It was finally time for her weekend away with Johnny. Hedy carried her weekend bag into the kitchen. "Johnny should be here in an hour or so."

Her mother carried a bowl of watery soup with a boiled potato to the table and set it down in front of Vater. Walking back to the stove, she ladled out soup into a second bowl. "Come sit down and eat before he gets here."

Hedy waved away the food. "No, keep it for yourselves. I am certain I'll have plenty of food this weekend."

A knock at the door interrupted them. Hedy opened the door to see Johnny and Steve standing there. She gave her fiancé a hug. "You're early!"

"We wrapped up a project earlier than expected." He looked around. "I hope that is all right."

Vater laid his spoon on the table. The embarrassment of not having anything to offer visibly showed on her mother. Hedy picked up her bag and ushered the men out the door. "I'm all packed. Let's go."

Johnny turned to her parents before walking out. "I'll bring Hedy back to Trier in a couple of days. I'm not sure of my office schedule, so I can't give you a definite day, but please don't worry. I will get her home safely."

They drove to the CIC headquarters, catching Hedy off guard. "I want you to meet my friends here in Trier. They can get information to me anytime you need me."

These were men who were tracking down the worst of her countrymen. How did they feel about Johnny marrying a German? Hedy's feet were lead as she trailed him into the building.

His co-workers jumped to their feet when Johnny brought her into the office.

"This is the famous Hedy?"

"Wow, I missed out never getting selected for a 'Finding Hedy' mission."

"Come join us for lunch."

Hedy could not believe their kindness. She glanced over to Johnny and whispered, "What have you been telling them?"

He squeezed her hand. "Only good things, obviously."

An agent pulled out a chair for her. "How did you two meet?"

"I saved her from the MPs one night." Johnny puffed out his chest.

Hedy tittered as she sat at the table. "Only after he had stalked me for a while. Scared me half to death."

With that, the crowd wanted to learn the whole story.

"Consider us your official mail carriers, Hedy," an agent volunteered.

"Swing by and say hello whether he's in town or not," another offered.

After the rather enjoyable lunch, the three drove off. Steve noticed a line of people at the base of the mountain holding armloads of personal items. "What is happening?"

Embarrassed, Hedy tried to explain. "Our food is rationed; however, there isn't enough food here in the cities to fulfill the rations. If we see a line, we stand in it assuming the store has food."

The men stared at each other surprised. The Allies had plenty of food.

"Is it really that bad?" Steve asked.

Hedy grimaced and nodded.

He continued, "But why are they carrying their belongings up the mountain?"

"The farming areas are on the other side. They line up in the mornings, hoping to catch a ride with anyone driving over the mountain. Once there, they barter whatever they have to the farmers for food. Then they try to catch a ride back down the mountain."

The men seemed uncomfortable and did not ask any more questions.

~

On their way to Wiesbaden, the travelers stopped at the Italian jeweler. The jeweler greeted them all as if they were long lost relatives. He and Johnny spoke to each other in Italian. Hedy and Steve watched the animated conversation for a while and laughed.

"Aren't they afraid they will hit one another with those arms flying everywhere?" Steve whispered.

"They wouldn't notice if they did," Hedy responded.

The jeweler positioned two ring boxes on the counter. Johnny showed his appreciation with a box of cigarettes, and the gestures began again. Finally, Johnny settled the bill, and after more friendly hugs, they headed back to the jeep.

"You two cuddle in the back. I know where we are going," Steve offered.

Neither Hedy nor Johnny argued, and they climbed in the back of the jeep together. Hedy snuggled up to him, before noticing he appeared to be upset. "Johnny, is something wrong?"

His face tightened. "Dammit, Hedy, every time I visit you, I ask, 'What do you and your family need?'" He stopped and drew a deep ragged breath. "You lied to me. You insisted you did not need a thing. Your family is starving and you won't tell me? What kind of relationship is this?"

Squirming, Hedy explained. "In Noviand, I could work on the local farms, and Tante Gisela had canned foods. It wasn't much but still better than here in the city."

"Why didn't you tell me?"

"I didn't want you to think I was dating you to get food." Hedy fought back the tears swelling in her eyes. "I never wanted you to question my motives."

He cupped her hand between his warm ones. "Hedy, that thought has never crossed my mind. Why would you consider it?"

"You have been extremely generous from the first evening we met, and I have nothing to offer in return. I love you, but I feel guilty for taking so much from you."

Taken aback, a hurt expression overtook Johnny. "*Mia amore*, how can you feel that way? You are giving me far more than a little food could ever repay." His eyes stared straight to her soul. "Do you doubt my love for you?"

"Of course not. Don't you see?" Hedy eyes pleaded. "I was more concerned about you doubting mine."

"Don't be foolish." He softened his tone. "I will love you forever, and I want you to promise me you will never ever question my feelings."

"Oh, Johnny, I promise." Hedy snuggled back against his broad chest.

After a few moments of silence, Hedy attempted to lighten the mood. "Did you not think it odd that Inge, Gerda, and I behaved as complete pigs at our first dinner?"

"I had been informed German women like their food. I assumed you were a good German woman." Johnny cracked a smile before becoming serious again. "You must understand if we are getting married, you have to be honest with me. If you and your family need help, ask me for it. In return, I will always be honest with you. Agreed?"

"Agreed." She considered their discussion. "Does this mean we've had our first fight?"

"No," grunted Johnny. "Wait, maybe. We have to kiss and make up."

With that, he pulled Hedy close to him and kissed her gently. Warmth flowed through her veins, and she hoped the drive would last forever.

~

Once in Wiesbaden, Steve drove Hedy and Johnny to the CIC villa. With no formal meals served on weekends, they prepared a snack of cold cuts and soup. Exhausted from all the driving, Johnny accompanied Hedy to the pastor's house and introduced her to Frau Hoper. He wished the ladies a good night.

Frau Hoper, a short, frail woman with lines etched in her face, insisted Hedy have a cup of tea and wanted to learn all about her and her family. After an hour, Hedy stifled a yawn.

"Oh, my. You poor dear. Come, I'll show you your room, and we can finish the conversation in the morning."

The widow led her to a large, tastefully decorated bedroom with a generous feather bed topped with a beautiful handmade quilt of pink and green fabrics, and lace curtains on the window. Scents of a floral potpourri wafted into the air.

"It is beautiful, Frau Hoper. I am certain to have sweet dreams tonight."

Beaming, Frau Hoper wished her a good night. Hedy snuggled into the fluffy quilt and drifted to sleep with dreams of Johnny's lips.

Wiesbaden

1946

...those who have fought longest and hardest should be returned home for discharge first.

US War Department—*Readjustment Regulations*—March 5, 1945

Frau Hoper greeted Hedy when she came down the next morning. "Johnny sent breakfast. It is the first time I've drank real coffee in years."

Hedy inhaled the flavor of such a treat, savoring every sip. The widow was a gracious, though rather chatty hostess. Consequently, Hedy rushed out the door when Johnny arrived an hour later.

The town was quiet on the sunny Sunday morning. Hand in hand, the couple strolled toward the twin steeples of St. Bonifatius, the mammoth church in the center of town. As they grew closer, Hedy realized all of the windows were gone. Stepping around the rubble, she squeezed Johnny's hand as they walked into the massive stone structure. She gasped.

The vault of the church had been badly damaged by bombing. The morning sun shone down on the makeshift altar. The debris had been cleared and the parishioners stood, waiting. The priest entered behind the cross bearer and the altar servers and began the mass. The stream of Latin washed over her. She closed her eyes to listen.

A waft of incense tickled her nose. She opened her eyes, noticing

Johnny gazing at her, love in his eyes. Her face flushed. He winked and touched her elbow. Edging as close to him as would be deemed appropriate, Hedy focused on the sermon as best she could.

After church, Johnny guided her on a tour of the town. The lake in the center was home to large, beautiful swans. Hedy laughed as Johnny fed crumbs to the majestic birds. When the birds climbed out of the lake and chased them, her benevolent feelings dissipated. Not finding any more food, the swans waddled back to the water.

Breathless, Hedy wondered. "How can such beautiful animals be so mean?"

Johnny shook his head as if distracted. Throughout the morning, he had been fingering something in his pocket. Sitting with Hedy on a bench near the water's edge, he pulled a box out and opened it. The sunlight glistened on the gold rings inside.

Handing the masculine ring to Hedy, Johnny kept the smaller one. Without a word, the two young lovers slipped the rings on each other's hand. Tears formed, but neither spoke.

The sunlight on the pond highlighted the small ripples of the water. The light summer breeze blew the hair from Hedy's face. Johnny grasped both her hands with his and kissed her fingertips. "Hedy, something important has come up. My overseas duty will end in six weeks, and I will be discharged from the army. They have already scheduled my transport back to the States."

"*No.*" Hedy stopped herself. Lines formed along her forehead as she thought of an unselfish response. "Sorry. I'm sure you are anxious to finally see your family."

"I am. I told the Army I didn't want to go back yet. Not until I take you with me." Johnny frowned. "Unfortunately, regulations still forbid marrying German nationals."

Hedy did not wish to think about that. "Do you have to go?"

He let out a long sigh. "Afraid so. My commanding officer—who you really impressed, by the way—recommends I sign up for another year of overseas duty before I leave. He will request I am assigned to the Wiesbaden office. However, I am required to go back to the States for at least four months."

She struggled to sound pleased. "Perfect. You will be able to visit your family and come back to me." Pausing, she raised her eyes. "You will come back to me, won't you?"

Johnny held her tight. "Of course." His lips kissed the hair covering her ear. "I told you never to doubt my love."

After giving Hedy time to digest the news, Johnny filled in more of the details of his planned trip. His anticipation of seeing his family burst through his voice. "I can't wait to tell my sisters all about you. They will be shocked to hear our big news."

"Is that good?" Hedy bit her lip and twisted the ring on her finger.

"They will love you. As will my father and brothers."

"Let me remember." She counted on her fingers. "You have three sisters and two brothers?"

"Good memory. Camilla is the oldest. I'm next, followed by Lucia and my brother Roberto. We were all born in the US." Johnny paused a moment and stared off in the distance. "But, my mother became depressed and begged my father to move back to Italy. As a member of the philharmonic, he had summers off, so he moved the entire family to Italy for a few months."

Hedy leaned closer.

"We enjoyed the ship ride over, and Mama seemed to get substantially better. At the end of the summer, she refused to go back to New York."

"How terrible."

"I was around nine when Papa decided I should stay with Mama while he took the others back."

"No." Hedy rubbed his arm gently, eyes questioning.

"It was fine with me. I became friends with a boy, Peppino Rosati and his family. We attended high school together and had a great time. Papa came back each summer. My brother was born after one year and the next year brought Maria."

"So your father supported two households the whole time?"

"Yes. Anytime a bassoon was needed at a recording session or a Sunday concert, Roberto Merenda performed. *Life* magazine featured him in an article." His pride was evident.

"Wow. I didn't realize I was marrying into a celebrity's family."

"I spent most of my time at Peppino's house. When my youngest brother and Maria were old enough to go to school, Papa sent them back to New York, but Mama refused to go. Her depression got worse."

Hedy eyes grew wide. His pain was evident. She rubbed his back, not daring to say a word.

He composed himself and continued. "I prepared to enter the Technical Institute in Naples to study engineering. By then, as you know, Europe was in turmoil. Afraid I would be drafted into the Italian army even though I was a US citizen, Papa moved me back to the States."

Johnny stopped speaking. The faraway look returned. "After spending half my life in Italy, the sudden change was difficult. I barely spoke English." He continued, "I accepted a job at the Lionel Train Company in their New Jersey plant. It was a short commute from downtown to where we lived."

"It must have been difficult moving back without friends."

He agreed. "I became a steady customer at a dance hall on 86th Street in the German section of New York." Johnny elbowed her playfully. "I guess I've always been attracted to German girls."

Hedy elbowed him back. He continued. "I liked dancing because I didn't have to talk much while I attempted to relearn English. After working a couple of years at the train company, I applied to a college in New York. They accepted me on the condition I attend two courses of English reading and writing."

"It makes me feel better that you struggled with English, too." Hedy linked her arm in his. "What did you study?"

"I didn't. Before I got enrolled, I received an invitation from Uncle Sam to join the army. When the army learned I was bilingual, they pulled me from boot camp and sent me to the University in Ithaca to study German." He smirked. "They assumed if I already knew one foreign language, learning a second one would be easy. It wasn't easy, but I stayed for a year of intense language immersion."

Hedy lightly stroked his arm. "It worked. Your German is flawless."

"The CIC branch wanted me. I landed after the invasion forces on the beach in Normandy and worked my way across France." He glanced away.

"That was when you lost your mother, wasn't it?" Her eyes grew sad.

Johnny pulled her hand close to his heart. "Yes, I am sorry you will never meet her. She was a good woman."

"She had to have been to raise a man like you." She touched his face with the back of her hand. "I'm glad you were able to visit her grave." Hedy narrowed her eyes. "How did you manage that with the invasion going on?"

He grinned. "It helped to be Italian. It required several planes, trains, and a bit of hitchhiking. I managed to get back to my unit before they fought their way into Germany."

They sat in silence. Pressing Hedy's hand to his cheek, he closed his eyes. "I want to tell you everything I can about my family, so you can start to thinking of them as yours."

The trees swayed in the light wind, and a blue bird chased another among the branches. Eventually, Johnny interrupted the silence. "I can't believe I found you. There is something I want you to promise me while I'm gone."

The serious tone startled Hedy. "What is it?"

"I need you to be more cautious. Your impulsiveness worries me. I don't want you to get hurt."

Hedy's emotions vacillated between "I can take care of myself" and "how sweet of him to be worried."

As if he could read her mind, Johnny added, "I am not trying to insult you, *mia amore*. You are a strong, intelligent woman who has accomplished amazing things over the past few years. You obviously can handle difficult situations. I am only asking you not to go out of your way to get into those situations."

Struggling for a way to respond, Hedy stuttered. "I can be impulsive. Mama has fussed at me all my life, but I don't go out of my way to get into trouble."

Johnny rolled his eyes. "Seriously? I am required to bring another soldier with me anytime I travel around the countryside, and I carry a gun. You, on the other hand, think it is safe for two young women to bicycle for days across the same countryside."

"I had no choice." Hedy became indignant. "How else was I supposed to contact you?"

"I believe you met Steve long before you arrived in Oppenheim. He would have gotten the message to me, and you could have gone home."

Pulling back her shoulders, Hedy leaned back and stared at him. "Would you have preferred I had?"

Affection still showed on his face; nonetheless, Johnny shook his head. "I loved seeing you, but you did put yourself at risk unnecessarily. It isn't the first time. Crossing the mountains at night from Traben-Trarbach—" He paused. "I hate to think of the adventures you haven't shared with me."

Hedy blushed. "The most irrational thing I have ever done was to climb in a jeep with an enemy soldier because he seemed polite."

"I certainly hope you are referring to me." Johnny tilted his head and raised an eyebrow.

"As far as the other things you've mentioned, I simply did what had to be done."

Johnny squeezed her hand. "I'm asking you; try not to do anything dangerous. You won't need to bicycle around the countryside searching for me, because I will come get you the moment I get back. I introduced you to my friends at the CIC office. They will help you with anything you need, if you ask."

She knew he was right about her impulsiveness; however, she must stay true to herself. What he perceived as reckless, she considered dealing with a difficult situation. "Johnny, the war is over. Life isn't back to normal, although it is livable. I'll help my family and neighbors in Trier as best I can. Don't worry. I'll be so busy, I won't have time to get into trouble."

~

When they returned to the big house, the local commanding officer and several of the other agents were there for a late meal.

"Now I understand why Johnny signed up for another year." The ranking officer's handshake was firm. "I am grateful to you. Johnny is a good man."

Hedy agreed. She and Johnny displayed their new gold bands

and graciously accepted the congratulations.

"I believe a toast is in order." The officer poured drinks and handed them around. "To Johnny and Hedy. May they have a long and fruitful marriage."

Though embarrassed by the attention, it pleased Hedy that most of Johnny's coworkers were happy for him. Only one man refused to look her way.

"Who is that?" Hedy elbowed Johnny and discreetly pointed to the scowling man.

"Ignore him." Johnny poured more wine in her glass. "Peter is convinced all Germans are evil and refuses to speak to anyone who might change his mind."

A chill rose up her spine. "Should I go? I don't want to intrude."

Johnny set down the bottle of wine. "There are jerks and bigots everywhere. We are going to ignore them and live our lives." He picked up his glass and called for another toast.

Hedy stayed in Wiesbaden for three days. Johnny worked during the day, giving her time to assist Frau Hoper around the house and to quietly explore around the town. Evenings with Johnny and the dozen CIC officers who lived in the big house were jovial and loud.

"You are in for a treat tonight." Johnny escorted Hedy from the widow's house to dinner. "Willie is quite a popular opera singer here in Wiesbaden. He offered to sing for us tonight."

As they walked in the door, Fred motioned for Hedy to sit beside him. She weaved her way through the room, with Johnny following.

"Willie is about to start. You will enjoy this." Fred told her as she sat.

Peter entered and scanned the room. His eyes rested on Hedy sitting between Fred and Johnny. Glaring, he sat in a rigid chair in the corner directly across from her. She squirmed in her seat.

Willie sang songs in both German and Italian for the group. As he began a particularly romantic love song, he offered Hedy a wink. Hedy blushed at the attention and squeezed Johnny's hand. Johnny beamed back.

~

The weekend passed by too quickly for Hedy's preference. While Johnny was driving her home, she advised him so.

He chuckled. "The men agree. Said the house hadn't ever been as pretty or charming as when you were there."

Batting away his compliment, she grimaced. "Except Peter. He'll be happy not to see a German in the evenings."

"Don't worry about Peter. He's been stuck in his depressed ways all of his life. It isn't you, it's him." Johnny glanced in her direction, concern written on his face. "Even as charming a woman as you cannot overcome everyone's biases."

She smiled. "I am not vain enough to try."

Arriving in Trier, Johnny explained to her parents his plans to go to the United States. Mama and Vater stiffened.

With his eyes displaying his earnestness, he promised, "I love your daughter, and I will be back to marry her. Please believe me."

"I do." Mama stood and embraced Johnny. "There is no doubt your feelings for each other are strong."

Vater rose. He wrapped his arm around Hedy as they said goodbye.

She gazed into her father's eyes and blinked back her tears.

~

Over the next six weeks, Johnny managed to get over to Trier several times to visit her. Hedy thanked him for parking behind the building. "We don't want the neighbors to tell the French we are getting food from the Americans."

Overwhelmed by the amount of food he brought, she looked around. "Is there anything left in the CIC pantry?"

"I'll be gone a while and want to make sure you retain your figure," he replied with a wink.

Mama hugged Johnny. "With all these gifts, we should start calling you *Sankt Nikolaus*."

Rubbing the back of his neck, Vater pulled him aside. "I appreciate the food. We don't want you to get in trouble."

"I am always careful," replied Johnny. "Forbidding other countries to send food to the civilian population is a cruel way for the politicians 'to teach the Germans a lesson'. Rumors are President Truman is rethinking the policy. I hope he hurries." He scanned the room before continuing. "The French are looking for ways to make life hard. Is there a way to hide the food?"

Leading Johnny to the cellar, Vater showed him the firewood container. Johnny surveyed the area. "I don't understand."

Grinning, Vater lifted the first three layers of firewood from the top, exposing a large inner box. Vater proudly displayed the hidden food storage.

"That is perfect," Johnny announced.

"It is." Hedy spoke from behind him. "Except, it is a lot of work to stack and unstack wood for a tuna sandwich."

~

The six weeks flew by. Johnny came to Trier for the final time before the troop transport carried him home. Hedy lead him into the woods for a long, private walk before he left. She did not want her parents and Steve to be a witness to their goodbyes.

Hedy wanted to be pleased for him, truly she did, but she cried, nonetheless. He touched her gold band and reassured her of his love. "We will be married when I return."

Their fingers intertwined as they took slow steps. Johnny squeezed her hand. "I'll write you. Remember it takes a long time for letters to come across the ocean."

"Your CIC friends will tire of being your mail carrier." Her weak smile betrayed her thoughts.

He reached for her other hand and leaned forward. They stood, bodies inches apart, lips lightly touching.

"Your tears are making our kisses awfully salty." His right arm wrapped around her and pulled her closer.

She let loose of his hands and wrapped her arms around his waist. Moving her hands up and down his back, she replied, "I don't care. Just kiss me."

The space between their bodies disappeared. Though sad, the kisses were passionate, meaningful, and fulfilling. Hedy never felt so complete before in her life.

Once they finally broke from the embrace, the couple wandered back, side by side, with arms around each other's waist. Her feet dragged as if in mud, as she walked with him toward the jeep.

With the salty tears streaming, Hedy waved as he drove off. *Father in Heaven. Keep him safe in his journey.* Twisting the gold ring on her finger she added, *and don't let him forget me.*

Waiting

1946

I feel that any boy in love with a girl over there should not be allowed to marry until he came home and had sufficient time to be quite sure that his love was not born of loneliness and propinquity in a strange country.

ELEANOR ROOSEVELT regarding American
servicemen bringing back wives from Germany.

The first letter from Johnny arrived almost a month after he left. Steve had relocated to the local CIC office and personally came to drop it off. "It is great to see you again, Hedy. I miss our excursions around the countryside with Johnny."

"I miss Johnny." She scrunched her face in an exaggerated frown.

Steve saluted her with a grin. "Have a great day."

The joyful letter explained how thrilled Johnny was to be with his family after such a long time away. He had shared the pictures of Hedy and told everyone all about her.

Now that she was back in Trier, Hedy found ways to be useful. Putting on her ever-faithful Red Cross uniform, she applied for a position at the hospital.

The hospital administrator was a skinny, forty-something French woman with her hair pulled back tighter than Hedy judged possible. She stared down her sharp nose at Hedy and inquired why she wanted the job. Hedy explained her desire to volunteer and her experience. The nurse interrupted. "You can be a nurse assistant; however, you must do exactly as you are asked."

Taken aback, Hedy blinked. Previously, the hospitals had been thrilled to have additional help. Here, the French made her feel rather unwelcome.

~

Once home, she described the administrator to her mother and the grocer's wife, who understood. "We saw that after the Great War. The French treated us Germans as second class citizens."

Vater arrived and overheard her comment. "Well, you can't blame them for being upset Hitler invaded their country."

"Fritz," Mama fussed at her husband, "it is not Hedy's fault Hitler occupied France. You think they would hold such things in perspective."

"Mama, don't worry. I'll perform my work, and it will be fine."

Hedy picked up a hefty container Johnny left on his last visit. Reading the label, she asked, "Has anyone heard of peanut butter?" No one had. "Here in the English dictionary Johnny gave me, it says it is *Erdnuss*. Why would you make butter out of that?"

She opened the lid. Two inches of oil pooled on the top. "This does not look appetizing."

"Pour the oil into a can, and we will use it to fry potatoes this week," her mother recommended.

With the oil off the peanut butter, the Weiß were left with three gallons of peanut paste. Hedy ate a spoonful of the thick, dry mixture. "It sticks to the top of your mouth and is dry, but tasty. It should keep us for a long time."

~

The next day, Hedy started at the hospital. After a week of mundane tasks, the head nurse decided Hedy could stay. "You are assigned to work on the third floor," the lead administrators explained to Hedy. "Your title will be *infirmiere assistante*. There are five rooms for you to cover."

She paused, her thin lips pursed. "Do not use the elevator as it is for the infirm. Also, as you will have access to medicines, your bag will be searched each day when you leave." With her nose in the air, the nurse marched away.

Hedy manned her station, taking patient vitals and changing bandages. Her patients were the soldiers from Morocco. Because she was not trained as a nurse, she had been assigned those with no severe injuries. Sitting on a stool at her post, she considered her position and sat up straighter. She was helping again. A smile spread across her face.

"Are you thinking of your lover?" A short, Moroccan solder with dark eyes teased.

Jumping up, Hedy reprimanded him. "Simo, that shoulder wound will never heal if you don't stay in bed instead of harassing the staff." She shooed him back to his room. "I swear you are the ringleader of the mischief in this hospital."

His short legs walked slowly and deliberately back to his room. "Mademoiselle, I have no idea what you might be talking about." He winked as he lay down.

~

Hedy's station became a popular place over the next week. After a particularly busy day, she stopped by Simo's room. "Simo, are you familiar with everyone in this hospital? My station constantly has people here looking for you."

"Mademoiselle Hedy, it is good to know lots of people. I invite them up here to entertain you."

"I must admit, you succeed. Though how are you going to get better if you don't get some rest? Besides you are getting me in trouble with the head nurse."

"What are those mean French blaming you for today?"

"You. I arrived at seven and you weren't in your bed. I left to search for you, and the nurse noticed my station was empty."

"I am sorry such a beautiful young woman like you landed in trouble because of me. She is searching for reasons to abuse a German." Bowing, he added, "The good news is there is finally a group the French like less than us Moroccan troops."

In spite of herself, Hedy was incapable of staying mad at Simo. His activities helped keep her mind off of Johnny's absence. She wagged her finger at him, but was interrupted by raucous voices and squeals from below. Running into Simo's room, she leaned out the window. On a large flatbed truck stood more than twenty women. They waved to the ever-growing group of French soldiers near them.

"*Yvette. Voir ici.*" One of Hedy's patients yelled down to them from his window.

Hedy pulled her head back into the room as Simo leaned out. "How do all these soldiers know those girls?'

"Simo, I enjoyed seeing you last night." A woman waved from below.

Hedy stared at Simo. "How do you know her?"

His eyes were focused on his feet, and he shuffled slightly. "Um, they are *les femmes du plaisir*."

"From the bordello?" Hedy's hands flew to her mouth.

Simo grinned.

"I understand." Her face caught fire as she recovered. "But why are they here at the hospital?"

"The French authorities encourage them to follow the soldiers and, um, assist. But they have to have a monthly health check."

"But they seem to recognize everyone. Even my patients."

Simo's eyes glimmered with mischief. "It is a thriving business."

Recovering, she tilted her head and scowled at him. "How are you getting out of the hospital at night?"

He raised his eyebrows, feigning innocence. "What could you be talking about, Mademoiselle Hedy? Your eyes are deceiving you."

"I know you snuck out last night."

Simo shook his head, "That would be very bad. I would never do anything like that."

The lack of sincerity caused Hedy to laugh out loud. "Just don't reinjure your shoulder."

~

A week later, her father received a letter from Onkel Randolph. He needed insulin, but could not find any. "Most of the pharmacies haven't reopened yet. The open ones don't have enough medicine."

"Papa, I may be able to help." Hedy patted her father on the back. "Let me ask."

When she arrived at the hospital, she inhaled deeply and approached the head nurse. "Madame, I have a request."

The nurse gazed down her sharp nose, saying nothing. Hedy continued. "The local pharmacy does not have any medicines. My uncle is in dire need of insulin. I would like to purchase the medicine for him from the hospital. I don't have much money but will work extra shifts to pay for it."

"Our medicine is for the patients. He will need to find another source."

Hedy stepped back, eyes growing wide. "But, Madame, he will die without it."

The nurse shrugged and walked away.

Within moments, the pharmacist's Moroccan assistant at the hospital stopped by her station to deliver medicine. "What is wrong, Mademoiselle? Why are your eyes red?"

She explained her uncle's predicament and the head nurse's response.

"Not to worry. My friend Simo tells me you are a good person." He bounced off.

Unsure how to interpret this, Hedy started to follow him, but refrained. She didn't want to get him or herself in trouble. Two days later, she noticed a small package next to her backpack. Opening it, she squealed with delight.

"What do you have there, Mademoiselle Hedy?"

Hedy jumped, almost losing her grip on the precious medicine as she spun around to discover Simo wearing an impish expression. "None of your business, Simo. You should be back in bed."

"No, Mademoiselle. You require my help. How are you going to get it out of the hospital?"

Hedy did not argue. The guards searched her backpack each night. "Can you help?"

He nodded. "You allowed me to get my *medicine*." Simo winked. "I would be honored to return the favor."

When her shift was over, the package was missing. Shouldering her pack, she headed to the control booth. The guard requested her bag. Hedy had never been so nervous in her life. It required every ounce of control to keep her body steady from shaking. In a matter of minutes, the guard handed her back her pack with a friendly, *au revoir*.

Once home, Hedy's trembling hands opened her backpack. There was the insulin. Her patient had come through for her.

~

A week later, the crisp fall morning air made Hedy pull her jacket a bit tighter over her uniform as she hurried to the hospital, but she didn't mind. She had received another letter from Johnny yesterday. They were few and far between; she wished the ocean wasn't so wide.

"Hedy. Over here. It's Günter."

She twisted around to see Günter waving at her from across the street. A gasp escaped from her as he strode to her side.

"I have found you again." Günter picked her up and spun her around.

She struggled to get away from his grip and steadied herself. "I didn't realize you were looking for me."

"Actually, I'm headed to work."

Hedy exhaled deeply. "So am I. I'm volunteering at the hospital."

"I knew your family would come back to Trier. I hired on with a construction crew to help rebuild this town so I could be closer to you."

Stopping in her tracks, Hedy caught her breath as Günter continued. "Let's catch up after your shift. A café has opened a few blocks from here."

Hedy hesitated. "I need to tell..."

Günter stopped her. "I have to run. Tell me at the café this evening."

With trepidation, Hedy agreed and rushed on to work. *I'm engaged. I shouldn't have coffee with another man.*

~

"Your ring may wear out if you keep twisting it around your finger." Simo's voice made Hedy jump. "What is the matter with my favorite German? You have been pacing and staring off into space all day."

She squirmed in her seat. "An old friend wants to have coffee with me."

"And that is a bad thing?"

"He has wanted to marry me since primary school."

"Oh." Simo squinted, knowingly. "But you are engaged to your American."

She nodded. "I hate to break his heart. He found a job in Trier to search for me."

"*Tsk, tsk.* You have feelings for him."

Hedy's body jerked straight up. "No." She stuttered, "I-I mean, only as a friend."

Simo tilted his head and squinted. "Is he not handsome enough?"

"Very." Hedy blurted. "I mean, I love Johnny." Sitting down, she buried her head in her hands.

~

The pace of work at the hospital the rest of the day kept Hedy from having time to think about Günter. At the end of her shift, she trudged down the steps to the door of the hospital. There by the curb stood Günter, his thumbs looped in his pant pockets. His broad shoulders and blond, blunt-cut hair accented his square jaw. He really was handsome. Hedy composed herself.

His long stride brought him to her side in seconds. With a wide smile, he linked his arm through hers and escorted her down the street.

Her legs felt mired in mud. She struggled to match his pace. "How is your family, Günter? Is Ralph in Trier too?"

"They are fine. Ralph is here. He will be thrilled to know I found you."

Arriving at the restaurant, Günter moved his chair closer to hers. "I am sorry it has taken me more than a year to find you. After the war, there was so much to do for my family."

She waved her hands to stop him. Instead he clasped her hands between his. "But now we are together."

"Günter, there is something—"

He placed his thumb and middle finger on the gold ring on her hand. "What is this?"

"Günter, I'm engaged."

Blinking rapidly, he gulped. "How is that possible?"

She pulled her hand away. "I am sorry. I tried to tell you this earlier."

"You said you would wait for me." His body sagged.

Shaking her head, she gently reminded him, "No Günter, you said that."

Crestfallen, he needed a moment to compose himself. "I want you to be happy. Who is the lucky man? Anyone I know?"

"I doubt it," Hedy answered, relieved he seemed to be taking it well. "He is an American officer."

His demeanor changed instantly. His face flushed with anger. "You are marrying the enemy?"

Shocked by the outburst, Hedy stared at the man sitting across from her. "Johnny is not the enemy. He is a good and generous man."

"The Americans killed thousands of our countrymen, including many of our friends. You don't consider that the enemy?"

Hedy glared at him. "The Americans did not ask for the war. Your Herr Hitler invited them." Her voice grew louder. "The Americans have been nothing but kind to us since they came to Noviand." Hedy attempted to regain her composure. "Besides, Johnny is counter-intelligence, not regular army. He wasn't shooting our countrymen."

"So he is a spy."

"I will not have this conversation with you." Hedy stood and started for the door.

Günter flew up and clutched her arm. Sneering, he stated, "You said he is a generous man. What is he using as bait?"

Rage shooting throughout her body, Hedy spun around and slapped him. He raised his hand in return, but stopped. Without a word, he pivoted and left. Hedy dropped to the chair and sobbed.

No Word from Johnny

1946

The United States cannot relieve Germany from the hardships inflicted upon her by the war her leaders started. But the United States has no desire to increase those hardships or to deny the German people an opportunity to work their way out of those hardships so long as they respect human freedom and cling to the paths of peace.

J.F. BYRNES, US Secretary of State—*Restatement of Policy on Germany*—September 6, 1946

Hedy and her parents settled into the new normal. Rationed food was practically non-existent. Johnny had been gone three months, and his care packages were almost depleted. A physical therapist had begun working with Simo, reminding Hedy of all she was unable to accomplish.

Worse, Hedy had not seen the officers from the CIC in weeks.

"The military has more to do than deliver love letters to you, Hedy." Her father tried to distract her. "Your aunt and cousin will be here before long. It will lift your spirits to see them."

"It will. I hate not hearing from him. What if something has happened?"

The arrival of Tante Gisela and Rosemary interrupted the conversation. Hesitantly, Hedy approached her cousin. Rosemary rushed to her, arms extended. "Hedy, I have missed you so much. Please forgive me for being so dreadful when you left."

Could Rosemary really have had such a change of heart? She squeezed her cousin back. "I have missed you, too."

As the women sat around the table, Vater excused himself. "I don't believe I am needed."

The women agreed. Tante Gisela wanted to hear all about Hedy and her fiancé.

"He is visiting his family in New York. I am confident he will be back any day."

"I hope so." Tante Gisela reached for Hedy's hand. "Mrs. Roosevelt doesn't want the American soldiers to bring back German wives. She doesn't think it is fair to the American girls." Her aunt's lip curled. "As if they have been waiting patiently for the boys to come home, while European temptresses distracted their men."

"I don't care what Mrs. Roosevelt thinks." Hedy pushed back from her chair and headed toward the stove. She glanced over and caught the smug expression on Rosemary's face.

Tante Gisela didn't seem to notice Hedy's agitation. "She is convinced the service men got engaged overseas out of loneliness. She wants them to go back to the US for four months before they get married."

Hedy's hands trembled. "Johnny has been gone more than three months, and he will be back to prove her wrong."

"Are you sure, Hedy?" Rosemary's voice dripped with sugar. "I can't imagine his family is excited he is bringing the enemy home instead of marrying a nice American girl. Or, better yet, an Italian."

Hedy's voice raised an octave. "I am not the enemy. Johnny said his sisters will love me. He should know."

Rosemary rose and came to her. Patting her shoulder, she cooed, "I am sure they will. Have you heard from him lately?"

"Mail is excruciatingly slow coming over the Atlantic."

Grabbing the tea kettle, Rosemary sauntered back to the table. "You don't need to worry. I am certain Mrs. Roosevelt's radio announcements are ignored in the States."

"Johnny will be back for me. He gave me this ring." She waved the gold band under Rosemary's nose.

Without conviction, her cousin glanced at the finger. "Oh, Hedy, of course he will be back."

Hedy stormed out of the apartment. The afternoon clouds darkened. Striding down the street, she ignored the two older women walking out of the grocery, passing them as she headed around the corner. "She's a fool if she thinks he'll return. I bet he's got a girlfriend who will never know of her."

Shocked, Hedy stopped dead in her tracks. The other woman shrugged. "She must be using her good looks for special privileges."

"Can you blame her? I haven't eaten a steak in years. I'd kiss all the soldiers in town for a thick, juicy slab of meat."

Was it her they were talking about? Was that actually what the neighbors thought? Surely they were speaking of someone else. Dizziness filled Hedy's head.

No! She ran her fingers through her hair. They chose to believe the worst. Maybe Günter and Rosemary were right. She was a traitor. Falling in love with an American did not help the injured soldiers of Germany. Volunteering in the field hospital had furnished her with a sense of usefulness to her country. Now she considered only herself.

A bolt of lightning arched across the sky, jerking her from her thoughts. The strong clap of thunder which followed was accompanied by stinging pellets of raindrops. Her drenched dress clung to her as she raced back to the apartment. Ignoring Tante Gisela and Rosemary, Hedy stormed to her room. Her eyebrows knitted together. Her frown deepened.

She pulled out her most recent letter from Johnny.

> *Dearest Hedy,*
> *How I am missing you. I am counting the days before I head back on the ship to you. There are plenty of people to see and much to do, but I would prefer to be with you. ...*
>
> *Lady Luck was good to me on the boat over. You will be pleasantly surprised with the results.*
>
> *My sisters have decided after the years of war, I need to be social again.*
>
> *Did I tell you I love to dance? My brother took me to the German dance hall the other night. We had a good time, except my favorite German girl is thousands of miles away.*
>
> *Besides parties and dances, my sisters have me playing card games. They are constantly bringing in different friends to challenge me. It is a lot of fun; however, I often*

*wish I wasn't the only man at the table. I'll have to teach
you some of the games when I get back.*
   With all my love,
   Johnny

Doubts and questions overtook Hedy's brain. Who was Lady
Luck? What was she doing on the transport boat? Why would his
sisters bring different women over?

Her imagination shifted into overdrive. She clearly saw Johnny
at his family's home in New York.

*Johnny is seated at a bridge table with three beautiful young
women. His sisters, Camilla and Lucia, walk around the room,
checking on their guests. The woman on Johnny's right flips back her
long blond hair and places her hand on his forearm.*

*"Johnny, I can't believe you have won again. You must have
spent the whole war practicing card games."*

He laughs politely. "I wish it had been like that."

*The red head on his left taps his shoulder and flutters her
eyelashes. "Well at least you are safe. Do you need a job? Daddy is
hiring over at the factory."*

*"No need, thank you. I am headed back to Germany as soon as
the army will let me."*

The blonde squeals. "No. Why? You just got home."

*"I need to get back to..." His sister Camilla rushes to him and
spills water on his lap before he can finish his sentence.*

*"Don't forget about the dance tonight." The red head dabs her
napkin on his lap. "I want to make sure you are on my dance card."*

*Gently pushing her arm away, Johnny studies his cards
intently.*

No, no, no. *Johnny loves me.* Hedy shook the scene from her
head. She was simply imagining it.

But he hadn't written lately. Doubt crept back in. What if Tante
Gisela and Rosemary were right? Did his sisters really want a German
for a sister-in-law? Another scene flooded her mind.

*Camilla is waving goodbye and closes the front door. She
glares at Johnny as Lucia is clearing the table. "I wish you wouldn't
ignore my friends."*

"What are you talking about? I played cards with them." Johnny's eyebrows pinch together.

"Any of them would love to escort you to the dance. Why don't you quit talking about that German girl and start having fun?"

Exasperated, Johnny shakes his head. "I am going to marry Hedy. Why can't you accept that?"

Lucia puts down the plates and walks over. She motions for Camilla to leave the room. Camilla hovers near the door to the kitchen.

Coming up behind Johnny, Lucia reminds her brother, "Camilla loves you. She only wants to be sure you will be happy."

"I will be happy when I marry Hedy."

Lucia pats him on the shoulder. "Of course you will. What will it hurt to dance with a few of the local girls? You have always loved to dance. I'm not suggesting you kiss them, just go dancing. Besides, Hedy is probably dancing with her friends.

Johnny stares at her in disbelief. "You truly do not understand how challenging it is to live in Germany since the war. No one is dancing."

Hedy smiled to herself. Johnny would stay true to her. She promised not to doubt his love, and she wouldn't.

But what if his sisters succeeded? She held her hands to her ears and closed her eyes, praying for sleep to take her away from her thoughts.

~

The next morning, Hedy woke up in better spirits. Johnny would return any day. He couldn't help the slow mail service.

With the day off, she offered to go up the mountain to trade for food. Making her way across town, she waved to the neighbors. Several stopped to chat. "When is your soldier due back?"

"Have you heard from him lately?"

"It has been a long time. Are you certain he's coming back?"

By the time Hedy arrived at the base of the mountain, she did not want to listen to another question about Johnny's return. Managing to catch a ride up in the back of a pickup, she appreciated the silence.

After successfully negotiating with the farmers for potatoes and apples, she needed to find a ride down the mountain. Burdened with her packages, she walked back to the highway to find trucks headed down. She bumped into someone, almost knocking him over.

"Watch it!"

"I am so sorry," Hedy glanced up to find a familiar figure. "Günter?" Frowning, she stepped away.

"Hedy." Surprise crossed his face. "No, please don't go." He touched her arm gently. "I must apologize for being such a brute last month. I practiced what I was going to say to you for over a year. In my mind, I had such a different scene ..." He stopped. "Please forgive me."

His sad eyes caused Hedy to reconsider. "No, I should apologize. I ought to have explained right away. No hard feelings?"

"Let me make amends. I've got a ride down the mountain. Come with me, and I'll buy you a cup of coffee."

Hedy's eyes narrowed. "As friends? I don't want another misunderstanding."

"As friends." Günter escorted her to the truck.

~

For the next two hours they laughed and talked as they had as children. He shared Ralph's latest shenanigans, and Hedy regaled him with stories from the hospital. Carefully, she avoided any mention of Johnny.

As they got up to leave, Hedy gazed at Günter, "I'm glad I was such a klutz today. It's nice to have you back as a friend."

Taking both of Hedy's hands, he responded, "No matter what happens with your American, I will be here for you."

Helping her with her purchases, he accompanied her home, much to her mother's chagrin. "Günter, this is a surprise." Mama's eyes narrowed, and she focused on Hedy.

"I literally bumped into him at the mountain top, and he offered me a lift home."

"It is a pleasure to see you again, Günter. How is your family?"

After some pleasantries, he left, and Mama confronted Hedy. "Why did Günter walk you home? Wasn't he extremely inappropriate before?"

"It is fine, Mama." Hedy waved aside her mother's concern. "He wanted to apologize for being such a jerk, so he bought me a cup of coffee."

"Do you think Johnny would approve?"

"He's playing bridge with other women. Why shouldn't I have coffee with other men?" Hedy's voice rose.

Mama's brow wrinkled. "What are you talking about, Hedy?"

Hedy broke down in tears as she shared her fears with her mother. Mama wrapped her arms around Hedy's shoulders and squeezed. "We do not always perceive the world in the same way. You are often impulsive. When Johnny asked for your hand in marriage, my first instinct was to tell you it was too soon; you were being reckless. Then I saw Johnny watching you with such affection in his eyes. There is no doubt in my mind he will make you happy."

Her mother pushed Hedy out far enough to face her. "I don't know why there haven't been letters lately. It doesn't mean he hasn't written or he doesn't care. It only means you haven't received them."

Hedy hugged her mother. "Mama, you are wonderful."

~

The work week began again. Work at the hospital was challenging, although not nearly as stressful as Traben-Trarbach had been. By the end of the day, however, Hedy was drained and ready to be home.

Heading out of the hospital, she started when Günter stepped out to greet her. "Interest you in a walk in the park?"

"I don't think it would be appropriate."

"Why not? We have been friends for years. Your fiancé a jealous type, is he?"

Not liking the idea of Johnny being portrayed negatively, Hedy agreed to join him.

After an hour of pleasant conversation, Günter asked, "So when does this soldier of yours return?"

"He should be back with in the month, and we'll get married."

"I can't wait to meet the lucky fellow. Be sure to introduce me when he returns."

The intensity in his eyes overtook Hedy. Günter's words, though polite and appropriate, did not ring sincere.

~

Several times during the next few weeks, Hedy crossed paths with her old classmate.

"I don't see you for years, and now I see you every week," Günter gazed down at her. "At least you didn't knock me over this time."

Hedy smothered her grin.

"Want to sit in the park for a moment?"

"I must be getting home." She stepped around him.

"Just as friends, Hedy. I want the best for you."

They sat and talked. The conversation revolved around the current happenings of Trier and the rest of the world. Günter showed his passion for Germany to be a great country again.

Hedy sighed. "I don't think the rest of the world wants that."

"I don't mean militarily. Don't you miss the pride we felt being Germans before this war started? We can get that back."

The friendly conversations continued. The uncomfortable feelings she had previously evaporated. She agreed to meet him in the park the next week.

~

"Hedy, over here." Günter called her. "I was telling someone today about going to school in Birresborn and realized you are the only person I've kept track of. Do you see any of our classmates at all?

Hedy recounted running into Gerda.

"You must be kidding. If she was living there, she must not be a *Weichling* anymore. "

"Johnny couldn't believe it either." Hedy stopped herself.

"It is okay to talk about your soldier, Hedy. All that matters to me is your happiness. Tell me how you met."

Surprised, she shared the story of how she met Johnny and their engagement. "Are you certain you want to hear this?"

"Hedy, I am your friend. That is the important thing."

~

Days went by and still no letter from Johnny. Hedy tried not to think about it when she stepped out of the hospital. The dark clouds headed ominously in her direction did not help her mood.

"You appear sad." Günter's voice made her jump. "What is wrong? Is your soldier not treating you well?"

She glared at him. "He is treating me fine."

"I am sure he is a fine man. I just don't want you hurt," he said tenderly, touching her cheek lightly with the back of his finger. "There are a myriad of stories of Americans making all kinds of promises to our girls, going back to the States and forgetting them. I don't want anything to happen to you."

Her anger subsided, and tears formed in the corner of her eyes. "He hasn't forgotten me. He gave me this gold band before he left. He will be getting back soon. She blinked back the tears. "His letters have gotten lost."

The boom of thunder made them jump. Günter positioned the hood from Hedy's coat onto her head. "We had better get moving. There is a huge storm brewing."

The two dashed up the block as the downpour started, drenching them. "Come this way." Günter pulled Hedy down a side street. "My place is right here."

They dashed into his apartment building and climbed to the second floor, shaking their jackets at the landing. Hedy shifted her weight from one leg to the other as Günter unlocked the door. "I should go home."

"Don't be silly. It is a monsoon out there. Ralph will be home any minute. Stay and let me make you dinner. I actually found sausage at the grocers."

"I shouldn't." She headed for the steps.

"As friends. I promise I will walk you back right after dinner."

A flash of lightening illuminated the interior as he opened the door. Günter's apartment consisted of a large room with a small cook stove on one side, two twin beds on the other, and a square table with two chairs in the middle. A narrow window let in the muted light.

Günter switched on the overhead light and pulled out a chair for Hedy. From a shelf in the kitchen area, he pulled out a bottle of *Moselwein.*

"I have been saving it for a special occasion." He set a glass in front of her and poured a substantial glass.

"What special occasion?" Hedy watched as he poured a smaller one for himself.

"You here having dinner with me." When she objected, he added, "As just friends, remember."

Clinking their glasses, they toasted to friendship. Hedy savored the bouquet. "This wine is almost as good as what we drank near the train station."

Günter lit the oven and placed the sausages in a pan, while throwing two potatoes in a pot of water to boil. "I agree. I wonder if the peaches in Birresborn have fermented yet." He topped off her glass.

Raising it, she offered a toast. "To the cavemen of Birresborn. May they enjoy fermented peaches."

He offered a different toast. "To the evening we spent together in the woods."

The heat rose in her face. "It was a pleasant evening. Thank goodness Ralph was there to protect my innocence. Where is he? You said he would be here."

"He will be." Putting down his glass, Günter lifted her hand and gently pulled her up out of her chair. With one arm around her waist and the other extended as if to dance, he whispered, "You don't need to be protected from me."

Before she could protest, he spun her around the room, dancing to a tune he hummed quietly in her ear. Her feet barely touched the floor. She hadn't danced in a long time.

He twirled her out from him and pulled her back. Heat rose within her body. The wine was definitely going to her head.

The arm around her waist tightened, and Günter whirled her around the room again. When was the last time she experienced the pleasure of Johnny's touch? Her head spun. Was it from the wine or the motion? Her grip tightened on his firm bicep.

Hedy shut her eyes. *Oh, John.*

Günter slowly dipped her back and kissed her. They weren't John's gentle lips. Realization washed over her. Her entire body went rigid. She struggled to stand and pushed herself away from him. "I am leaving." Hedy headed for the door.

Günter grabbed her arm and spun her into his chest. Eyes blazing, he leaned down to kiss her again. She slapped him. Surprised, he loosened his grip, and she sprinted to the door, slamming it behind her.

The storm had increased. The thunder reverberated. Hedy raced through the dark, drenched in rain and shame. Once at her home, she ran straight to the bathroom and rinsed her mouth, spitting wildly into the sink.

Shaking uncontrollably, Hedy stared into the mirror. What had she been thinking? Why had she let him take her there? Covering her face, she rushed to her bedroom and propelled herself on the bed, sobbing.

~

Hedy did not go to work the next day. She refused to leave her room. The hollowness of her chest overwhelmed her.

"Dear, why don't you brush your hair and walk with me?" Mama sat on her bed, stroking her arm.

"I'm too tired. I don't want to go anywhere." She rolled away from her mother.

"Please tell me what happened, Hedy. I'm worried about you."

She refused to answer. Eventually Mama left the room. Hedy locked the door behind her.

Another day passed, and Mama became more concerned. "Why don't you see if Gerda or Inge are coming to town anytime? You haven't seen your friends in a while."

Hedy gazed out her window. The weather was beautiful. If she biked fast enough, maybe she could escape her conscience.

The Return

1946

"The American people want to help the German people win their way back to an honorable place among the free and peace-loving peoples of the world."

JAMES BYRNES, U. S. Secretary of State — *Speech of Hope* in Stuttgart—September 6, 1946

"Hedy. What a surprise," Gerda jumped from the flower bed she was weeding. She wiped her hands on her slacks before giving Hedy a hug. "Inge will be sorry she missed you. She is back in Berlin trying to discover if the medical school will reopen soon."

They walked into the house together. Gerda washed her hands and filled the pot with water for tea. After filling Hedy in on the happenings in Traben-Trarbach, Gerda inquired how the wedding plans were progressing.

Hedy sighed. "I don't know. I haven't seen a letter from Johnny in two months."

Gerda reassured her. "He loves you. He will be back any day."

"Even if he does, I can't face him." Her hand cupped her mouth. The words tumbling out of her in confusion and sobs, she confessed what had happened with Günter.

Gerda almost dropped the tea pot. She set it down and rushed over to her friend. "Günter is a jerk. Always has been. It is about time you noticed." Her voice softened. "That wasn't your fault. There is no reason for you to dread facing Johnny." She stopped and scrutinized Hedy's expression. "Unless you are contemplating not marrying him."

Jerking back, Hedy vehemently replied, "I want to marry Johnny more than anything else."

Gerda patted her friend on the arm. "Then what are you worried about? You have done nothing wrong. Spend your time looking forward to seeing him, silly."

Raising her head, Hedy managed a smile. "Oh, Gerda. You are such a friend." She laced her arm with Gerda, and the two ambled towards the river. "What have you been doing all summer?"

Gerda grew serious. "I went to Auschwitz to see the concentration camps for myself."

"You cannot be serious."

"I am. Obviously it is no longer a camp, but you can grasp the idea of what occurred." Gerda's features harden. "An Allied soldier didn't want me to go near it. I talked him into letting me walk through." She faltered.

"Hedy, the place was horrible." She broke into tears. "The cramped barracks. The blood stains. The pits in the back." Shaking her head as if to knock the memory out, she continued. "I was convinced it was Allied propaganda." Her shoulders quivered. "How could we have done this?"

They sat on the bank. Hedy examined her friend's face for some sort of understanding. "Gerda, *we* didn't do this."

"We should have known. Remember Rachel Rosen, your Jewish friend from Trier?"

"Oh, Gerda, no." Hedy pulled back.

"Her father's name, the jeweler, was on the list."

"But my father assumed they had gotten away."

"Maybe *she* did, but her father didn't." Gerda paused. "We should not have let this happen. I am going to finish my medical training and move to the Eastern part of Germany."

"Why, Gerda? There are terrible reports of rapes and murders from the Russian controlled areas."

"That is why I need to go. I ignored the stories of the atrocities, refusing to believe it. People are suffering in the East. I am not going to ignore it. As a doctor, I can try to help heal the wounds."

Hedy gripped her friend's shoulders. "How can you make amends, Gerda? You had nothing to do with it."

"If I don't help, I am no better than the damn Nazis."

Struggling for a way to respond, Hedy gripped Gerda's hand. "It isn't safe. Putting yourself in harm's way is not going to make up for the past." She paused for a moment, thinking. "Come to America. Become a doctor there instead of the east." She stood and pulled Gerda up beside her. "We will prove to the world not all Germans are monsters."

Gerda sank back down. "No, Hedy. That is the path you should take. You will make a wonderful ambassador of the good in Germany. I must go my particular way."

Sitting beside her, Hedy stared down at the ground. "I want to talk you out of this." Gerda tilted her head and gave her a significant gaze. Hedy exhaled deeply. "But I realize you are as stubborn as I am."

The women sat in silence. The sun set over the lake. After the fiery red ball and its reflection disappeared, Gerda lead Hedy back to the house.

~

The next morning Hedy awoke to find Gerda's bed empty. She slowly worked her way down the stairs, stopping when she overheard Frau Schmitt in the kitchen. "I can't believe a nice girl like Hedy is going to marry an American."

Pouring coffee into a cup, Gerda fussed at her mother. "Ma, you met Johnny. He is a delightful person and is good for Hedy.

"He seemed relatively nice. It probably doesn't matter anyway. You know how those foreign soldiers are. Promising everything to bed a girl and then leaving town."

Gerda slammed her cup down. "Ma. It isn't like that at all."

"Of course it is. They give them food and promise to take them to the land of milk and honey. It is enough to make anyone lose their allegiance."

"Our country lost its allegiance to us," Gerda shouted. "Think about what the Nazis did. We sat back and pretended it wasn't happening. Hedy should get as far away from Germany as possible."

Backing up the steps, Hedy crept back to the bedroom and laid face-down on the bed. Is that what she was doing? Running away from her country?

She stood and glared at the person in the mirror. Maybe Günter and Rosemary were right. Maybe she was a traitor.

Walking to the window, she gazed out at the sun shining on the flowers below. She threw open the window and leaned out, scaring a couple of rabbits across the garden. The sunlight warming her face brought the clarity she desired. Maybe her father's expression should have ended with the *Brighter the morning*. With her chin held high and shoulders back, she marched down to the kitchen.

Standing tall, she addressed Gisela's mother. "I am a proud German, and I always will be, Frau Schmidt. I did not sell my loyalty or body for food." Frau Schmidt's mouth dropped open. "I will make a difference in this world; however, I am going to make a difference alongside the love of my life, Johnny Merenda."

"I am awfully glad to hear that." Johnny poked his head into the open kitchen window.

"Johnny." Hedy sailed out the door and flung herself at her fiancé, nearly knocking him off his feet. In his dress uniform, he was even more handsome than she remembered. Catching her in his arms, their lips met. The long, passionate kiss made Hedy weak in her knees.

Coming up for breath, Johnny wondered, "Do you always have to leave town when I'm looking for you?"

"When did you get in? How did you find me?"

"Slow down, *mia amore*." Between showering kisses around her face, Johnny explained. "I got to town last night expecting a welcoming committee. I sent a message to the CIC office to tell you when I was arriving. Imagine my surprise when your father informed me you weren't there." His eyes sparkled. "Actually I should have expected it. I'm beginning to think you hide from me on purpose."

"They didn't tell me. I've had no mail forever. If I had realized visiting Gerda would get you home, I would have come months ago."

A distinct cough interrupted them. Gerda stood on the stoop, arms crossed, watching them. "Would you two like to come in the house, or would you prefer to continue the performance for the neighbors?"

Hedy glanced around sheepishly. The elderly woman next door stared at the embracing couple with a frown on her face. "We should go inside."

Gerda's mother offered coffee and biscuits. Gerda pelted Johnny with questions as they ate. Though polite, Johnny toyed with his fork. As soon as the last roll was eaten, he suggested they return to Trier.

Sitting in the jeep, Hedy let out an extended sigh. "I'm sorry you needed to track me down again." She twisted in his direction. "I was worried you would never come back."

Johnny stopped fidgeting with the key in the ignition. A slow, disbelieving look crossed his face. "Why did you worry? Haven't I always come back?" Disappointment replaced disbelief. "Don't you recall all of those trips, hours across Germany simply to spend a few minutes with you?"

"The letters stopped, and people said horrible things." She shivered at the thought. Throwing her arms around him, Hedy cried, "I will never doubt your love ever again."

He kissed her once more and started the engine. "Hedy, I wrote you every week. I warned you the mail is slow across the ocean." His eyes narrowed. "I will find out what happened to my arrival message. You ought to have been told."

"I was a fool. I knew you would come back." She beamed at him.

The summer sunshine glistened on the ripe fields as the jeep traveled the bumpy roads. Hedy didn't mind the bumps. They brought her closer to Johnny.

"You had better hold on or you are going to land on me one of these times." Johnny patted her knee.

Winking at him, she replied, "Would that be so bad?"

~

Back in Trier, Mama ran out to greet them. Linking her arm through Johnny's, she ushered him up to the kitchen. "There is no need for you to go back to Wiesbaden tonight. You can sleep in Hedy's room, and she can stay on the couch. You two have a lot to talk about."

"Thank you, Frau Weiß. But I'll take the couch." He gazed around as they sat at the table with Vater. "How is your food supply holding up?"

"It was kind of you to have left us so much food. We are doing fine," Mama responded.

Johnny glared suspiciously at Hedy. "Your mother sounds remarkably like you. I will bring more next time I come."

Hedy grinned. "We did enjoy the odd thing you left—peanut butter. Tasty, though it was awfully dry."

"It shouldn't have been dry." Johnny scratched his head. "Wasn't it sealed with the oil?"

"Yes, we poured it off and used it for frying."

Johnny's shoulders jiggled as he attempted to hold back the laughter. "You ate the peanut butter without stirring the separated oil back in?"

Realizing her mistake, Hedy winced. "We didn't know, but we liked it anyway."

Johnny patted her leg. "You will need to learn to love peanut butter. When you get to the States, you will discover it is quite the staple." Seeing the incredulousness on Hedy's face, he added, "Wait until you try it on bread with jelly."

His hands twitched. "Mr. and Mrs. Weiß, I hesitate to ask this, as Hedy is your only child. I would like her to move to Wiesbaden immediately."

Mama clutched Vater's hand. Johnny continued, "The army still has the regulations forbidding me to marry her. From what I heard in the States, it should change soon. If she is living in Trier when they release the restriction, Hedy will need to get a visa and permission from the French authorities." He tilted his head. "The French are not known for their openness for Americans, or anyone else, marrying German citizens."

"We know," Vater explained. "We tried to announce your engagement in the local newspaper. When the French administrator realized the groom was an American, they wouldn't let us publish the banns."

Johnny understood. "I would like to get Hedy away from the hospital."

"The French don't bother me," Hedy chimed in. "I ignore their attitude."

"There is another reason." He placed her hands in his. "Hedy, you must work on your English. I am only signed up for one year here in Germany, and then we will be moving to America. I have found an English widow for you to live with." Twisting his gold band, he added. "You will be required to know English if you still want to go to school for physical therapy."

Jumping up, Hedy threw her arms around him. "Oh, Johnny."

"Mr. and Mrs. Weiß, I realize I am asking a lot. I promise you, Hedy will be safe and chaperoned. We will visit every three weeks."

Vater and Mama exchanged sad, but knowing looks. Vater broke the silence. "Hedy, your mother and I understand you need to become more acquainted with your fiancée and his culture before moving to another country. If you would like to move to Wiesbaden, you have our blessing."

"Thank you, Vater." Hedy jumped up and kissed her father on the cheek. She hugged her mother. "And you, Mama."

With that settled, Johnny shared news from the States. "The US government should be releasing the restrictions on food presently. President Truman is talking about allowing the Red Cross to come back to Germany and bring food supplies."

"I hope so." The creases in Vater's forehead deepened. "This year's harvest is expected to be horrible. I am also worried about the winter. There isn't enough coal and wood left."

"I'll help out as much as I can. The non-fraternization rules have been relaxed." Johnny stared at his hands. "But we still need to be careful.."

Moving to Wiesbaden

1946

8. Suspected War Criminals and Security Arrests:

a. You will search out, arrest, and hold ...chief Nazi associates, other war criminals and all persons who have participated in planning or carrying out Nazi enterprises involving or resulting in atrocities or war crimes.

Directive to Commander in Chief of US Forces of Occupation
Regarding the Military Government of Germany—Released October 17, 1945

"Let's grab a bite and then you can unpack." Johnny pulled in front of the CIC house.

She stepped into the house. The aroma of bratwurst and sausage made Hedy's stomach growl. She hoped the animated conversation of the agents had kept them from hearing it. "What were you doing in Birresborn, Peter?" Fred asked.

Remembering her childhood years in Birresborn, Hedy smiled.

Peter set his fork on the table and leaned back. "Looking for Jaeger Wo–."

Hedy entered the dining room and interrupted Peter. "Jaeger Wolf? How is he?"

Five heads turned in her direction. No one said a word.

Johnny gaped, "You know Jaeger Wolf?"

"Of course." Hedy waved her hand in the air, feeling a touch of unease as they all continued to stare. "He was the grocer's son, from my hometown. The last time I saw him he looked so handsome in his new black—Oh.'

It dawned on Hedy why everyone watched her so oddly. She fled the room, hands to her mouth, hearing Peter proclaim, "I told you so."

Collapsing on a low brick wall outside the house, she lowered her chin to her chest and shut her eyes. Johnny joined her on the wall without saying a word.

"I understand it is your business to track down war criminals." Hedy suppressed her sobs. "It never occurred to me they may be people I knew."

Putting his arm around her shoulders, he lifted her chin with his other hand. "Wars change people. Especially when they are surrounded by such evil."

"How can I go to America with you?" She twisted from him. "People will assume I am evil too."

Johnny pulled her close. "No one who spends more than a single moment with you would believe that." He drew back. "Listen, Hedy. You are a strong woman. I heard you putting Gerda's mother in her place. You will do fine in America."

She held him tight and rubbed her face against his shoulder. "I don't think I can face the men just yet."

"We'll go to Mrs. Walker's and get you settled. We can get a bite to eat later." He drove her to a beautiful but aging two-story house with sky blue forget-me-nots growing in the flower bed. A tall, silver-haired woman with a lively step welcomed them at the door.

"I am so pleased to have you stay with me. It has been lonely since Mr. Walker died." Mrs. Walker ushered Hedy to the kitchen and sent Johnny on his way. After putting on a kettle for tea, she said, "I am a war bride, too, dear."

"Really?" Hedy straightened.

"Oh, yes." Mrs. Walker pulled a teapot from a shelf and measured in the tea leaves. "It was the Great War. He was strong and handsome." She lifted her face towards the ceiling. "It was love at first sight. I moved here to Wiesbaden after the war." Returning her gaze to Hedy, she confided, "My German was terrible. Luckily, he was remarkably patient."

Hedy lifted the singing kettle off the stove and poured water into the pot. "Your German is excellent."

"Thank you, dear. Mr. Merenda tells me I am not allowed to

speak German to you after today." She playfully shook her index finger at Hedy. "You have to prepare for America."

Hedy trembled. "I am nervous. He's asked all the agents to only speak English to me." She grimaced. "I will be the laughing stock of the CIC."

Mrs. Walker poured the tea into cups. "As pretty as you are, they will find it charming. Besides, you will pick the language up quickly."

"If only I could believe you." The two women sipped their tea and chatted. When they finished, Mrs. Walker accompanied her upstairs to her room.

A thick feather bed invited her to climb in. The window opened to a flower garden below. Lace curtains fluttered in the light breeze while sunshine highlighted the pale colors gracing the walls. Best of all, there was no low eave for her to hit her head upon in the mornings. "It is perfect, Mrs. Walker. I don't have much, but I'll unpack when Johnny brings my bag."

As if on cue, there was a knock on the door. The ladies laughed as they walked downstairs. When Mrs. Walker opened the door, Johnny lugged in two heavy suitcases. "Hedy, these are for you." His grin was that of a Cheshire cat.

"What are you talking about?" She followed him into the living room.

He laid the bulky suitcases on the floor and knelt beside the first one. "My sisters were so excited to hear about you, they dragged me shopping." Snapping the latch open, he flung back the top. Inside lay more new clothing than Hedy had seen in years.

Gasping, she sank to the floor next to Johnny. He pulled out a white dress with black lace sewn on in a spectacular pattern. "Lucia is about your size, so she tried it on. She said you would like it." Johnny gazed at her expectantly.

Hedy held the dress to her chest and squeezed. She stood and twirled. It was the most beautiful dress she'd ever seen. "Oh, Johnny. It is perfect."

Leaning against his back, she wrapped her arms around him. He tried to stand, but stumbled before straightening. He watched her hold the dress up for him again. "I'm glad you like it."

She carefully folded the dress and placed in on a chair. "I can't believe I was imagining your sisters trying to talk you out of marrying me."

He kissed her hand. "Quite the opposite. They couldn't wait to go shopping for you. They said to tell you to let them know what else you need and they will send it over."

"Umm," coughed Mrs. Walker. "I'll go refill my tea." Hedy had forgotten she was in the room.

Johnny knelt back onto the floor. "Wait. There's more." He pulled out shoes, skirts, and blouses. Reaching the bottom of the suitcase, he paused. "I will be in uniform at our wedding—" White satin fabric draped his arms as he rose. "But I want you to be dressed as a real bride."

Hedy released the shirt she was holding and touched the lengths of silky fabric. "Thank you." The tears in her eyes blinded her as he engulfed her in his arms, pressing the soft fabric to her back. After a few moments, they moved to the couch.

Nestling next to him, she became serious. "You are too generous. You shouldn't have spent so much money on me."

"Don't be silly. You haven't had any new clothes in years." His eyes sparkled. "I can't have you walking around the CIC office in nothing can I? What would the agents say?"

She swatted his arm playfully. "I mean it. You can't afford all that."

"Don't worry *mia amore*." He shook one hand and tossed something imaginary to the floor. "Lady Luck smiled on me."

Hedy stiffened. She remembered him mentioning a woman on the boat in his letter.

The crow's feet around his eyes deepened. "What's wrong, Hedy?'

"Who is Lady Luck?" She squirmed away from him. "I thought the ship was a troop transport, not an ocean liner."

After a loud belly laugh, Johnny teased, "You aren't jealous are you?"

Hedy clenched her jaw. "Why are you laughing at me?"

"Dice, Hedy." He repeated the tossing motion with his hand. "We say Lady Luck was smiling when we win at dice."

"Oh. I feel foolish." Hedy hid her flushing face. "When you wrote about Lady Luck and all the girls your sisters brought for you..."

"Hedy."

She dropped her eyes. He stroked her cheek with the back of his hand. "Would you like to know what actually happened when I got home, *mia amore?*"

She nodded, afraid to open her mouth.

He leaned back on the couch. "After Papa picked me up from the docks, we drove home. Everyone, all my extended family, was there. Remember, they hadn't seen me for years. Everyone was talking at once, arms were flying."

Remembering Johnny communicating with the jeweler, Hedy tittered. "I can only imagine."

"Before I would answer a single question, I called for their attention and pulled out your picture. Holding it up, I shouted, 'This is the girl I am going to marry.' There was absolute silence for about 30 seconds, before the floodgates opened. 'Who is she? Where did you meet? What is her name?' I passed around a couple of other pictures of you and answered everyone's questions."

His animated story gave Hedy the feeling she was there with him. "They were almost as upset as I that we couldn't set a wedding date yet. By the time I stopped talking, my sisters had already planned the shopping trip for you. Everyone was excited."

With his enthusiasm increasing, his arms acted out the story. "Maria and Lucia wanted to do something special for you. They picked out shoes and clothes. Luckily Lucia is close to your size." He gave an exaggerated cringe. "They took me to dress shops all around the city. Lucia would model the dresses for me to see if I thought you would like it."

"She sounds wonderful." Hedy clapped her hands together. "I always wondered what it would be like to have sisters."

"You won't have to wonder for considerably longer if the rumors are true. I wrote letter after letter to the Pentagon asking for the restrictions to be lifted. It probably won't help, but I had to do something."

"Oh, Johnny." She squeezed him. "I can't believe I ever doubted you."

"I brought back what I could." He lowered his head. "We weren't allowed more than two bags on the ship."

"But if these two suitcases are for me, where are your clothes?"

He winked. "Don't worry about me." Turning serious, he said, "It will be winter soon. You'll need heavier clothes as my sisters only sent lighter ones."

"I'll make do, especially with all this. Besides, my uniform has always kept me warm."

Johnny stiffened. "Your Red Cross uniform is officially retired. You no longer need to work for the French for food." He thought for a moment. "The agents can tell me where to find a local tailor, and I will have some clothes made for you."

She folded her arms across her stomach. "The stores are empty. Where will we get material?"

With a sly grin, John answered, "Leave that to me. It is almost time to go to dinner. Will you model one of your new outfits for me?"

"Give me ten minutes." Hedy blew him a kiss as she gathered the clothes and bounced up to her room.

~

Dinner at the CIC house was a jovial affair, with Peter noticeably absent. Everyone agreed Johnny and his sisters had done a good job shopping for Hedy. "I feel like St. Nicholas has come early this year," Hedy beamed.

His commanding officer cleared his throat. "Johnny, perhaps you could explain why you requested replacement uniforms?

One of the agents raised his glass and shouted, "Seems to me like he didn't have space for them."

Johnny blushed a bright red. Hedy's eyes grew wide as she tried to tell if the officer was upset.

"To Johnny and Hedy," the officer toasted.

Her fiancé exhaled deeply as she squeezed his hand.

~

A few weeks later, they started out for Trier. It was her first visit since moving to Wiesbaden. The unrest in the country had settled down enough to allow the couple to travel without another soldier accompanying them.

"It will be good to see your parents, but—" Johnny hesitated "—I am worried about crossing into the French sector."

Hedy wasn't worried. "I should be fine. My papers prove I live in Trier."

"My concern is not getting you in, but getting you back out." He kissed her cheek. "They don't view German women favorably who ride around with American soldiers." Johnny pulled an official-looking paper from a pouch on the seat. "Carry this with your regular papers."

The document included more stamps and official seals than Hedy had ever seen. "What does it mean?"

Johnny chuckled. "I may have begged a signature or two to say you are an employee of the CIC." He helped her into the jeep. "We have to make one stop before we head to Trier." Without another word he drove into Wiesbaden and stopped at a small shop.

After retrieving a package wrapped in brown paper from the back seat, he helped Hedy from the vehicle. "Fred said this tailor should be able to fashion winter clothes for you."

"Out of what?"

The short, thin tailor removed his round wire glasses. "How may I help you?"

Johnny handed him the package. "I would like you to make these into women's clothing."

Unwrapping the package, the tailor pulled out a pair of pinkish-green trousers from an army officer's dress uniform. He glanced at Hedy and back at the pants. "That should not be a problem." Motioning to a woman in the next room, he instructed Hedy, "If you will go with my wife Clara, she will take your measurements."

Hedy did as requested and minutes later walked back to her future husband. As they were leaving the building, Johnny stopped and called to the tailor's wife. "Frau Clara, if we bring you fabric, can you design a wedding dress?"

Clapping her hands, Frau Clara beamed. "I would love to."

"But, but we aren't allowed to marry yet," Hedy stammered.

"We will, *mia amore*, and we need to be prepared." He put his arm around her waist and escorted her to the jeep.

~

Pulling behind the apartment in Trier, Hedy bit her lower lip.

"Is there something wrong?" Johnny reached for her hand to assist her out of the jeep.

She hesitated. "It just dawned on me; Trier will never be my home again."

Stroking her arm, he watched her for a moment. Then, silently lifting the giant box of food from the back seat, he followed her up the stairs.

"Welcome home, dear." Her mother opened the door and kissed each of them. Her bones were less obvious, and her skin reflected a healthy glow. Even the streaks of grey which had surfaced over the past few years seemed more attractive.

Vater received the couple warmly. "Did you have any problems getting here?"

Smiling, Hedy showed her parents her new document. "The French soldiers at the checkpoint gawked at all the different stamps and waved us through."

"So glad. Come, sit down." Vater focused his attention on Johnny. "Any changes in the army regulations?"

"No, sir. We are still waiting." Johnny set the box of provisions in the kitchen and joined them at the table.

Mama bounded to her bedroom. The others waited for her, curious. She came back out carrying a small ring box. "Here is your piano."

"My piano?" Hedy opened the box to expose a beautiful rosette diamond ring. "It is exquisite. I don't understand, though."

Vater chuckled. "Do you remember seeing our apartment after the bombing?"

Hedy shuddered. "All that was left was the piano teetering on the second floor."

He nodded. "We weren't supposed to go into the building, but I climbed in from next door and pitched a tarp over it. I prayed the weather wouldn't ruin it. Eventually, we received permission to start clearing the rubble." Eyes glowing, he continued. "I had to figure out how to get the thing down without hurting it or myself."

Mama interrupted. "Why he bothered, is beyond me. We barely had enough room to move in here without a piano."

"Well, stories of the piano passed around town. Nightclubs are reopening. Last week, a couple of young musicians came to me and said they had heard about the piano. They had a job in a club if they could bring their own instruments." Vater threw up his hands. "I asked how they could pay and they offered their grandmother's ring."

"But, sir, how did you get the piano down?" Johnny leaned forward in his chair.

"I located a truck and hired several strong boys. We climbed into the building next door." Vater leaned back, eyes bright. "The boys were like squirrels. They scurried across the support beam and tied ropes around the piano."

Mama crossed herself and gazed up to the sky.

Patting his wife's hand, Vater continued. "After a few close calls, we managed to lower the piano into the bed of the truck and climbed back down." He pointed to the ring in front of Hedy. "Now you can take your mother's piano with you to America."

The four laughed. Hedy examined the ring closely. "But, Vater, this is a valuable ring." She placed it back in the box and pushed it toward him. "You can use it to buy food."

Her father shoved it back in front of her. "Consider it your dowry." He cracked a grin. "If I had tied your hope chest onto the truck correctly, it wouldn't be laying in pieces alongside the road."

Mama got up and placed her hand on Hedy's shoulder. "Don't argue with your father. It is our gift to you."

Hedy thanked her parents. Mama ladled soup into pottery bowls for each of them. "Konrad is coming from the farm tomorrow to visit. He wants to meet his cousin's fiancé."

Johnny grasped Hedy's hand. "Should I be concerned?"

"He is the closest thing to a big brother I have." She raised an eyebrow while tilting her head. "How would you handle your little sister's boyfriend?"

"I am in trouble." His grimace caused Hedy to burst into laughter.

~

The next morning, Konrad strode through the kitchen door with such confidence, that it brought memories of the cocky teen to Hedy's mind and tears to her eyes. "Hey, Cousin." He punched her on the arm.

"Ouch." Hedy punched back with a hug. "It is great to see you. Johnny has gone out with Vater. He'll be back soon."

"I can't wait to meet him, though I doubt he is good enough for you."

"Come on." She linked her arm through his. "Let's go walk." She grasped his arm and guided him down the steps and toward a nearby park. They caught up on the happenings at the farm as they walked. Once at the park, she paused. "I'm glad you came back."

"What about you? Are you moving to America?"

Hedy swallowed. "I am."

"You will enjoy the States. There are good people there."

"If they are all like Johnny's family, I shouldn't have any problems. You wouldn't believe all the lovely things his sisters picked out for me when he explained I hadn't had a new dress in five years. They sent so much, Johnny had to leave his uniforms behind." She attempted a smile.

Konrad chuckled, but his eyes narrowed as he studied her. "They sound nice. What are you worried about?"

She tightened her grip on his arm. "Am I doing the right thing?"

"What do you mean? I thought you loved this fellow." Konrad stopped to look directly at her.

"Oh, I do. That is what makes it so difficult. It's just—" Hedy stammered for a moment and stared at the ground. "I feel like I'm deserting my family. There is so much to be done here in Germany, and I'm leaving it all behind."

"For love," Konrad reminded her.

"For love." Hedy peered upward from her downcast face. "Does that make me a traitor?"

He motioned for her to sit down on a bench and pulled her hands from her face. "The traitors to Germany were the ones who got us in this damn war."

Hedy wiped her eyes with her free hand as he continued.

"Hell, I took up arms and fought for those monsters." He paused and added, "It is time for you to take charge of your life. We can't change what has happened, but we can learn from it. Go to America. Show them the good that comes out of Germany."

Letting her head fall back, Hedy smiled at her cousin. "You have always had a knack for making me feel better."

Konrad shook his head. "I'm not so sure about that. I believe I got you in trouble on the farm." They laughed together at the memory of the ox.

Feeling more relaxed, Hedy still had one more concern on her mind. "Do you think they will like me in America?"

"I can't imagine anyone not liking you, but, remember, there are jerks everywhere. Don't worry." He punched her lightly on the arm. "You have practice standing up to a bossy cousin."

His lively tone quieted. "Here is the real question. Will your feelings for Johnny outlast other people's hateful comments?"

Sitting up straight, Hedy answered defiantly. "Of course. I have already heard so many ugly things from our own people."

"Then you should be used to it." He looked around. "Which reminds me, I am here to meet this fellow. Where are you hiding him?"

She clasped his arm and they strolled back to the house.

New Year's Eve

1946

Now, therefore, I, Harry S. Truman, President of the United States of America, do hereby proclaim the cessation of hostilities of World War II, effective twelve o'clock noon, December 31, 1946.

Proclamation 2714—Cessation of Hostilities of World War II

Biting her lip, Hedy dabbed the cold, damp cloth on Johnny's forehead. "*Schatz*, my dearest, I pray this fever breaks."

Johnny tried to respond, but his words were mumbled and inarticulate. Hedy touched his shoulder. "Shush. Don't speak."

The door opened "Excuse me, Ma'am." Upon seeing Hedy, Fred began scolding her. "You shouldn't be here."

"I realize it is New Year's Eve, but I am not here for a date."

He shook his head fiercely. "We can't have you getting the mumps too."

Laying down the cloth, she straightened her shoulders and stepped toward him. "I need to get his fever down. He's getting delirious." She stopped and pointed to the door. "Now you get out and let him sleep."

Chastised, Fred started to leave. With the door open, he glanced back. "Your outfit seems familiar."

She swayed from side to side. The pinkish-green material swung with her. "It should. It is made of the same material as your dress uniform."

"So it is. I wondered what happened to my extra slacks."

After pantomiming throwing a glass at him, Hedy focused her attention back on her patient. She poured water for Johnny. The door burst open, causing the liquid to spill. It was Fred again.

"What are you doing?" She set down the glass and brushed the water off of her skirt.

Fred grabbed her by the waist and spun her around. "You are getting married."

She pushed herself away from his grasp. Had he lost his mind? "Of course I am getting married. Johnny and I have been engaged for months."

"No." Fred's eyes were glowing as he clasped her hands. "I mean you *can* get married. It just came over the radio. The army has lifted the restrictions. You can marry."

Hedy hesitated, unable to believe what she was hearing. "Are you sure?"

"Yes." Fred's eyes sparkled. "You can finally get married."

She danced to Johnny's bedside. "Johnny, *Schatz*, we can marry."

Tossing in bed, his only response was "Uh, huh."

Fred glanced from Johnny to Hedy and they broke out into laughter. "We will have to share the news in the morning."

~

Over the next few weeks, Johnny's health improved, and, luckily, Hedy did not contract the mumps. Though the army had lifted the regulations on marrying German civilians, they required a ninety-day waiting period.

"Ninety days is March 29th." Johnny kissed Hedy on the cheek. "I'll take care of the paperwork, but you need a wedding dress."

~

A month later, the tailor welcomed them with open arms. "Wait until you see them, Fräulein Hedy." He exited and came out with slacks made from army fatigues. "Johnny said you required something comfortable for an extended boat voyage."

Smiling at Johnny, he motioned to the door. "You must go. Clara needs Fräulein Hedy to try on her wedding dress."

Johnny waved goodbye. "I'll be outside."

Frau Clara brought out the dress. Hedy gasped as she touched the silky satin gently. Her fingers followed the gown's long sleeves to the dress body. A thin band of satin around the neck was attached by transparent lace. Yards of lace flowed down the skirt, leaving an extensive train. "I am a princess in a fairy tale." Hedy went to the back room where Frau Clara helped her into the dress. She wanted to spin it around, but dared not move.

The tailor agreed. "You are beautiful. We will sew the final touches and send the dress to you."

Hedy changed back to her street clothes and found Johnny. "The end of March cannot come soon enough." She kissed him and practically skipped down the street.

"I have something to tell you." Johnny stated so seriously, it stunned Hedy. He accompanied her to the bench at Swan Lake where they had exchanged rings the year before. "Last year, when they sent me back to the States, I signed up for another year of service."

"I know." Hedy gazed lovingly into his eyes. "So you could come back to me."

"The year is almost up." He gulped. "They have my transport scheduled back to New York in late April."

"Perfect. We will be married by then."

The creases in his forehead deepened. "The problem is we don't have your travel papers yet. There is a backlog with the immigration side." He stopped and held her. "I may have to ship out before you do."

Her stomach churned as she bit her lower lip. "What do you mean? I thought the army approved us marrying."

"They have. We need to work out the visas and paperwork. I am pulling all the strings I can to get us on the same boat over, but I wanted you to be prepared if I have to leave first."

She frowned and twisted the gold band on her finger, imagining herself on a large ship crossing the ocean alone. *Please God, keep us together.*

The Weddings

1947

Section 13.

1. The marriage is concluded by the contracting parties declaring personally and in the presence of each other before the registrar that they wish to marry each other.

Enactments and Approved Papers of the Allied
Authority Germany, Volume 2—January 1946

The young American chaplain rose from his chair. "I am Father Stephan Titian. I understand you wish to marry."

Squeezing Johnny's hand, Hedy nervously nodded.

He motioned for them to sit in the overstuffed chairs against the back wall before pulling up a straight-backed chair for himself. Leaning forward, he addressed Hedy. "Are you comfortable with English or would you prefer we speak in German?"

"English will be fine." She tilted her head towards her future husband. "He doesn't want me to speak German any longer."

"Wait a minute." Johnny sat upright. "Only so you will be more comfortable when we get to New York."

Hedy patted his knee. The priest grinned at her before settling in his chair. "How long have you two known each other?"

Johnny considered for a moment. "It was April of '45. Before the war was over."

Wringing her hands in her lap, Hedy added, "He has met my family numerous times. They all approve."

The priest exhaled slowly. "I needed to ask. Since the army lifted the regulations, you would not believe the number of people wanting to marry who barely know each other."

They had passed the first question with flying colors. She hoped the others were as easy. From the expression on Johnny's face, he was having the same thought.

The conversation lasted an hour. The priest offered to reserve the chapel at the convent for March 29th. After thanking him, they rose to leave, but he stopped them. "Don't forget. The German government requires a civil marriage separate from the church ceremony. Be sure to schedule your civil service at the courthouse before the 29th or I won't be able to marry you."

Nodding, Johnny ushered Hedy out.

~

Inge and Fred sat on either side of Hedy and Johnny in front of an enormous mahogany desk in the Wiesbaden official's chamber. The dark paneling cast a somber mood. Inge elbowed Hedy. "I've never been to a civil ceremony before, Hedy. How am I supposed to act?"

"I haven't any idea. I assume someone will explain." Hedy fidgeted.

To their right, a door opened, and a short, elderly gentleman dressed in a dapper cutaway greeted them in German. He opened the wooden shutters, allowing sunlight to flood the room. "That is better." Lifting his perfectly-round wire frames from his desk, he positioned them on his thick nose and peered at the wedding party. "Are you the persons with an appointment for a civil law marriage?"

"We are." Johnny replied.

The official required each person to identify himself by name and birthdate. "Do not take this event lightly. The Civil Law Marriage is a legally binding contract that cannot be broken at will. Do you understand the significance?"

Everyone acknowledged their understanding. The short ceremony required Fred and Inge to be sworn in as witnesses and concluded when all four signed the register. Expecting to be dismissed, Hedy started to stand. The gentleman motioned for her to remain seated.

He switched to imperfect English. "Out of respect for the two Americans," he pointed to Johnny and Fred, "and as this is a legal contract, I would like to repeat the ceremony in English hence there will be no misunderstandings."

The bridal party stared as the official began the service over in English. Frequently, he opened a drawer in his desk and referred to it. Once completed, he requested they stay for another moment while he left the room.

"How sweet of him," Inge gushed.

Hedy put her hand on her heart. "I can't believe he learned English for us."

Returning to the room carrying a stunning bouquet of a dozen red roses, the official handed them to her. "*Viel Glück und Gottes Segnen*. Good luck and God bless you." He waved goodbye and left the room.

Hedy buried her head in flowers and blinked back the tears. Johnny stroked her face and linked her arm in his. Inge and Fred trailed behind.

Standing on the street outside, Fred shook Johnny's hand. "Well, you are finally married."

"Only for the Germans." He winked at Hedy. "I've got to wait another month for God and the Army."

A tingling sensation sweep up Hedy's neck and face as she playfully turned away.

~

"The chapel is almost full." Mama was attaching the flowers to the front ring of the veil and fiddling with it on Hedy's head.

Hedy squinted and twisted her body to peer into the church.

"Stop fidgeting, dear, or I'll never get this right."

"But Mama, we only invited our family and John's friends. Why is the chapel so full?"

The priest coughed behind them. "We ran the announcement of the wedding in the bulletin last week. The locals want to see how Americans marry. Is that a problem?"

Her hand waved in the air. "I am pretty anxious to see how an American gets married too."

Father Titian touched her arm. "You and Johnny will do well."

Choking back tears, Mama fussed with the lace, placing it and replacing it on Hedy's shoulders.

"Mama, it is perfect. Go take your seat in the chapel." She pointed to Fr. Titian. "We are ready to start."

Leaving her daughter, Mama sat in a pew at the front of the church. Rosemary stood up from positioning the long train behind Hedy. "If I ever get married, can I use your dress? It is stunning."

Hedy reached out her hand to her cousin. "Of course." She pointed into the chapel. "If you change your mind about Americans, Johnny has some handsome friends." Rosemary blushed and sat next to Tante Gisela and Onkel Marcel.

Hands shaking, Hedy accepted the bulky spray of white hyacinths and greenery from Gerda. "I can't thank you enough for postponing your move to the East. Are you sure I can't talk you out of it?"

"The only person as stubborn as you is me, Hedy."

"I still don't like it." Hedy frowned.

Gerda hugged her. "Oh, Hedy. Don't worry about me. Today is about you. You will have a great life."

"You really think so?"

"Because you will make it happen." Gerda kissed her on both cheeks.

Fr. Titian lined up the altar servers and the cross bearer. Hedy caught a glimpse of Inge waiting near the altar, across from Fred, shifting her weight from one leg to the next. The church organ began its march. The priest followed the procession to the altar.

Left alone with her father, Hedy kissed him on the cheek. "Well, Vater. It is just us."

He blinked back tears, obviously trying to steel his emotions. "It is, dear. I hate to be losing you."

She had never seen her father appear so anxious. "Never, Vater. I will always be your little girl." She linked her arm through his and strode into the room.

Johnny in his dress uniform stepped from a side door and stood in front of Fred. The love on Johnny's face shone across the room, taking her breath away. Her step quickened.

"Slow down, Hedy. I can't keep up," her father whispered as he plodded beside her.

~

The ceremony was performed entirely in English. Hedy had practiced her responses and her vows, but still trembled when Fr. Titian called on her. Her anxiety dissipated as she gazed into Johnny's eyes. She stated her vows clearly and passionately.

This was the perfect day.

After the ceremony, the CIC agents chauffeured the wedding guests to the CIC villa for a luncheon while the wedding portrait was taken. When she and her new husband arrived at the villa, Hedy was met by an old friend.

"Kiki. I can't believe you made it to my wedding."

"Your mother wrote my aunt." Helping maneuver the long, flowing train, Kiki steered her to a chair and sat beside her. "She wanted to surprise you. You are truly stunning."

After giving her mother a loving smile, Hedy quizzed her friend. "How is the Duchess?"

"Still as clever as can be. My aunt was right about getting away from Eastern Germany." Kiki shivered. "I'd hate to think what it would be like if she lived there."

Unsure how to respond, Hedy placed her friend's hand in hers. Kiki's mood lightened and she shared her good news. "I've met a brilliant man and we will be marrying. He travels extensively; maybe we will be able to visit you in America."

Hugging her friend, Hedy squealed. "That would be wonderful."

Various CIC agents surrounded them. Steve yelled, "Time for a toast."

Another agent helped her stand and gently shoved her next to John. A dozen men circled them.

"John, you owe us." Fred elbowed his partner.

He laughed. "I am sure I do. What for this time?"

Motioning to the agents around the room, Fred explained. "We have all been members of the 'Search for Hedy' expeditions. Without us, you would have never been able to wear her down enough to marry you."

"Here, here," Steve shouted. "Especially me." He stuck out his chest gallantly. "I saved her from getting arrested."

"You are right. I needed all the help I could get to land my beautiful bride." Johnny's bright eyes lit on Hedy. Every inch of his face displayed his love for her. "Break out the champagne. It is time to toast my expedition mates."

The corks popped and the champagne flowed. Hedy surveyed the room and hugged each of the men. She glanced back at Johnny. His back was going to be sore from all the slapping.

Grimacing, Johnny winked at her. Now she was convinced he could read her mind.

~

After the champagne was gone and the couple had received more congratulations than they could count, Hedy changed into her traveling clothes. Mama pinned a rose corsage onto the repurposed army uniform before giving her a tearful goodbye. Rosemary, Kiki, and Inge all promised to keep in touch.

Hedy squeezed Gerda's hand and whispered, "Please take care of yourself."

Blinking back her tears, Gerda reassured her. "I only get arrested when I'm with you."

With the goodbyes complete, Johnny picked up her small suitcase and escorted her to the train station. He had been given three days off to take Hedy to their choice of one of the three resorts within an overnight train ride. With the war over, the resorts were available for visitors again. Hedy chose Garmisch near the Alps so that her new husband would see the beauty of Germany. She didn't want his memories of her homeland to only be of war and destruction.

"It is probably too late in the year to get skiing in," Johnny remarked as they walked towards the train station.

"It doesn't matter," she reassured him. "I never learned to ski anyway."

"All these years, living next to the mountains, and you didn't go skiing?"

Hedy tilted her head and looked sideways at her new husband. "The war got in the way of a lot of things. Besides, Hitler confiscated all the skis when he invaded Russia." She motioned towards the tracks. "The train is pulling in."

An American soldier saluted them as they entered. Noticing her corsage, he asked, "Are you celebrating your birthday?"

Johnny responded before she had a chance. "We just got married."

"Congratulations, sir." They passed him and found their designated compartment. After greeting the two other travelers already seated, Hedy stowed her travel bag below the bench. The door to the compartment opened, and the American soldier motioned for Johnny to follow him. Johnny kissed her on the forehead. "Stay here for a moment, *mia amore*. I'll be right back."

She observed the people on the platform through the window, wondering if any of them were as happy as she was right now. Twisting her ring, warmth rose through her body.

Johnny interrupted her thoughts by retrieving her bag. The dimple in his left cheek was pronounced and his eyes reeked of mischief. "Hedy, follow me."

Head cocked to the side, she grinned back. "Why?"

"Come on." He crooked his finger at her.

As she stepped into the hallway, the soldier from the door saluted her. "Right this way, Ma'am."

Hedy giggled. She was a Ma'am.

The soldier led them to a separate car and opened the door, displaying the sleeping berths. She offered Johnny a questioning look.

"I told them this is a very special trip." His eyes sparkled.

With her stomach doing flip-flops and her face burning, Hedy entered the room.

"Happy honeymoon." The soldier saluted and closed the door behind them.

Going to America

1947

To expedite the admission to the United States of alien spouses and alien minor children of citizen members of the United States armed forces.

The War Bride Act approved by the US Congress —December 28, 1945

Their perfect honeymoon was straight from a storybook. The weather was perfect and Hedy had never been happier. The stress of the war and not being able to marry was gone, allowing them to focus solely on one another. Though they had dated for two years, they had experienced very little time alone. Johnny's giddiness about introducing her to his family soon was contagious. The newlyweds returned to Wiesbaden and waited for Hedy's papers.

Housing for CIC agents was not designed for wives; therefore, Hedy remained at Mrs. Walker's house. "Some marriage," Johnny groused.

For another week, Hedy spent her days assisting her hostess and her evenings with Johnny at headquarters. Every day, she would search her husband's face for news of her transit permission. Every day, she was disappointed.

Her jaw ached from clenching her teeth. Her husband was becoming more irritable by the hour. "I'm sure it will work out, *Schatz*," Hedy promised as she rubbed his shoulders.

His transport to New York was scheduled to leave the next day, but there were still no documents for Hedy. When he could delay it no longer, Johnny held Hedy in his arms and kissed her. "I'm headed to Bremerhafen. I've made arrangements with the other agents to check the mail for the paper work every day. They have promised to arrange your train to the port when the papers finally come through."

She squeezed him as tightly as she could. "You know they will take good care of me. With any luck, I will be right behind you."

"I'll look for you at the docks in New York. Fred will let me know which boat you are on." He kissed her again. "I will be there every day until you arrive."

With one last passionate kiss and a wave goodbye, he left. Loneliness engulfed her almost immediately. She prayed for his safety and for her papers to arrive.

The other agents endeavored to buoy Hedy's spirits. They invited her to the CIC house each day for dinner. "We will keep you so busy, you won't have time to think about him." Fred promised.

She appreciated his efforts, but she knew that would not be the case.

~

A week later, Fred rushed into Mrs. Walker's house without knocking. "Hedy. Hedy."

"My dear, what is the matter?" Mrs. Walker almost lost hold of the pot of tea she held in her hand.

Hedy hurried down the stairs. "What is it, Fred? Is Johnny hurt?"

"No. Good news." Fred waved a stack of papers in front of her. "Your travel orders arrived. I need to get you on the next train to Bremerhaven."

"Oh, Fred, thank you." She practically bowled him over with her hug.

"Save it for Johnny. Go get packed. Your train leaves in four hours."

She raced up the stairs and tossed everything into her suitcase. Closing the latches, she surveyed the room. As she sank into her desk chair, the realization she was leaving Germany hit her. She pulled out a piece of paper to write to her parents.

Dear Mama and Vater,

I am headed for the ship to take me to America. Though we have been planning on this for a long time, I find my heart is heavy. I don't know when I will see you again. When I think back to all of the aggravation and stress I caused you, I am ashamed. I was especially hard on you, Mama. You always forgave me and welcomed me home.

I will finally be able to study physical therapy. Johnny has researched the universities there and will help me get enrolled. He thinks my English is strong enough to handle the coursework.

My new home may be far away from you, but you will always be in my heart. Johnny and I pray you will be able to visit us before long.

I love you both.

Your devoted daughter,

Hedy

Large tears smeared the ink as Hedy signed her name. She blew on the letter and waved it in the air to dry before folding it into an envelope. Sealed with a kiss. Hedy carried the envelope and her bag downstairs.

Mrs. Walker hugged her goodbye with a sob. Fred drove her by the CIC office to bid farewell to her friends from the previous year.

"We are so happy for you, Hedy."

"Damn Johnny is the luckiest guy on the planet."

"Take America by storm, Hedy."

"Don't worry about your English. You are doing great."

The men hugged and kissed her. Even Peter gave her a quick embrace, before turning away. She would miss them all greatly. "Don't forget to look us up if you visit New York," she said, peering at them through wet lashes. "Johnny and I want to see you."

Fred ushered her out of the house. "I don't want to have to explain to Johnny you missed your train because you were kissing all his friends."

When they arrived at the station, Fred handed her a piece of paper with a phone number. "Would you call my wife and tell her I'll be home next month? I never trust the mail."

"I would be honored to speak to your wife," Hedy tucked the paper in her bag and gave him one last hug before boarding the train.

For the next six hours, she twisted her wedding band and imagined her life with Johnny in New York. The car became more crowded with each stop. Soon there was standing room only.

"Last stop. Bremerhafen," the conductor called. Everyone stood. Hedy was jostled out onto the crowded platform. Where was she supposed to go? How would she locate her ship?

Working her way through the crowd, she tried to calm her anxious feelings. Hundreds of other young women held suitcases. Could they all be war brides too?

She moved out of the station, away from the crowd. One of three women behind a table with a red shield motioned to her. "Do you speak English, dear?"

Hedy hesitated. "Yes. Some."

"You look a bit lost. Can I help you?"

The tension from her shoulder's evaporated as she let out a strong sigh. "That would be lovely. I am supposed to be on a transport to the States, but I don't know where to go."

The woman reassured her. "No one is going anywhere these days. There is a strike in New York, and no boats can get into the harbor. It has been more than a week since a ship sailed."

Hedy was unsure what the strike was about, but she did understand no ships had sailed in over a week. "Johnny may still be here." She dropped her bag as her hands flew to her mouth.

The woman nodded. "He may be." Noticing the ring on Hedy's hand, she asked, "Is that your husband?"

"Yes. He was scheduled to leave a week ago. Can you help me find him?"

"Of course." She called back to the women behind the table. "I am going to help Mrs. —?" Turning back to Hedy, she raised one eyebrow.

"Weiß. Uh wait. I mean Merenda."

"I'll be helping Mrs. Merenda." She came back to Hedy and directed her toward a building. "I take it you are a newlywed."

With her cheeks burning, Hedy explained they had only been married a short time.

"I am Nikki Smith. Do you know his rank and unit?" She weaved in amongst the throngs of people.

"I do." Hedy pointed to a wall covered with pieces of paper where people were jostling each other. "Why are all they staring at the wall?"

"That is where the ship manifests are posted with the passenger list. I hear they are going to let one to two ships leave a day starting tomorrow. Everyone is trying to find out if their names are on the lists."

Hedy shuddered at the idea of fighting that mob. "Where does everyone stay while they are waiting?"

Miss Smith pointed to rows of barracks in the distance. "The men are housed there." Rotating, she pointed to the other side of the compound. "The women and children sleep there."

"But we are married. Where do we stay?"

Shaking her head, Nikki answered. "The honeymoon will have to wait until you get to New York."

The sheer size of place overwhelmed Hedy. How was she ever going to find Johnny? Finally, Nikki stopped at an administrative building. Lines and lines of people filled the space. The racket was deafening. Nikki had to yell for Hedy to understand her. "Stay in line, Mrs. Merenda. They will assign you a place to sleep and help you track Mr. Merenda."

"Merenda? Who's looking for me?" A familiar voice yelled back.

"Johnny." Hedy's heart leapt in her throat. She bounded up and down to try to see over the mass of people.

"Watch it."

"What is going on?"

"Bud, wait your turn."

The crowd shifted as a familiar, handsome figure pushed his way to her. "*You're here.*" Johnny picked Hedy up and kissed her. Her feet barely missed hitting the next man standing in line.

"Johnny." Hedy patted him gently, her face flaming. "Everyone is staring."

"I don't care. When did you get here?"

"Just now. Miss Smith..." Hedy motioned to Nikki. "Miss Smith led me here to find you. I assumed you would be long gone."

He squeezed her again. "Thank God for the strike."

Nikki chuckled. "You are the only one in this compound saying that."

After thanking Nikki for her help and getting a sleeping assignment, Hedy slipped her hand in Johnny's. He directed her away from the crowds. "Even though we are together here, there is no guarantee they will put us on the same ship over," Johnny warned her.

"Surely they wouldn't tear us apart again. It's bad enough we have to stay in two different buildings. I would hate to be on a different ship too."

He cuddled close to her. "We'll have to make the best of it."

~

Each morning, they met at the ships' manifest posting site, elbowing their way into the throng of passengers to discover if either was sailing. The waiting was tedious, but at least they were together.

On the fourth morning, Johnny let out a whoop. "We are sailing this afternoon on the SS Goethals." He pulled Hedy out from the horde and spun her around. "Together."

"Stop it." She laughed. "You're making me dizzy."

"Meet me in front of the ship with all your things in an hour, *mia amore*." Johnny left her to pack.

~

Boarding the ship was no easy task. Their papers were inspected, they were checked for lice, and asked all kinds of personal questions by medical staff. "Mrs. Merenda, are you pregnant?" The doctor glanced at her midsection.

Hedy folded her arms over her stomach. "Of course not," she huffed. "We just got married."

The doctor waved his hand. "Too bad. We place the pregnant women in the staterooms. You will be in the women's steerage compartment."

~

Hedy had never been on a ship before. She clenched Johnny's hand as he guided her up the metal gangplank. "This is massive. How will I ever find you?"

He rubbed her hand gently. The men's steerage compartment where he was assigned was on the other side of the ship. "We only have to be apart at night. There are deck chairs on the upper decks. The fourth deck, starboard side will be our meeting place." He guided her to the stairs leading down to her compartment.

"Which is the starboard side?" Hedy called back up to him.

"Right side when you are facing the bow." Johnny hesitated a moment. "The front of the ship."

Reassured, Hedy left him to stow her suitcase. She crept her way down the steps to the hull of the ship. Bunks piled high stood against the walls and a row of bunks in the middle was anchored to the floor and ceiling. A few small bulbs lit the room. She worked her way through the crowd to find an open berth and stowed her suitcase.

The ship hadn't left dock yet, and she was already nauseous. This did not bode well for the trip. Hedy climbed to the fourth deck to find Johnny. Standing at the edge of the railing as the ship pulled away from the dock, they waved to those waiting. The coastline gradually disappeared. "Goodbye, Germany," she whispered.

Johnny pulled her to his chest. "On to America."

She rubbed against him and sighed.

~

At their designated time, Johnny accompanied Hedy to dinner. They descended to a dining hall below the waterline. The meal, though uninteresting, was satisfying. "It is rather odd to watch the water in my glass move when I am not touching it," she observed.

Johnny touched her cheek. "You will get used to it. Let's go to sleep early tonight." He led her up to an open air deck and pointed to the moon. "The ocean swaying will put you right to sleep. Tomorrow you will be amazed by the vastness of the ocean. We may see a whale."

The bright stars reflected on the calm waters. After a long kiss goodnight, they parted ways. Hedy climbed into her bunk, expecting to be lulled to sleep by the sound of waves lapping at the side of the boat. Instead sleep escaped her. Children cried and women vomited. As more passengers used the buckets, the rancid smell wafted throughout the compartment. Hedy hid her head under the pillow and prayed for morning to come quickly.

~

When the morning finally came, she dressed and met Johnny for breakfast. A plate of eggs and sausage sat in front of her. She pushed the food around, unable to bring it to her mouth.

"Isn't it great?" Warmth radiated from her husband as he beamed at his bride. "I have always loved ocean voyages." He frowned at her untouched plate. "Finish up and we'll go breathe the salt air."

Hedy didn't think she could speak. She took one glance at the uneaten food and felt her face becoming a putrid shade of green. Her stomach churned and she fled from the room up to an open deck.

Johnny caught up with her at the railing. "Oh dear. Are you all right?" He sat her down on a deck chair and brought her a glass of water. "Ocean voyages take a little getting used to."

~

She didn't seem to be getting used to it. Hedy was unable to eat anything that day or the next. Johnny brought her crackers to settle her stomach and lemon slices to suck on. "It will stop your gag reflex."

"Johnny, I can't survive five more days feeling like this."

He ran his hands through his hair nervously and stared intensely over the horizon. "I understand you've never been on a boat before, but this is the smoothest I have ever seen the ocean."

Sinking further into her chair, Hedy pulled up the blanket Johnny had laid across her. "You mean it won't get any better?"

He laid his hand against her forehead. "Are you sure you don't have a cold?"

"I wish I did. Then I'd think I'd live." She covered her head and groaned.

Two more days passed, and Hedy did not improve. Johnny begged her to visit the ship's doctor. She refused. "I didn't like him. He asked too many personal questions that were none of his business."

"What do you mean?" Johnny gently stroked her hair.

She pulled back her shoulders. "He wanted to know if I was pregnant."

Snickering, John replied, "Well, we are married, Hedy."

"I couldn't believe he asked."

Johnny sat for a moment, deep in thought. "Um, Hedy. You might not be seasick."

She glared at him, barely able to temper the scorn in her voice. "What do you mean? I've been sick since the first morning on this thing."

An odd smile replaced his concern. "Sick every morning, huh?"

What was that grin for? Why would her queasiness make him happy? She paused and slapped her forehead with the heel of her hand. "Oh, no. I couldn't be."

Kissing her on the forehead, Johnny disagreed. "You most certainly could be."

"I guess my physical therapy plans will be put off one more time." She wrapped her arms around her husband and whispered in his ear. "I love you."

"On to America, *mia amore*. On to America."

The couple who inspired the story, John and Hilde Sensale.

Acknowledgements

First and foremost, my thanks goes to Hilde Sensale for letting me incorporate the fascinating events from her life into my story. If my readers would like to know more about this amazing woman, check out DarkerTheNight.com where I've posted interviews with her and other fun tidbits.

In case you are wondering, the woman on the cover is nineteen year-old Hilde in the dress John brought her back from the States. The bomb scene on the back is a picture John took as he followed the troops through France after landing in Normandy.

Without the patience, guidance and humor of my editor, Susan Sipal, I would have given up a long time ago. Thank you, Susan, for everything.

Thanks to my loving husband Skip, who thinks I have forgotten how to cook since I started this book. In spite of the fact he refuses to read it, he has helped tremendously, especially with the historical facts. My voracious reader of a daughter, Adair, and her friends, Alex Saunders, Michelle Hayes, Victoria Herschel, Owen Piehler, and Rhett Simpson, acted out several of the scenes for me, which brought laughter and insight.

Huge thanks also go to Sabrina Beasley for her editing skills as well as the numerous early readers who offered suggestions, improvements, and support.

And most of all, thank you, my readers. I love sharing stories, and you make it possible. If you enjoyed the story, please consider posting a review on your favorite book website and sharing it with your friends on social media.

Questions and Topics for Discussion

1. *Darker the Night* shows life in World War II from the point of view of a German civilian. What did you learn about the war? Did anything surprise you?

2. Fritz and Marlene obviously sheltered their daughter from their political views and what was going on in their country. Do you think they ought to have been more forthcoming? Why or why not?

3. Each chapter began with a quote from a speech or piece of propaganda from the time to give the reader a feel for what the citizens of Germany heard were the reasons for war and the government's expectations. As the war wore on, the propaganda became more about sticking to the fight, all the way to Hitler's suicide note. Which quote affected you the most?

4. Hedy felt she should be able to travel as desired even if the country was at war or occupied, because, "It's our country." If you had a teenage daughter, how would have handled her traversing the countryside?

5. The Red Cross uniform becomes an important piece of Hedy's life. What does the uniform symbolize in Hedy's journey?

6. The woman whose life the story was based on said she had no idea at the time what was going on in the concentration camps, only that the political prisoners and Jews were taken to "serious" camps. Should she and the other German civilians have known? What could they have done if they did?

7. Gerda, whose character was based on an actual person, was horrified by her country's behavior and moved behind the Iron Curtain to help. What do you think happened to Gerda?

8. The Allies kept food relief from entering Germany for some time after the war. Do you feel there was any justification?

Glossary

Achtung: Attention.
Alles Gute zum Geburtstag: Happy birthday to you.
Alliierten: Allied forces.
Amici: Friends. (Italian)
Anschluss: Annexation. Nazi propaganda term for the invasion and incorporation of Austria in March of 1938.
Arbeitsdienst: Compulsory six-month work service for men and women from 18-25 for civic and land improvement projects, dating from the early 1930s. Once the war started, personnel also assisted on the farms. This was separate, and usually served before, their *Kriegsdienst*.
Au revoir: Good bye. (French)
Bund Deutscher Mädel (BDM): League of German Girls, a Nazi –sponsored organization for girls aged 14-18; an offshoot of the Hitler Youth.
Bruderkrankenhaus: The hospital in Trier.
Ciao: Informal greeting. (Italian)
Clausewitz, Carl von: Prussian general and military theorist from the 19th century who stressed the moral and political aspects of war.
Danke: Thanks.
Deutsches Jungvolk: German Youth—the Hitler Youth for younger boys.
Deutschland, Deutschland über alles: National anthem of Germany. Translates to "Germany, Germany above all things."
Donitz, Admiral Konrad: German admiral who took command after Adolf Hitler's suicide.
Eins, zwei, drei: One, two, three.
Eintopfgericht: A basic stew. Nazi administration required civilians to eat stew one night per week and donate the money saved on the meal to the government.
Endhaltestelle: Last stop.
Enkelin: Granddaughter.
Erdnuss: Peanut.
Frau: Woman.
Frau bait: Slang term for food and supplies offered by Allied troops to a woman in exchange for sexual favors.
Fräulein: Girl or unmarried woman.
Führer: Leader. Adolf Hitler granted the title to himself.
Gau: Shire or country subdivision.

Gaupropagandaleitungen: District propaganda office.

Goebbels, Joseph: Reich Minister of Propaganda.

Göring, Hermann: Founder of the Gestapo and commander of the *Luftwaffe* (air force).

Gott: God.

Gott sei Dank: Thank God.

Gratulation: Congratulations.

Guten Appetit: Enjoy your meal.

Guten Morgen: Good morning.

Guten Tag: Good day.

Hallo: Hello.

Hase: Rabbit.

Heilgymnastik: Physical therapy.

Hitlerjugend: Hitler youth for boys aged 14-18.

Hochbunker: High rise air-raid shelter composed of large concrete blocks above ground and huge lintels over the doorways.

Hohe Domkirche St. Peter: The High Cathedral of St. Peter in Trier.

Ich bin verlobt: I am engaged.

Infirmiere assistante: Nurse assistant. (French)

Invasionsarmee: Invasion army.

Ja: Yes.

Jewish Bolshevist: Communist Jews. The term was used by the Nazis to imply that Jews were behind communism and wanted to take down the German government.

Jungmädel: Young Girl's League— Nazi organization for younger girls, age 10-14; offshoot of the Hitler Youth.

Juwelier: Jeweler.

Kameraden: Comrades.

Kein Arzt in der Stadt: No doctor in town.

Konzentrationslager: Concentration camp—a place to hold and torture political prisoners. Some were converted into extermination camps.

Kriegsdienst: Required war service for both men and women.

Kristallnacht: Night of shattering glass, November 9-10, 1938. Paramilitary forces and German civilians attacked Jewish-owned businesses and synagogues in retaliation for the assassination of a German diplomat by a Polish Jew. German authorities did nothing to stop them.

Lass doch: Leave it.

Les femmes du Plaisir: The women of pleasure who followed the French troops with the government's blessing. (French)

Luftwaffe: Airforce.

Marketplatz: Market street.

Mein Herr: Sir.

Meine apolgies: My apologies.

Meine Mutter ist krank: My mother is sick.

Mia amore: My love. (Italian)

Mittagessen: The main meal of the day, served early in the afternoon.

Moselwein: Wine from the Mosel region.

Nein: No.

Oberschwester: Head nurse.

Onkel: Uncle.

Opa: Grandfather.

Our Hitler: Annual speeches broadcast over the radio by Goebbels on Hitler's birthday.

Panzer: German tank.

Pfarrer: Priest.

Porta Nigra: Large ancient Roman city gate in Trier.

Potsdam Conference: US President Harry Truman, British Prime Minister Winston Churchill, and Soviet leader Joseph Stalin met in Potsdam, Germany, July 17-August 2, 1945 to work out the terms for ending World War II and how to manage post-war Germany.

Prost: May it benefit you. Used as a toast.

Reichstag: Parliament.

Ruhr: Urban and industrial region of western Germany in North Rhine.

Sankt Nikolaus: Saint Nicholas.

Saxe-Meiningen: An area in central Germany. The last duke abdicated in 1918 and the area was incorporated a few years later into Thuringia.

Schatz: Sweetheart. A term of endearment.

Schwester: Nurse.

Sieh um Dich: "Look behind you." Used as the name of an ancient prison in Trier.

SS: *Schutzstaffel*— A guard unit based on an ideology that commitment and effectiveness instead of class or education would carry you in the organization. They stressed loyalty to Hitler and obedience to orders and were entrusted to carry out the worst of the atrocities of the war.

Strasse: Street.

Stille Nacht: Silent Night.

Stollen: Dense sweet bread coated with powdered sugar served at Christmas time.

Sudetenland: Land in the northwestern part of the Czech Republic, given to Czechoslovakia after World War I.

Süße: Sweetie. A term of endearment.

Tante: Aunt.

Third Reich: The third empire. Term used by the Nazis to refer to a continuation of a German empire; the first being the Holy Roman Empire and the second of the German empire in 1871.

Tommies: Slang term for the British troops.

Vater: Father.

Viez: Spicy apple wine, usually served warm.

Volk: The people.

Weiblicher: Female.

Weichling: Slang term for softie, wimp.

Weinstube: Wine bar.

Weiß: White. As a last name, is also spelled Weiss.

Wir haben die Briten auf die Knien gebracht: We have the British on their knees.

Wir haben's geschafft: We did it.

Wo sind die Deutschen Soldaten?: Are there any German soldiers?

Yanks: Slang term for the American troops.

About the Author

Lisa London is the author of the best-selling *Accountant Beside You* series of books for nonprofits and churches. Hearing her next door neighbor's tales of growing up in Hitler's Germany motivated Lisa to research civilian life during the war, and *Darker the Night* was conceived. It is her debut novel, written in hopes people's eyes no longer glaze over when they ask what she is currently writing.

When not writing or assisting nonprofits and churches, Lisa enjoys spending time with her husband Skip and their four children on the beautiful North Carolina coast, paddle boarding, kayaking, and sailing.